MURDER IN THE TETONS

By J. Royal Horton

MURDER IN THE TETONS

By J. Royal Horton

Jackson Hole Mysteries by J. Royal Horton

Murder in Jackson Hole

Murder in the Tetons

Murder in Moab

Other books by Jon R Horton

Gib

Snuffy Johnson's Cowboy Christmas

ISBN 978-0-96-439785-9 (pbk/Amazon)

978-1-7375024-2-5 (hc)

978-1-7375024-3-2 (pbk)

Cover art by Malcolm Furlow, Michael McCormick Gallery Taos, NM

Book Layout and Interior by Suzanne Fyhrie Parrott

SUNLIGHT PUBLISHING LLC
Colorado Springs CO 80903

Printed in the
United States of America

PRAISE

"With its elegant descriptions of modern Western culture, Murder in the Tetons *is more than a mystery. J. Royal Horton has joined such illustrious company as Theresa Jordan, Gretel Ehrlich and William Kittredge. strength...passion...superb characterization."*

—W. Michael Gear and Kathleen O'Neal Gear,

Authors of *People of Silence.*

"Praise for Murder in Jackson Hole*: "Different! Captures Jackson Hole's unique sense of place."*

—Warren Adler, Author of War of the Roses—

Contents

"Better to die on your feet than live on your knees."

—Emiliano Zapata —

Prologue

West of Jackson Hole, Wyoming, a summer sun drops behind the Big Hole Mountains into neighboring Idaho. The encroaching night nudges pink light to the summit of the Grand Teton mountain, then the pinnacle gutters out like an immense altar candle.

Far below the peak of the mountain named the Grand Teton, the smells of freshly mown hay and the acidic smell of cottonwood in the air are redolent of summer. Among other large homes sprawled at the feet of the mountains and the ski area named Grand Targhee, one house is notable for an avant-garde design that speaks of an uncommon mind. In the basement of that idiosyncratic home, a man sits in his laboratory, examining what should be a priceless cultural artifact. But, in fact, he is engaged in doing exactly that—setting a price for an auction to be held in Dubai in two weeks' time. The Heart of the World. Every time he holds it, his hands grow damp with excitement.

As an uncut emerald alone, the enormous gem is worth something in the neighborhood of a million dollars or more. However, as a legendary cultural piece, it is virtually priceless on the international black market for antiquities, so only some of the very richest men in the world will be participating in the auction.

History had it that the Heart was pounded to dust in 1557 by a Dominican missionary priest, Fray Benito Hernandez, in the Sierra Madre Oeste of southern Mexico. In 1674, another Dominican, Francisco de Burgoa, wrote, "*and of their infamous altars, the Mixtecas had one devoted to an idol, called* The People's Heart, *that was a great veneration object and a greatly appreciated matter because it was an emerald as large as a big chili pepper from this earth, that had carved on it a little bird, with great gracefulness, and top to bottom coiled a little snake, done with the same art. The stone was transparent, and it shined from the bottom, where it seemed like a candle flame burning. It was a very ancient jewel, that there was no memory of the commencement of its worship and adoration.*"

The vandalism was meant as an object lesson to his neo-Catholic congregation. However, the pagan priests of the Society of Ancient Guardians had substituted a fake made of dark-green obsidian from the volcano, Mount Orizaba. The zealous but ignorant priest hadn't known the difference, so neither had the history books. It was only when he had lived among the Mixteca people that he learned the secret of the emerald's continued existence. And now, after untold years, it was his.

The thief put the gem down next to another near priceless object of the Mixteca people—the vellum book that tells the story of Lady Three Monkey. It, too, has to be priced, and that means consultations with other antiques smugglers.

When he presses a button on his desk phone, a female voice answers.

"*Si*, Nataniel."

"Please bring me a carafe of the Jamaican coffee; I'm going to be working late. Call me when it's ready, and I'll unlock the door to the lab."

"I will make it now."

"Are your brother and his friend still there?"

"*Si.*"

"Damn it! Tell him to go back to Mexico; I won't talk to him under any circumstances."

"I will tell him, Nataniel. But he is bein' ver'...dramatic." The person stands on the east side of the house and admires the expensive furnishings that includes antique Southwest chiefs' blankets, large original figurative paintings and landscapes, and collectible guns and swords from America's military history.

In one corner, an ornately silver-dressed antique Mexican vaquero saddle is set on a stand, while a collection of Molesworth furniture is arranged around a big stone fireplace.

Above the mantelpiece is a bas-relief black fossil garfish at least six feet long, half-liberated from a sandstone matrix where it had been captive for 100 million years. And there are people to be seen inside this enormous house too.

The voyeur sees three olive-skinned people, two small men and a small woman with black hair and dark eyes. One man wears a poor man's palm-fiber cowboy hat while the other is hatless, revealing a coarse mane of hair. He speaks earnestly to the woman, who resembles him. She sits nervously on the edge of the couch, then suddenly turns her head as if responding to some person's voice.

The woman leaves and soon returns with a tray set with cups and a coffee server. After serving the two men, she walks to an adjoining room, then descends a stairway with the tray in her hands.

Our observer has drawn close enough to hear through a side window opened for ventilation. The men are speaking a language unlike the Hispanic dialects often heard in Jackson Hole. They appear to be Mexicans or Central Americans, but the language is not Spanish.

The woman reappears from below and excitedly engages the men in conversation. Startled, they leap from the couch and hurry down the stairs. The woman follows cautiously to the balustrade and peers down.

Our silent witness presses her face near the window and hears an unintelligible argument growing in volume—loud voices clash. There are cries, shouted cursing, then the cry of a man in great pain.

Soon, the same two men reappear, each of them grasping an object protectively. They pause to speak to the woman, then a large white man with blood on his face charges up from the stairwell. He grabs at a leather-bound book held by one of the men, sending his rude hat flying.

The small Indian man lies down with the book in his arms, wrapping himself around it in an attempt to fend off the white man, but the large man falls to his knees and tries to pry the book from the little man's grasp.

The woman, who fled to the kitchen, returns just as the second Indian man swings a piece of cordwood taken from the fireplace, knocking the white man away from his friend. The big Anglo falls to the floor. She screams and rushes to the downed man's side, then apparently tells one of the small men to go to the kitchen for a wet towel as he returned with one.

Some moments go by as the woman nurses the big man back to consciousness. As soon as he has his wits back, he thrusts her aside and attacks the two smaller men, who have retreated to the main room.

In the melee, one of the small, muscular men jumps on the tall man's back and wraps his arms around his throat. The gringo swings his shoulders while pulling at his attacker's arms until his grip is broken.

The big white man jumps to where the leather-bound book fell on the floor and retrieves it. But the second little man has picked up another piece of firewood from the nearby fireplace and, raising his hands high, brings it down again on the wounded man's head.

The victim falls, and his legs began to twitch so that any observer would surely know that he has been very badly hurt. The woman cries softly, her hands over her mouth, then she staunches the blood from his head with the towel. She is heard praying, this time in

Spanish, the prayer language of the Catholic Church in the lands south of America, from where most of the labor in the Jackson Hole area comes.

The two men begin to converse in their native language. They occasionally gesture toward the window, past our observer, apparently talking about the great mountain now lit by a moon as bright as a statue of The Virgin. Though the viewer could have no way of knowing for sure, they are speaking of the tall mountain above their village in distant Mexico, the one named Nindo Tocoshu—the home of their Mixteca Indian god Dzaui.

The woman stands and addresses them tearfully for some minutes. Then, suddenly, the injured man scrambles to his feet and staggers outside through a side door! The two Indians run across the great room and follow the man outside.

Our observer now moves to the side of the house in time to see that the big man is down again, this time never to rise again. She watches as one of the Indians checks the pulse on the victim's neck as the other man reaches inside the house to douse the rear door in light.

The watcher stops to calm her racing pulse, taking several deep breaths. She pauses in the dark as the three fall to their knees and bow their heads in prayer. She takes that opportunity to hurry from the property and cross the Targhee Road to another large neighboring house that sits next to the summer rush of Teton Creek.

The three Indians pray to their native god, Dzaui, and to the enormous moonlit mountain that rears above the valley. Our observer might have been puzzled by the fact that the small people crossed themselves in the fashion of Catholics during their pagan prayers because few know how deeply native beliefs in southern Mexico had long ago wedded themselves to Catholicism. In accordance with both traditions, the three had dedicated the dead man and his soul to the mighty mountain, the Grand Teton, at whose foot they would bury him. They also prayed to spare themselves retribution from the imported God, Jesus, and Holy Ghost.

As the three little people offered their prayers in the fashion of innocent people all over the world, the night was cut by the sound of a *swish* of night wings. An owl? A nighthawk? Or perhaps the sound of a soul flitting its way to Hell.

CHAPTER ONE

It was very dark in the southern Mexico state of Oaxaca as Lauro Osorio Cruz picked his way carefully over a rocky path. A smoky moon hung overhead in a sky full of lusterless stars. The moon was an angry orange because the dry season continued far into what should be a rainy June. Lauro was a young Indian boy, and he didn't understand that the orange color came from the pall of smoke in the air. To him, the color was another sign of the rain god Dzaui's ruddy anger.

In the late afternoon, Lauro fell asleep because of a sickness in his stomach and awoke in darkness. Then he set out for home, full of fear. In the Mixteca Alta of southern Mexico, the night is full of things that one should fear—most of all *hombres volandos*, the Flying People.

Lauro made his panicky way through the smoky night until he reached the dry riverbed that meandered below his village of San Miguel Achiutla. The sounds of his steps whispered in slight echoes as he neared the other side, and he whimpered with fear as he entered the *barranca*, a very large gully that led up the hill toward his father's *ranchito.*

He looked fearfully over his shoulder, and the glance took in the dome of a sixteenth-century convent's nave that barely whispered of moonlight where it sat on the hill high above him. The Catholics had built it on the site of the ancient pyramid city of Achiutla whose ruined mound had once been the temple of his ancestors.

Like the site itself, the conquerors superimposed their influence on the ancient civilization only superficially. In place for more than four hundred years, that influence was not much more than a veneer. Lauro Osorio believed in more than one god, and he also believed in the beings and things that populated the nights of San Miguel Achiutla—Flying People, the blood-sucking *chupacabra*, and others even more terrifying—like the fiery god, Dzaui.

Lauro was a goatherder, and for many of his fourteen years, he moved his father's goats along the barranca he was about to enter. It was part of his home territory, and he knew it by touch—by second nature—but only during the day. He crossed himself and kissed his fingers for luck, then, sweating, entered the Willow grove that marked the mouth of the barranca and the springs above, which were barely a trickle this dry year.

He felt better after a few minutes as his feet recognized the familiar feel of the ground. He kept his head down as he walked with determination. He got closer to his house by the moment and dreaded the sound of swooping wings every second of the way.

He turned right up a branch of the gulley, his head still down and his eyes on the ground to pick up the faint light reflected by the white limestone rock that marked the deeply worn footpath. He hardly noticed when the white rocks grew gradually brighter and appeared to take on the smoky orange color of the moon above. He didn't look up until he was stopped in his tracks by the wet smack of a whip and a man's scream.

At first, Lauro wanted to run back down the *arroyo*. But after a few panicky steps, his fears of the dark returned. He was also curious why someone was being whipped here in the *barranca* rather than in the jail. It was a common enough punishment in San Miguel, meted out for serious breaches of the local laws. His curiosity drew him closer to the circle of torchlight that illuminated the scene.

Marcos Albino was being whipped, and each time the *anciano* brought the *quirt* down on Marcos's bare back, the young man screamed. In between the strokes, he cried out for mercy, for help.

"*¡Ayudame! ¡Dios mio, Ayudame!*"

The whips used by *ancianos* are made by twisting together the two halves of a split penis of a slaughtered bull. When dry, they made a whip about a meter long with hard and exaggerated twists that have a terrible effect on human flesh.

The men laid Marcos face down on the ground, one man holding each arm and two men restrained each leg, and, at first, each time the whipper brought the vinza down, the men had to exert all their effort. However, after a dozen strokes, Marcos no longer screamed, and the men no longer had to exert effort. But the man with the whip still threw all his weight into his work. The men who held the arms and legs turned their faces away at the last few strokes, not because they were squeamish but to avoid light sprays of blood.

After twenty-five strokes, it was over, and the anciano who had wielded the whip removed it from his wrist. Lauro had crept forward during the lashing and now, in the dancing torchlight, saw that the anciano face was wet with tears. It was Venustiano, the victim's father.

The old man knelt, turned his son's face toward his own, and bent to kiss it. Then he said a few quiet words to the others who held the young man. They dragged the limp figure a few feet to the spring that barely trickled from a small limestone grotto rimmed with ferns. Using clean white cloths, they dipped him in the water, then bathed his ravaged back as Marcos moaned.

Venustiano removed his hat and raised his wet face to the smoky sky, to the sick moon, "This man has paid for his sin against you, Great One. He is redeemed according to our customs and yours. Our crops lie waiting in the ground for your mercy, and without your mercy we will starve. Forgive us. Please bring us your rain."

The powerful old man put his hat back on and motioned to the other men. They put Marcos on a rough stretcher, and Venustiano led them up the arroyo and across the dark and dusty fields toward their adobe casitas that squatted in the hot and stinking night.

To the north, above the mountain called Nindo Tocoshu, a forked bolt of lightning flashed, and thunder rolled. But it was dry lightning. The little people below knew that the blood sacrifice of Marcos Albino had not appeased Dzaui, and this night He would not pour down rain on the mountains of the Mixtec world, but more fire.

MiT

It was morning in Riverside, California, as two people got out of a big green 1970s Chevrolet. It was parked under an enormous avocado tree next to the driveway of a white stucco house in Spanish Colonial style. The man was small—an inch or so over five feet—and the woman was even smaller.

"*Seguro?*" the man asked nervously.

"*Si, aqui . . . seguro.*" And then she said to herself, *I am sure this is the place.*

She went to the front door while the man waited on the lawn. He looked back at the car where another Indian man sat behind the steering wheel. He shrugged his shoulders helplessly at him, and the driver took off his palm fiber cowboy hat to wipe his forehead.

The little woman knocked on the screen door, but there was no answer, so she pulled it open and rapped on the door. In a moment, it opened.

A tall woman with graying hair and half-glasses perched on her nose looked at the couple and said, "*Buenos dias.*"

"*Muy buenos dias, Señora. Yo soy Concha Osorio,*" the small Mexican woman answered, identifying herself, "*¿Usted Profesora Roberts?*"

"*Si, si, yo soy Señora Roberts.*" The woman motioned to the man on the lawn, and then she stepped back inside and waved them both in, saying, "*Por favor, mi casa es su casa. Y el otro?*" inquiring about the man in the car.

The little Mexican woman switched to English and said, "We can stay not so very long, but perhaps he could have some water for drinking?"

"Of course, of course, let me get you all something." She turned and shouted toward the kitchen, "Mariana?"

A Latina wearing an apron came out, wiping her hands.

"*Si, Señora?*"

"*Por favor, agua de limon por' los.*"

"*Si, Señora,*" she said and disappeared back into the kitchen.

The woman went to a table, picked up an envelope, then returned and handed it to the little Mexican woman. "Here is the money that Señor Garcia asked me to get for you, Concha. Is there anything else I can do?"

"No, Señora, I am very thankful that you could do this for us. Now we can return home and save our world."

"I am always glad to help any of the Mixteca people who need me."

"You are famous for your generosity, Señora. The people say you are a saint."

The woman tilted her head back and laughed. "Hardly a saint, Concha. Just an old *profesora* who loves the Mixteca and its people."

"The money will be paid back, though it may take some time. I will get it from the *ejido* elders when I am home in San Miguel Achiutla. Do not fear for this, Señora."

"There is no hurry. Ah, here is the lemonade."

Maria had come from the kitchen with a gallon jar full of ice and lemonade. She was also carrying a bulging brown paper sack.

"*Tamales, frijoles negros, y tortillas gorditas. Salsa tambien,*" she said.

The little man smiled broadly, his eyes disappearing into his moon face. "*Bien, bien . . . muchas gracias a usted, Señora.*"

"*Para servirle, y gracias a Dios,*" the woman returned.

"*Si, si, gracias a Dios,*" he said and took the food.

Concha went back to the door, and Maria opened it.

The tall Anglo woman followed them to the lawn and waited until they were in the car, then she waved and said, "*Buen viaje!*" as they pulled out of the drive.

When they were gone, she added to herself, "And luck . . . *suerte.*"

"*Si,*" said Mariana from the front step, "*mucha suerte.*" She crossed herself and kissed her fingers before she went back into the house.

MiT

In Berkeley, California, Ozro "Oz" Gertner was signing books at the Shambhala bookstore. He was a big man with a long silver ponytail dressed in sandals, homespun white pants, and a white poncho secured by a wide brown belt. He was an impressive figure, but his eyes were even more impressive. They were a rainy gray to match the rainy gray day outside, and there was something else about them—a profundity—like looking down a well to pinpoints of black water far below.

He signed a book and underlined the signature with a flourish before handing it to an expensively dressed older woman. She protested mildly, "I was hoping you'd dedicate it to me personally."

"The jaguar is powerful but has no ego, and you do not need one either. Let your life be egoless and powerful!" Oz said and emphasized the last word with a verbal flourish.

Let your life be stoned to the max, you mean. Detective Sergeant Pete Villareal was in an ironic mood as he waited in line to have the police department's book signed.

He observed the others in line as he waited and saw they were almost all well-to-do people in their forties and fifties, maybe a few in their late thirties.

They were Berkeley vets of the sixties and seventies, people like himself. Except he hadn't gone off on a vision quest to Mexico or Central America on his Diner's Club card and been ripped off, as some wealthy and influential people said had happened to them. They'd signed formal complaints to the local PD, and he was investigating them.

Oz had conducted a couple of the rips, and Pete was assigned to find out what had gone on. He needed to find out more about the folks who took the *ricos* to some remote place, got them stoned on various substances, and made them very, very angry when their "trip" turned into a "bummer."

It was just more of the same sort of thing Pete had seen twenty-five years earlier when dealers promised Panama Red and delivered dirt weed to upscale dink students at the university. Now it was upscale, boutique freak-outs instead of some raunchy kids in Hashbury screaming their asses off in free clinics.

Villareal grew up in south San Francisco and was a minor student radical at Cal State San Francisco during the time of the Free Speech Movement here in Berkeley. He was a part of it all and witnessed the riots around the People's Park. In fact, he was one of the students who ran from the tear gas and buckshot of the police back then. Now part of his job was to infiltrate the action that took place in that same park, in student housing, and just about everywhere else in a town proud of every stripe of minor sedition.

Pete worked undercover and did it well. His cover had been broken because, as one of the street intellectuals who orbited the vast university campus, he hung out at the Cafe Med, Cody's Books— before it was driven out by universal gentrification—and other shops that line Telegraph and the other capillary avenues.

Pete had long known the action that took place in those places, and he now made small deals in the back rooms of the trinket shops, ethnic restaurants, and other interesting corners of the city as he gathered intel for the PD. He knew the scene and its history personally, and that was what made him an excellent cop, his badge his graying ponytail.

Oz had been a part of the scene since the late fifties and was a minor figure during the history of that time. He has known Kerouac, Casady, Ginsberg and was supposedly to be found in the poem Howl!

He was also a historical figure in the drug underground of Berkeley. By reputation, he'd been a source of the best Mexican dope at the time, and he'd moved LSD for the legendary Owsley. A friend forever of The Grateful Dead and the other legendary Bay Area bands, he was now a *paterfamilias* to the most exclusive part of the Bay's boutique drug world.

Still, on the cutting edge of The Scene, he appeared to be a conductor of souls to the underground—Pluto and Charon's buddy. But, unfortunately for him, the trippers didn't drink deeply enough from the River of Forgetfulness when they found themselves in Hell. Instead, they returned to file criminal complaints. Some serious crimes were apparently committed in foreign countries, but fraud had been initiated in California when credit card transactions were processed through a terminal in Panama. Now Pete needed to see if he could arrange a little trip with Oz and see exactly what was going on.

Pete put his copy of POWER PLACES OF THE AMERICAS on the table and said, "Hey, Oz."

"Hey, Pedro," Oz said in his husky whisper, "how goes?"

"Beautiful. Thanks."

"There you go, my man," he said as he signed in his meticulous science hand.

"Can I buy you some coffee at the Med when you're done?"

"Gotta go. Got some people to see at five. Soul tourists."

"Where you going this trip?"

"Southern Mexico. There's a power place in the Oaxacan sierra that you wouldn't believe. We're going there for the summer solstice—ancient Mixtec astronomical observatory. One of the most powerful places on the planet."

"Sounds trippy."

"Blow your mind, man."

"Sounds like something I'd be interested in doing. Got any room on the bus for another soul?"

"I can check with my partner, Olga, but I'm pretty sure we're booked. Maybe overbooked if these folks all want to go. Perhaps next time we'll be going to San Bartolo in the Guatemalan jungle for the Autumnal equinox—the Mayan temple with an Olmec foundation—the most powerful spiritual combination in this hemisphere." Oz gestured at the book in Pete's hand. "I cover it in the last chapter of the book."

"Well, keep me in mind. Hey, thanks for the autograph."

"Pleasure. See you 'round the campus."

Pete put the book under his poncho, pulled up the hood, and walked out onto the rainy avenue. He looked at his watch: 3:50. Lots of time. He was due to make a buy at 6:00, so he had time for a cup of coffee and smart talk at the Med.

"What a job!" he said and then grinned. He was getting paid

a lot of money for doing exactly what he was doing when he was seventeen years old and looking to be a member of another of California's multiple generations of perennial university students.

MiT

The ax came down directly into the center of the Douglas fir round. The blade split the sinewy pink wood into two near-perfect halves.

Detective Tom Thompson of the Teton County Wyoming sheriff's office stooped to right one of the halves then cut it into quarters with another quick slash of the ax. The summer morning sun shone on his back, and he felt good from the past hour's work. He split the second half and threw the four pieces onto the growing pile of redolent wood.

He and his son, Jackie, had fallen the trees and bucked them into eight-foot lengths. Working together, they loaded then hauled the logs to Tom's place in the mountains west of Jackson Hole where, they blocked them into sixteen-inch rounds for the wood stove in the front room of the new house.

Tom took out a bandana, mopped his face, and smiled. The memory of his son's slim, sinewy strength made him feel good. The boy was growing, and in more ways than one. The two had joked and laughed easily as they worked, and it had seemed a miracle. One year earlier, most of their communications had been composed of painful silences and neutral conversations that left them both emotionally stranded. The divorce from the boy's mother was hard on them both, but the last year proved that life goes on and time does heal.

He bent, rolled the last round into place and split it, then tossed those pieces on the pile and drove the ax into the chopping block. It had been a perfect morning.

Thompson was in good shape, now. He had lost thirty pounds since the year before and his new relationship with a California woman who believed in fitness. She had put him on a diet and started him running in the hills around their house above Jackson Hole. At six feet tall and a sturdy one hundred and ninety pounds, he was big enough to handle himself in the occasional physical scuffle his job demanded. He wore his dark hair, streaked with silver, a little long. Before he put on his T-shirt, he fingered two thick scars on his stomach—souvenirs of a knife attack shortly after he had reunited with Polly. He had another one, the one that had almost killed him, on his back.

On the way down the wooden walk to the house, he paused for a moment, said, "Thank you, Lord, for my new life," and he meant it. He was thankful for many things, but this morning he was most thankful that he *could* feel his feelings. For most of twenty years, he had primarily felt nothing. Those years were leavened mainly through flashes of anger and blossoms of violence. Being a cop gave him ready access to the violence, and he took a perverse pleasure in the release that the violence had given him. Being happy was something relatively new to Tom, and it had come from his wife, Polly.

After he showered and slipped into walking shorts and shower clogs, he went to the kitchen and mixed some tuna salad. It was four o'clock in the afternoon Pacific standard time, and he was expecting a call from Polly, "Sugarbritches." It still made him pulse with happiness when he thought of her.

She reappeared in his life the summer before. They were hot lovers almost twenty-five years before the previous year's reunion, and nothing was lost in those long intervening years. They rekindled immediately, and nothing had cooled since. The thought of her hot body and clean mind made him flush all over. Shivers ran over his bare shoulders, and he shrugged them away.

"Zowie," he said, smiling at the feelings that thoughts of her raised in him.

He was spreading the tuna salad on a slice of buttered bread when the phone rang, and a thrill ran through him as he picked it up.

"Hi, Sugarbritches," he said breathily.

After a pause, a male voice said, "Gee, Tom, the last time I looked there was only a streak there. Will brown sugar do?"

Tom looked out the window and said, "Well, shit!"

"Embarrassed, huh?" It was Sam Harlan, the Teton county sheriff, and Tom's boss.

"Yeah . . . what's happening?"

"I just got a call from the other side of the mountains, and they've found a dead guy in a cave above Alta. I need you to run over there and investigate."

"Dammit. This is a comp day for me, Sam."

"Sorry, but this looks like a strange one, and you're the only guy I have who understands strange."

Tom sighed. "Tell me about it."

"Some local hikers were screwing around in the woods and smelled something dead. They thought that it might be a bull elk or something that they could get some horns or ivory off of, so they poked around until they found some rocks piled up in front of a small cave. That was odd enough that they pulled the rocks down and found a body."

"That sounds more like a burial."

"Bingo. It was a burial."

"Weird."

"Weirder than you think. This guy was buried in strange clothing with things piled around him—ritual things. He even had dealies braided in his hair. I'm afraid that it might have something to do with the Satanism that occasionally hear about over there."

"Hell, I hope not. You say he had *dealies* braided in his hair? What kind of dealies?"

"They tried to explain them to me, but it didn't make any sense. Get over there and take a look. It's in the forest, so there will be some rangers involved. They're waiting for you at the district ranger's office and will take you up Teton Canyon where Elvin Hansen is doing the preliminary investigation."

"Okay." Tom looked at the clock. "Tell them I'll be there in about an hour."

"Take your digital camera."

"Will do. Bye."

"Bye."

The drive over Teton Pass was steep and beautiful. It wound over the south rampart of the Teton Range and then dropped into Idaho's Teton Valley. Soon after reaching the bottom of the pass, Tom entered Idaho. The highway gradually swung north, passing through Victor and running up the middle of the broad green valley and into the main town of Driggs.

It was a whole different world on this side of the mountains. This was Mormon country with big ranches and dry farms rather than the federal land—a haven for the rich—and condominiums of Jackson's Hole. A different mentality ruled here. Jackson was yuppie country where the environment as rabid politics held sway. On this side, it was still bucolic, an artifact of the *laissez-faire* nineteenth century. A T-shirt often seen in the valley bragged, "Dogpatch of the West" because here, they liked to get down and roll in the disdain of the intellectual and upscale folk from the other side of the hill.

Once in Driggs, he went to the US Forest Service office. Two rangers were waiting outside in the morning sun. Tom got out of his car and introduced himself to two guys in green federal uniforms. They introduced themselves and then climbed into a government

4-wheel drive SUV, headed east through Driggs toward the mountains.

When they reached the head of Teton Canyon, Tom saw the white Teton County Sheriff's vehicle parked on the side of the road. The ranger, keeping his eyes on the road, pointed toward the canyon.

"Those buttresses up there are called The Ten Sentinels, supposedly named by the local Indians a long time ago. The cave is at the base of them."

They parked the vehicle, put on their backpacks, and started up the side of the hill. When they neared the base of the buttresses, Tom saw four men sitting under a tree. They had just sat down and were digging their lunches out of their backpacks.

"Hi, Tom." The local deputy, Elvin Hansen, was lying down in the shade of a large pine, and he didn't look happy.

"Hello, Elvin. What we got?"

"A friend of mine, Tom."

"Sorry. Who is he?"

"Doc Ward. He was a caving buddy."

Elvin was a local, born and raised in Driggs. He was also a mountain climber, spelunker, skier, search and rescue expert, and general backcountry person. It was why he'd took this job. A lot of what went wrong on this side of the mountains happened in the vast backcountry, including the Jedediah Smith Wilderness.

"What happened to him?"

"Head trauma, depressed right-rear quadrant, and deep scalp lacerations. We haven't moved him very much, been waiting for you and the coroner."

"We heard on the radio that he's right behind us with another ranger, so he should be here in a few minutes. What do you know about the subject?"

"Nice guy and a PhD in anthropology. Hell of an athlete—expert climber, caver, skier. He was an ex-Army Ranger and a loner, but good company for someone who doesn't like a lot of talk. He had money, going by the house he built and the fact that he didn't seem to have to work for a living. Probably inherited his bucks. He spent a lot of time out of town, mostly in Mexico."

"Married? Family?"

"No. He had a housekeeper, a little Mexican gal that I'm pretty sure he was intimate with, but she's gone."

"Gone for the day or just plain gone?"

"I don't know for sure. I asked one of the Idaho deputies to go to the house, and he said that there was no one around."

"How about other family, like parents? Where was he from?"

"Maryland, I think. I've heard that, but I don't know exactly where."

"What's with the burial? The Sheriff said that it might be something Satanic."

Elvin nodded his head at one of the Forest Service officers eating his lunch under the next tree. "Kelly says that it's nothing like that."

Tom looked at the other man. He said, "My degree is in archaeology. I worked a couple of digs in Central America and this guy is buried with some Mexican or Central American artifacts, as near as I can tell."

"Artifacts?"

"Yeah. The hair decorations are a fairly common practice among the indigenous people of the older civilizations and he's wearing an interesting gorget. There's a couple of pots whose decorative style looks real familiar, and the textiles will be fairly easy to identify, I'm sure. Very distinctive needlework."

"Also, he's wearing white cotton peasant clothing, and the style, if I'm not mistaken, is Mexican or Guatemalan."

"Both Central American and Mexican stuff?"

"I'm no expert."

"Where do I find an expert?"

"I went to school at the University of Idaho, and they have a real good grad school up there. It'd be easy to get someone down here to take a look and give us some expert opinions."

"That sounds like a good idea. Would you give me some names?"

"Be glad to."

"Thanks." Tom took a deep breath and opened the top of his backpack to dig out his jar of Mentholatum because it was hot, and the guy was sure to be ripe. "Where is he?"

Elvin stood up. "About a hundred yards up the slope, there's a small cave in the base of that limestone outcrop. I'll take you there."

CHAPTER TWO

"Ritual strangulation?" Tom asked.

"Yeah," said the Coroner. "He was knocked unconscious, or into a coma, but he died of suffocation."

He held up a hand-twisted cord. "This is not just your everyday twine. See this decorative knotting? And it also has a clever one-way slipping knot that was designed for strangulation."

"I don't want to have to deal with any ritual stuff. It's evil."

"I know," the coroner said. "In this time of space shuttles and space travel, people have a hard time believing in a literal Satan. Evil, as such, simply doesn't exist anymore for most Americans."

"If they ever got to see the things we see, it'd make believers of them."

The man nodded. "It gets me down sometimes."

"Me too," Tom said, and the old sadness crept into his heart. This was his job, and someone had to do it. But he had a hard time not turning his heart off when he had to deal with things like this.

Hoskins shook his head and said, "*The heart is deceitful above all things, and desperately wicked: Who can know it?*"

"Is that from the Bible?" Tom asked as it sounded familiar.

"Yes. Jeremiah 17:9. C'mon, let's zip him in, then get him on the Stokes litter and back to town where I can cool him down."

"Yeah, he's getting pretty ripe." Tom turned to the Forest Service people who stood at a distance. "Would a couple of you come over and give us a hand getting this guy down to the ambulance?"

After the litter bearers started down from the cave, Tom turned to the archaeologist ranger. "Let's get this stuff tagged and put in my backpack boxes. I will need you to give me a brief description of each item, and the more detailed the better."

MiT

After they took care of Ward's body, Tom drove to the man's big house to wait for another Teton County deputy to come over with the official order from Judge Herschler to open "Doc" Ward's house. When he and Elvin arrived, Tom used his burglar set to slip the locks. No sense in waiting now that they knew Jeff was on his way with the warrant.

When they entered, Tom was immediately impressed with the huge picture windows that filled most of the east end of the room—framing the Teton's magnificent view. Yet, they appeared a bit strange to Tom—like a mirror image. But while most everything was different on this side of the Tetons, some things remained the same.

"This guy had very serious money," Tom said.

It was decorated in a tasteful, expensive western decor, with lots of wood showing on the walls and floors. Tom knew from his interest in the American southwest the style included museum-quality rugs, like an antique Navajo chief's blanket on one wall, a Beyeta serape on another, and a big Wide Ruins on the floor. He also saw a sizeable original oil by Charlie Russell, which led him to believe that the Frederic Remington sculptures were originals.

However, what caught his eye was a large glass case holding a collection of kachina dolls. They were something that Tom knew something about, so he went to the display and examined the contents. His maternal grandfather served a Mormon mission in the southwest among the Pueblo Indians and brought back a few.

The only two dolls that he recognized were Salako and Bear kachinas. He remembered that the bear doll represented a powerful healing spirit, but the others weren't at all familiar.

He turned his attention away from the glass case. This part of the house was immaculate. No sign of struggle, nothing obviously out of place.

"You say he had a full-time housekeeper?" he asked Elvin.

"Yeah, a little woman from Mexico. Real cute."

"Think there was anything going on between them?"

"Like what? Sex?"

"Something to do with passion."

"Looking for a crime of passion? I thought we had a ritual murder here."

"Just running all the possibilities around in my mind."

"I don't know for sure that anything was going on between them, but you know how it goes—a good-looking woman a long way from home in the house of a good-looking guy. And the winters get long out here." Elvin shrugged his shoulders. "Who knows? I always try to give 'em the benefit of the doubt."

Tom sighed. "And I'm a suspicious prick. Can't help it." Another one of the character defects he was trying to work on.

Tom was a card-carrying alcoholic. The card was in his wallet and had the 12 Steps and 12 Traditions on it, a talisman against his vulnerable side. The upstairs included two large bedrooms and bathrooms, as well as an entertainment center. The man had a collection of jazz and classical music that was impressive as well.

Tom went to another large case. "Media freak."

"Yeah, he always had a digital camera with him. He recorded a lot of our explorations and grotto functions in Idaho Falls."

Tom saw an unlabeled DVD player and almost absentmindedly turned on the TV and machine. A naked, sweating woman came into focus. Her mouth was open, her eyes wide and defocused. Moving her hips and gasping audibly, she was sitting on the pelvis of a naked man with a beard. He was open-mouthed and sweating too.

Tom pushed the stop button on the player and turned off the TV. "Well, that probably answers my question." The woman had been small and Hispanic. "Was that the housekeeper?"

Elvin smiled self-consciously. "I don't remember ever seeing her like that but yeah, that was her. I'll put the DVD in an evidence bag."

Suddenly, they heard a shout from downstairs. It was the other deputy, Jeff.

"Sounds like Jeff found something," Elvin said.

They went to the stair landing and saw the tall blonde deputy in a doorway that led to the basement.

"You won't believe what I found down here," he said.

They all went down the stairs where Jeff led them past a work-table with camera gear on it to a door obscured by a large gas furnace and air conditioner. That door opened into a small, tiled foyer, and in the back wall was a vault complete with a spoked handwheel to drive the tumblers. On the door in florid, nineteenth-century script was painted "First State Bank ~ Sydney, Montana."

MiT

When they finished their initial survey of the house, Tom found what they were looking for in the side yard when two magpies took a couple of hops, looked over their shoulders, and reluctantly flapped away.

Tom walked to where the birds had been tugging at the grass and found a patch of dried blood. Not too far from the blood was a piece of bloody firewood that also had hair and thick tissue, presumably from the victim's scalp.

"Hey, Elvin!" he hollered.

Elvin came around the side of the house and said, "What?"

"Bring me a big evidence bag."

"Whatcha got?"

"Looks like the classic blunt object, a piece of firewood with boogers on it."

"Bingo! I'll be right there. Just a sec'."

Tom sighed and looked up at the mountain spires. They were lit by the afternoon sun, and it made the residual summer snows turn a soft pink and lightened the dark granite to light purples and lavender. Early evening was ordinarily a good time for him, but this murder weapon lowered a pall on the view.

"Here ya go," Elvin said as he walked up with Jeff. "You secure it, please."

Tom turned to Jeff. "Let's do a careful search of this area and see what else we can find. The grass hasn't been mowed for a while so let's take our time and not miss anything."

"Ten-four," the tall man said.

About ten minutes later, Jeff hollered, "Come take a look at this!"

When Tom and Elvin reached the front of the big house, they saw Jeff holding up a license plate.

"Got a license plate—Oregon car." He pointed at the garage. "If you look you can see where the garage was backed into. Looks to me like someone banged into the building, knocked the plate loose, and then lost it when he cut the corner on the driveway and bounced over these rocks. Looks like someone was in a hurry to get out of here." Jeff pointed to where tires had spun in the gravel drive.

"Good work, Jeff. Run the plate and see who it belongs to."

"Already have." He handed Tom a slip of paper.

"Cenovio Osorio. Wilsonville, Oregon. Green 1974 Chevy Impala."

"Whoa," Elvin said. "That was the housekeeper's last name. Osorio."

"You positive?"

"I'm not positive, but I'm pretty sure I've seen it. Oh yeah, she ran the stop sign at the Targhee road and banged into Cappy Capellen's car. Her driver's license said her last name was Osorio. I remember because it was so different from the Sanchezes, Hernandezes, Garcias—the usual Latino surnames."

"Was it a Wyoming license or an Idaho?"

"Uh, Idaho."

"Jeff, run the last name Osorio in Boise and ask for a last name sort. I'll bet one of them is a box number in Driggs."

Elvin nodded. "Yeah. Mail here is a mess because they make the Alta, Wyoming, post office use the Idaho zip. If there were more people here, it would be a real mess."

Jeff touched Tom's arm. "Here comes the boss." Sheriff Harlan's car was coming up the lane toward the house.

The car stopped when it reached the wide yellow perimeter tape, and Big Sam uncoiled himself from the driver's side. Bob Bilyeux got out the other door.

"Good afternoon, gentlemen."

"Hi, Sheriff," Elvin said.

"Whatcha got? I talked to the coroner when he got to town, and it sounded like this is going to make a bunch of noise in the media." Tom took out his notebook.

"The man's name is Amos Nathaniel Ward, 42 YOA. Originally from Owings Mills, Maryland, with degrees from William and Mary, and a Ph.D. in Anthropology from Vanderbilt. That's according to the framed certificates on the walls in his office.

"Also, he has one that says he was a vet. Army Rangers. Expert outdoorsman—climber, kayaker, caver, and who knows what else.

Has an equipment room chock full of outdoor gear, and Elvin knows him personally as an expert outdoorsman."

"You said on the phone that you'd found something real interesting in the basement."

"Yes. Also, we've since found what appears to be a bludgeon. And Jeff just found an Oregon license plate and ran it. The registered owner may be related to the housekeeper, who seems to have disappeared."

"Good. You guys did a real good job for such a short time. I know you're following up on all that."

"We will, don't worry."

When they reached the basement, Sheriff Harlan looked at the vault and said, "Phone DaddyO at Teton Locksmiths, and get him over here." He then bent over a plate fixed to the front of the safe. "Write this down: Schwab Model 7840-6, serial number 2411617, relocking device number 7514."

He turned to Tommy. "I'm going to get the judge to give us an order to have this thing opened. If we can't get the registered combination from the manufacturer, we can try to coax or force the lock. We'll meet here at eight o'clock tomorrow and open it, one way or the other.

MiT

When Tommy got home, it was dark, so he went into the house and turned on the kitchen light. His dog, Millie, came into the kitchen and stretched, then went to Tom's feet and sat to smile up at him as her bobtail slipped quickly back and forth on the tile. She was an Australian blue heeler with the personality of Cocker Spaniel and the heart of an alligator.

"Hi, Mil. Glad to see me?" She stood on her hind feet and placed her forepaws on his thighs so he could scratch under her collar. "Did you miss me, Girl? I'll get you some food in just a minute."

Tom went to his answering machine and saw the light blinking. Both messages were from Polly.

When she answered the phone, Tom felt a sense of relief. He sat down on one of the stools at the breakfast bar and said, "Polly, I love you."

"You sound tired."

He stretched one arm over his head. "I've got another murder investigation going."

"Oh no. I'm sorry." She knew the toll a murder could take on his emotional life because they had been through a lot of this together. The past year had been a mess for both of them.

"This is going to be a sick one, too, I'm afraid."

"Sick?"

"Ritual stuff, maybe satanic."

"Oh, Thomas."

He swiveled the stool and looked out the glass doors at the ballpark lights in town, far below in the valley. It was beautiful.

"I'll be okay. How are you doing?"

"A lot better, now that the divorce is going to be finalized at some real point in time. August first." She sighed.

"I still don't understand why it's taken so long."

"If you had ever lived in California and knew about real estate, state taxes, and the court system down here, you would understand, believe me. We have the most intrusive legal system in the civilized world. And then there are the lawyers."

"You'll like Wyoming a lot better. Life is still livable here."

"There are a lot of things that I love about Southern California."

"Like what?" Tom couldn't think of anything except the ocean. He loved the sea, especially the sight of large ships sailing along the coast at night with their lights ablaze.

"Well, for one thing, it has 171 museums . . . and Disneyland. Ask Jackie about that one—as if you didn't act like a kid there, too! And it's one of the most spiritual places in the world."

"It's also one of the sickest, most murderous places in the world." He had murder on his mind for some reason.

"The second thing I love about the place are the contradictions, the tension of opposites. It may be why the oriental philosophies and religions flourish here. The yin and yang are part of everyday life. You have to be able to accept the contradictions and let it go."

"You're really saying that only a philosopher could love the place."

She laughed. "Maybe that's true. It's true that the place is hell on cowboys."

It was his turn to laugh. He had taken his son, Jackie, to California the previous spring, and the traffic, among other things, had driven Tommy crazy. Too damn many people for his taste.

"If it hadn't been for the AA meetings, I'd have gone nuts."

"Now, there's an example of the spirituality. You forget too easily."

She was right. In California, there were five times the national ratio of people kicking addictions and meeting their personal monsters head-on. Churches were sprouting like mushrooms in a wet summer.

"Are you sure you're going to marry me? How are we going to have a life if you live in California and I live in Wyoming?"

"Yes, I'm going to marry you, and the second part is up to fate. We'll see what You Know Who has on his mind. Mind your own business and take a lesson out of your own book."

"That's why you want to be married at Christmas."

"No. It's because you're such a sentimental sap that if we marry at Christmas, you'll feel so indebted, obligated, and be so saturated with the romance of it that you'll never be able to say a cross word to me. The guilt will keep you in line even when it has worn transparent from use."

"I'm so glad that we're both as manipulative and dishonest as we are. It makes things so much easier." He was smiling. He tickled Millie under the chin with his toe.

"Thank God for alcohol." There was a smile in her voice. "If our fathers hadn't decided to drink, we'd be so bored and boring that we'd have to live in front of the TV set to have a life."

"I love dirty talk."

"Cable television, Glenn Beck, Geraldo Rivera . . . Bill O'Reilly!"

"That's a little too obscene, even for my sick mind."

She giggled, and he closed his eyes. He could see her little blonde head, her hair falling forward, and her pulling it up with her free hand as she talked. "God, Polly, I love you so much . . ." A quaver slipped into his voice.

"Oh, Thomas, I wish I were there. I can tell you're hurting."

He took a deep breath. "I'd give anything for you to be here. This one is going to get me down. I have to admit this satanic stuff scares the crap out of me."

There was a silence. "I'm going to fly out."

"You can't do that."

"Yes, I can." It was a statement. "I can come out for a few days, and Christina can handle things here." Christina, their daughter through youthful indiscretion, was a real estate agent in the family brokerage.

"Are you sure?"

"I'm sure about everything I do."

And she was. In some ways, they were complete opposites.

CHAPTER THREE

At eight in the morning, the locksmith unloaded his equipment, and Jeff helped carry it downstairs. They made their way through a small bunch of curious local law enforcement types from the Driggs PD and Idaho's Teton County sheriff's department who had nothing better to do.

Tommy followed DaddyO, the nickname for Mark D'Addario, the locksmith from Jackson, to the vault and watched as he surveyed the vault.

He turned and looked at Tommy, then pointed at the hand-painted script on the door. "This came from a bank so it's going to be a tough one, especially if it's a retro-fit."

"Retro-fit?"

"Yeah, you can have the wheel pack modified to work around your schedule. For instance, this type had a mechanical clock mechanism as original equipment. See where the key goes in? Well, it looks like it hasn't been used for a long time so that means they probably put a battery-driven wheel pack on this one."

"Why would they do that?"

"Well, when the wind-up mechanism winds down, the door opens and that could be, oh, seventy-two hours. With a battery pack it could be set to take months, depending on the guy's schedule."

"So chances are you're going to have to force it?"

Mark smiled and gestured toward the door. "I'd rather try to manipulate it."

"Manipulate it?"

"Yeah, if it's a Group Two lock, I may be able to listen to the mechanism with a stethoscope and try to get the tumblers to fall by listening. If it's a Group One, which is most likely, I'll have to do something else." He waved at the Looky Lou's who were now standing around. "But I'm going to need dead silence."

Tom turned and saw that Sheriff Harlan was in the group. "Sheriff, Mark needs dead silence while he tries to manipulate this lock."

"Okay, guys, let's give the man some room," Sam herded the onlookers out of the basement.

For almost an hour, Tom watched as Mark worked. He held the stethoscope next to the lock as he moved the dial slowly and methodically back and forth. Finally, he sat back in his chair and said, "I'm going to have to try something else."

Tom looked at the big variable speed drill with its magnetic mount that lay on the floor. "Like drill?"

"Well, it's not that simple. Let's get the sheriff down here and talk it over a little before I start that."

When Sheriff Harlan came down, he asked, "What's happening?"

"I may have to drill, it looks like."

"Okay, so drill."

"First, let me run through some of the back-up, the re-lock mechanisms, that this guy could have in this door. Drilling could cause big problems."

"Shoot."

"First, there are lead linkages, and they're fairly common in older doors like this one. If you try to burn through the door the lead melts and the re-locks pop into place. In case of a re-lock you'll have to go into the vault through a wall."

"But you're not going to try to burn into it, are you?"

"No, I thought I'd try to drill, but we might have a glass plate backup which can shatter and do a re-lock too."

"Will drilling break the glass if you're real careful?"

"Well, I'm familiar with this kind of door because they had one at the school I graduated from, as an example of things we could run into. If they are the same, this one is magnesium/cobalt with carbide chips embedded in the matrix. The only way to get through is to drill until you get to a chip, and then pound on the carbide, which is brittle, then blow the carbide chips out and drill some more. It means a lot of drilling and pounding, and that could break the glass to trip the re-locks."

The sheriff nodded and said, "Go to it. If we have to go in through a wall, we'll go in through a wall. Are you going to have to drill the whole lock out? How long will that take?"

"No, no. I drill through and then use my orthoscopic bore scope and a dental mirror to look at the slots in the wheel pack. I put one slot where it belongs and then extrapolate the other numbers to get the combination."

"How long is it going to take?"

"I don't know. It could take two hours and it could take four." He shrugged.

"Well, go for it. Do you need any help?"

"I could use one man."

"I'll get Elvin or Jeff down here to give you a hand."

"Thanks. I'm going to seal this door with tape, and I want you to initial it. That way you'll be sure that I didn't go into the vault before you got here."

The man sealed the vault with a special flimsy tape, and Sheriff Harlan initialed it with a Magic Marker. Then Mark and Elvin mounted the drill next to the dial, and Mark started to drill. The noise was an incredibly high shriek that drove everyone not wearing ear protection out of the basement. Tom closed all the doors and went upstairs.

When he entered the front room, he saw Kelly Dittus, the Forest Service archaeologist, making annotated drawings of the kachina dolls in the glass case, which Tommy noticed the day before.

"Pretty interesting, huh?" Tom said as he walked up to the man's elbow. The drawings were excellent renderings.

"More than interesting. I worked in the district office in Taos, New Mexico, for four years and got to know a lot about kachina dolls from a man who owned a gallery there." He began to draw another doll.

"I have a few antique dolls that my grandpa collected back in the late 1920s in New Mexico," Tom commented.

The man looked at Tommy and smiled. "I'd love to see them sometime."

"Any time."

"Thanks. Maybe you have some unknown ones too. Wouldn't that be something?"

"Unknown ones?"

Kelly pointed at two dolls on one of the shelves. "I have all the published research materials on kachina dolls and neither of those two appear anywhere in the literature. They are priceless."

"Really?"

"Yeah. And almost all the rest of them are known only from late nineteenth century to earliest twentieth century collections." He pointed. "That one is Tuma-oi, White Chin Kachina. The last known collection of that one was in 1895." He pointed at another. "That's Chowilawu, Terrific Power. It's known from a collection dated 1901. Those three are Owangaroro, Stone Eater Kachinas—the last year their dances were performed was in 1909 and 1910." His voice trailed off in awe.

"You know a lot about these."

"These dolls were very important in the education of the people. The kids learn to recognize the spirits through the figurines, and later, they learn the oral history and medicine ways that corresponded to each doll. It's a wonderful way to teach.

"The men make them from the dry roots of cottonwood trees because the wood is easy to work. The paint scheme is pretty simple—there are six directions and a color to represent the direction from where the kachina comes. Yellow is north, red is the south, white is east, blue-green is the west, and all the colors combined mean up while black means down.

"Distinguishing decorative symbols fall into six classes too: animal and bird tracks; celestials like clouds, lightning, sun, moon, and stars; vegetable such as corn, flowers, cactus and the like; phallic symbols for fertility; inverted V's for kachina officials; and pairs of vertical lines under the eyes represent the footprints of a warrior.

"There are thirteen costume classes, and there's a lot more to it too. It's fascinating stuff."

Tom said, "I'd really like you to take a look at my dolls, I have three and my sister has five, but she lives down in Salt Lake City."

"I'd love it. Maybe I could get another monograph out of it."

"Another?"

"Yes. Those unidentified dolls are going to get me published, no doubt about it."

"Well, have fun. I'm going to run into town and get a burger. Looks like they're going to be working on the vault for quite a while."

When Tom returned, all of the law enforcement tourists were gone. He didn't hear any drilling or pounding when he entered the house, so he went downstairs where Elvin, Jeff, and Sam were watching DaddyO looking into his borescope, manipulating the dials.

Elvin looked at Tommy and gave him a thumbs-up. After fifteen minutes or so, Mark spun the wheeled handle and gently tugged the door until the tape seal barely deformed.

Sam Harlan stepped forward, and when he pulled the vault door open, he was surprised. Instead of the storage vault he had expected, he saw that the room behind the door was large, much larger than anyone had anticipated.

He stepped inside and slid his hand along the wall until he found a double switch plate, flicked up the two buttons, and filled the room with light.

The first man to follow Sam and Tommy into the room was Kelly, and the man instantly drew in a sharp breath at what he saw. Then, after a moment, he said, "Man, this son of a bitch deserved to die."

Chapter Four

The back of the vault was a virtual library with banks of shelving that ran around three walls of the room over rows of filing cabinets. On the wall next to the door was a computer workstation with its own library of software reference works.

The center of the room featured two rows of back-to-back glass display cases displaying beautiful objects fashioned from gold, silver, feathers, enamel, and other precious materials. Enclosed shelving contained more artifacts. They looked familiar only because Tom subscribed to National Geographic magazine, and that was about it for him. But the archaeologist was shaking his head in awe as he strolled around the room.

He finally stopped in front of a glass case at the center of the room. It contained a mummy, obviously the collection's showpiece how it was presented using special lighting inside the case.

The mummy sat with his knees drawn to his chin and wore a headdress made of a wonderfully woven cloth wrapped about his head. Encircling the headdress were several iridescent midnight blue bird plumes. He wore a magnificent cape made of small bird feathers, probably breast feathers. The top third was a checkerboard design of iridescent, yellow, and green feathers.

The bottom two-thirds of the cape was a field of white feathers with a broad stripe of orange and occasional yellow checks ran through it just above the hem. The feathers looked as though they'd been taken from the birds days ago rather than several hundreds of years.

In front of the mummy were ceramic boxes and little leather sacks. At his side was a pouch from which protruded bone and stone instruments.

Dittus's voice was awestricken when he began to speak. "This was the archaeological scandal of the century, and it happened about five years ago. A local guy who ran the government warehouse in Peru supposedly lost a box bound for Washington University. He was a former grave robber, so everyone knew that he'd probably sold it. The shipment included this shaman mummy. They planned to send it north to be curated, then returned to Peru. Nikki Clark, the woman who is on her way down here to look at the textiles in which Ward was buried, was on that dig. She is going to die when she sees this."

He sighed and turned to point to a glass case on the wall. "That is a world class turquoise mask, and it looks real familiar to me, so it may be another stolen piece. Those jade *hachas*, axe heads, are also the kind that you find on display only in Mexico City or Berlin, or the Smithsonian."

He went to a cabinet and pulled a drawer from the wall. Tom was familiar with the design; it was the same in the sample room of the geology building at the University of Wyoming.

Kelly leaned over and looked at the ceramic pieces in the shallow drawer. "*Adornas*–lobe earplugs. My god, this one still has quetzal feathers sticking out of it! I've never seen any that were in this condition before. They look like they were just taken out of someone's ears and set here while they went to the river to bathe."

He opened another drawer and straightened up in shock. Tommy peered around him and saw bracelets, armbands, pectorals, and other pieces. Solid gold.

"Sheriff, we need to get this thing organized."

"When did you say your professor friend was going to get here?"

"She should be here today, but I'm going to phone and make sure she's left. And if she hasn't, I want her to know what she's in for. She may want to bring someone else down with her to help—she isn't just going to be working with a dozen pieces of low-grade burial objects."

He returned to the mummy and stared at it again. "Everyone in the academic world was interested in this guy. He was buried with his medical instruments, as well as his whole pharmacopoeia."

Dittus pointed at the leather sack at the mummy's side. "He had llama leg bones which he used for giving drug enemas too potent to be taken orally. He was buried with over sixty different kinds of drugs that were in all the little boxes and sacks there. The drug industry was drooling at the possibility of examining the contents." Dittus shook his head again. "He even had trepanning instruments used to do brain surgery."

He stared at the dried-up little man for a long moment and added, "This guy was a brain surgeon." He wagged his head in wonder. "They were more advanced in their knowledge than we will ever dream."

MiT

Tom was late meeting Polly's plane, but she didn't seem to mind. She sat in the airport snack shop with a soft drink, sunglasses, and a Mirabella magazine on the table. She wore a chocolate-colored cowboy hat, but the rest of her clothes said it was a fashion piece.

Her clothing was simple: Wrangler jeans, a khaki safari shirt, and expensive brown cowboy boots. But the Hopi silver button earrings and the antique concho belt set them off perfectly.

This beautiful woman had class, and it did not escape the notice of the men in the room. When he entered the airport lounge, more than one stared at her.

And so was Tom. Polly glanced up with a neutral look in her eyes meant to discourage his stare, but when she recognized him, a slow smile spread over her face. She was happy to see him, and he was more than happy to see her. She was perfect.

He walked to the table and said, "Hi."

She just maintained the loving look and took his hand. Not saying a word, just looking up at him for a few seconds, then she said, "Sit down, Cowboy."

He placed his hat on a chair and sat down next to her, taking her hand and raising it to his mouth for a light kiss. "You are one very beautiful woman."

"Thank you. You are one tired man."

"Huh? I don't feel tired."

"I can see the stress in the lines around your eyes. Sure you're not tired?"

He shrugged. "No. Not really."

She stood. "Good," she said and smiled a languorous smile.

"Damn," he muttered and looked around the room, then put his hat over his lap.

"You're gonna have to carry one of them suitcases your own self, Lady," he said.

When she looked over and saw that Tom was hiding the front of his pants, she said, "It seems like the very least I could do. My, my, but aren't you an excitable man." She put on her sunglasses and giggled.

"Excitable ain't the word."

"I hope that doesn't go bad before we get it to the house, Thomas."

"Don't worry, Sugarbritches, Blue Steel doesn't go bad. It may get a little rusty from time to time but it never, ever, goes bad."

In the hot desert, a hundred meters ahead of the car, a soldier with a slung rifle walked out onto the roadway and held up his hand for their vehicle to stop. When the car was near enough to identify the license plate as American, the soldier turned and called to another soldier who sat in the front seat of a battered, olive, drab pickup. Propped against some greasewood was a crudely hand-lettered sign made of tattered plywood that read **Policia Judicial**.

The young soldier in the truck grinned, put on an officer's garrison hat, and walked toward the car. He said something to the man with the rifle, and that man smiled also.

"*Buenos tardes*," he said as he walked to the driver's side of the vehicle and bent to look at the occupants. He recognized them as Indians, and his face took on an arrogant look.

"Get out of the car and open the trunk," he said to the driver. "Everybody out."

The occupants looked at one another, and the driver nodded, almost imperceptibly, as they prepared to get out.

The driver went to the trunk and opened it. The officer nodded, and the soldier took out two cardboard boxes secured with twine. Once the cartons were on the ground, the soldier leaned his rifle on the bumper and took out a knife. He cut the cord on the first box and threw the contents—women's clothing—on the ground. He cut open the second box and took out a flat object wrapped in cloth.

Throwing the cloth on the ground, he looked at a large book made of leather. He opened it and looked at the drawings. "It's a comic book," he said to the officer and tossed it back into the trunk.

Then the soldier stooped to retrieve a third box from the trunk of the big Chevrolet and placed it on the ground. He grunted and said, "Heavy," and then bent to saw at the twine, then opened the flaps.

The three Indians glanced at one another, the officer taking note of their nervous looks. He pushed them aside and walked to the soldier's side. He knelt in the dirt to reveal the object in the box and grunted as he lifted the thing into view.

It was a large piece of rock crystal, and the sun flew out of it in a thousand beams as it was revealed. Its brilliance made him shade his eyes.

"What is this?"

The woman said, "It's the Heart of the World."

"Ahhhh, and where did you steal . . ."

Cenovio's machete sliced through his neck to cut off his voice. Instead of the rest of the sentence, a whistle escaped from the wound as his head dropped onto the asphalt and rolled onto its side, the man's eyes wide with shock.

The officer dove for his rifle, but one of the men grabbed the barrel, and they wrestled for a moment, but the machete wielded by the grim driver cut the young soldier down as well.

The Indians dragged the dead into the roadside brush. One of the men tossed the head onto the bodies then kicked dirt over the bright pool of blood by the edge of the black asphalt. The woman quickly returned the objects to their boxes, set the crates back into the trunk, and slammed it shut. Then the trio jumped into the car and threw rooster tails of dirt into the hot afternoon air as the car screeched onto the road and disappeared into the shimmering distance.

Chapter Five

Tom woke at daylight with Polly in his arms. The resident Steller's Jays were already doing their Ralph and Alice Cramden act in the big fir outside the bedroom window.

He lay in the pale room filled with peace. This feeling was the definition of serenity.

He moved his head on the pillow to look at the gradually growing luster of the summer morning as it worked its way through the trees on the hillside below the house.

It was amazing what intimate human contact could do for one's soul. Giving, taking, sharing in the physical sense opened one to an infusion of what we chose, so poorly, to describe with the word love. It could not last for long because it is not what life is. Life is hard; life can be brutal, but there is such a thing as love, and at that moment, he had it. He thanked God that he could feel everything for this one blessed moment, then picked up a lock of Polly's hair and dropped it. In the magic light of dawn, it seemed to fall in slow motion to her white, fragrant neck. He raised his hand toward the ceiling and wiggled his tingling fingers as he moved his arm in a small arc. His hand left traces and flares of ghostly light behind it.

A bubble of joy rose in him. He moved the hand in a figure eight. It was limned with a faint luminescence that left the lazy eight to flare for a moment against the dark wall. He smiled.

It was almost unbelievable that this woman could raise his consciousness so much that his perceptions took on added dimensions.

It was wonderful. She gave him powers he could not know alone. She was magic.

He put his hand on her thigh under the covers, running it up to the small protuberance of her hipbone. Her hand came down languorously from her pillow and placed itself on the back of his, mimicking it in miniature.

Tom moved the hands very slowly down the thigh and then back up, moving to the inside of her leg as the hands approached her mons.

Polly rotated her hips slowly, making a soft smacking sound with her lips as she spread her legs. Together, he pushed gently down and entered her with his middle fingers. She gave a little start and gasp of pleasure as her mouth opened and her small hand guided his gently, slowly, up and down, in and out. Her eyes were closed, but her mouth was now tense.

She whispered, "Thomas . . . *ahhh!* . . . you'd better hurry if you want to get in on this!"

He rolled on top to enter her, and her pelvis pushed once, taking all of him. She groaned, "Now!" and they climaxed together.

MiT

"We need to be there by eleven o'clock," Tom said as he tossed the dregs of his coffee in the sink and ran some water from the tap.

"How long does it take to get to the ranch?" Polly asked as she ate a spoonful of yogurt.

"It's, oh, fifteen minutes from Bondurant, so about an hour from here, I guess."

"What exactly is a jackpot rodeo?"

"It's a rodeo where the public isn't invited. It's for just the locals—for fun and a dab of money."

"How does it work?"

"Oh, it's lined up by a stock contractor or subcontractor, maybe a rancher. It costs about fifty bucks to enter. There's the roping and bulldogging rodeos or there's rough stock, which is bareback, saddle bronc and bull riding. This one's going to be rough stock. Jackie will be riding in the bareback event."

"Aren't you worried?" she asked with a slight frown.

"About what?"

"That he will get hurt. He's young."

"He might get hurt, but that's part of it."

"I don't understand that at all."

Tommy shrugged. "You'd have to be from this part of the country to understand. Heck, you used to watch me ride, way back when."

"Yes, but explain it to me, in the here and now."

Tommy turned his coffee cup around and around, then said, "I don't think it's really accessible, intellectually speaking."

"Try me."

"Trust me. You have to be raised in it to have any feel for what it means to us."

"Who is *us*?"

"Us is the people, the culture, that is being subsumed by the influx of strangers with their money, their ideas, and their lack of generosity for the people they found when they moved here. They've left damn little room left for us, and the way we do things."

"Is that really so?"

"Yes, hon, it's really so. We are living artifacts of the human past, and instead of being treasured, we're sneered at and called 'rednecks.' Except in the bars and at the tourist rodeos—then we're interesting. That's why we have these private little shows as a way of getting right down in it and letting go.

"We have our own antiquated values and seeing that our boys become men is a real part of it. Being a man in our little world still means knowing physical fear and physical pain and knowing you can rise above it. That's something I want my son to have. Being a man is something that still has value and that means something to all of us, including our women. Hell, in the rest of this country anyone can be a man, including a lot of wannabe women."

"You don't have to be a cowboy to be a man?"

"Nope, but I don't know any men from my little corner of the world who dance around bonfires on weekends, whacking a drum with a rubber tomahawk to feel like one."

"If they weren't getting something out of it, they wouldn't be doing it."

"Pol, God bless them if that's what works. What I'm saying is what those men are searching for is still part of everyday life. We are still horsemen, herders, and hunters, all of which make civilized people go nuts. They can't stand the fact that we still exist—and I am not talking about those dickheads with the doilies around their necks down at the Rancher Bar on Saturday night." He paused. "But it will only be a matter of time."

"Before what?"

"Before they get their way and we're just recent history. They'll invade every last corner of these mountains and grub us out with their money, their politics, their higher sensibilities and their 'no trespassing' signs." He stood up. "But today we are here, and we are real. Let's drive out to Bondurant and see how it's still done."

When they turned through the ranch gate, Polly could see fifty or so pickups and horse trailers parked in the big yard of the ranch. Some of the vehicles were new and expensive, some were crummies in the five-hundred-dollar range, but most were somewhere in between—the vehicles of working-class men and women of the rural West.

The ranch sat in a quaint valley all its own. With its broad ribbon of green willows, Dell Creek ran near the outbuildings, and the snow-laced Gros Ventre Mountains stood in the background. Fragrant, newly swathed hay meadows ran to the sagebrush hills and quaking aspen groves in the middle distance. The vista was stunning and prompted Tom to say, "The Shining Mountains. That's what the Mountain Men called them."

"And these people have it all to themselves. Amazing."

When they pulled up and were looking for a parking spot, Tommy grimaced and said, "There's Holiday's outfit."

"Holiday?"

"Ed Holiday. He and Beth are seeing each other, I heard."

"I'm glad Beth found someone."

"Ed's no good for her, but I guess that's none of my business now that she's my ex." He pointed at a new white Ford pickup and horse trailer with 12-county plates. "There's Wid's truck."

"And who's Wid?"

"One of Beth's brothers. He's the one PRCA, professional cowboy of the bunch, but he's second or third best of the six boys."

"Why didn't the better ones become professionals?"

"Wives, babies, responsibilities. Ford is the best, bar none, and he was on his way to the top. The jukebox says, 'He loves that darned old rodeo more than he loves me,' but when Pattycake moved to the valley from Idaho and Ford saw her, that was it for his rodeoing. Besides, the boys aren't comfortable outside Star Valley. Things make sense to them at home. There's a place to park right behind Kathy Jensen." The truck bore a bug deflector with Cowboy Crazy painted on it.

"Do you know everybody's vehicle on sight?"

"Just about."

After parking the truck, Tom opened the camper shell, dropped the tailgate, and Millie jumped out to start smelling tires. He slid a big Coleman cooler onto the gate and then put a leather rigging on top.

"What's that?" Polly asked.

"My old bareback rigging. Millie! You get back here." The dog trotted back to the truck with her head down. "You stay close, dammit. I don't want no dogfights."

"Looks like that rigging has been shined up quite a bit."

"It's been 'treated', my dear."

"Sorry, I guess I'd better learn the lingo if I'm going to marry you. Or is it 'get hitched'?"

"Hitched."

"Hitched it is."

"You seem awful damn positive for someone who doesn't even have a ring."

She looked up at the perfect summer sky with its puffy cumulus clouds sailing east over the Gros Ventres. Her smile was serene. "You'll marry me," she said. "And I don't need a ring."

"Well good then, let's practice being married." He pointed. "Tote that durn cooler over to where the women are getting the food ready and stay there till I get done here."

"Okay." She slid the cooler off the tailgate and started toward the cooking area. Then she stopped to holler back, "Just don't forget to bring my purse with you, along with that bucking thing."

"Yes, Dear," he hollered back and then grinned as he slammed the tailgate shut. "She'll do," he said to himself.

When Tom walked to where the hamburger grills were set up, he realized that he sent Polly into a crowd of strange women and realized how thoughtless he had been. But when he found her, she had her sleeves rolled up and was making hamburger patties at the side of the valley matriarch, Sis Mulholland.

It was quite a contrast. Sis had short white hair, mammoth denim pants, homemade blouse, and orthopedic shoes and stood beside Polly, who looked like nine hundred dollars. They laughed and acted like neighbors while the other gals smiled at the exchanges between the two women.

"Tommy!" Sis said, "Get your butt over here."

"Hi, Sis."

"Where did you find this girl?"

"She found me. About twenty-five years ago."

"Now, that's a damn lie! No decent girl would pick you, especially with the sorry bunch you used to run with before you married Beth. Oops!"

"It's all right, Mrs. Mulholland," Polly said. "I was lucky enough to get him back after Beth had knocked the corners off him."

"And it was work enough for her, I tell you that," Sis said. She reached up and pinched Tom's cheek with her suety fingers. "But he was the prettiest boy in the country when he was cowboying around here. The girls all thought he was special. If my husband, Ralph, hadn't been home all the time, I'da sneaked him down in the willows my own self."

"Momma!" said a graying, sun-worn redhead who had walked up holding a tray of deviled eggs.

Sis winked at Polly, nodding her head toward her daughter, and said, "But Jolene would know a lot more about them willows than me. Ask Tom some time."

"Momma!"

Tommy decided he'd better get the hell out of there. Women didn't give a hoot what they said or who they said it to, when they were bunched up like that.

Jolene! That was Jolene? That woman had very little to do with his memory of a thin, expectant and opalescent body lying in the fragrant grass of his youth, highlighted by a coppery little patch of hair glinting the summer sun.

When Tom reached the chute area, he picked out the Snow brothers and headed to where they stood with the few non-drinkers. Jackie looked up and smiled when his Uncle Doug nodded his hat brim at Tom and mouthed, "Here comes yer Dad."

"Hello, Son."

"I was afraid you wouldn't make it. Have a Coke."

Tom popped the can top and said, "Wouldn't miss it for the world. Here, this is yours," and handed the boy the bareback rigging.

"That was your riggin'."

"It was your grandpa's. Now it's yours, like the .30/.30 I gave you last year."

"Gol', Dad, thanks."

Tom put his arm over his son's shoulders and was glad for the muscle he felt. Working on his Uncle Doug's ranch was doing the boy some good.

"Hi, Doug. Hi, Wid. Deloy. Ford. Ernest." He shook hands with each of the brothers in turn. Though none of them said anything, they all had smiles on their faces, and their eyes were real friendly. That made him glad because they had been brothers to him for a lot of years.

"Look what Dad gimme," Jackie said.

Wid reached out, took the rigging, and whistled as he looked at the stamp on the rigging skirt. "Jackie, this is a Pete Dixon riggin', probably made in the '40s. It belongs in the King Ropes museum over in Sheridan. I'll give you five hundred dollars for it right now." He reached in his pocket and took out a wad of 100s.

Jackie's eyes got big, and he looked at Tommy.

"It's yours to do with as you please," Tom said.

"Nah, Uncle Wid. It's worth a lot more than five hundred ol' dollars. This was my grandpa's . . . and my dad's." He took the rigging back from his famous uncle. Wid smiled and winked at Tommy because the boy had passed the test with colors flying. All the brothers were grinning.

"You're putting some muscle on this kid, Doug," Tommy said and squeezed the boy's triceps until he winced.

Ford reached out and took the boy's hat. "Dougie, if you paid the kid once in a while, he might be able to get himself a decent hat." Ford stuck his finger through a small hole in the front of the crown, and the cheap felt parted like cheese. Ford added two more fingers and then punched out the whole top of the hat.

"Now look what you done, Ford," said the boy's Uncle Ernest. "You ruined the kid's dang hat. Shoot!" He reached into the back of the pickup he was leaning against and retrieved an expensive Panama straw cowboy hat that Tommy knew cost at least sixty dollars. "Guess I'll have to give him one of mine." He took the protective plastic off the hat and handed it to the boy, whose mouth was hanging open.

"Put it on," said Deloy, "it'll keep the sun off yer face and save you some freckles. Heck, you already look like you been walking behind a horse that's been eatin' bran."

Jackie put on the hat, and it was a perfect fit. Tommy's eyes were wet for some reason.

"Only one thing, Jack," said Ernest.

"What?"

"You pull it down real tight, so that snaky little horse don't whip it off you and get it dirty."

"I'm gonna try, Uncle Ernie."

"What horse did you draw?" asked Tom and took a swig of the cold Coke.

"A mare named Peter Breath," said Jackie. "What a dumb name."

Tom blew Coke through his nose while the uncles dropped their heads and toed the dirt. Except for Uncle Wid, who was grinning like a possum eating shit because he was the one who named the horse after buying her at the BLM horse auction in Rock Springs.

Tom closed his eyes and dropped his head so Wid's grin wouldn't make him irrigate his sinuses again. He swallowed, wiped his nose, and said, "Pretty snaky horse, huh?"

Wid's own eyes were watering when he choked out, "Yeah, she's a swivel hipped bi . . . cuss. I rode her both times I drew her, but she's a triple A bucker for sure." He took out his handkerchief and wiped his eyes as a puzzled Jackie watched the men.

"What's she do?" Tom asked.

Now serious, the brothers leaned in and watched Wid's hands as he made the motions that followed his description of the horse's bucking habits.

"First, she's bad for rearing in the chute. Second, she's small enough that she'll try to bang your legs on the chute just as the gate is about to open. Jackie, you gotta get your spurs up and keep 'em up once you've got your seat. Are you paying good attention?"

Wid was now looking right into Jackie's eyes, and the boy was meeting the man's earnest look and concentrating on what was said. He was drinking it in.

Tom leaned back and took another drink of soda. The boy was in better hands than his own. Thank God for family.

CHAPTER SIX

Tom was talking to Clement Meeks when Ed Holiday walked toward them. The hair stood up on the back of his neck when he saw the man even though they'd been acquaintances for years.

Ed had a can of Coors in his hand, and he switched it to his left when he stuck out his right to shake. Tom took his hand.

"Hi Tom, thought I'd come over and say hi."

"Hi, Ed. Good to see you again."

"Hi, Clem."

"Ed."

"Tom, I'm seeing Beth. I wanted you to know that."

"I knew, Ed. Jackie told me."

"Yeah, I guess he would do that alright." Ed stared at Tom for a moment and said, "I hope this doesn't cause any hard feelings."

"It doesn't, Ed, trust me. I'm glad that Beth has someone, she's not herself unless she has someone to do things for."

Tom was aware of the irony in that statement. Beth was a caretaker and people pleaser to a fare-thee-well.

"Anyway, I've got someone, too, and Beth has told me that she's happy about that. As a matter of fact, that's my lady coming now."

Polly walked up, and Tom said, "Polly, meet Clem Meeks, an old friend of mine, and Ed Holiday."

"My pleasure, gentlemen." Polly stuck out her hand and shook with the men.

Clem pinched the brim of his hat and said, "Ma'am." Holiday took his off when they shook.

"Tommy, come and get something to eat," Polly said.

"Okay, Hon." Tom turned to the men and said, "See you when they get the bulls out of the way and the saddle broncs ready." The bull riding had been scheduled first because two riders had other rodeos to get to.

"Hey, Thompson." It was Ed.

"Yeah?"

"You gonna ride today?"

"Nope. Jackie's going to have to hold 'er down for the Thompsons today."

"I'm gonna be riding for one of the Thompsons—Beth. Saddle bronc."

"Then you'll be riding against Deloy and Ford Snow, and Beth is a Snow too."

"And Wid, don't forget Wid."

Tom felt the blood filling his face in spite of himself. He knew that Holiday was trying to get a rise out of him in front of Polly, and the prick was getting it done.

"Well, you got your work cut out for you. Maybe you should try bareback, instead. Then only Jackie will put you in the sack."

Holiday's face went pale. He glared, took the last swig from his beer, pooched his cheeks, and swallowed. Then he flipped the can between Tommy's feet.

Clem squinted, looked at Tom, looked at Holiday. "No fights, period. Them's the rules." Clement was one of those good old boys with fingers like bratwursts who meant exactly what he said and could back it up a hundred percent, plus change.

Holiday spun around to leave, and Tommy felt his pulse racing.

"Gonna go get himself some more of that spurring fluid, I guess," said Clem. He looked at Tommy. "Go get yerself something to eat with your pretty friend, Tom. He's about a dumb head."

"Dumb enough to think he can ride with the Snows."

"Don't write him off. Ed's a hell of a rider, drunk or sober. He may be a prick, sorry ma'am, but he does know how to ride buckin' horses."

"See you over at the chutes, Clem."

The big man pinched the brim of his hat again and walked away toward the crowd at the corrals.

Tommy looked at Polly for the first time since the confrontation began and saw she was pale with anger.

"Sorry about that," Tommy said.

"You had to give him that dig, didn't you?"

"Yup."

"You men and your damn male strut. It was juvenile."

"Yup, you're right. Lots of juveniles around here. Little ones, big ones, and some about this tall." He held his palm over his hat. "But don't expect an apology."

When it came time for the saddle bronc event, Deloy was the first cowboy to ride, scored an eighty-two, and that number wins a lot of money, even at big shows. It takes the combination of a very good horse and a very good rider to make that score.

Two more riders came up. One got bucked off, and the other scored a lowly 60. Wid Snow, who made more than a half-million dollars a year as a pro cowboy, was the next rider. He made it look easy, his left hand moving up and down, keeping the pressure on the animal. He predicted the animal's actions through that arm, tied to the animal's muscular neck and head. And where the horse's head went, the body was quick to follow.

Wid kept his knees hooked under the saddle's swells as he raked the horse's shoulders and ribs, sawed the rope up and down as though he were playing a living instrument. He scored an eighty-two, just like his older brother.

When Ed Holiday got up, he grinned like a jack-o-lantern. And he was drunk. Tommy was helping with the animals, and when Holiday straddled the chute and looked into Tom's face with his spooky smile, Tom smelled his breath, and it reeked of alcohol.

"Keep your eye on this one, Thompson," he said as he took hold of the bucking rein.

When the gate swung open, the big, powerful gray horse blew out into the arena as though he'd been levitated. His first jump ended with an insane squeal of rage, a ripping fart, and the squealing, slapping sound of tortured leather as the animal propelled himself into the arena. The men at the chute heard Holiday's grunts and curses from thirty yards away.

The horse jumped again, straight into the air, and landed with all four hooves in an area no larger than a dishpan. Holiday's body compressed like an accordion, and his hat whipped down onto the ground as the big gray vaulted back into the air and twisted himself so that his front legs were almost opposite his back legs. Ed stayed in the middle, but the force of the landing was hard enough to make the rider groan from the shock, and Ed's bared his teeth in a grimace of pain. A big bubble of mucous ballooned out of his nose then popped and flew away.

The horse spun, throwing his head down. For the first time, Holiday seemed to lose control, and Tom thought he was going down. But Ed stabbed the horse viciously with his spurs and powered the bucking rein. The animal gave one more twisting buck then went across the arena in great bounds. The rider stroked him with the spurs and played him as though he were now a frisky stable horse. The horn blew on the second bound, the pickup men took Ed off his back, and it was over.

"I'll be a son-of-bitch," said one of the chute men. "If that ain't a eighty-five I'll kiss your ass 'til your hat flies off."

He was close. It was good for an eighty-six.

Tommy felt like hell. He'd goaded this man and said that his fifteen-year-old son could out-ride him. If the goading inspired the ride, then he kicked himself for doing it. If the man were really that good a rider, then he'd made himself look like a fool. Either wa,y Holiday had made Tom look foolish.

He turned to Clem, who stood beside him and said, "I guess I let my mouth overload my ass."

Clem smiled wryly and said, "Looks like. That was one helluva ride."

The next rider got dumped right in front of the gate, and the horse leaped across the ground like a frolicking colt until they hazed him out of the arena.

The rider after him drew a lazy snip-nosed sorrel that made him look bad.

Then it was Ford's turn.

He had drawn a big line-back buckskin with insane eyes. As Tommy twisted his hands into the animal's black mane and gripped the animal's chin with all his might, he could feel the animal's power. The animal was big, and he was crazy. This was either going to be really good or really bad.

"Who is this spooky son-of-a-bitch?" he asked through clenched teeth.

"Rum Runner, a proud-cut mustang. He's a gooder," said Wid, who was working across the chute from Tom. "He'll make you money or he'll stomp a mud hole in your ass. He don't like people, and that's a natural fact."

Tom looked at Ford's face and saw the slight smile that was always there. His eyes were serene as he winked at Tom, giving him the nod. The gate flew open.

The horse put his head down and screamed, then threw himself on the ground to crush the rider's leg. Ford calmly put his boot out, giving a push on the ground that seemed to vault both him and the animal off the dirt and back into the air.

As the animal came down, he twisted himself into a huge knot of muscle and man. Ford reached out and ran a spur down the whole length of the animal's neck, and the horse damn near turned himself inside out. He flew into the air with another squeal of rage and almost threw himself over backward as he pawed at the air, then flew eight feet high as he brought his hind hooves almost to his nose.

The whole while Ford hooked him on one side as he hooked the opposite side to stoke the horse into a frenzy. One side of Ford's brain was doing one thing while the other did another to force the animal to galvanize one acrobatic leap after another.

Tom could see the art in it, as could all the other experienced riders.

The horse balled himself up again, this time coming away from his contact with the ground in a sideways vault. Ford lifted the bucking rein high over his head and raked the horse evenly, effortlessly, while he flew through the air at a forty-five-degree angle.

When the horse landed at the eight-second horn, he seemed to crumple in the middle because his mind had been blown. He'd been ridden and knew it. The ride earned a score of ninety-four and was the winner by a mile-and-a-half.

Polly had straddled the top rail only a few feet from the chute. She'd been with Deloy and Ford's wives, and they'd explained what was going on. When Tom walked, over Polly's eyes were wide.

"I had no idea. When I used to watch you ride, I was always in the grandstands. It looked . . . I guess athletic would be the word. But over here close you can see the power, the tension." She smiled a wan little smile. "I had no idea." She took his arm.

"Did you like it?"

"Honestly?"

"Honestly."

"No."

Tom stopped and looked at her in surprise. "How come?"

"Thomas, this may come as a great shock to you, but there is a whole world of people out there who don't enjoy this kind of action. It's too much, it's . . ."

"Scary?"

"That and more. It's simply too much for someone who isn't familiar with this world."

"It's the only world I ever knew, except the military."

"And that was more of the same kind of thing, wasn't it?"

"In a way, I guess."

"It's violent."

"It's real." He crooked a finger under her chin. "That's it. It's real—it makes you feel so much more alive."

"Well, you're welcome to it. My idea of feeling alive is a steam and a massage."

"Different strokes for different folks. Welcome to my world."

"Well, the people are nice. And honest! They all come right out and say what they're thinking, don't they?"

"Except when it wouldn't be polite." He patted her hand and said, "There's Ed and Beth. I owe him an apology. You stay here."

She gripped his arm, and he felt her fingernails dig into his arm. It hurt like hell. She muttered, "If you don't think I can handle meeting your ex-wife you are sadly fucking mistaken."

He was shocked. Polly never swore.

"Then let's go."

Ed leaned against the fender of a pickup, not getting too far away from the beer tub or the jug of Black Velvet the boys were passing around. It brought back a lot of bad memories for Tom.

Beth had her back to Tom and Polly. It was Ed who noticed their approach. Tom saw him drop his head and say something, and he saw Beth stiffen. She didn't turn around until Ed looked over her head and said, "Quite a show, huh Thompson?" He was really drunk now.

"Yeah. They sure rounded up some winners for stock."

Beth turned around, and her face was pale, even under her tan. She took off her sunglasses, and her eyes crinkled as she attempted a smile.

"Beth this is Polly, Polly this is Beth." The women shook hands, and then both turned their eyes to Tom. Suddenly, he felt terrible.

"Ed, I owe you an apology. That was one hell of a ride."

"Thanks." He took a big swig of his beer, and Beth grimaced, then lowered her head and put her sunglasses back on.

There was a very awkward silence for a moment before Polly said, "Let's go." Simple. They turned and left.

When they were a few yards away, Tom said, "Thanks."

"You know, that really embarrassed her. You do the dumbest things."

"No shit?"

"No shit."

What a night, Tom thought as he swept through the lazy ess turns of the Hoback River canyon road on the way home. It was midnight, and a big moon was blanching the cliffs and trees before it dropped down to scallop the cold river's undulating surface with light.

"And what a day," he added aloud.

He looked down at Polly's sleeping face. She had folded his jacket for a pillow, put it on his lap, and was asleep before they hit the ranch gate. Now her mouth was open, and she was breathing deeply. All the lines were gone from her face, and she slept in an innocence he hadn't seen since his son had slept on his mother's lap the same way, years and years ago.

Tears came to his eyes as he looked back through the windshield at the road and moonlit canyon. The memories of those lost nights when he had driven this same canyon as they came back from some local event made his heart hurt.

He sighed and wiped his face, then laughed at himself. Things were better now than they ever had been.

He turned his mind to the little miracles of the day. He saw Jackie get a deep seat in his dead grandpa's rigging. He hung onto the top rail of the chute with one hand and, with the other, gripped the handle as his thin muscles stood out in his forearms. Spurs high, his face was white as he nodded at his Uncle Wid's last-minute advice on the mark-out rule.

He'd been smooth, so smooth, as his genes took over. He lay back against the horse's rump and spurred the animal at will. He looked just like Ford, and Ford was the best in this corner of the country. And he won it with an eighty-four! He'd won the damn thing. Tommy's throat tightened with emotion.

And then he laughed out loud as he remembered something else that had happened, the gust of laughter making Polly stir on his lap.

Tom had stood with the whole Snow bunch and seen his dog Millie bristle up and growl as she circled with the red heeler that belonged to Ernest. He started to holler at the dog, and then he remembered that by some horrible act of fate, he'd been given a half-grown dog whose name was the same as his ex-mother-in-law. And the woman was standing about three feet away from him.

"Uh, Jackie, go get that darn dog. Please."

His son had just looked at him with those big innocent eyes, took a sip off his soda, and said, "Heck, Dad, why don't you just holler her name and she'll tuck her tail."

Tom had seen red, spluttered and growled, then strode over to get his dog.

Score one for the kid. He knew he was going to hear that story a few times during the years he had left.

And Beth.

It had been dark, and the musicians, locals, were grinding their way through *Queen of the Silver Dollar* as their pudgy platinum blonde singer gave it her all.

Tom had felt a light touch on his arm and looked down to see that Beth stood next to him. She leaned around him and said, "Polly, can I borrow Tommy for a minute or two?" Polly hadn't even paused, just smiled and said, "Of course, Beth."

They'd walked out past the vehicles and stood next to the corral. The moon was rolling up over the Hoback Rim to silver the new-mown hayfields and fences.

She'd cried, and he'd held her. She was so small, so cold, and he'd put his jacket over her, then waited until she could speak.

"Tommy, now I know now that I have a problem. Finally."

Tom said nothing. He couldn't say anything because he was praying.

"I picked Ed, he didn't pick me. I can see that."

She wiped her face with the backs of both hands. "When he found out I was seeing Ed, Jackie told me that I was getting someone who needed fixing, and someone who couldn't be fixed. He told me right there and then that I had Alanon."

Tom smiled a little smile and didn't say anything. He'd told her before that Alanon was an organization, not a disease, but it had gone over her head.

"Where do I go, Tommy? God, what do I do?"

"Look in the paper for an address and go to ninety meetings in ninety days. Let those people love you 'til you can love yourself, instead of everybody else. And pray for understanding."

"Lord, but Ed embarrassed me. The drinking was bad enough, but picking a fight with one of my own brothers . . ."

"Well, Ernest made short work of that. Do you remember patching me up and taking my side even when I was more wrong than Holiday was today?"

"Oh, hell yes!"

They had laughed, she'd wiped her nose on his jacket, and he'd smiled as she apologized. And then she'd broken his heart: she looked up at him and said, "Come home. We need you."

The big lump came back to Tom's throat as he remembered kissing her wet, cold cheek and said, "I can't. I've changed."

He picked out the Sulphur Springs Bridge as it came up in the headlights. They rumbled across it and broke out onto the sagebrush flat across the river from Willow Creek where he saw that the moon had washed it all clean and bright.

And Tommy felt clean because he'd said the right things to Beth, and he'd said the right things to his son. He'd told Mom Snow that he loved her and her children and always would. He'd thanked her for her love all those years, and she'd cried with happiness and kissed him. Then he'd danced with all the girls, Polly danced with all the men and charmed their asses off. And now the prettiest girl at the dance was going home with him.

If he didn't have a flat tire before they were home, the day was going to be as close to perfect as it was possible to get.

Chapter Seven

Sunday morning was also perfect. Tom rose early and did his exercises on the deck as the first rays of sun came over the mountains. The jays swooped down on the sunflower seeds he'd piled at the edge of the deck and brazenly ate as Tom did his sit-ups less than ten feet away. Then he left for his morning run along the trails that laced the mountain behind his house.

He was reading on the deck when Polly came downstairs, poured herself a cup of freshly ground coffee, and then joined him. She took a sip then reached over to tug at his hair where it touched his neck.

"Good morning."

"Good morning." He leaned down for a kiss, and her mouth opened slowly and took the kiss with lazy sensuality. He moved his head back and looked at her face. Her mouth was still open, and her eyes had darkened to a cobalt blue. He shook his head. "Drink your coffee, Hotpants."

"I thought my name was Sugarbritches."

"Same thing. Drink your coffee, I've already had my exercise this morning."

She laughed and took another sip. then stood to step onto the deck where he joined her.

He reached out with one arm and put it around her. "Beautiful, huh?"

The valley was full of light as it broke down the morning fog above the Snake River and limned the tall cottonwoods that crowded its course. Green trees, green pastures, green mountains. Twenty shades of green, at least. It wasn't Ireland, but it would do.

Polly kissed his forearm and said, "I love this place. You done good."

He took another drink of coffee and said nothing.

"What a pair we were last spring, me trying to nurse you and the neighbor's nanny coming over to nurse me when I couldn't help myself. A real sick ward." She reached down and traced his scars with her finger.

Tom nodded. He remembered lying on the couch as he slowly recovered from his stab wounds and looked out through the French doors, day after long day, as Polly did her best to nurse him. She had used a walker as she recovered from a smoke inhalation-induced coma.

He knew they were getting better when she emptied his bedpan off the deck and said, "So this is what it feels like for you guys."

When he asked what she meant, she'd smiled and said, "I've always wanted to pee off a deck, and now I've done it."

It had made him laugh and then cry out from the pain that flared in his wounds. It hurt like hell, but it was funny, even after all this time.

He put his face on her breast and kissed it lightly. "Have I ever said 'Thank you' enough?" he asked.

"Of course. Uh, maybe not, now that I really think about it."

"Then I would like to thank you again. Inside, on the couch."

She smiled and flipped her coffee dregs into the brush below. "If you feel up to it, Exercise Man."

MiT

They drove to the Snow King Hotel at one o'clock that afternoon to meet the expert from the University of Idaho, Dr. Clark.

She turned out to be a small woman with sharp eyes and a ready smile.

Tommy asked, "Have you had a chance to look at the burial objects at the sheriff's office, Doctor Clark?"

Polly broke in. "Wouldn't we be more comfortable out by the pool?"

Dr. Clark smiled, "Yes, I was out there this morning, and it's very pleasant. No kids running and screaming, just this clean mountain air and sunlight."

Once they gathered around the table beside the blue pool, Dr. Clark said, "Yes, I've looked at the artifacts as well as the clothes the victim was wearing, and I'm sure that they are Mexican. The pants and shirt are plain peasant-hand manufacture still popular only in some remote mountain areas. Unfortunately, most Mexican men now wear cheap American athletic-style clothes.

"I would say that they were made special for the dead man because he was an Anglo and very tall. Most Mexican people in the south are quite small. Something significant is that the cloth and workmanship is very fine. It is embroidered, and I'm guessing that the clothing is actually a wedding 'suit'."

"Why do you say 'south'?" Polly asked.

"He was buried in a woolen serape typical of Oaxaca state. It's black with vertical red stripes and a stylized corn plant motif." She smiled and shaded her eyes against the bright mountain sun. "It's interesting because Dr. Ward is notorious in the field of cultural studies of the Mixtecs, one of the major indigenous cultures of Mexico. Generally speaking, it is also the least appreciated of the major peoples and their ancient world. They were highly respected by the Aztecs for their astronomical and astrological skills.

"For instance, when the Spanish were advancing on the capital city of the Aztecs, named Tenochtitlan, Montezuma was carried hundreds of miles to a place called Achiutla to consult with their priests and to find out what the Aztecs' future held."

She looked around the table and added, "They are one of the most under-appreciated cultures of the western hemisphere."

Dr. Clark now pursed her lips, hesitant to speak. "As for Mr. Nathaniel Ward, let me begin by saying that a *codex* is a manuscript volume, usually one from antiquity. The name comes from *caudex*, which indicates that they were originally written on tree bark or wooden tablets. There were six known codices from the ancient Mixtec culture, the people then known as the Cloud People." She looked at Polly. "They are the gentlest people you will ever meet, and their state, Oaxaca, has been, and still is, the poorest and most repressed by the government in all Mexico.

"Anyway, those six codices were the basis of most of the studies of the literature of the Mixtec culture until about five years ago, when Ward announced he had possession of a codex Lady Eight Eagle that is named for himself—Codex Ward. It's the generational history of a line of people who appear in no other known codex. But there is internal evidence from his papers that there is at least one other codex that corroborates the line of caciques, rulers, described in Codex Ward." The woman's brow knitted, and her voice trailed off.

Deeply engrossed in the conversation, Polly leaned forward and observed, "It sounds like he did something very wrong as far as you experts are concerned."

Dr. Clark grimaced. "It's not that he did anything really wrong, it's just that he wouldn't let anyone study the codex except to have it authenticated, and a British auction house did that! Perhaps you are familiar with the controversy over the refusal by Israeli scholars to broadly disseminate the Dead Sea Scrolls for many years after their discovery.

"Well, this is a similar case. The difference is that Ward has a reputation for dealing precious artifacts, and there are rumors that the Codex Ward may be on the market! The recent sale of the priceless Gospel of Judas is an example of what unscrupulous men like him will do.

"Scholars around the world, including myself, would kill for the chance to examine the codex or codices, which, incidentally, he has used as the basis of some original and brilliant scholarship."

It was Tommy's turn to be interested. "Did you say kill?"

Dr. Clark looked surprised for a moment. "Why, I guess I did say 'kill'. And I've been talking about the man as if he were still alive. He has been murdered, hasn't he?"

"Yes. And murdered in what may have been a ritual manner too. Does that sound like the handiwork of an academic?"

"Only in a very, very meticulous and poetic way—speaking of poetic justice." She looked around the table to see if the black humor had registered, but it had not. "Is there more, besides being buried with ritual objects?"

"He was knocked unconscious and then asphyxiated with what has been described to me as a ceremonial strangling rope," Tom answered.

"That's very interesting. Ritual strangulation and mutilation were common to most of the ancient cultures in the southern two-thirds of this hemisphere. As a matter of fact, it's reported that it still goes on among the remnant Tiahuanaco people in the Lake Titicaca area of Bolivia-Peru, and in Chile."

Polly gasped. "It's still going on?!"

Clark nodded. "It has been reported reliably. No one has come forward as an actual witness, but it's possible that there are academic people who have been witnesses. But they won't report the ceremonies because it would be too controversial, and it would end their academic careers."

She leaned back in her chair. "We must remember that most of the world hasn't changed as much as the northern half of this hemisphere and Europe. As a matter of fact, there are still many people whose fundamental life and customs have changed only superficially over the last few thousand years. When one goes into these ancient cultures, one has to be very careful about looking at what goes on through our late twentieth century, especially American politically correct, eyes."

Dr. Clark added, "And underline 'American.' Ours is doubtless the most intrusive post-colonial culture. Just like the British, French, Dutch, Portuguese, and Spanish colonial times, we will probably have to learn our lesson in turn."

Polly was interested. "What lesson is that?" she asked.

She answered. "That, in most instances, we should keep our values to ourselves."

"That's been my experience, God knows," Tommy said, thinking about Southeast Asia and his experiences there.

"I would like to take a look at the collection before the place is swarmed by agencies and people with legal stature larger than our own," Dr. Clark said.

"Okay then, let's go." Tom went to pay the bill. As he was leaving, he overheard Polly say, "Oddly enough, I have business interests on the coast of Oaxaca at a beautiful place named Huatulco."

When they had parked at Ward's place, Tommy asked, "Doctor Clark, something you said has been bothering me. Do you think that an expert would actually murder Ward for the book you were talking about?"

"Not an academic type, I'm sure. However, the codex does have an enormous value as an artifact. Underground collectors spend untold millions, perhaps billions, each year for rare things plundered around the world. The codex is one-of-a-kind, and there might be a rich collector whose passion for literary items could be enough to warrant it in his own mind. Or another might have it done if enough value has been ascribed to it. Who knows?"

Clark shook her head. "There are collectors out there who will spend more money for a few small items than my whole department's annual budget." She looked at Tommy, and the smile was gone. "From my point of view, and that of many, many others, it is a catastrophe. More knowledge of ancient civilizations is lost in any given year than is generated at universities and government institutions, worldwide, in decades."

"You are angry about that, aren't you?"

"I'm damn mad!"

"Mad enough to kill?"

Dr. Clark's smile returned. "Not me, but nice try."

"But someone else in the academic world, perhaps? Sorry, if I keep pursuing the point."

She grimaced. "I honestly don't know. It's not inconceivable that some academic with an aberrant personality might be driven over the edge by the illegal or immoral activities of someone like Ward.

"But, if I were you, I'd look for someone from that underworld I spoke of. When there is that kind of money changing hands, it's realistic, I think, that men would kill or contract out for a killing."

It was Tommy's turn for a grim smile. "It doesn't have to involve millions, and I know that from personal experience. Life is so precious, yet people are capable of throwing one away like a candy wrapper out a car window."

Chapter Eight

Tommy stood on the porch and stripped his T-shirt, then took down a towel that hung from a nail on the side of the garage, then dried himself after his morning run through the woods. It was another wonderfully cool early morning, and songbirds filled the woods with their songs. The Western tanager he often saw flitting through the trees sang his lovely melody from a nearby tree. Tom went to the end of the walk to scan the pines for a glimpse of its brilliant black, white, orange, and red plumage but had no luck at glimpsing the furtive bird.

"C'mon, Millie," he said and opened the screen door for his dog. She smiled up at him and stepped slowly over the threshold. Her short Australian heeler legs were a distinct disadvantage when running any distance, though her dingo blood made it possible to trot all day.

In the shower, he went over the Ward murder in his mind. He received a personal phone call from the FBI agent now in charge of the federal part of the Ward affair. While the murder was still Tom's responsibility, all the rest of Ward's sins were now the government's business, and much of the man's interests involved interstate commerce, which is the Feds' field of play. In the two days since Dr. Clark returned to Idaho, much more had been discovered, and the range of the man's activities impressed everyone.

Tom smiled at the memory of Dr. Clark's gasps as she opened drawer after drawer, box after box of Ward's collection—some stolen from government and university collections, but most had been unique and priceless pieces collected from the field. The bulk of it equaled the best public collections while the best rivaled the crowning works of the world's best museums.

Experts linked Dr. Ward's computer workstation directly to the National Security Agency, and it gave up its trove in short order. The entries in a master file had been formulaic: "It 347: Pec multi Tol, 93.2 Au, 52.1cm/120.4cm, 22.3cm/38cm, 40.8 T; CusKSI.1 11-9-06 700,000Eu/Ref METO-05 #79, VenJBL.1."

One of the crypto experts had broken it out almost at a glance: "*Item 347: Chest ornament with multiple elements; product of the ancient Toltec culture; 93.2 percent pure gold, measurements of the main elements in centimeters; weight in Troy ounces; code for buyer and date sold; selling price in Euros, catalog number for Mexican/Toltec collected in 2005 the 79th item received that year or the 79th Toltec, or even the 79th Toltec gold item received that year, code for vendor.*" The IRS was having them break out the whole record so they could attach Ward's estate.

But it was another encrypted file that the NSA cryptologists broke out that interested Tom and a few other people. Ward was deeply into the study of hallucinogens. He had a virtual library on the chemistry, use, and religious practices associated with them, and he had found a way of helping to fund their research by selling them. He was a select dealer in exotic drugs that were unknown to any other researchers. With the new interest in native religions by moneyed Americans, Ward found a way to make money from something that interested him and excited the antisocial aspect of his personality.

Dr. Clark had made a brilliant connection when she proposed that the Peruvian mummy's pharmacopoeia might have contained viable remnants of unknown hallucinogenic mushrooms and other plant materials that Ward's lab had been able to cultivate. A lab at a Florida university was now investigating the idea.

Ward funded legitimate research through a foundation in Florida that sent people all over the world to collect them. He also funded research into mystical practices of indigenous peoples from the Arctic to the other extremes of all continents, even being welcomed into various rites of groups as diverse as Siberian Eskimos and Colombian jungle peoples. Bogus or genuine, it appeared he was a practicing shaman, so he doubtless indulged heavily in his own products.

Tom turned off the shower and pushed the curtain aside to retrieve a towel. As he dried himself, he smiled. As an ex-addict himself, this was a side of Ward he wanted to know more about because addictive personalities, in general, interested him. He liked to study what drove them, how they functioned, and their behaviors when whipped by their personal demons. He liked to compare them with his old self in order to check how far he had come by comparison.

Addicts are too often people given exceptional powers that they turn against themselves. Usually smart, sometimes brilliant, always self-destructive, they make fascinating criminals when their genius runs athwart the running sea of the law.

However, artifacts dealing and designer drugs weren't Tom's main deal. Ward had been murdered in Tom's territory, and his murder was what really concerned him, and the Feds were welcome to all the rest of it. Jackson Hole was a small place, and a guy like Ward may have been exotic and a genius who deserved to die, but you couldn't kill him and get away with it. Not here, not yet.

MiT

Tom was running late when he got to the law enforcement center. He walked past the reception desk and paused when he heard hysterical laughter coming from his office. When he went in, he found his two partners laughing so hard they had tears running down their faces.

"Please stop!" Lewis said to the other detective, Brad.

"What's so funny," he asked.

Brad groaned, "We arrested a shoplifter at the Albertsons store last night."

"Yeah, so?"

Brad said, "You see, Tom . . ." His hand appeared from below his desk with a turkey baster.

He went directly to Sam's office and knocked on the door.

"I'm busy."

"Sorry Sam, it's important."

"Well come in then, but make it quick." The sheriff was sitting behind two substantial stacks of paperwork, and Tom glanced at the calendar on his watch. Last day of the month.

"I don't dare say anything about waiting until the last day of the month to do all the department's invoices for the month. That would probably piss you off to no end, huh?"

The storm cloud that built instantly on the sheriff's face made Tom feel really happy.

"You can bet your sweet ass it would. What the hell are you doing in my office jerking my chain?" Then the storm blew over as Sam leaned back, and a half-grin warmed his face.

"I got a call from Failoni, the FBI's Agent-in-Charge."

The Sheriff looked blank.

"The Ward murder and all that other federal stuff over in Alta."

"Oh, yeah. What's up?"

"They think they know who did Ward. They're doing an interview of him this morning and I'd like to be there. Some other stuff has come up too."

"Maybe I'd better slide over there too. The papers have been splashing a lot of ink over this, and I don't want to look like I'm not on top of it."

As he walked out to his car, Tom shook his head. Being the sheriff and having to sit behind piles of paperwork, ride herd on almost a hundred people, constantly deal with self-serving politicians on the make, and keep your feelers out for every little change in amplitude of public opinion had to be a royal pain in the butt. He was glad he didn't have to carry that burden.

Chapter Nine

When Tommy and Sheriff Harlan walked into the courthouse in Driggs, they saw a major stir in the building. The Assessor offices, County Clerk, Clerk of Court, and just about every other county department were on the first floor of the old brick building, which is typical of the rural west. It didn't take much to excite a town this size, and if the two-dozen people who worked in the building gathered in whispering groups, then the whole city would be too. The questioning of the Mormon bishop's First Councilor would be big news.

The accused man was a dairy farmer in a marginal business who had branched out into real estate development during the recent property boom. He was intelligent and had an impeccable reputation. If local authorities had handled the investigation, he'd been shown the respect due his position in the community and approached in the privacy of his own home. But federal agents are always cut off from the communities they work in and seldom know the proper etiquette in small towns like Teton Valley, Idaho.

They had not arrested the man but publicly escorted him to the courthouse, paraded down the main corridor while being held on each side by the arms, and prepared for a voluntary polygraph test. When Tom and Sheriff Harlan arrived, the man was sitting in a room where the polygraph expert from the nearby city of Idaho Falls was setting up his machine.

When the sheriff of Teton County, Idaho, saw the sheriff of Teton County, Wyoming, in the hallway, he motioned for him to come into his office.

"Hi, Sam. Hello, Tom," he said and motioned his two guests to sit.

"Hi, Terry. What do you think about this?" Sam waved at the small crowd outside the door.

"Oh, it's horseshit—federal horseshit. If LeRoi Metcalf is a murderer, I'll kiss your ass on the sidewalk right out there in front of the building."

"They must think they have something."

"The man told Ward he would beat his brains out, but that doesn't really mean anything." He grimaced sourly. "Well, you can't ignore the fact that he said it, but to haul him down here and disgrace him in public...."

Tom said, "The agent in Jackson said that Metcalf had done more than just threaten him. He said that he'd attacked Ward."

"Knocked him on his ass alright. Did it at the pizza place in front of a few folks, but you have to remember that we're talking about Metcalf's teenage daughter. You know how us Mormons feel about our kids, especially our daughters."

"Was Ward messing around with her?"

"No, but she had to be taken to the hospital for a psychotic episode. One of the local boys gave her something like LSD, and she went crazy. He got scared and dropped her off at the hospital, then ran. When I questioned him, he said that his big brother got the drugs from Ward while they were backpacking together—gone out on some kind of vision quest thing together in the Jedediah Smith Wilderness.

"I talked to Ward, and he denied possession of anything illegal, of course. I couldn't prove anything, but LeRoi didn't need any more proof than the boy's story. After that, the girl had a flashback and had to be taken home by the school nurse. When LeRoi ran into Ward in the pizza place, he told him that if his daughter had one more problem associated with the drugs, he was going to take a club and beat him to a pulp."

"Well, someone did just that," Tom said. "But he wasn't buried in Mormon temple garments, at least none that I'd recognize, so it sure as hell wasn't anyone who was Latter Day Saints."

Sheriff Rogers grimaced. "We're all sure that Ward's wife or someone else did that. The Feds tell me that it was a Mexican-type burial, and she was a Mexican. Don't make fun of Mormon garments."

Tom colored. He knew that Rogers was LDS, most officials with the confidence of the valley communities were. "I apologize, I shouldn't have said that. I didn't mean any disrespect."

Sheriff Rogers waved his hand in dismissal. "It's okay, I understand."

"So you think this is just a lot of . . ."

"Horseshit, excuse my French," Sheriff Rogers said as he finished Sheriff Harlan's sentence.

Sam stood. "Well, that's good enough for me."

Once they were outside, Sheriff Harlan stood for a moment and pinched at his bottom lip.

"Let's find Elvin," he said. "He spent quite a bit of time with Ward on rescues and in training. I want to make damn sure one of my deputies isn't ingesting psilocybin mushrooms and running around in the woods calling on Wakan Tanka or Timothy Leary to drop a celestial staircase into the Jed Smith Wilderness. It sounds like this guy was giving lessons."

When they met him, the deputy looked apprehensive. As the Sheriff led up to the real question, the deputy paled, looking at the mountains out the window.

Finally, Sam asked, "Elvin, did you ever eat any of any damn magic mushrooms? I'm asking you straight out, and don't lie to me."

Elvin's brow wrinkled, his face resigned as he looked directly at his boss. "I don't lie," he said. He paused and nodded slowly. "It wasn't mushrooms, it was peyote, and yeah, I ate a piece of one of the things. You can have my job if you have to because it was worth it."

Sheriff Harlan's face took on a perplexed look. "Tell me what happened," he said, and his voice had a mournful tone.

"Doc and I went on a conditioning run-and-scramble—just daypacks, running shoes, and shorts. We were up in Alaska Basin taking a break when Doc started talking about native religions and ceremonies he had taken part in. The guy had been everywhere and done just about everything."

Elvin looked out the side window, and Tommy knew what the young man was thinking—that he'd never been anywhere or done anything interesting.

Elvin went on, "I know that peyote is illegal and all that, but I also know the Native Church over at Fort Hall, and a lot of other places, use the stuff in their religious ceremonies."

He raised his hand against Sam's objection. "And I know that I don't belong to that church, so it doesn't make it right for me. But I'd been going through a real long dry spell with my church, and I felt alone. My family life was falling apart because I'd quit going and was feeling cut off from life . . ." His voice trailed off.

"For whatever reason, I ate a segment of this nasty-tasting mushroom button Ward had brought. After he built a little fire, burnt a sweet grass bundle, he had then sang in some other language . . . and I met God. I couldn't see him, but he was just as present to me as you are now."

The statement seemed to echo in the car and set up literal vibrations in Tom. There was a long silence unbroken by either Sheriff Harlan or Tommy. Then Elvin went on.

"Something happened to me that I can't explain. You see, I'd always believed in God, mostly because I was raised in the church, and it was a major part of the community and our lives. But the God I was raised with carried a very big stick, while the God that I came face-to-face with out there in Alaska Basin loved me. He flooded me with love.

"I thought I'd known what love was, but in fact, I didn't know how *big* it was. I had an experience that day that has changed my entire understanding of who I am and what this world is about. I now go to church, and I can see who stands behind the men who are the authorities, the ones who supposedly know all about God and what he wants for me—and it makes them look pretty small.

"Now I know that I am truly loved, and I'm part of the spirit that animates the whole of the universe. I know that I am more real and much larger than this limited body I occupy. That afternoon with Doc Ward was exactly what I needed. It changed my life, Sam."

Sheriff Harlan shifted uncomfortably in the car seat. "You know what happened with the Metcalf girl."

Elvin's face registered real pain. "Yes. I talked to Ward, and he said that Boyd Van Dusen stole a button, then his little brother stole it from him."

Sam straightened up. "That's no excuse. I'm putting you on administrative leave starting tomorrow. I want you to come over the hill tomorrow, and we'll have a meeting to work this out."

Tommy was momentarily shocked at the quick decision, but that was Sam's style. Elvin's story had moved him, and his own quest for spirituality had responded to it. Tom doubted that the man had had a revelation of some real sort, and that showed in the man's face, though at the moment, that face was very troubled. Losing a good job in Wyoming is a damn serious thing for a man with a family. Life can still be very hard for a workingman in these mountains.

Elvin nodded. He looked at Sheriff Harlan and asked, "Am I going to lose my job Sam?"

"I'll be honest with you—yes. I promise I'll do everything I can to find something else for you with the county, but you're through as a law officer. We'll come up with something medical, like stress or a bad knee. Something.

"Elvin," the sheriff looked at his deputy, and his eyes were cold, "you really screwed up. This is the real world, and I have to operate in it according to real world rules. You broke the law, and that's something I won't accept, even though only the three of us here know it."

His eyes warmed a bit. "I understand something of what you must have been feeling when you did what you did. But God doesn't spend a lot of time sowing love in law enforcement agencies, courts, jails, and prisons. We handle the devil's share of the business."

MiT

It was hot in Huajuapan de Leon as the sun's blaze blasted the limestone hills to a brilliant white. White dust covered the few leaves of the trees, turning them from green to a dirty gray as traffic on the mostly unfinished roads lifted the powdered limestone into the languid air. It added dust from stone buildings shaken down by an earthquake the day before. White powdered work gangs of small, dark-skinned men worked to clear stone and wood debris with wheelbarrows and odd assortments of pickups and trucks.

On a tall hill in the center of the modern city stood an ancient pyramid of the Mixtec civilization that flourished a thousand years before, but the trembling earth had not shaken it down. It shone in the hot sun and hazy air like a beacon, but it was a beacon that had lost its significance in the modern world of southern Mexico.

In an ordinary year, regular pulses of wet air move west from the Gulf of Mexico. Cooled by its precipitous rise on the backs of the coastal range and interior sierras, rains wrung from the resultant clouds drench the heartland with abundant afternoon rains. The rainy season begins in early May, but it is now the middle of a stifling June, and with the cloudless washed-out sky, the Cloud People suffer.

Huajuapan is a major city of Oaxaca state that lies halfway up the highlands from the plains south of Mexico City. It is a city of the dry Mixteca Baja characterized by eucalyptus trees, tall cactus, and whitewashed stone walls that form the northern edge of the ordinarily wet Mixteca Alta. Higher up the mountains, Mixtec pine and highland oak forests are now ablaze in a hellish acceleration of the seasonal spot fires that cleanse the forest environments during normal years. Even on the northern margin of the Mixteca Alta, there is a smoky taste mixed with the tang of fine alkaline dust from the fallen buildings whose destruction the people blame on the angry god, Dzaui.

Concha Osorio and her brother, Cenovio Espinoza, sat on a stone wall and shared a glass of a sweet rice drink called horchata and ate pink Isleta bananas they bought with the very last of the money they received from Señora Robertson. Too much of it had been spent on bribes to corrupt petty officials who victimized them once they recognized defenseless Indians.

"All we need is one more tank of gas," said her brother.

"Yes."

But the money for that one last tank seemed impossible. Not that they believed it was impossible, given time. But they had no time. Their one hope was that their companion Valerio Trujano would return with some money he'd gone to borrow from an uncle who owned an electrical supply house and was rich by provincial standards.

"I sincerely regret the death of the soldiers," Cenovio said. It was the first mention of it since the incident on the road outside Culiacan.

Concha nodded and wiped her sweating face with a handkerchief. "There was nothing else to do. They would have taken our money, and probably the car, but they could not take the holy things of the people. Dzaui himself lent stealth to your feet and strength to your arm."

"Perhaps, but I feel the need to repent. In the sanctuary." He pointed his chin toward a colonial-era chapel that had withstood yet another severe shaking of the earth since it was built hundreds of years before. The black square of the door had been beckoning him ever since he'd parked the car across the plaza from it.

"Of course. Go." Concha was also a believer in both her native religions and she heartily approved of her brother's impulse. "I will wait here for Valerio. Pray for his success as well as for absolution."

The small woman waited on a plaza cement bench in the shade of a lime tree as she watched the car and its precious contents. Concha thought of very little as she moved into the endless continuum of peasant time. Her life in *El Norte*, her dead husband, and his riches were forgotten. She was going home, and in the trunk of the car were two treasures of her people taken for his money by two weak men. She was bringing the items home to her family, who were custodians of the powerful objects before the time of the Spanish *capitanes*.

The theft of those objects by her husband's agents, one of them her older brother, had turned the world of the Mixteca upside down and set it on fire. But all that could be righted with the return of the Heart of the World.

In the old days, a great artist-priest was inspired to fashion it when the calamity of the Conquistadores and their new religion had fallen on the heads of the people. The old gods had been greatly offended when the blood of the Mixtecs had almost been drained to the last drop. The artist-priest had fashioned the Heart of the World from a large and flawless rock crystal. Then what remained of the priesthood of the old religion convened in the Cave of the Dead Kings near Chalcatongo, where they practiced the old rituals and sacraments that took days, as they called to the old gods to return. And those gods had returned to restore the strength of the people.

The Catholic Church had built their edifices on top of the old religious sites of the Mexican Indians, hoping to obliterate their power and wipe them from memory. The Heart of the World was hidden for hundreds of years in a grotto beneath a deserted convent that once dominated the landscape from a mount above Achiutla. But now, the god that overcame the Church had been plundered, and Dzaui was furious.

It was a time of earthquakes, fire, spilled blood. A period of great calamity, like the coming of the Captains and their agents—the present Mexican government—eventually followed by a long time of tranquility. And she and her brother were privileged to be agents in one of those intimate cycles. As a descendant of the great Mixtec princess, La Cacica Maria, she understood the eternal symmetry about it all. That was the way the world worked down here. *But not in El Norte*, she thought. There, with all its riches, it is always a time of calamity because the people do not love God. They only love the world.

Valerio Trujano walked up to Concha, and from the smile on his face, she knew he'd gotten the money. He said, "My Uncle Mario Pacheco is generous, and he has given me the money."

Concha held out her hand, and Valeriano passed her the folded money as he glanced around. It was a lot of money in this barrio. "Where is Cenovio?"

"He is praying, asking for absolution."

Valeriano crossed himself. "Yes. And I will pray also, but later. Now I will get my things."

He went to the car and took his suitcase and laundry bag from the rear seat. "You will go north again?" he asked.

Concha, her hand shading her eyes, shook her head. "No. I am a widow now."

Valeriano sucked on his teeth in the Indian way of expressing disgust. "You are young. Just because you are back in Mexico does not mean that you have to take back all the old ways. You can find a good man."

"I am going back to Achiutla. My husband was responsible for a great wrong to the Cloud People, and I will not be looked upon with respect."

"But you bring back your family's story and The Heart of the World. That is a very great thing to do."

"Yes, but I am not a man."

Valeriano looked sad. "Yes. That is true."

He picked up the poor suitcase and the laundry bag. "I must leave. I have found a ride to San Jeronimo. Tell Cenovio I will see him sometime at the Friday market in Tlaxiaco, and we will make a plan to go north again," he said as he turned to go.

Concha raised her hand over her head and motioned good-bye and thanks. He had given up much to help them bring back the people's things. The odyssey north and south again was a courageous thing to do for oneself, but to do it for someone outside one's *ejido* was a much braver thing.

Now that she had the money for gasoline, Concha was anxious to go, so she crossed the road, put a handkerchief on her hair, and then stopped at the threshold. Before entering the chapel, she glanced nervously at the car with its treasures, then turned and stepped inside.

Inside the chapel, she crossed herself and waited for her eyes to adjust to the dark. Halfway to the altar, her brother knelt in the aisle. She could see his shoulders shaking, and she knew that he wept silently.

He always was the gentlest of the boys, the one who rescued puppies from emaciated, feral bitches or from the tortures of the other children. It moved her to know that this man was not above his suffering and that life had not turned him hard like most men of her race.

She knelt and asked for absolution for her part even though she felt there had been something moving them from the very beginning.

After a moment, she rose and hurried back to the door. She paused before the blinding light at the chapel door, then stepped outside.

The trunk of the big green Chevrolet yawned open, and in an instant, she understood. She jerked her head to the side, and her eyes caught the flash of heels as they disappeared around a corner. Once they had seen the license plate on the front of the car, the street urchins had waited for their moment and taken it when she entered the church!

She ran across the hot, dusty road as her heart drove spirals of spots through her vision. When she reached the car, she looked inside the gaping trunk and saw the boxes were gone. Concha shrieked and raised her fists to the stinking sky, then collapsed into the orange peels, bottle caps, and candy wrappers of the hot and dusty street.

Chapter Ten

Tom set Polly's bags on the airline scale while she gave her ticket to the Delta guy. Then they walked to the waiting area and sat down.

"I wish you could stay for the weekend."

"Sorry, but business like this doesn't wait. It's a great chance for our brokerage." For two years, Polly's real estate company worked on a deal with the largest commercial bank in Mexico and a Mexican development group. Now it looked like their work had paid off.

Polly's ex-husband was Hispanic, and his family were Spanish land-grant Californios who had kept their ties with the elite of Mexico, from whom they were descended. They were related to "major Mexican money," as Polly had put it.

In the beginning, Tom's had a strained relationship with the man. Yet, Ferdie was a gentleman in the Spanish style and had finally decided what was done was done, and their relationship was politely correct.

He had been habitually unfaithful to his wife, considering that a privilege of the Hispanic male, and Polly had struggled with it at the beginning of their marriage. But when the women's movement had first stirred in California, she embraced it and began a quiet campaign to become her own woman and demanded an end to the philandering. However, Ferdie was not the kind of man to change the way of a privileged Latino male.

When Polly needed room to grow, he responded by reining her more tightly and eventually caused the end of the marriage. He still could not accept the power of American female politics, so he was left with his money, his daughters, and his vanity. But when Polly was in the room, it was obviously not enough. The man was still very much in love with Polly, and to watch him stare at her was painful.

As the inheritor of the windfall, Tommy tried to be as generous as possible to the man who, for over twenty years, had raised Christina as his own. Christina was the fruit of a summer romance long ago, something Tommy found out only the summer before. He met the girl twice—in the hospital when Polly had been hurt and when Tom went to California with his son.

The meeting had been strained. Christina once thought she was the product of a perfect family—well-to-do, educated, influential, and blue-blooded Californians on both sides. To discover that her birth father was a small-town detective from the sticks of Wyoming had been a shock for everyone.

It made Tom sigh inside. One of his burdens was to wonder what he could have been if his family had had money or a tradition of higher education. He wondered what it must be like to have a family where each generation stood on the shoulders of the last. In working-class Wyoming, most children struck out on their own down the first, or widest, path that presented itself after high school.

Polly reached up to smooth Tom's forehead and bring him back to the waiting area. "You get in trouble when you think, Thomas."

It made him smile. "Strong back, though."

"Yes. The back is strong and that is good." She grinned. Then her face changed, and she touched his chin. "Leave yourself alone. You are a good man, and I love you."

Tommy said, "Which reminds me," he looked around for a clock. "When's the flight due in?"

Polly glanced at her watch and said, "Twenty-one minutes." When she looked up, Tommy took her right hand to put a wide gold band on the ring finger.

Her face melted. Her mouth turned down, her nostrils turned white, and tears flooded her face. They ran buckets. Her nose began to run too, and in an instant, she looked a mess.

She raised her hand and stared at the ring.

"It's French," Tommy said.

"What's French, you nincompoop?" she squeaked. "I can't see a thing."

He took the hand, which had a dollop of something, tears or mucus, on it and read the inscription: *Vous et nul autre*, butchering the French.

Her mouth turned down even further, and she looked like Plastic Man as she raised her face to the ceiling and a squeaky little cry came out of her mouth as more tears ran down her face and jaw.

"It means 'You and No Other'."

"I know what it means, Thomas," she said and hit him so hard on the chest it made him wince.

She put her face on the back of his hand. He felt the wetness from her face and the shaking of her body. People began to notice.

"Pol!" he said, indicating at all the onlookers. "People think I've done something bad to you. They're staring at us."

"Screw 'em," she said into his shirt and snuffed what sounded like a whole cup of stuff back up her nose. "This is Wyoming—where everyone thinks a crying woman is a happy woman."

MiT

"There was a Mexican police officer here to see you," Rhonda said when Tom returned from the airport and stood in front of his message box. "He said he'd be back at two o'clock."

"Mexican? Like from the country Mexico?"

"Like from the Attorney General of Mexico's office in the national capitol, Mexico City, state of Mexico, country of Mexico, our neighbor to the south," she said with one eyebrow arched. Tom took the business card he held out.

"You have every National Geographic that was ever printed, don't you?" Tom said sweetly.

"No. I'm missing the one with you and your relatives in it—the Jane Goodall issue."

She turned and walked across the room, leaving Tom with the sure knowledge he had been insulted in some obscure way. The name Jane Goodall did ring a bell. He looked at the card.

Rigoberto Sandez Sanchez
Official
Oficina de Avogado General
Mexico D.F.

The guy was from the Attorney General's Office, alright. Tom took three years of Spanish in high school. It was only to get as close to Edie Kline as he could get the first year, but she hadn't given him a tumble. However, he'd taken a real interest in the language and stayed with it. The skill came in handy, qualifying him for a Vietnamese language course and Army counter-intelligence school.

Tom was at his desk when Lewis stepped through the door and said, "Hey, Tom."

"Huh?"

"The chili belly is here. Do want me to bring him in?"

Tom's blood pressure went through the roof. "Who?" he said through clenched teeth.

Lewis realized his mistake instantly. Raised in Texas, he thought everyone shared his prejudices. "Uh, sorry. I'll go get 'im."

"No! I'll go out there myself."

"Okay, have it your way." He stood aside as Tom pushed his way past, genuinely pissed.

"Sheez," Lewis said.

When Tom reached the reception area, it looked like there was no one there. The lobby area looked vacant from where he stood behind the counter.

"Hey Rhonda, where's the guy from Mexico?"

Before she could answer, a head and shoulders appeared above the reception counter as a small-statured man stood up from the couch on the other side.

Tom walked to the gate and asked, "Mr. Sanchez?"

"Sandez. Sanchez was my mother's family name, and we use the one in the middle, which is our father's name. It's kinda confusing, I know. Also, the names are real close."

He straightened his tie, took out a well-worn wallet with a badge pinned to it then handed it to Tom. He had a dark complexion, thick hair parted on the side, stood about five-foot-four, and was built like a wedge.

Tom pushed the Dutch door open and said, "C'mon back, my office is down the hall on the right." He returned the badge.

"Thanks, I appreciate it." The guy had no accent whatsoever. His English was perfect and inflected like an American's.

Tom walked to his chair and sat down once they were in the detectives' room waving at a chair. Sandez looked suspiciously at the deeply upholstered chair across the desk from Tom. Then he spotted a folding chair that leaned against the wall.

"May I?" he asked.

"Sure, lemme get it for you."

"Nah, sit down I can get it for myself. Man, when you're as short as I am, life can be a bitch. All American furniture is built for people twice my size." He gave a little sigh as he opened the chair and put it down. "But, what the heck, nothing you can do about your genes. My mom was an Indian—four foot ten. My dad was pretty tall, and my sister is almost five foot six. Ain't that a bitch—your freaking sister is bigger than you are." He smiled. Tom liked the guy. He was confident, even a little cocky, which can be a real asset for a good cop.

"You born in Mexico?" Tom asked and then was immediately embarrassed at the personal question. "I mean, you sound like you were born in the States."

"Yeah, but I went to junior high and high school in Southern California. Sis and I were kind of adopted by some people who took us north and got us educated. My mom and dad still live in Baja, in a town called Guerrero Negro."

"Then you went back after high school?"

"After college. Didn't have any choice. I'd've liked to stay, but the *pinche migra* caught up with us. But it turned out all right because they were the ones who got me my job. They introduced me to a colonel in the Mexican Federal Police, and that's how I ended up a cop. Juana works for the government too—tourist muckety-muck in Mexico City."

"What is your job, exactly?"

"And why am I here, right?"

Tom smiled and opened his hand, meaning, *You said it, not me.*

"Cenovio and Concha Osorio Espinoza—that's why I'm here."

Tom looked surprised.

Sandez laughed at the expression on his face. "We're pretty good at this stuff."

"What stuff?"

"Murderers are high on our priority list at the Attorney General's office, but smugglers of these people's caliber are even higher."

"These people are wanted in Mexico, too?"

"Yeah, especially Concha. We want her real bad because she's the one who made all this possible. With her brother's help, of course. She's real smart."

Tom thought of the pretty woman in sexual abandon he'd seen on the videotape. Difficult to get an impression of a person's intellect in that state.

"Are they wanted for more murder? Or smuggling?"

"Both. But I guess you know all about their expertise in smuggling, which is what we are mostly interested in."

"Well, the reports aren't even close to being finished on all the artifacts. And I have no idea where the Feds are on the dope deal, either."

"Dope?"

"Nothing major, really. Hallucinogenic mushrooms, but it's all tied up with the artifact smuggling that Ward was dealing in. I guess that's what really interests you, the artifacts?"

"For sure. Some of the things that we have been missing are apparently in the collection you found at Ward's. If I can speak with your promise of confidentiality . . ."

Tom nodded. "Of course, go ahead."

"The importance of some of the items can only be appreciated when considered from a Mexican perspective. Corruption is, and always has been, a way of life at home, but there is a limit. Some of the people involved in this artifact trade have far exceeded our idea of what is acceptable. They have given away whole sections of our cultural foundation. Priceless is an inadequate term to describe the things stolen by Ward with the help of our countrymen.

"There are very important names and academic titles involved on both sides of the border, so there can be no breath of this made public. We will handle it on our side and in our own way. But we must depend upon the discretion of all the American offices, and their officers, involved while we make our case. Unfortunately,

Mexico hasn't assigned a real priority to this activity until recently, and enforcement has been very, very lax. But that's changed." He smiled and spread his hands wide. "And here I am!"

"Well," Tom said, "you can depend upon me, and I think I can speak for the sheriff, on our department."

Sandez smiled grimly. "That will make the Attorney General, and the people he reports to, very happy."

Tom guessed that the Mexican Attorney General only reports to the President of the Republic of Mexico.

Sandez asked, "Do you have any preliminary stuff I can look at? We're going to have to work together on this, make it as airtight as possible. If we catch them in Mexico, we are going to want to have as much information on their activities as possible. And, of course, we want to help you catch them. Then it will be a matter of extraditing them to my country."

"But first we have to catch them," Tom said. "In the meantime, I can get you what we have. The Federal Bureau of Investigation office here is handling the federal stuff in Jackson. The agent's name is Failoni, if you want me to contact him for you. But the evidence pertaining to the murder, which is mine, is yours to examine also, if my boss approves."

"Great. Let me digest the info you have, and then I'll work my way up to the federal folks. Also, is it possible to look at the scene, at Ward's place?"

"I don't see why not. The Feds have sealed the place and are finishing an inventory, but I think I can get you in. How does tomorrow sound?"

"Tomorrow's Saturday."

Tom waved his hand. "No big deal. My girlfriend left town today, so I don't have anything planned."

Sandez stood up. "Great. What time should I be here?"

"Where are you staying? I'll pick you up."

"I'm at The Rusty Parrot."

"Nice place."

"Yeah, it is. Great massages. What time do you want to take off?"

"You like big breakfasts?"

"I may not look it, but I love to eat, man."

"Good, we'll slide over to Bubba's. Pick you up at eight, how does that sound?"

"Just right, I'll be waiting."

Chapter Eleven

Jeff was keeping watch on Ward's house, and he got out of his patrol car to stretch as they drove up.

"I don't suppose you brought me any coffee?" he asked with a tired grin.

"As a matter of fact, I did. I even got you some Colombia Supremo with all the caffeine still intact—size El Supremo Magnifico." Tom handed it to him out of the car window.

"Alright! You're a helluva guy, Thompson."

Tom and Sandez got out of the car, and Tom introduced the men. Jeff was six-foot-seven, blue-eyed blonde. The contrast with the Mexican detective was almost comical. But Berto, as he'd asked Tom to call him, didn't turn a hair at Jeff's size, just shook Jeff's hand and began a conversation. It was apparent that the size of other men didn't bother him in the least.

As Tom looked at the two men before him, he came to an understanding. Sandez, like Jeff, could be a terrifying guy when it came right down to it. He would be a good man to have on your side when the shit came down. The day before, Tom noticed he carried the small frame 9-mm automatic pistol Smith & Wesson made for women. The gun and the holster both looked like they had seen a lot of use, just like the man.

They raised the yellow plastic ribbon strung around the property and entered the house. When they stepped into the front room, Berto stopped in his tracks to shake his head and whistle in a very American way. He was impressed with both the view and the house.

"Damn! Those are some kinda mountains!"

He spun around and took in the huge picture windows, the expensive furniture, and lavish interior decorations. "And this is one helluva house." Then he sucked on his front teeth, making a sound of disapproval. "The money that went into this house would support a community in Mexico for years." He smiled wryly and added, "But that's the way the tortilla crumbles, Man. The rich get richer, and the poor get babies."

After a quick survey of the upstairs, Tom took him downstairs to the vault. He whistled again in appreciation as he took in the depository, its cabinetwork, and the computer workstation.

Tom said, "Looks like all the artifacts have been packed up and are on their way to Washington for inventory and identification. I guess you'll have to go out there to do that. Failoni can probably get you an inventory, though."

Berto shook his head. "People from the embassy will be handling things there. I'm here for the Osorios. It sure would have been nice to see the collection for myself though. I'm into that kind of stuff." He grinned at Tommy and added, "Have they developed any leads on customers and sellers? The Attorney General is really interested in finding out who was selling our heritage to this guy."

"Not that I'm aware of. The computer records just had three-letter and one-number customer and vendor designations, but we haven't yet found a key for them. There's probably a notebook somewhere, but we haven't found it."

"Damn, that's too bad. But that's how the tortilla crumbles, like I said." And he grinned.

On the way back to Jackson, Berto asked, "What do you know about the Osorios? Any ideas where they might be, for instance?"

"The law enforcement people in Idaho and Oregon are looking for them real hard. But we have put out an APB for all the states between us and Mexico too."

Berto shook his head and said, "You need a national APB. There are a lot Mixtec *colonias* in the States now."

"*Colonias* means colonies, right?"

Berto looked at him and smiled. "*¿Entiendes español?*" he asked.

Tommy laughed, pinched his index finger and thumb together tightly, and said, "Oh, I understand about that much. I took Spanish in high school, but that was a helluva long time ago. Anyway, what were you saying about Mixtec colonies in the States?"

"Well, I'm a product of this little history, so I know something about it, and it starts in the late fifties, early sixties sometime, when they first started growing tomatoes in Baja—across the border from California. The unions in California were pushing for higher wages and better conditions. The price of produce was going up and up, so they started growing tomatoes and lettuce in Baja. There were a lot of Indians from Oaxaca living there, and they became the labor for the fields. The demand grew, and the fields grew too. And bigger fields needed more labor, so more colonies of Indians from Oaxaca came there to work.

"At the same time, a lot of the women were working as street vendors in Tijuana, and the cops were demanding crippling bribes, *morditas*, from them. They got organized, formed unions for protection, and it spread to the fields. Long story short, there was a bloody time, but the Indians finally won, then Oaxacan Indian colonies quietly formed in the north as the labor market grew here. There are a lot of them, and the Osorios could be hiding out in any one of them."

Berto paused for a moment, looking out the window and the fields passing by. Then he said passionately, "Man, if you think there's prejudice in this country, you need to go to Mexico and see how they treat the Indians down there. I know."

Tom said, "Believe me, we treat them about the same. All this stuff about the great spirituality of the Native Americans in the media is just following a fashion. They make a big fuss about the American Indian's kinship with the earth, but it hasn't changed the realities on the reservations. All the crystal gazers, vision questers, and the people doing all the writing about "Our red brothers" don't contribute as much as the guy who sells 'em junk cars. He's just ripping them off for a couple thousand bucks while the others are ripping off their culture by popularizing it."

Berto grinned. "*Bien, tu eres simpatico*, podna."

Tom waved his hand. "Nah, the drum-pounding, flute-blowing yuppies just give me heartburn, that's all."

"You a redneck?"

"I came by it honestly, believe me. I'm working class from my neck down to my boots." After a moment, Tom added, "Watsonville, I wonder if that's a colony."

"Watsonville? Where's that?"

"Watsonville, Oregon. That's where the license plate was from."

"What license plate?"

"Oh, I forgot to tell you. We found a license plate to a car owned by Cenovio Osorio at Ward's place."

"No shit!" Berto was visibly excited. "How far is it to this place? Can we drive there?"

"Oh, it's only about a thousand miles."

"Damn."

"Well, it could have been lost when he was on a regular visit to his sister too We can't tie him to the murder on the strength of a dropped license plate."

Berto grinned. "In Mexico I could make it stick." Then he waved his hand, "Nah, just kidding."

Tom said, "You said you grew up in Mexico but went to school in the States. How did that happen?"

"I was born in Baja. My dad was a game warden at Scammon's lagoon, the place where the Gray whales go to get it on." He grinned. "My mom and her family went down there to scavenge on Junk Beach. They heard you could sell the fishing net floats, and other stuff that landed on the beach in Tijuana and Ensenada for some good *jing*. She met my dad there."

"So, you were raised at Scammon's Lagoon?"

"Yeah. But it wasn't as romantic as it sounds. We lived in a stick shack, and before there was a road to the place, the only time they would get stuff to us was when the fisheries people bothered to remember we were alive. We lived almost exclusively off the ocean, and there was a bunch of us kids. Eight."

"Not the same place now, huh?"

"*Turistas, hombre. Muchos turistas* and *dinero*. Now."

Tom laughed. "There wasn't a whole helluva lot around here when I was growing up either. But by the end of the summer, we called them "terrorists." There's even a T-shirt the locals wear that says, "Why do they call it 'Tourist Season' if you can't shoot them?" But it would be pretty cold and hungry around here without them.

"Hot and hungry without 'em at Laguna Scammon, *Chavo*."

The two men laughed together. They shared a lot, it seemed, considering the cultural chasm Tom had expected when he'd first met the man.

"But my next youngest sister and me got lucky. Two of the first tourists to come down wanted to do something for the family, so they brought us back to the States and educated us all the way through college. We thought we were going to be able to stay . . . ."

"What happened?"

Berto smiled grimly. "Ronald Reagan. Man, those Republicans are hard on us Mexicans. Maybe I should stay here and organize the *paisanos* to vote Democratic, what do you think?"

"Hell, no one represents the working man anymore. Save your energy," Tom said. "Catching killers on the run somewhere in two counties is a hundred times easier than finding a populist politician who means what he or she says."

MiT

Concha and her brother stood in the big house garden and watched the servants come and go. She thought about the American movie called *The Godfather*. It had come as a great shock to her that the *cacigazco* system existed in El Norte too. She felt the caciques were needed only in developing countries where the poor needed protection from the government. That it existed in a country as wealthy as America surprised all Mexicans when they found out.

In many ways, it was *una desgracia* how the caciques acquired power and took advantage of that power, but life without them was hardly possible for the poor in many parts of Mexico.

She and her brother were fugitives from two governments, but only because they were on a mission to preserve the very life of their people—to defend the earth itself against the corruption that the power of money brought to her village and the mountains in which it was isolated. And she had been a part of it all.

"*¿Señor Osorio?*"

The voice of the cacique's secretary jolted her back to the large patio of the big house in Huajuapan de Leon. With his hat in hand, her brother beckoned her to follow him. The tall, bald man in the suit disappeared through a large double door at three meters high.

Inside it was very cool. The damp air from the lush garden and its fountain acted as an air conditioner, and the black and white tiles of the floor were cool on the bottoms of her bare feet. It felt wonderful as she padded after the men.

"Dear God, we are ever in thy hands. Keep us safe, deliver our people's fate back into our hands which are clasped in your very own," she prayed to herself.

They entered through another door, then into an office where a large man, whose thick glasses magnified his eyes, sat behind a desk piled high with papers.

He stared at the two small Indians in front of him and said nothing.

Finally, the secretary said to Cenovio, "Tell Señor Pacheco what you are here for."

Cenovio dropped his face and waited for Concha to speak.

"Señor Pacheco, I am from the village of San Miguel Achiutla, and my name is Concha Osorio Espinoza. This is my brother, Cenovio."

The large man blinked at Cenovio, then moved his owlish eyes to Concha. It is unusual for a man to defer to a woman concerning serious business in Mexican society, but certainly not unheard of.

"We have been living in the north for some time. I myself was married to a very important gringo, a professor of great distinction who made me proud to be his wife. But something happened, something of which we are greatly ashamed for; it has brought disaster to the whole world of the Mixtecos: earthquakes, fires . . ."

The cacique looked at his secretary, the hunched man with a sharp, vulpine face. The man nodded.

The cacique looked back at Concha and nodded to encourage her to continue.

"My husband was a man who achieved fame as a scholar of the ancient Mixtec culture. Ten years ago, he came to our village, which has a famous *convento* and a great pyramid of the *ancianos.* Neither has been excavated nor desecrated, so the ancient gods still reside there.

"At first, we were afraid that he was there to begin an excavation, which would have disturbed our dead, but he was not there for that. He moved into the village and talked to the people about our history. At night we would see him writing, sometimes all the night. And because they admired him, people began to bring El Profesor Ward things of the ancianos. Little things at first, but then things of value."

"One moment," the big man broke in. "Please bring these people chairs, Pancracio."

Concha was greatly impressed by the deep voice of the cacique.

"I can tell that this is not a short tale. Uh, and Pancracio . . ."

"Yes?"

"Bring us all some *Agua de Sandia*."

"Yes, sir."

The man moved two chairs to the front of the cacique's desk and left the room as the cacique motioned them two to sit.

"Please continue," said the man behind the desk.

Concha described how some people brought Nathaniel objects they'd found in the fields. At first, *hatches* and *maniacs*, the little dolls made of fired clay. Then Nathaniel paid them for small items fashioned out of gold. Fathers and grandfathers of the men who sold them had found those things. And when it became known that the professor would pay enormous amounts of money for items of the *anciano*s, people began to come in with a few objects held in trust for centuries by their families.

But it had all been with the consent of the families. Money had been so hard to come by, and Nathaniel was paying in American dollars. It was so much money for the isolated little village. This was before the road was built, and life was so very hard.

Concha told of Ward coming to the *cocina* of her mother, where he often ate. Concha had been thirteen the first year Nathaniel had come to the village on the big sorrel mule. He spoke perfect Spanish and even a good deal of Mixtec. She had fallen in love with him the first day he ate at her mother's table.

He came back for three more years and spent three or four months of each summer talking, writing, talking, writing, and buying things from the people.

But it was when her older brother Demetrio had shown Ward the deerskin book, Ward became visibly excited and wanted to take the book away. When they explained to him that it was part of the family's heritage, from the time before the *capitanes*, he still wanted to take the book away. He promised to bring it back the following season.

However, this was different. He did not want to give them money for the book and keep it for his own. He only wanted to take it to the north to show to his *compadres* at the university. But that was not acceptable to the family, either. Not until the following year, the year that Nathaniel took Concha for his bride, and he became part of the family.

"Señora, Señor," said the secretary as he entered the room. He gave Concha and Cenovio their drinks and left the room after a dismissive motion of the hand from the cacique.

"Please go on with your story," he said.

El Profesor Ward was thirty-five and rich, and she was freshly eighteen. He gave her father the big sorrel mule and a blooded stud horse from the Oaxaca Valley to breed her for sturdy animals that could be sold for excellent prices. There were other things in the bride price, some of which Concha was not told. But there was gossip over the whole countryside that no girl in memory had brought such a price as El Profesor Ward paid for Concha Marisol Osorio Espinoza.

The book made of deerskin with the pictures of her ancestors went to Ward to complete her dowry, but only as a loan for one year.

"Uh, Señora," the cacique broke in. "Could you describe to me a bit more about the book? And why the professor was so interested in it?"

"Yes. I learned a great deal about artifacts and such things while I was in the north. This book was our family's history told in pictures and symbols. It was the story of Lady Eight Deer who was the cacica of the area of Teposcolula long before the Spanish came to our country. She came from a great family in the Oaxaca Valley which is mentioned in others of these books."

"And this is important? This made the book very valuable, *sí*?"

"Oh, yes. But not as valuable as The Heart of the World."

"Oh? And what is this?"

"It is the most important thing that the Mixtec people have . . . had. It was the personal possession of the rain god, Dzaui, and was kept in the cave of the spring beneath the convento, except when it was moved to the Cave of the King near Teposcolula for the rain ceremonies. He misses it so much that he has brought this drought and has tumbled the houses of our people in his anger." She gestured at her brother. "My brother and I were returning the Heart and stopped here because we had run out of money. Your nephew, Valeriano, borrowed it from you, then the priceless objects were stolen. Here in Huajuapan, we are beseeching you for help."

"And your husband had bought this *Heart of the World*, also."

"Yes. Our brother and one of our first cousins, Marcos Albino, took the piece and sold it to two men. They then sold it to my husband, who sent the men to buy the Heart. They are famous agents, and thieves, who buy and steal from Indians all over the state of Oaxaca. It is said they are corrupt *Federales*. But my husband was the man most guilty for the theft of the Heart of the World. This we know."

"What makes you so sure of that?"

"His death proves it!"

At the outburst by Cenovio, the cacique's leonine head swung back toward Concha's brother.

"Ah, and you killed him—your wife's husband."

"Yes, but not with a glad heart. He was mostly a good man, and he was generous to my family in many ways, but to take the Heart of the World and plan to sell it was a very great sin."

The cacique turned his enormous eyes back to Concha. "And you two," he waggled his finger at them, "you are wanted by the American police for your husband's death?"

"Yes."

The big man leaned back in his chair, and it squealed from his weight. He pushed his bottom lip out, took off his glasses, and rubbed his eyes and forehead with a huge hand.

"When was this crystal stolen from Achiutla?"

Concha replied, "Last September, then sold to the *Federales* from Oaxaca City. It made Dzaui very angry."

The cacique nodded his head. "There were many fires in the mountains and many villages fell to the ground when the earth was shaken. This I know."

"And the country has burned almost continually since that night," added Concha.

The cacique nodded in agreement. "Yes. And you say that the two earthquakes are a sign of Dzaui's anger." He gestured toward a great crack that ran down the plaster wall to his left.

Concha nodded. "And they will get stronger, worse. That is how he expresses this anger. This is known in the stories that have been told in my family since long before the *capitanes.*"

The man leaned back on his desk, crossing his big, muscular arms. "You know that the police would think that this is all superstition—stupid Indian superstition. And that you have killed a man for nothing."

"Three men!" Cenovio's angry voice cut into the cacique's speech.

He leaned back in his chair again, and again the chair wailed in protest.

"Three." He said simply.

"Two officials in Michoacán who tried to rob us of the Heart," Cenovio said unapologetically, as Concha put a restraining hand on her brother's arm.

"Hmm, this is very serious. Policemen are dead too." He pinched his lips and stared at the two sitting in front of him. He then knocked loudly on the top of his desk with his knuckles. His secretary opened the door immediately.

"Yes?" he said.

"Send someone for two bus tickets to Tlaxiaco. When you come back, give these people some money. Five hundred pesos should do."

"We have money, your nephew gave us enough money to get back to San Miguel."

"Very well." He turned to the secretary and waved him out of the room, saying, "Tickets, tickets."

"You are very lucky, you two. I am also a descendent of the famous Cacica de Teposcolula. You are my kin, and I must take care of my kin above all.

"You will be driven to a highway stop outside of Huajuapan because the federal police may be looking for you at the bus station. When the bus comes, wave it down, and once you are in Tlaxiaco, go to the Hotel Cristobol Colon where there will be a room waiting for you. I have family who own a *ranchito* near Santa Catarina Tayata, and they will come for you at the hotel as soon as I can get word to them.

"Santa Catarina is not far from San Miguel Achiutla, and your people can contact you there. You will be under my protection as long as you are in Santa Catarina. Do not leave the *ranchito,* for any reason, before your people are notified and it is safe for them to come for you. It is possible that *Federales* will already be swarming San Miguel searching for the two of you."

"But what of the book and the Heart?" Concha pleaded.

The cacique waved his hand. "If street urchins have taken them, it will be no problem. There are only a few places where they could get money for items such as those. We can only hope they have not destroyed the Heart and angered Dzaui even more. Once I have them, they will be returned to San Miguel, and Him."

He gestured at the cracked wall. "My house is very strong, but it cannot stand much more of this."

CHAPTER TWELVE

At Berkeley police headquarters, Pete Villareal reached in the pouch of his hooded sweatshirt, took out a plastic bag, and then dropped it onto the watch commander's desk.

"There it is. I finally scored one."

"What?" the Captain said.

"The Gate to Heaven."

"Looks more like The Gate to the Dog Run to me."

"That's because it's been dried," Pete clarified, taking a seat.

"Okay, so a dried dog turd. What are you trying to tell me?"

"This is a mushroom developed from spores maybe a thousand years old. It's supposed to be the 'shroom that the royalty of the Inca used to visit the gods."

"This is the one they're feeding the soul tourists down south?" The Captain looked up in surprise.

"The same one, and it's real powerful stuff. The ones who have freaked on this have apparently freaked in a real big way—full blown psychotic episodes that require hospitalization."

"Who's peddling this shit anyway? Where did you find it?"

Pete leaned forward. "I got it from my connect. But the story behind the mushroom is really interesting. The guy who grows them is named Baret Froehlich. He's another campus freak genius—thirty-two years old with two B.S. degrees, one M.A., and works up at Lawrence Berkeley Labs as a computer whiz while he's getting his PhD in paleomycology. You know the type."

The Captain grimaced. "Yeah. He has an IQ of 200, lives with a Billy goat and four dogs in a shingle-sided house he designed and built himself. He also made all the stained-glass windows. He lives with two women, one in her forties who's a potter and weaver, and another in her twenties who is a grad student—and he's doing them both. Another progressive little household in the hills."

"Nah. This one apparently hates people in general. He's brilliant, but a mental case."

"So the goat's the lucky one. Tell me the rest of the story."

"The guy has a little lab somewhere in Oakland, and he gets his research money from a foundation in Florida. He developed this mushroom by resurrecting the DNA of psychedelic stuff found on a South American mummy then welding it to the cells of viable hallucinogenic mushrooms. He's come up with a winner on the Marin County dope scene." He pointed at the object in the bag. "Guess how much."

"For this?"

"Yeah."

"Two hundred bucks."

"Lots more. Guess again."

"Five hundred bucks."

Villareal rolled his eyes to the ceiling. "You got no imagination. I'm surprised you didn't start at fifty bucks."

"I was going to, but I changed my mind."

"Shit, Cap." Pete picked the bag up and stared at the black object, then said, "Two thousand dollars."

The commander grabbed the bag. "Gimme that!" He turned it over and looked at the other side. "Still looks like a dog turd to me. What the fuck makes this thing worth that kinda money?"

"Two things. People with Silicon Valley money who think two-grand is chump change. Plus, this turd will put you in a place you can't even imagine. Even the freak-outs say it was the most important thing that ever happened to them."

"Going nuts is important to those dickheads?"

"No, but going on a guided tour of heaven was."

"So now what?"

"I'm going to find the lab so we can bust it, for one. Unless I'm nuts, this drug is going to find its way to the streets, and we'll have kids flying out of dorm windows like bats out of a cave."

"I remember the days when kids were tripping out, and not coming back. I helped pick up a dozen of 'em when I was a patrolman. One walked out onto the freeway in a rainstorm, and he musta been hit ten times before it was over."

Villareal reached down and picked up the mushroom, but the Captain snatched it back. "I gotta show this to the guys. Two thousand bucks! I'll do the chain of custody and get an evidence locker for it. It'll be in there."

"Okay, but don't even handle it without latex gloves. If it's as powerful as they say, you could freak out just from the spores on your hands. As old and straight as you are, I'm surprised you didn't run screaming from the room when you laid eyes on it."

The man smiled and waved him away. "At least I don't get paid to smoke dope. Go write your report."

"I'm not done for the day. I'll finish things at the house."

Pete walked down the hall to the front door of the police station. He got into his Porsche Speedster and started the engine to let it rough idle as he reached into the front of his sweatshirt. He took out another plastic bag then held it up to the lights of the passing cars. Inside was another black and orange mushroom, and just looking at it made the hair on his arms spring up.

He drove down Shattuck to Channing and turned left, then moved slowly past People's Park to frat row and right to Dwight

Way. He lived above the city in the old neo-Colonial Smythe House that had been divided into two large apartments. When he was in his upstairs digs, he went to the fridge and poured himself a glass of apple juice.

He crossed the large front room and opened the big French doors, then went out on the verandah to look out over the city.

Across the bay, the lights of San Francisco pricked and punctured the night, and above it was a pale green aureole. The orange glow from the long bay bridge sutured SF and Berkeley together, where it draped across the black waters of the bay.

Pete sat down and put the glass of apple juice on the table. On the way from his score to the police station, he decided to eat the second mushroom.

All his training had taught him this was a line he was not supposed to cross. If smoking a little dope meant building a case, it fell within the boundaries of good police procedure in California. But to keep a controlled substance like this for personal consumption meant crossing a line, one that could not be untaken if he were caught.

He'd never had the problems that many of his fraternity had, sampling the cocaine and money that turned up by the bushel at some busts. But tonight was different for some reason. He simply felt compelled to eat the mushroom from the instant Oz tossed in a second as a freebie.

He went back over the time he had spent with Gertner when he'd made the buy early that evening. It brought back a flood of memories and a lot of strong feelings. Good old feelings. Old young feelings of the '70s. Maybe it had been the stoned girl with the long brown hair, long dress, and Patchouli perfume that triggered it all and made him want to get really high.

He felt the most alive when he was in college. When he felt real. His mind had been engaged, and his body had been healthy and strong. And there had been all those hot, slippery, and redolent young female bodies. He had comrades whom he would have died for during the riots that swept through the now tranquil streets below.

Pete took the mushroom out of the plastic bag and bit the cap in half. It was bitter and had a rank, musty taste. He drank some apple juice, washed the taste back, swallowed, and finished the 'shroom and the juice. Then he relaxed into the chair to wai, as he turned his mind back to the time he'd spent with the old hippie earlier that night.

The apartment on Walnut had been filled with books, and there was a magnificent collection of framed Fillmore posters. The pretty girl with a paisley scarf wound around her head had excused herself when Pete arrived. Her little breasts with their erect nipples were visible beneath the bodice of her long dress, and she wore Indian sandals with the leather ring around the big toe. Her eyes were large and fixed. Stoned.

The scent of her perfume made her an apparition from the hell-roaring days when the parks and streets of San Francisco and Berkeley overflowed with young people, new ideas, brass timbrels, grinning dogs wearing red bandanas, falafel stands, and bewildered cops. Then it ended in tear gas, billy clubs, blood and, on one very bad day, buckshot and brain matter.

Oz offered him a chair and gave him a beer. Then he tossed the mushrooms in Pete's lap, reached under the easy chair, and brought out a cleaning tray with a half-dozen pin joints. He removed four and laid them on the lamp table next to him, retrieved one, lit it, took a big toke, and passed it to Pete.

He took a long drag and held the smoke in his mouth for a moment, then let it slip out both corners of his mouth. It was a trick they'd taught him at the law enforcement academy. Not getting smoke into your lungs was the idea, and too bad because he could tell by the taste and smell that it was probably Hawaiian red bud. No wonder the girl had such big eyes and a fixed smile.

"I remember you, Man."

Pete jerked his attention back to the room.

"Huh?"

"I remember you. You were one of the young, smart guys from the other side of the bay."

"You Beats call us Radicals, but that was just a lot of posturing intellectual horseshit. But it was great to be alive then . . . *really* alive."

"It will never be like that again, and it's way too bad." The old hippie's raspy voice gave Pete the impression that time was slowing down and getting softer.

"It was a great time to be alive."

"All that passionate music, the street scene, the young pussy." He sighed.

Pete nodded at the other room and said, "Looks like you're still doing alright."

"Nah, man, that's my kid."

"Sorry 'bout that." Pete felt his face flush with embarrassment.

Oz waved his hand in dismissal. "Don't worry about it, no big deal. If she weren't mine, I'd probably be strapping her on. Pretty chick, and smart too—environmental law at Boalt Hall.

"Like I was sayin', I remember you the first day I saw you. It was October '67, and we was standing out in front of the Oakland induction center, screaming at the kids with the haircuts to join us, to not get on the buses. But they just kept smiling and walking through those doors, and right into Hell."

After popping the roach into his mouth and swallowing it, Oz said, "Yeah, I know you, Pedro."

Pete looked at Oz, and there was something genuinely spooky about the stare the guy was giving him.

"I was no Mario Savio. I don't know why you would remember me, particularly."

"Well, one thing I do remember is that you were the first one to wear an Army helmet liner to Oakland, to keep your scalp intact. After that, everyone started wearing them, and hard hats. Good idea." Oz lit another joint, burned it halfway down, and passed the joint to Pete.

When he noticed Oz staring at him, he took the smoke in and held it. What the hell, he'd been wanting to do it, and from the suspicious stare he had just gotten, he figured it was time to be judicious.

"Man, that's enough for me, I gotta drive. It's gotta be Hawaiian red bud, huh?"

"You know your dope."

Pete smiled. "But getting back to the scene, it was no revolution, not even close. When Bardacke and Rossman and those other rads crowed, that there was a revolution going on, I looked around and thought, *What fucking revolution? Where are the barricades, the sickles, and the people happy to die? This is a jack-off scene.* I dropped out of the dropout scene right there."

"What did you do then, man?"

"Split for the north. Hung in the woods, grew dope, then went back to school at Humboldt State."

Oz nodded. "Arcata. Pretty country up there."

"This'll make you shit."

"Try me."

Pete narrowed his eyes and watched the man carefully as he said, "I majored in Criminal Justice."

Oz snorted the smoke he'd just inhaled and went into a coughing fit. He finally quit coughing and choked out a stoned little laugh. "A lotta good it did you."

Pete smiled and tipped his beer. He smiled a mean little smile at the old hippie and said, "Man, you'd be surprised at the shit I learned. A lot of it still comes in handy."

"I bet." Oz spits a glob onto a finger to douse the roach, then popped it into his mouth and swallowed.

"You weren't in the war either, huh?"

Pete looked at the floor. "Nah. And I still feel like shit because I skipped out on it."

Oz shook his silvery, leonine head. "Not me, not for one fucking minute."

Pete smiled a grim smile. "And that was the difference."

"What difference?"

"Between the rads and the heads . . . you guys had no real conscience."

Oz's face took on a slow smile. "That's funny. All these years I thought it was just the other way around."

Pete stood and dropped the money for the shrooms on the coffee table, next to the remaining joint. Then he touched fingertips with Oz and left. Now one mushroom was in an evidence locker downtown, and the other was sitting in Pete's stomach, running its elegant DNA up to his brain.

Pete sipped the last of the apple juice and put down the glass, then stood to walk to the low wall of the verandah. He looked out at the city's lights again, and the old feelings came flooding back on him—the camaraderie, the clandestine meetings, the sense of power, and the real possibility of changing the world.

The night. A night sweet with the scent of the large tulip tree downhill, in the middle of the steep yard. And there were the scents of other night-blooming flowers that made it all so sweet to his radically blooming senses. Sweet, softly flaring, and beckoning . . .

Pete stepped onto the low wall of the verandah and looked down. The bulb on the wall next to the downstairs apartment door dropped a delicious cone of custardy light onto a pair of woman's running shoes. The laces drooped in a languorous pile between them—pulsing in luminescent red and white like twin hearts on the concrete.

His running shoes were blue, white, and luminous. The scene below took place between the toes of those shoes, and that was significant because he was in them, and he was alive.

Pete wondered if Courtney was home, the girl who owned the shoes and lived downstairs with her boyfriend. Cute Courtney, with the perfect bottom.

Pete stepped out onto the night, and there was a faint crack as his weight came down. He took another step and looked between his legs to see the light was on in her room. She must be studying.

He looked out over the sloping yard, then over to the student apartments next door to the left. The kids' swings hung stiff and bright, and the chains glinted in the damp night air. The crescent-shaped seats appeared like smiles suspended from the chains.

To the right, prayer flags at the Nepalese Buddha house were vibrant, and their folds and drapes breathed in and out. Alive and serene, as if in deep meditation.

He took a few strides more and stood directly above the tulip tree with its fleshy flowers. The scent was potent, a pillar of exotic perfume.

Across the water, Coit Tower and the Transamerica building were rampant, brilliant. The bay and city were breathing and alive too.

He was doing the impossible, but anything seemed possible at the moment. This was the feeling he had wanted. This was the possibility he hoped he was going to find when he had decided to eat the mushroom after he'd gotten into his car at Gertner's place.

In the 1970s, everything seemed possible, and he'd never been afraid because he felt immortal. All the doubts, the fears, and other tentative feelings that attended life came later. And with it, the numbness that he needed to keep banging away at life day after day. But this night's mushroom magic sloughed off that shell, and he felt new as a butterfly coming out of its case. He was reborn! Pete strode out over the hill toward the apartment building across the street.

Some students were having a party on a fourth-floor balcony, eating from huge pizzas and drinking beer. The Grateful Dead sang and played. He walked by and saw a young woman put a slice of pizza to her mouth as she looked out into the night. Her face froze, her eyes widened. Pete smiled at her and kept walking.

The next building was more apartments. Someone played the piano, someone cooked food . . . curry. Yeah, curry and fish. Exchange students. In another apartment, the smell of hot starch meant someone was ironing shirts.

On the roof, a guy lay on a sleeping bag, smoking a joint as he looked at the stars. He didn't even see Pete even though he was no more than fifteen feet away when he passed by. Probably too stoned. Or maybe he saw, and it made perfect sense, a man walking by on the night air.

Hey, this is pretty neat, he thought. What a perspective. What a great way to see the world that you see every day, from seven stories up.

The next building was dark, probably a commercial or university building. On the next corner was a church. And above the church, a horse and rider.

Pete was not afraid because this was what he had come to find. He'd known something was waiting for him when he'd first stepped off the verandah and onto the night.

The horse was white and had huge, expressive eyes. There was a great deal of love in the eyes, and he was trying to communicate with Pete.

Stop there, the horse was thinking. So Pete stopped.

The rider nudged the horse with his heels, and the animal started toward Pete, prancing in the air above the intersection in front of the church. His hooves made a very soft chuff, chuff, as though he were strutting his beautiful hooves in the soft earth of an outdoor stadium.

The horse stopped, and Pete looked at the rider's foot, his eyes drawn by the silver-mounted *tapadero* and the silver piping that ran up the man's pants.

The man's hands were strong, and the reins ran through his muscular fingers. The fingers twitched the reins, and the horse made one prancing step forward, then turned sideways.

Pete looked up to see the rider looking down at the street below. Pete also looked down to see an Asian man who stood at the corner looking up, his face slack and mouth open. The man dropped the large sack he was carrying, and Chinese food cartons tumbled to the pavement. He froze in place and did not move, just looked up with his mouth open.

Pete and the rider simultaneously looked at one another. The big sombrero was a midnight blue, with flashing rosettes of silver thread. The rim of the hat rose until Pete could see under it and, in the darkness there, shone a full moon.

The moon was blood red, and Pete knew that the color was communicating something to him. That something was deeply significant! But what was its meaning?

Pete moved his eyes away from the rider's night face and looked at the horse just as it spun slowly and began to pace away with a *pasofino* gait that was so beautiful Pete found himself crying. Tears coursed down his face because the profound and formidable beauty was all he could stand.

The vision melted away. Pete wiped his face, turned around, and walked toward his house that he could see in the distance. It was a beautiful white with red tiles, warm windows, and his waiting bed.

He stepped onto the verandah wall, a ceramic tile cracked, and this time the crack was real. He stepped down onto the deck and went to the kitchen to dispense a glass of fresh mountain water from the five-gallon bottle. The liquid fell into the container in delicate blues, aquamarines, pink and apricot-colored ribbons. When he drank, the water tasted like music and rainbows.

In the bathroom, he washed his face as the water glittered as it dripped from his hands in waves of light and sound. It swished down the bowl and fell into the drain with tinkling sounds that made him laugh aloud. Pete flicked drops out into the room, and they arced, bounced, ran around the floor, and trickled out under the door. He went to the verandah and looked out into the night. The cities were still beautiful, still breathing and alive. Above the town and a faintly dappled bay hung a bony crescent moon.

But the full and bloody moon of his vision—what could that mean? As he lay down on his bed and into a kaleidoscope dream, Pete knew its meaning would be important at some point.

CHAPTER THIRTEEN

After a busy morning, Tom drove to the Rusty Parrot and picked up Berto for a drive. The guy wanted to look at the area's famous scenery, and Tom chose a drive up the Gros Ventre River road, to see the Tetons from the spectacular east side of the valley.

To make conversation, Tom asked, "So, what are you here for, exactly?" as they turned off the highway and onto the river road.

Berto frowned at Tom. "Huh?"

"I guess what I'm asking is, what can we do for you?"

"I want you to help catch these guys so I take them back to Mexico, then we'll give 'em a fair trial and shoot 'em." He had a huge grin when when Tom glanced his way. "I got that from one of your movies, Tomas. You might be surprised to learn, Amigo, that we actually have judges, juries, and all that stuff. Heck, we even have a Supreme Court!"

Tom waved his hand. "Don't put words in my mouth. You sound pretty sensitive about how Mexican justice is perceived up here."

Berto sighed. "Actually, I'm pretty sensitive about how Mexico in general is perceived up here."

Tom grinned. "Don't feel alone. America perceives the whole world in pretty much the same way—we have the franchise on rectitude. Hell, we think that ours is the only way to live, and that the whole world should follow our example—and just look at us. Vietnam and now Iraq . . . .shit."

Berto grinned. "I like you; we think the same. To get back to why I'm here. My people want the Osorios just as much as you guys do, probably more. Cenovio was the biggest smuggler in Oaxaca state. And he's a cold SOB too. Got a lot of blood on his hands. Plus, now that Ward is dead, they may be the only ones who can tell us what was stolen and where it went. One of my government's priorities is stemming the flow of our national heritage to other parts of the world, so it's a pretty sensitive subject anymore."

Tom nodded. "Not a month goes by that you don't read something about the richness of the prehistoric period of Mexico and South America, and how advanced their early societies were. Hell, the mummy Ward had in his case was a brain surgeon!"

"Yup. To say nothing of the fact that the Maya invented the most accurate calendar ever made by pre-technology man. They weren't just standing out there in the dark looking at the sky and picking their butts; they were scientists in the very real sense. And God only knows what the Osorios and people like them have sold to other crooks like Ward. It could have been something just as important as the Aztec calendar stone, for all we know."

"So they are pretty high up on your AGs shit list, huh?"

Berto smiled. "Somewhere in the top three, I'd say."

"Well, let's run through this. One, Teton County would probably not insist that we spend our money on two murder trials when you guys are willing to do it. Plus, we aren't going to welcome any political crap that might come with interfering in an international extradition. Two, our federal government seems quite interested in repatriating other country's national treasures, so you'll probably get all the cooperation in the world there Three, our government would probably do all it could to involve you guys in the drug stuff, hoping to learn what we can there."

"What drug stuff?" Berto seemed suddenly quite animated.

"The mushrooms and all that."

"Mushrooms?"

"Ward was financing some pretty esoteric research on the regeneration of hallucinogenic mushrooms and plants the shaman surgeon had in his pharmacy bag. California thinks it's the beginning of a whole new drug scene. I guess they've been looking at it for a while now."

"Huh. Nobody told me anything about that."

"From the little I've heard, Ward's people have been using state-of-the-art science to clone DNA from the organic materials. It involves using living bacteria to resurrect genetic material, I guess. The technology didn't even exist until some genius working for Ward discovered it."

Berto shook his head. "I'll give you gringos one thing."

"What's that?"

"Nobody else in the world even comes close to what you people do in science."

"I guess."

"Actually, Tomas, this country is probably the most admired country in the world when it comes to most things."

"Well, that's nice to hear."

"Now if we could all just figure out some way to like you guys." And he grinned his big grin when Tom looked across the car. He leaned forward. "Hey, this place looks just like Oaxaca."

Tom looked out at the valley of the upper Gros Ventre. "Here?"

"Yeah."

"I thought Mexico was all cactus and desert."

Berto waved his hand back and forth. "No way. The border area is like that, for the most part. But Mexico is mostly mountains, and in the south it's real jungle."

"You mean Mexico has mountains like these?"

"Hell yes. A lot of Mexico is mountains with pine trees and the whole nine yards. Only the big volcanoes snow on them, but the mountains in Oaxaca have pine and oak forests just like these."

"Those trees aren't oaks, they're Quaking aspen."

"They look the same from here, Amigo. Only those flat places below would be fields, and there'd be some guy there guiding a wooden plow and poking oxen in the butt with a stick to make them go."

"I'll be darned, you learn something every day. I had no idea there were pine trees down there."

"Yep. Mixtec pine, and real people doing real work to fill their bellies with corn, beans, chilies, and gourd fruits like watermelon. Amigo, damn little has changed down there for a thousand years."

"Like your mother's people?"

"Yup, named for the Indians."

"I never heard of them before yesterday."

"Yeah, nobody up here has. And they were one of the most famous of the ancient people—Olmec, Aztec, Toltec, Zapotec, Mixtec. The Mixtec are pretty much the only pure bloods left, except the Maya, Trique, and the Zapotec. The Zapotec mostly don't practice their folkways anymore but the Mixtec do. Their fundamental mentality hasn't changed all that much since the Spaniards showed up."

"Not very many of them left, I guess."

"The mountains are full of 'em," Berto snorted.

Tom noticed more than a little contempt in how the man said it, which was odd when half the blood in his veins was Mixtec.

CHAPTER FOURTEEN

The bus roared down the long hill and left the pine-forested mountains, leaving a pall of blue exhaust smoke behind. It broke onto a vista of fields and red-roofed houses on the outskirts of Tlaxiaco, as the driver pulled the bus to the middle of the road to avoid people walking on the shoulder in the early morning mist.

Children waved from the doorways of wooden huts as they blinked in the wood smoke from breakfast fires. Concha saw the weather was chilly because the people wore their heaviest clothing. It made her want to open the window so she could savor the mountain air of her home. It would be damp and thickly redolent from pinewood smokes of a hundred breakfast fires. Tears welled into her eyes because she was so close to the home and the family she had not seen in almost five years. Today she would get word to San Miguel Achiutla that she and her brother had returned.

"It will be so good to see Mama and Papa," she said to Cenovio.

"But Don Mario told us that we could not see Papa and Mama until he sent word—that we would be wise to not even contact them," her brother whispered emphatically. "Remember, the police may be looking for us, even down here."

Concha sighed. "There must be some way that we can get word to them, to let them know that we are all right. But it will not be hard once we are in Santa Catarina Tayata; it's only fifteen kilometers away."

The bus entered the town and climbed the little hill to the main intersection. A dozen truck taxis waited to leave for the scattered small communities to pick up and drop off passengers at the side of the dirt roads that laced the mountains.

They rode down the hill, then the bus turned right toward a terminal on the south side barrio, astride a rutted dirt street busy with chickens, dogs, and Indian people.

Cenovio took their small bags and walked across the street to a rough-board stand where they bought sugar bread and two cups of the strong Oaxacan coffee.

After eating, they began the steep walk toward the Hotel Cristobol Colon. They waited at a corner for a truck to pass from the side street into the main traffic. They stepped from the sidewalk, then froze in the middle of the road. Two policemen exited the shop on the corner and two more appeared behind them. One of the men in front of them was huge, two meters tall. He carried a shotgun slung over his shoulder and wore a mean smile on his face.

Cenovio bolted, making it only two steps before a policeman struck him down from behind. He started to rise, but the man stood over him with his rifle butt raised.

"Do not move again or I will break your head."

Slumping onto the stone roadway, Cenovio groaned. They had come so far, only to lose everything. He thought of the three men who gave up their lives in his hands, and his strength fled from him.

God forgive me, please, he said to himself. *Absolve me of my sins, for I did not kill them for myself, but for my people.*

Thus, he began the preparations he knew he must make before these men took his life and that of his beloved sister, as they surely would. There was precious little mercy for Mixtecos in the land of his fathers when the *capitanes,* and their heirs, took the reins of power.

MiT

When Tommy entered the Law Enforcement building on Monday, he noticed that something was wrong. It was too quiet, and everyone was in their offices with the doors closed. Usually, there was a little joking and grab-ass that went on around the coffee machine. But today, it was as quiet as a Sunday.

"Morning, Rhonda."

"Morning."

"Uh, what's wrong?"

"What are you talking about?"

"It's like a hospital around here. What's going on?"

"Don't ask me."

"As in 'Don't ask me, ask someone else'?"

"Go ask someone else."

"Thanks, Rhonda, and by the way . . ."

She looked up quizzically and said, "What."

"This weekend I remembered who Jane Goodall is."

A hint of a smile played on her face, and she said, "Good work, here's a treat." She picked out a piece of candy from a bowl on her desk and tossed it to him.

He said, "Oo, oo, oo," and scratched under one arm, then walked to his office. He was sitting at his desk when the door opened, and Lewis stuck his crewcut head inside.

"Can I come in?"

Tom waved at the chair across the desk and said, "Sit."

"Nah, that's okay. I was just wonderin' if you'd been in to check on Sam."

"No. Why?"

"You haven't heard, huh?"

"Lewis, you know damn good and well I haven't heard, or you wouldn't be in here. You're just aching to tell me something juicy, what is it?"

"Sam got tossed in jail in Big Piney this weekend."

Tom's mouth fell open, and coffee ran onto his chin. He wiped it away with the back of his hand and said, "What the hell are you talking about?"

"He got to feeling bad about the suicide in the jail last Thursday—the girl who managed to smother herself with a plastic bag because we don't have enough personnel to post a suicide watch. Too bad he didn't bust up the county commissioner's chambers when they cut the SO budget last year. Anyway, he went over to Big Piney and got in a bar fight. They took his ass to jail and made him spend the night."

"Did they book him?" Tom asked instantly.

Lewis waved his hand, "Nah. The chief there knew it would mean the end of Sam if there was any public record of him being arrested. They just put him in the tank and let him cool down and sober up."

"Has anybody here talked to him yet?"

"Who's gonna take that chance? You, maybe?"

"Is he in his office."

"Yup." Lewis smiled. "But I don't think they're allowin' any visitors." He made a wide grin. "I guess it took every cop in that part of the county to get him cuffed and stuffed. He's still a horse, you bet."

"I wouldn't pee on his leg," Tom said and grinned too.

Tom pushed the intercom button when it buzzed. "Thompson here."

"Get your ass in here." It was the sheriff.

"Be right in, Sam."

Lewis leaped to his feet. "Gotta go." He put his thumb and little finger to the side of his face to pantomime a conversation later.

Tom just looked at him.

"Sheez," Lewis said and left.

When Tom knocked on the door, Sam hollered, "Come in, dammit!"

Tom glanced at Rhonda. Her eyes were wide, and her face pale. Then she mouthed, "Good luck!"

Tom tried to think of what could have inspired the summons as he opened the door and stepped inside.

Sam had his boots on the desk, a cup of coffee in his hand, and wore a raccoon eye that defined what one should look like. He also wore a big grin on his face.

"Siddown, Tom. How you doing, anyway?"

"Uh, I'm fine," he flicked a finger at Sam's huge shiner, "but how does that feel?"

"You know, it feels real good."

"I bet it does."

"No, I mean it. I haven't felt this good in years."

"Got the shit out of your system, huh?"

"Yeah, I did."

"What's the other guy look like?"

"Oh, probably about the same. We always did end up about even."

"You tangled with this guy before?"

"Yup, both of 'em. It started when we were kids, out on the Hoback Rim."

"There were two?"

"My twin cousins. Aunt Rea's boys."

Tom felt a smile growing. "Tell me about it."

"I stopped at the Green River Bar in Daniel and visited with some folks I hadn't seen in years. Then I stopped at Waterhole #3 in Marbleton and had a few, and when I got to the Silver Spur, I was feeling no pain." He took a sip from his cup of coffee, and his face softened at the memory of the moment. "It was perfect. I walked in and there they sat—Pat and Mike."

"Pat and Mike."

"Yup, big ol' Pat and bigger ol' Mike. They never saw me coming."

"Just sitting there minding their own business, having a quiet beer . . ."

"Yeah, it was great. They had no idea I was even in the room till I popped them two big ol' round heads together. Tom, it was beautiful. Pat spit his beer all over the bartender, Mike's teeth popped out on the bar . . . .It couldn't have been more perfect. Now I know that there really is a God and that he loves me, just like you keep saying."

"I assume they didn't just take it as a joke."

Sam smiled as the swollen eye winked like a black mule's ass. "Oh, hell no. They both hate me, always have. Their mom liked me more than either one of those dumb bastards, because they were just like their big no-neck dad."

"And the fight was on," Tom prompted.

"It was a beauty. Pat's the smallest of the three of us and he weighs about two-ten. We broke every damn thing in the place before the cops got there."

"Just the kind of nightmare every cop dreads."

"Yeah, a family fight. Nothing like it."

"I'm glad you had a good time."

"Couldn't have been better. It's gonna be expensive, but what the hell. Now I'm in the mood to drag those commissioners' asses through the fire. We're going to have the two jail positions I've been sniveling about. And while I'm at it, I'm going to wring some other things out of them that I've wanted for a long time."

"Like what?"

"None of your damn business. Don't you have any work to do?"

"Hell, Sam, you're the one who invited me."

"And now I'm the one who's dis-inviting you. Get out of my office."

"Sheez," Tom said with a grin and got up out of the chair. "You know, I haven't seen an eye like that for years."

Sam touched the swollen eye and winced. Then he smiled again. "Ol' Mike's got two of 'em. He never did learn how to duck the punch behind the jab. You know, I haven't felt this good in a very long time. I think I'll take Rhonda out to lunch today."

Tom left the office. When he closed the door, half a dozen people stood casually in the reception area. All eyes turned toward him. Rhonda raised her eyebrows in question. Tom drew his mouth down in a look of horror and shook his head. Everyone left, except poor Rhonda. When Tom left, she stared at Sam's door with a look of dread on her face.

MiT

"Hey, Pete. What you up to? Come in." Oz opened the door and stood aside, so that Villareal could enter.

"I didn't know how to get in touch with the company you work for, and I didn't have your phone number, so I thought I'd drop by."

"That's cool. The company isn't in the phone book, and neither am I. You want some coffee?"

"Nah, I'm about coffeed out."

"This is some Oaxacan like you've never tasted before. It's the best; it'll knock your socks down on your shoes."

"Sounds more like a description of some new kind of smoke."

"Heh, heh," Oz wheezed, "you're not far wrong. Caffeine is the popular drug now—that's why we got into it."

"You're growing coffee?"

"We're hybridizing it, making it more flavorful and stronger. This is some of the first crop."

"You're always right in the middle of the scene, aren't you?"

"It's not hard to see where things are going. This coffee thing was as predictable as sunrise, once the Starbucks started popping up like dandelions."

Pete followed him into the kitchen. The coffee brewer spluttered its last gasps, and the fresh coffee smelled wonderful, especially after the stale Safeway house brand he'd been drinking down at the police station.

"Hey, that does smell like some good stuff. Maybe I will try a cup."

Oz opened the cupboard and took down another cup. It had a picture of a 1930s girl, and the black script under the graphic read "Ozma of Oz." Pete turned the old hippie's cup around and saw a picture of the Wiz himself.

"Cute."

Oz grinned as he poured the fragrant brew. "I got the whole set—there's a dozen altogether."

Pete picked up his cup and breathed in the aroma. "Hmmm, you're right. This doesn't smell like anything I've ever drank before." He took a sip and let it run slowly down his throat. "It's smooth, but still bitter. I don't know how to describe it."

"It's semi-alkaline, the opposite of acidic. Easy on the stomach."

"But it's got a kick. You're right."

"Come in the front room, I just rolled one."

Pete smiled to himself. Life was invented, pretty much, in the Bay Area, and Oz was going to live it right to the end. And why not? It worked for him, and he was happy with it. Too bad Pete was here to put an end to it if he could. He liked the guy, but what he was doing was dangerous to folks with lower tolerances than he had, which was probably the whole rest of the world. Anyone who could still be doing the quantities of dope that this guy ingested and still be functional had to make him a world-class something. Jerry Garcia had learned his lesson the hard way too.

Oz licked the number and fired it up, then took a monster toke. With a slight nod, he offered it to Pete as he held the smoke deep in his lungs.

Pete waved it away. "Too early for me." He smiled in genuine admiration at the guy's tolerance.

Oz shrugged, let out the toke, and said, "You want to do some business?"

"Yeah. I want to make this Mexico scene that you talked about."

"The solstice gig."

"It sounds like something I'd like to try." He looked out the apartment window at the bay bridge, now a lacy gray over the blue waters of the bay. "I ate one of those 'shrooms . . . ." His voice trailed off.

Oz's eyes twinkled as he held in another toke. He raised his eyebrows and pantomimed a question mark.

Pete shook his head, and his voice was awed when he spoke.

"I never experienced anything like it, and I've eaten some kick-ass veggies in my time."

"Who showed up on your trip through the Gate of Heaven?"

Pete's heart missed a beat. "You mean someone was supposed to show up?"

"It wasn't a hallucination, Pedro. Tell me what happened."

"I walked on air, Man. I walked right out onto the freaking air. And I met some Mexican guy riding a white horse, and someone else saw him too—a delivery guy who dropped his order. That's what convinced me that it was, well, real."

Oz leaned forward. "You walked out in the air, and someone saw you do it?"

"A chick with a slice of pizza hanging out of her mouth, and then the delivery guy."

Oz leaned back in his chair and smiled beatifically. "Congratulations, you had the primo trip. I've only heard of two other people making that one." He shook his head in admiration. "You're a real advanced soul, Pedro. The egotists and egoists drop when the trapdoor of their petty illusions about themselves, based on their money and status, opens under their feet."

"They drop?"

"The big drop with the sudden stop. They survive it, of course, but the crash and burn is real enough. I should have warned you, but honestly, I thought you would have one of the garden variety of experiences—riding your body music, seeing into people, stuff like that."

"Body music?"

"Yeah. Everyone's a symphony. Hearing your own composition, the unique music that is God's signature for your soul will wring your heart, Man. It'll make you whole, just like being born again, but without the monotonous snare drums of Yahweh. It comes from a place higher than heaven."

"I wouldn't believe you if I hadn't walked."

"You surprise me, Pedro, you really do. On the outside you seem like . . . oh, a narc even." He raised his hand as if to ward off any protest. "I don't mean an actual narc-type narc. I mean you came across as someone who wouldn't catch the *merkaba*."

"What's that?"

"The Sky Sleigh—tripping out onto the ether is the big trip because that's where you meet eternity's messengers."

"Messengers."

"Yup. The beings with the messages."

"What messages?"

"From the future."

Pete's scalp tightened, and goose flesh stood the hairs on his arms. "He didn't talk to me; he didn't say anything."

"They don't talk. What did he look like?"

"He was wearing a sombrero, one of those ornate ones with silver embroidery—"

"No, not the man. The animal."

"The horse?"

"Yeah. The messenger is always the animal, the man was the message."

"But no one said anything, there couldn't have been a message."

"Think."

"There was a beautiful white horse, and rider in black and silver, a Mexican, waiting for me. The horse pranced up and stopped, the guy looked up and instead of a face . . ."

"Yeah."

"There was a night sky—stars, a full moon."

"Was there a particular constellation of stars?"

"None that I recognized."

"You need to remember the configuration of the stars and moon. I'll bet that that's the message, Man. You gotta get that down."

"The one thing that was really different was the moon looked bloody."

"What?"

"It was really red, a blood red. I got the feeling that it was bleeding, dying even."

Oz stared at him. "There's something seriously wrong in the Alta. We need to get down there and help them."

Pete let out a deep breath he had been holding. "When do we leave?"

"Huh?"

"When does the group leave for Mexico?"

"Full up." Oz doused the number and popped the roach back.

"What do you mean, full up, can't you see? The guy was a Mexican!"

"We booked the last place days ago."

"Hell, I'll be glad to pay extra if that's what it takes."

"You'd make thirteen, Pedro. We can't go down there with thirteen."

"Book another one, that'd make fourteen."

"I hate to disappoint you, but it ain't gonna happen. We got the group we need. You see, not just anyone can go. We weed 'em real careful—no nuts, no nothings, and no thirteens. You should have committed when I told you about the trip."

" 'Nothings'?"

"People with no personalities who are looking for one. They freak every time."

"I guess they would. I damn near freaked myself when I came down and thought about what had happened."

"Next time, Pedro. Sorry." Oz stood up. "Gotta go."

Pete walked with him to the door. "Oz, I have to go with you. I have this feeling, a knowledge, that I should be in Mexico."

Oz put his big paw on Pete's shoulder and looked deep into his eyes. The man smelled like a thousand years of smoke, and his eyes mirrored this ancient look—as if they witnessed the building of Egypt's pyramids.

"If you're supposed to go, you'll go. Relax."

"How?"

"If you're supposed to be down there, you'll be there." He paused. "Your spirit animal, the horse, will see that it happens."

Chapter Fifteen

Tom phoned Polly in California just before his lunch hour, and his daughter, Christina, took the call for her mother.

"This is Christina Anaya, Mr. Thompson."

A lump came to his throat. This was the daughter he had always wanted yet had never known. And it looked like he never would because she kept an enormous emotional distance between them. Tom might be her biological father, but that didn't change one whit her relationship with the man who raised her, Ferdinand Anaya.

His whole life, he had looked at little girls, especially the three- and four-year-olds, and ached for one to hold. He loved his son as much as he loved anyone or anything. But having a little girl to hold and receiving the special kind of trust they give was one thing he always longed for.

"Is your mom there?"

"She is."

"May I speak to her?"

"She's in a meeting right now, an important one. I just stepped out to get a file or the receptionist would have told you to phone her at home tonight. Try about eleven o'clock, coast time."

"No way that I could just talk to her for a minute, huh?"

"Mr. Thompson, we have people here from Mexico at the moment, very important people. We will be talking business until early evening, and then my father . . . *my* father and I will be hosting them, and our associates, at dinner. You can expect her to be home around eleven, or perhaps later."

Tom felt a stab of irritation. Keeping an even voice, he asked, "You'll be sure to tell her I phoned, won't you?"

There was a moment's silence, and then she said, frostily, "Of course I will."

"Thank you."

"You are welcome." *Rattle. Click.*

Tom felt his face flush with anger. He knew that she had good reason to resent him but having to deal with her unpleasantness was unbearable. He wanted to know her, but there seemed to be no way, now or ever.

Then he remembered the ring. Polly was undoubtedly wearing it, and the ring probably served as a symbol of his intrusion into their life. Oh well, they could like it or lump it because Polly was his now, and he didn't care if it hare-lipped every sheep in Lincoln County. He left the office, pulling the door shut. Turning around, he saw Sheriff Harlan talking to Berto, who was waiting to have lunch with Tom.

"You going to have lunch with us, Sam?"

"Can't, Tom, gotta go to a Rotary meeting. Wish I could though, we're having another talk by some expert on limiting growth. If it were up to me, I'd give the developers five years to build anything they wanted and then cut 'em off at the ankles—tell 'em to go back to where they came from. I wish we could get this whole damn thing over with, I'm tired to death of listening to it."

"You're not the only one. All the same, they're going to shit this nest full, and right to the brim just like they did where they came from. It's inevitable."

Sam rubbed his thumb back and forth across the tips of his fingers. "Money."

Tom nodded. "Money."

Berto smiled. "Doesn't matter where you go, it's the same—"

"The rich get richer, and the poor get babies," Tom finished for him.

"You got it. Where we going to eat?"

"Let's go out to the Bunnery and see if we can get a couple of stools at the counter in back."

Miraculously, there was an empty table waiting when they got there, which was rare as the place was small and usually packed with tourists.

After the waitress took their order, Tom asked, "What did you and Sam talk about?"

"More of the same stuff that you and I have talked about—how to catch the Osorios."

He went on, "I gotta tell you, this waiting is getting real old. I thought they'd be picked up by now."

Tom shrugged and took a sip of his coffee. "They could be in Mexico by now."

Berto shook his head. "You'd think that as hard as it's getting to cross the border, there'd be a real slim chance of them being missed. There's thousands of cops between here and there."

Tom smiled. "Yeah, but no one's trying to stop anyone from heading back."

He saw from the sour look on Berto's face that he'd interpreted the statement as a slam, but he decided to let it stand. The truth was the truth.

"If I thought they had gone back, I'd be down there. My guess is that they've gone underground up here. And I'll bet they're in California somewhere."

"I've checked with the agencies in both those places, and I've done it every day. Heck, you've been in my office just about every time I've phoned."

The little man sighed. "Yeah, yeah. But I hate sitting around like this."

They'd finished their meal and were standing in front of the restaurant picking their teeth when Tom saw Sheriff's Harlan's car pull in. He waved them toward the car and then said, "Get in."

Tom opened the front door for Berto and then climbed in the back.

Sam pulled out into the traffic and drove toward Wilson, not saying anything for several minutes. Finally, he said, "I don't like secrets."

Tom waited for him to go on.

"I got pulled out of my Rotary meeting to answer a call from Senator Enzi. He was afraid that what he had to say might be sensitive. He asked me to keep it under my hat until he could smooth things out with the folks at the Mexican Embassy in Washington. I told him that Mr. Sanchez—"

"Sandez," Tom corrected.

"—Sandez was here and waiting. He said he thought that it would be better if I didn't say anything for the moment."

"But you aren't going to do that, are you?" Tom said.

"No."

"What's the deal?" Tom asked.

"Doctor Nathaniel Ward was the nephew, the favorite nephew and namesake, of the Honorable 'Nat' Ward."

"Stud congressman from Virginia," Tom added.

"Well, he's an ex-congressman because he just retired, but he still has a lot of stroke in Washington. Enzi says that the guy is kind of a dickhead, but he's influential, and if we can do him the favor, the senator would appreciate it, strictly as a personal favor and nothing more."

"The Senator called the Congressman a dickhead?" Tom smirked.

"Mike's been back there long enough to know one when he sees one and he calls 'em the way he sees 'em. You know that," Sam said.

"So?"

"So, until now, we've had an understanding, an *informal* understanding, with Mr. Sandez that we might not pursue the murder charges against the Osorios—that we would not stand in the way of an extradition request from the Mexican Attorney General's office, depending on how the federal case went." Tom said.

"Yes. The murder charge supersedes any other processes—smuggling, trafficking in national treasures, anything. And Congressman Ward wants them to face the music in the States."

Berto became agitated. "But they are citizens of Mexico."

"And they killed an American citizen," Sam said emphatically. "And it looks like they killed one who had a hell of a lot of influence in the center of power here. I guess his family is related to just about everybody who came over on the Mayflower."

Tom leaned forward in the seat and said, "We think that they may have killed an American citizen. The evidence is only circumstantial."

"I have some other news for you, Tom," Sam said.

"What?"

"Jeff just phoned from Alta and we're headed over there. We have a witness to the murder."

MiT

In Tlaxiaco, the policemen led Concha and Cenovio up the hill to the Municipio building, then through the central courtyard to the regional police offices.

Once inside the office, the Commander dismissed all the men except one—the giant with mean eyes carrying a shotgun.

"You are Cenovio Osorio Espinoza."

Concha's brother said nothing until the giant put the muzzle of the shotgun gently behind his ear.

"I am Cenovio Osorio, yes."

The man was looking at a piece of paper in front of him. "And you are Concha Ward Espinoza, the wife of a man who was murdered in the States."

"I am Concha Ward Espinoza."

"And you are both from San Miguel Achiutla?"

"Yes," Concha answered.

The policeman looked at Cenovio and his face flushed. "If you do not find your tongue, Señor Osorio, we will find it for you."

"I am Cenovio Osorio Espinoza from San Miguel Achiutla."

"You are a bloody one, Osorio. From this information I have here, I know you have killed two policemen." The Comandante looked up from under his eyebrows. "And this is true?"

Cenovio's face was pale. If he admitted to the killings, he was a dead man. If he did not answer, he was in mortal danger from the huge dog of a man with the shotgun.

"Uh, Comandante?" Concha ventured.

The man turned his flushed face to her. "Yes."

"May we have a lawyer before we answer any more questions?"

The man leaned back in his chair and stared at her for a moment. "Señora Ward, you are no longer in the north. In Mexico we deal in the truth, not in the handiwork of law mongers. I will decide when, and if, you talk to a lawyer."

"Sir, surely you would want my brother to give you the truth willingly, and from a good heart."

"You mean that if he had a lawyer, only then he would tell the truth?"

"Yes, certainly."

"As I have just said, lawyers do not deal in the truth—they deal in the words of the law, not necessarily the truth."

"And are not they the same, the law and truth."

The man smiled. "Either you are naive or coy with me."

He picked up the piece of paper from his desk. "I am interested if what is written here is true. If it is true that your brother is the murderer of two, and possibly three, men. At this moment, I want only the truth of those matters."

Concha looked at the paper the man was dangling. Curiously, it was handwritten, and it occurred to her that if it were an official report, it would have come from a machine of some kind.

"This report has nothing to do with you, and for that reason I am letting you go."

"What?"

"You may go." He nodded to the huge man against the office wall who leaned over and opened the door.

"I would like to stay with my brother."

The man behind the desk looked sinister. "Believe me, you would not like to stay with your brother. You would not like it at all, I think. He appears to be a stubborn man."

Concha looked at her brother. The look on his face was flat and devoid of emotion.

"Cenovio."

He didn't look at her.

"Cenovio . . ." She felt hot tears run down her face.

He looked at her, and his eyes said, "Save yourself. And our people."

Concha felt the huge man's hand on her shoulder and knew she must leave while she had the chance. Once Cenovio was put in jail in the basement, there was a real chance he'd never be seen again. She must be the one to go for help.

She picked up the plastic grain sack that held all she owned and left as the massive wooden door slammed with great force behind her. The giant was warming to his work.

Sheriff Harlan pulled into the driveway of a large log house, across the county road from Ward's place, where Jeff's patrol car was parked.

He met them at the door and took them to the maid's quarters at the rear of the house, where a woman in casual but expensive clothes waited. A petite Latina, a plain young woman in her mid-twenties, sat next to her.

The moment they stepped into the room, Berto started a torrent of Spanish as he walked directly to the woman and began to interrogate her. The effect on her was startling.

The little woman fell back into her chair. Her eyes widened, and her legs trembled so badly that she looked as if she might lose control of her body functions.

"Whoa, WHOA! Wait just a damn minute." Sheriff Harlan had seen the effect of the interrogation on the woman, and from the look on his face, he was not happy with it, and neither was Tom.

Berto looked up at Sam, and it appeared that he was going to stand his ground for a moment. He suddenly smiled and said, "Lost my head. For a moment I thought I was in charge, like I would be back home." He shrugged. "Do you want me to translate?"

"Does she speak English?" Sheriff Harlan asked the owner of the house.

"Yes, her English is good. At least it is when she is not scared to death."

Sam turned to the little woman and said, "Don't worry, no one is going to do anything to you. I am the Sheriff of Teton County, and you can trust me."

The frightened woman looked at Berto and didn't offer a word.

Sam glanced at the Mexican officer and said, "Señor Sandez is an officer of the Attorney General's office in Mexico City. He is here to help us." He saw the words were doing little to reassure her.

"Jeff, what did she tell you?"

Jeff looked at his notebook and said, "Apparently, she had a boyfriend who was a friend of Ward's maid's brother. When he came to visit, he'd bring this Valeriano with him, and she'd go over there."

"Concha, she was my fren'," the woman offered.

"What was the name of your other friend, the man?" Sam asked.

"His name Valeriano Trujano," she said.

"Tell me, what do you know about the murder of Doctor Ward?"

"It was in the night after I do the dishes from supper. I know that Valeriano is at the house because Concha phoned and say that he is wanting to see me when I am done with my working. So I am walking across the road to the house when I see in the big window there is much trouble in the house . . . they are making loud talk, and then the mens is fighting over something. Cenovio an' Valeriano an' *el Profesor.*

"Then Cenovio is hit Señor War' with e-stick, an' Concha is feeks him. But Profesor War is come back awake and is fighting again an' runs outside, an' then the door is go open with broking, breaking window . . . ."

Jeff explained, "It's the side door to the living room, the one that opens onto the side yard where we found the piece of firewood with the boogers."

Sheriff Harlan shook his head at the deputy, "Let her go on. You can fill us in later."

The woman looked back and forth at the men.

"Please, go on."

"El Profesor Ward is come out of the house, and he fall down. He is holding his head and is making bad noises—like he is . . ."

"Crying?" Sam asked.

The woman shook her head. "Is differen', not crying."

"Moaning. She told me that he was moaning," the owner said.

"Go on," Sam said gently.

"He is get up and walking funny . . ."

"Staggering," the woman interpolated.

"Then is coming out of the house, Cenovio and Valeriano. Cenovio is have some wood in his hands and he run to el Profesor Ward and push him so he is fall down on his knees."

"Ward falls," Sam said.

"*Si*. Then Cenovio is shout to *el profesor,* but he is only moan an' hol' his head. Then he fall down and do nothing."

"Then what happened?"

"Cenovio is cry. He shake El Profesor Ward and shake him. He say, 'Wake up, wake up!' Then Valerio say, 'Oh, Cenovio you have kill him, *'sta muerto'* and Cenovio say 'No, no, he is not dead he is only . . . *inconsciente.*'"

Sam turned to Berto.

"Unconscious," he supplied.

"Then what happened?" Sam asked.

"They pray over heem for long time."

"Pray?" Tom asked.

"Yes. They are pray to Dios, and to the big mountain."

"The Grand Teton? Why?"

"They are believe in that is where God lives. Like at their home in Mexico. They are Indians and have strange beliefs."

"Then what?" the sheriff asked.

"They pull on him into the house. It was taking them long time, an' I leave."

"And did they know that you were watching them while this was going on?"

She shook her head emphatically. "No, *Señor.*"

"Why didn't you tell us this before?"

The young woman looked at her mistress, and the older woman put her hand on her shoulder. "She said that she was afraid of the police, was afraid that she might have to go to jail."

"Well, she is definitely not going to jail, this is America. What I want, though, is that she tape-record her statement. Jeff, can you do that for me? You might want to get a few more details too."

"Sure, Sheriff. Be glad to."

"Thank you very much, ma'am," Sam said. "And thank you too," he added to the owner.

"You are quite welcome. I hope it helps."

"When and if we catch them, it will help a great deal toward getting a conviction."

"If you don't catch them, it will be just as well," she said.

"Why do you say that?"

"Doctor Ward was not our idea of a desirable neighbor."

"How so?"

She shrugged. "Stories."

"Stories?"

"Yes. Rituals, drug use . . . and other highly illegal things. He was not a nice man."

"What about his maid?"

"Oh, she was very sweet. I enjoyed it when she visited. But she was not his maid, she was his wife, although he didn't marry her."

"No?"

"She was a bartered bride."

"What's that mean?"

"It means that he didn't marry her, Sheriff. He bought her."

MiT

Pete Villareal sat in the Cafe Med, drinking coffee and reading the Berkeley Barb newspaper. There were always clues to illegal activity in the form of personal ads that alluded to sexual activities that traversed the spectrum from end-to-end, so to speak. Also, outright ads for products flagged businesses as likely hubs for trafficking in just about every substance and item governments felt compelled to control. It was the source of some of his best intelligence.

He put the paper down at his table and went to the counter for a refill when he felt a hand on his shoulder. He turned and looked into the mysterious gaze of Oz Gertner.

"The horse is looking out for you, Pedro."

"Huh?"

"You're going to Mexico. We had a last-minute cancellation."

"The horse decided I could go, huh?" Pete said lightly and retrieved his coffee.

Oz stared at Pete for a moment, then carefully said, "Don't joke. If you don't respect what is going on, then maybe you shouldn't be with us. This is very serious business."

"Uh, sorry. It's just that this all real new to me. Hell, I've never been involved in anything like this, outside of reading a book or two for amusement."

Oz walked back to Pete's table with him. When Pete sat, Oz leaned forward with his hands on the table and whispered in his smoky voice, "This is not for amusement, it is not for pleasure, it is not a pastime, and it is definitely not a hobby for me and my partner Olga Blavatsky."

"C'mon Oz, you make it sound like a life-or-death deal."

Oz pushed his weight from the table and smiled mysteriously. "Nothing so trivial, this is larger than either life or death. Get that straight."

Pete watched the man walk out the door and into the slanting afternoon light. The smoke-grimed windows gave the effect of vanishing into the light. The hair on his arms rose, and his scalp tightened like a drumhead.

MiT

Tom was reading a magazine, and petting Millie, when the phone rang. At the sound of Polly's voice, he snapped his fingers and waved Millie down. Polly didn't like the dog on the collector's quilt she'd picked out for their bed.

"Sorry I couldn't phone sooner, I know it's late there," Polly said.

Tom glanced at the clock and saw it was twenty-five after eleven. "How are you?"

"I'm fine, but a little tired. It's been a long day. How are you?"

"A little tired too. Busy, huh?"

"Yes. This development deal with the Mexican group is really quite complicated. We are in the middle of a re-negotiation."

"Why re-negotiate?"

"Because we can see the potential for improving our position."

"How so?"

"Ugh, please let's not talk business. Let's talk about us instead."

"What's to talk about?"

"Are we really going to be married, finally, Thomas? Or is this ring just your way of trying to get in my panties?"

"Hon, in case you haven't noticed I have been in your panties so many times I get winded thinking about it."

"Surely not winded, Thomas, you run almost every morning. Perhaps you get exercised when thinking about my panties."

"If you keep talking like this, I'm going have to take a break. Phone me back in fifteen minutes, okay?"

"Don't you dare. You can exercise later."

"You know I've been thinking. I want to come back next time as a whale."

"A whale?"

"Yes, with a tongue four feet long, and able to breathe through the top of my head."

"Oh, stop it," she giggled. "But seriously, how have you been?"

"Oh, this Alta thing took an interesting turn this afternoon."

"Uh-huh, go on. Oooh, that feels good."

"Get your hands on top of the covers and keep them there!"

"I was kicking off my shoes. Go on."

"Senator Enzi phoned and said that the victim was the favorite nephew of the distinguished 'Nat' Ward."

"The congressman from Virginia."

"Well, ex-congressman, but he still swings a big stick in Washington, apparently."

"And what did the senator want?"

"He wants us to get hot on the case and bring the felons to the bar as quickly as possible. I guess this is major news back east because our Nat Ward was a yuppie prince with a permanent niche on the social register. And from the evidence we've recovered so far, he was also a major supplier of world-class artifacts to some of the richest collectors in America. All in all, a potent mix of influence."

"Do you have any clues as to where the suspects might be?"

"Berto—he's the guy I told you about when I phoned you Sunday—thinks that they are here in the States. Personally, I think that they're back across the border."

"What makes you think that?"

"Nothing more than a hunch, really. But let's not talk about my business either. Let's talk about your panties some more."

"Let's talk about a wedding."

"Simple. I meet you in Vegas, we get hitched at the Chapel Chez Bugsy Siegel, then do it standing up in the Caesar's Palace fountain."

"Sounds like fun, but we're getting married in The Chapel of the Transfiguration in Grand Teton Park. We'll honeymoon in a new hotel that's part of a complex we're investing in down Mexico Way, and once we're married we do it once a month—and that's in our snug bed between comfortable flannel sheets while wearing sensible flannel night clothes."

"With the lights off and wearing sensible shoes too, no doubt."

"Of course. It's the way decent people comport themselves."

"We're going to quit doing it and begin comporting. Sounds safe enough."

"Safe sex—it's the rage."

"Californians have a way of perverting everything, even turning safe sex into dumb sex. Is James Dobson your new guru? And Focus on the Family our future?"

She laughed the effervescent laugh that he loved, and they talked for more than an hour.

MiT

When the phone rang again, Tom was startled out of a dead sleep. The large, phosphorescent numbers on the clock radio read 2:11.

"Thompson here."

"Hey Chavo, you awake?"

"Berto, what the hell's up? It's two o'clock in the damn morning!"

"I just got a call from Mexico, and I'll be leaving on the first plane south."

"What's happening?"

"You were right about the Osorios."

"What about them?"

"They scooted back across the border."

"Where are they now?"

"He's in jail. A place called Tlaxiaco, down in Oaxaca."

"And the sister?"

"Looks like she and the other guy have disappeared, Man. Maybe they didn't make it."

Chapter Sixteen

Once awakened by Berto's phone call, Tom decided to stay up. By sunrise, he'd done his exercises on the deck in the crisp June dawn, then gone for a jog up the road above the house.

When Polly first set up his exercise regimen, he'd bitched and complained. He had also ragged her about California-izing him and his house. He'd resisted running, the collector's quilt on the bed, expensive rugs on the floor, and flower beds around the house. However, the exercise made him feel better than he had in years. He also felt better when he walked into the bedroom and saw the antique Dresden Plate quilt that dominated the decorating scheme. She'd even gone to Tom's mother and dug up old family pictures taken in 1860s Utah, had them copied and enlarged, then framed them for the walls. It was a real personal and thoughtful touch that gratified the woman to no end. Polly got along fine with the older woman, something Tom couldn't manage, no matter how hard he tried.

At six o'clock, he went to the Exxon station for a large blueberry muffin and coffee, then decided to go for a drive before work. As the sun lit the dew-laden fields, he decided to take a turn down the back road between Teton Village and Moose, then make the loop back to town. The road, mainly in the Teton National Park, had not changed much over the years. It was one of the few places left that had retained a bit of the valley's earlier character.

Once on the dirt portion of the road, memories of his childhood came back. The special rhythms and motions that old dirt roads impart to cars made him nostalgic.

The road was built in the early twentieth century, and the equipment used was motor-driven but primitive, and the engineers designed roads within the small capacities of the machines. After World War II, the narrow, switch-backed byways grew wide enough to accommodate two fast automobiles, but the bridges were still narrow enough that a car had to slow down and give way to any larger vehicle. This road was a relic of that time.

The song of the tires spoke of the developments that came in the 1950s when the surface changed to asphalt. Even America's new prosperity reached its fingers even into places as remote as Jackson Hole. Now, wider cars had to stop and wait for one another to negotiate the sharp turns in the narrow roadway. It all spoke of change, and change was the name of the game in the new scheme of things.

Tom shook his shoulders because he didn't want to fall into the chain of thought that usually followed his consideration of what a second millennium meant for his home. Change was the only real given, and everything was subject to swoops, turns, accelerations, and stalls, but it kept right on coming, despite all the wishing to the contrary.

Tom turned his thoughts to his business, reminded by the increasing traffic coming over his radio as the night troops checked in on their way back from their patrols.

He had to close the three cases that the judge had disposed of the past week. Three burglaries, all done by teenage males paying for their meth habits. More shade of the larger America falling over the little towns in the western mountains. And everywhere else.

He also had better let Sam know about the arrest of the Osorio guy and the disappearance of the other two. And he wanted to catch up with Berto before he left for Mexico. The first flight out was around ten o'clock, so he had time. He just wanted to see the prickly little guy before he left. Tom liked him.

What else? Oh, he had to phone his son Jackie and tell him he'd rented the canoe for their fishing trip on Murphy Lake this weekend. Suddenly, a call came for him over the radio.

"Dee-One this is Jackson. Do you read me?"

Tom picked up the mike and said, "Jackson, Dee-One. Read you five-by."

"Dee-One please come to the center. Tee-One wants to see you. Stat."

"Roger." Tom looked at his watch. "Give me fifteen, uh make that twenty."

"Roger, roger. Over."

"Over."

Tom pushed a little more gas to the big engine. There had been no one on the road so far, so it probably wouldn't hurt to pick it up a little. There was always the chance that a Park Service ranger might be patrolling the back. He hoped that he didn't get a ticket because there were no professional courtesies extended by the gimlet-eyed guys and gals in green and gray. No way, José. They each were sworn by the President, ordained by God Almighty, and bound only by the poorly surveyed borders of the parks. They jumped on everyone like a duck on a June bug.

MiT

When Concha walked out of the Municipio building to cross the Plaza Mayor, she was stopped by two men who told her to come with them. They put her in a taxi and headed for Santa Catarina Tayata.

Once on the highway toward Boca de Perro, they explained that Don Armando Pacheco had sent them to pick her up and take her to the rancheria that had been her and Cenovio's original destination when they left Huajuapan. When she said that the police chief himself had let her go, they remained adamant, saying that there were still the federal police to consider. Apparently, Professor Ward's murder had become a matter of interest between the governments of Mexico and the United States of America.

Once at the little ranch, just west of the jacaranda-shaded town, they showed her the little room where she was expected to stay until Don Armando sent word that she could continue on to San Miguel. The man and woman who owned the place were friendly, simple people. One man was ordered to stay behind, and he was not so simple. And not so nice. He had told her in no uncertain terms what he expected, and she had no doubt that he meant every syllable of it. She could see that he was a man who followed the orders given to him to the letter.

When she had dissolved into tears at the news that she would not be allowed to contact her parents—even though they were so close and she had not seen them for five whole years—he was unmoved. "Don Armando would be told of her feelings," he said. When Don Armando said it was alright to contact her parents, then she would be allowed, but until then, nada. Nothing. She must be patient.

"We will stay here," the man explained, "until El Cacique finds the things that were lost. In the meantime, he expects that there will be federal police looking for you all over San Miguel, and if even a rumor of your whereabouts is known, you will be arrested. He cannot protect you from some people, despite his power."

Sitting in the morning sun next to a vibrant Bougainvillea, she gazed at the eastern mountains, comforted that she was so close to the valley of her birth. But the thick haze of smoke hanging over the valley and obscured the view of her home mountains troubled her. Even as she watched, she could see a flare of flame on the side of a hill, not more than a kilometer away.

Cenovio had told her of the fires, but she had not imagined how general they were. On the way between Huajuapan and Tlaxiaco, they had never been out of sight of fire for more than ten or fifteen minutes. Black stumps in areas several kilometers wide were the only evidence of previous woodlands. Also, since she had been here in Santa Catarina, the ground had jerked, shuddered, and sent a shock of dread through her. When the earth was restless, it left nowhere to go, nowhere to feel safe. It was worse than she had imagined.

Now she understood the urgency of her brother's plea for the return of The Heart of the World—why her gentle brother had turned into a man fierce as *el Tigre*, the jaguar. When Nathaniel shouted that the crystal was bought and paid for, and the money was in the hands of their cousin Marcos Albino and brother Demetrio, she understood now it was the insult to their family that cost Nathaniel his life. The disaster from the fires and temblors, the guilt over the theft, and this final insult proved too much for the normally passive and good natured man.

A-i-e-e-e, that had been a terrible night. Her mind turned from those thoughts in reflex at the memory of it. Instead, her mind sought comfort in memories of better times and one particular event when she had been not much more than a girl.

She could see the mountain that had interested Nathaniel—Nindo Tocosho—the one whose summit she and her brother, Demetrio, led him to in search of the old astronomical observatory. Nathaniel became excited when they found it, discovering the building's foundation stones barely visible in the little meadow atop the mountain.

It had been a wonderful day as they sat on the stones, and he told them stories of Achiutla in the days of the ancient ones. Stories she had never heard before. As a young girl of thirteen, she had been mesmerized by the gringo who knew so much about her people, even about her own village. They had been stories from a time that she had thought lost to her people. Years later, she discovered just how much her people remembered and the secret customs they kept from almost all outsiders.

MiT

Sam was waiting when Tom arrived at the law enforcement center. "Morning, Tom, where's Berto?"

"He's over at the Rusty Parrot, packing."

"Have you talked to him?"

"Yes."

"He wants to leave today, right?" It sounded more like a statement than a question.

"Yeah, how did you know?"

"I got a phone call from someone who told me that our probable felons have been arrested in Mexico. I assume that he is going to be heading that way."

"Who phoned you?"

"You don't need to know that."

"Why not?"

"Tom, you don't have a need to know."

Tom understood instantly. Need to know was a term taken from the vocabulary of the intelligence community to indicate that the source of information was secret. When in the military, Tom had been a member of that community, and so had Sam during his turn in the Korean War. It meant 'shut up and don't ask any questions' when used between fraternity members.

"Okay, Sam, I understand."

"Good. Now, those folks have apparently been picked up down there, and that brings us back to where we were the other day. Senator Enzi's colleague wants them brought back here, and they are doing everything they can back in Washington to make that happen. In the meantime, I want you to go down there with Sandez to keep an eye on things. I want you to try and make sure that those folks stay healthy until we can get them back to the States for trial. Especially the wife, or whatever she was. Congressman Ward was apparently very fond of the woman and believes that she had no part in the murder."

"Sam, I hate to tell you this, but when Berto phoned me this morning, he told me that she had disappeared, or was dead. He sounded pretty sure of it."

Sam frowned. "My understanding was that both had been picked up. I'll have to call back and have the source in Mexico check the facts. In the meantime, get your stuff ready."

"You want me to head for Mexico," he glanced at his watch, "with two hours' notice?"

"No one's leaving today, you'll have time enough."

"How do you know he's not leaving? He told me that he was flying out today."

Sam smiled. "His reservation got canceled. He'll be leaving tomorrow, and you'll be sitting in the seat next to him."

Tom smiled. "Well, at least I'll have time to pack. What about a passport? I don't have one."

"Just take your department ID and badge. That, and the tourist visa you get on the plane will do for thirty days or more, which will be plenty of time."

"How about my pistol?"

"Deputy Roark at the airport substation will handle all that with the airline, and with Mexican customs."

"So, Sam, what am I supposed to be doing? Be specific."

"You and this guy get along pretty well, don't you?"

"Yeah, I like him, and I think he likes me. We get along."

"Keep it friendly, but keep your eyes open. You know Spanish, don't you?"

Tom waggled his hand. "So, so. It's been coming back to me a little bit at a time."

"Well, play dumb and keep your ears open. Phone me when you can, and let me know what's going on until I can get you some backup."

"I'm going to need backup?" Tom asked and felt a flutter in his chest.

MiT

Pete Villareal walked into the office of Jaguar Travelers and looked around. There was no one behind the receptionist's desk, so he sat down and picked up a copy of Shaman magazine.

From the articles and ads in the magazine, it appeared that magical mystery tourism was a pretty good business. As he browsed the contents, it became apparent that there were two crucial elements for a successful tour: a geographical location purported to have concentrated mystical powers and a guide with spiritual abilities obtained either through extraordinary experience or through long and arcane study. When combining these two factors with an American company, like Jaguar Travelers, and customers with a Diner's Club card, one had the promise of an instant way onto the hallowed grounds where the likes of the Dalai Lama dwelled. It struck Pete as being very American—another shortcut, this time to heaven, made possible by the liberal application of dollars.

He was musing on Oz's warning about bringing any cynicism to the trip when a voice broke into his thoughts.

"Are you Mr. Villareal?"

He looked up and saw a blonde woman in her mid-thirties. She was wearing a vest covered with exquisite cut-glass beadwork with a motif of lizards, or salamanders, Pete wasn't sure which. Somewhere in the back of his mind, he remembered that the salamander was a component in some old mystical tradition that he could not place.

"Yes, I am."

"Padrito Gertner said that you would be in to pay for your journey. Cash or credit card?"

"Credit card. How much is it going to be?"

"Eleven thousand dollars."

"For ten days?!"

Cripes, the city accountant is going to shit his pants when he gets this one, Pete thought, *even though it would be financed by confiscated drug money.*

"That's a very reasonable price, given what you will be privileged to experience," the woman said with a frown.

"No, I was surprised that it was that cheap. Really."

The smile returned to her face. "Yes, the business is attracting some real rip artists and frauds," she said as she ran his card through her magnetic strip reader and waited for the approval and receipt.

She returned his card and looked up at him. "Your wife won't mind you going?" she asked.

"I'm not married."

"Oh," she said in a small pleased voice.

MiT

Tom phoned Los Angeles in the middle of his packing, and when the receptionist tried to stonewall him, he had to bully her into getting Polly to the phone.

Her voice sounded worried when she answered. "Is something wrong?" were her first words.

"I'm sorry, Pol, about breaking you out of your meeting but I'm going to be leaving tomorrow for Mexico, something important came up. I wanted to make sure I got in touch with you before I left. Are you going to be home tonight?"

"This is so strange."

"What's strange?"

"Something came up down here too. I'm leaving for Mexico this evening. I was looking at my watch, trying to figure out what would be the best time to phone you, when Marta broke in on the meeting."

"Where are you going?"

"Mexico City and then a place on the Pacific coast called Huatulco."

"I'm going to a place called Tlaxiaco down in Oaxaca state."

"Thomas!"

"What?"

"Huatulco is in Oaxaca too!"

"How weird. I wonder how far it is from Tlaxiaco."

"How do you spell it? I'm going to look it up," she said.

"T-l-a-x-i-a-c-o, and it's pronounced Ta-la-kee-a-ko. How long are you going to be down there?"

"I'm not sure, it's one of those last-minute deals. But if we can arrange it, I'll meet you at one or another of the places."

"Where will you be staying?"

"Our hotel project is in the hills above the beach and the new Sheraton. I'll be staying there, at the Sheraton."

"Is Ferdie going?"

"Of course."

Tom paused for a moment, giving Polly enough time to say softly, "Thomas?"

"Huh?"

"I love you. I'm wearing your ring."

That made him feel good way down deep inside, in the place where only Beth and Polly had ever been.

"Yes Ma'am. I apologize."

"The girls are going to be there too It would be nice if we could all get together."

"Well, I trust your judgment. If you think it's a good idea then it's a good idea, but my last reunion with your family made me feel like a turd in the punch bowl at a society ball."

"It is just going to take a little time, that's all. You are a decent man, and they are good and generous young women. Give them time."

"Sure. But I don't have the slightest idea what's going to happen once I get down there. Real estate isn't exactly the same game as Cops 'n' Killers."

CHAPTER SEVENTEEN

"How long will it take us to get to this town from Oaxaca City?" Tom asked Berto when the plane had leveled out and the seat belt sign turned off.

Berto stared at the magazine he was holding. For a moment, Tom thought he might not answer the question. It had been like this since Tom showed up at the Rusty Parrot the day before to tell him he would have company to Mexico.

"We'll change planes at Mexico City, then fly to Oaxaca City and spend the night at a hotel right by the first-class bus terminal. Tomorrow we'll take the bus to Tlaxiaco. That ride takes about four hours."

"You're not going to stop in Mexico City and talk to your people at the AG's office?"

Berto had a sour look on his face when he answered, "I don't have to check in, I've been phoning in my reports every evening. Besides, I'm a field guy, and my boss will be waiting when we get to Tlaxiaco. He's going to be one really unhappy dude when he gets a load of you tagging along."

Tom took the in-flight magazine from the pocket in front of him. It looked it was going to be a real long, chilly trip.

Suddenly, Berto's voice broke into the conversational void.

"You know, this is just a damn good example!"

"Of what?"

"How you Americans operate. You elbow everyone around like you own the whole damn world. You walk into my room, tell me that you are coming to my country to commandeer the arrest of a felon, one who is a priority prisoner wanted for multiple crimes in Mexico. Then you smile and ask, 'Where do you want to go for breakfast today?'

"Who in the fuck do you people think you are, anyway? No wonder you're in the shit up to your eyelashes in Iraq, it's a disease with you bastards!"

Tom could see his point, but he also had a job to do. Sam had put him in a tight place with this guy and his agency as well. This was not going to be a picnic unless he found a way to make peace with Berto.

His mind turned to an old controversy over the FBI's kidnapping of a doctor who had subsequently been convicted in assisting in the murder of an American DEA agent named Camarena. It had caused a major rip in Mexican American diplomatic relations, and if the folks who were pressuring the Mexican Government about Ward weren't damn careful, Tom could be caught in the middle of another one like it. The thought made his ass work buttonholes.

"Hey, Berto, let's try to be friends. I got called into the office and pretty much had a plane ticket shoved into my hand. I assume that the same kind of thing happened to you when you were sent up here and had to walk into my office cold.

"Not to mention that you had the advantage of having been pretty much raised in the States, while I've only been to a couple of border towns when I was in the Army, and on one fishing trip to Baja. I'm going to have to throw myself on your hospitality while I'm down there because I don't know diddly-squat about the realities of your country. I'm just doing what I've been ordered to do, and I have no choice."

Berto looked Tom directly in the eyes and said, "Okay, you have a point. Just tell me, what is it you were told to do. Be honest with me."

Tom nodded and said, "Sam told me that I was to go with you and keep my eyes open but my mouth shut. The muckety-mucks in Washington D.C., the ones applying pressure, are working on your diplomats there, trying to get them to concede to an extradition. If it works, I assume that I am to escort the prisoner back. If it doesn't work, then I suppose I get a free vacation on the county's money. Which, come to think of it, ain't such a bad gig, really."

Berto finally smiled that big smile of his. "Yeah, I got to have a nice little break in Jackson Hole, and now you get one in Oaxaca. Maybe this is a good little deal for both of us. As long as you do like your boss said—eyes open, mouth shut."

Then he nudged Tom and added, "Hey, what a country-y-y!"

Tom's butt began to relax.

MiT

Pete met Oz and the rest of the group at the Oakland airport. From what Pete picked up from the introductions and conversations as they waited, the other people were Silicon Valley types or old San Francisco Bay Area money. He made himself known as another rich skid, a California type who would go mostly unremarked in this group.

Oz and the blonde from the office, Olga, were the conductors for the group, and there was excited talk about a man they would be meeting in Mexico named José Gorostiza. Oz called the man *El Viejo*, which was an affectionate Spanish term for any respected elder. He was to be their spiritual guide once they were in the southern mountains. Apparently, the man was famous in the places where these people circulated.

"How you doin', Pedro?" Oz asked when he eventually made his way to Pete.

"Fine. This is quite a group you got here."

"Nice people. Only one or two, besides you, are advanced enough to be taking this trip, but that's about average for one of these things."

"How do you mean that?"

"Oh, most of them think that they are on a genuine spiritual quest, but they have no real aptitude for it. It takes a special kind of person to get anything out of it, to advance to a higher astral plane."

"In what way?"

"You know how the blacks talk of someone having soul?"

"Yeah."

"Pretty much the same thing. They saw it in their churches—recognized the people who really had the capacity to receive what the Christians call the Holy Ghost. They are the ones who find themselves moved mightily, what is called 'slain in the spirit'. That's when someone is struck to the floor by the force of receiving the spirit. Unfortunately, that sort of thing is all too often faked, but the people can discriminate between the ones who fake it and the ones who make it by saying that the genuine recipients have soul. You are one of the three here who have soul, by our lights."

"Because I could see the man and the horse?"

"Yes. And some other things I have noticed about you."

"Like what?"

Oz just gave Pete what he'd come to think of as the man's "mummy stare" and walked away.

Once Pete had boarded the plane and found his seat next to the window, he saw Olga walking down the aisle to count heads and hand out reading material. She finally made her way to Pete's aisle and handed him a brochure with Jaguar Travelers on the top. Then she sat down next to him and put on her seat belt.

Pete returned her smile and buckled his belt as well. Up close, he saw that she was pretty in the way that women in their late thirties or early forties can look if they take care of themselves. Her skin looked healthy, even under the light makeup, and she smelled terrific—like jungle flowers.

MiT

In Los Angeles, the Anayas were making themselves comfortable in the first-class section of their plane. The stewardesses bustled efficiently, flitting through the aisles as they prepared for takeoff. The low electric hum of the airplane spoke of efficiency as well.

Polly's younger daughter, Maria, saw to it that her father's little office was set up in the seat next to the window. His laptop computer would be on the tray the instant the seat belt light went off, the Wi-Fi ready to go. She saw him staring out the window, deep in thought, and she knew that look. It hurt her.

She retrieved her copy of Elle magazine and leaned back. After a moment, she glanced again at her father's troubled face, then moved her gaze across the aisle.

Polly had her hand on the arm of Christina, Maria's sister, and was talking to her in a low voice that could not be heard. Still, she knew the subject of the conversation—Tom Thompson, the detective in Wyoming whom their mother planned to marry and who was, unimaginably, Christina's birth father.

That was the reason for the weary and depressed look on her father's face. He had hoped, just as the girls had hoped, that this thing with the man in Wyoming was only a passing, painful episode in their lives. It didn't seem possible that their parents were divorced in some genuinely irrevocable way. Through the whole process of the dissolution of the marriage, there had been hope in the hearts of everyone that it could be resolved in a positive way. But their mother had not shared their hopes. She had gone to a place called

Jackson Hole, for God's sake, and run into this man Thompson, and the whole appalling truth had come out.

Maria looked at her sister's face and saw the resolute look signifying she had dug in her heels, not about to be budged. It was the same look that Maria and Ferdie recognized in Polly's at times—one that brooked no compromise and promised no peace.

As she gazed at the two, Maria was conscious of the symbolism that the wide aisle represented. On the one side were Ferdie and Maria, the dark-haired, olive-skinned ones who loved the lighter approach to life. They were Latin to the core and loved the superficial expressions of life. They loved to put on parties, go to social events, eat in restaurants, and rejoiced at having their pictures in the Los Angeles Times Lifestyles section. Polly and Christina had been happiest when their home appeared in Sunset magazine, and there wasn't one picture of the family in the whole article, just the house and the gardens! Maria hadn't seen the point of it.

The airplane released its brakes and began to accelerate down the runway, shuddering, rattling, and making her stomach queasy. Maria glanced again at her father's troubled face, confirming the distance between the two halves of what had once been a close and happy family.

Who was this man Thompson who had somehow gained so much influence over one of the most influential businesswomen in Los Angeles? And what in the world was this about him being in Oaxaca at the same time they were?

Chapter Eighteen

Ildegardo Osorio was making pottery on his wheel when his wife, Lilia, called to him.

"Ildegardo, I see José Gorostiza coming this way, and he has his sons with him."

"Eh, what brings him to this side of the barranca and up this steep hill? His spindly legs will fail him if he is not careful."

He chuckled and rose to wash the clay off his hands. He loved bantering with the old man, a friend and fellow artist from his childhood, who would starve except for the labor of his wife and strong sons. The boys' blood had come from their mother, thanks to God, or José would have died from hunger onto his papers and pen long ago. Unlike pottery, there was honor in poetry, certainly, but nothing for the belly.

Ildegardo walked around his hut and stood to look down the hill at the approaching men. He waited for them to near, but it took some time because the boys had to support their father every five meters or so, grinning up the hill at Ildegardo as they waited for him to catch his breath. Only the natural reserve of the people of the mountains kept him from shouting insults down at the friend of his childhood. He could wait.

Only when the men had a few moments to sit did Ildegardo say, gently, "Surely, José, you taunt the devil when you strain your heart with a visit to me. You must be more careful, *Viejo Amigo*, for you might burst something if you do more than push that pen of yours across the paper and lap at your bowl of pulque."

"A-e-e-e, *cabron*, you insult me when I come with news of your daughter Concha. You are shameless."

At his daughter's name, Ildegardo froze. Lilia gave a little cry and came to the door of the hut, wiping flour from her hands onto her dress.

"You have news of Concha?"

"Yes. My son here, Socratio, saw her with his own eyes! She is in Santa Catarina Tayata, and it is said that she is a prisoner there."

Lilia gave a cry and put her face in her hands to hide her emotion.

"A prisoner, you say," Ildegardo said, his voice full of genuine bewilderment. "A prisoner of whom, José? Who is holding my daughter?"

"A powerful cacique, it is said."

"A cacique? What cacique?"

"The godfather of Huajuapan de Leon."

Ildegardo's wife gasped. This was more than a mystery; this was incomprehensible. And coming on the heels of the federal police's search of the whole village for their children days before, it was also a shock. Shame and infamy seemed to be falling steadily on the heads of the Osorios. Steadily as the fine gray ash from the burning mountainsides.

The surprising news, for which there was absolutely no explanation on the face of this earth, startled all of them into silence. It was indeed a mystery of great proportion.

Finally, Ildegardo asked, "How long has she been there?"

Socratio said, "Since yesterday. She is guarded by one man only, but she is surely a prisoner."

"And how did you come by this news?"

Socratio motioned at his brother Plato and said, "We were waiting for a ride in Santa Catarina when we remembered that it was getting time for tomatoes, and that the Mendezes had the best ones in the valley. We walked down there to see when the tomatoes would be ripe, thinking that we might be able to get some for the market in Tlaxiaco—the Mendezes are old, and one can take their tomatoes to the market for shares. When we approached the house, we saw Concha sitting under the ramada. But when we hailed her, saying only *Buenos Dias* because we were not sure it was her, a man came out of the house and beckoned her inside. She stared at us and her eyes spoke to us, though she said nothing."

"This man had been shaving so had his shirt off, and he was wearing a gun," Plato added.

Ildegardo nodded. "Surely then, she is a prisoner. Surely." He rubbed his hands on his pants and said, "How do you know that she is the prisoner of this cacique?" he asked Socratio.

"We know that Mrs. Mendez has one friend, another old woman, and she tells her friend everything. After we had inquired about the tomatoes, we went to *la soltera* and asked her what she knew. She told us that Concha was being held for the godfather of Huajuapan, and none other. Why, even I have heard of this Don Armando Pacheco."

From the hut, where his wife had gone, the men could hear her sobs and little squeaks as she tried to hold in her fear.

Ildegardo said, "I do not understand why she was brought so near to San Miguel, why she is not here with us. And if they meant to harm her, surely they would have done it in some other place and not brought her to Santa Catarina. Perhaps they are keeping her far enough away that the federal police, or their informants, will be ignorant of her presence. A-i-e-e-e, there are many things here which my poor mind can make no sense of."

He ran the backs of his fingers over the silver stubble of his strong jaw, making a heavy scratching sound. "What should we do, what can we do?"

"Simple. We go get her! We can do nothing less," said José, the poet, said in an iron voice.

All the men turned toward him and were startled by the fire in his rheumy eyes.

"Go get her," said Ildegardo. "Of course. There is only one man, so we could take her from him, surely."

José raised his hand. "But he is armed, and we must not lose anyone's life to his gun. So it must be done at night."

His sons nodded, observing their father. Thinking was not their strong suit, but they were not known for their cowardice either. They were as brave as the fighting cocks they bred, cocks whose fame had spread the names of the brothers throughout the mountains of the Mixteca Alta and beyond, even to the state capitol itself.

José turned to the young men and said, "Go to Santa Catarina and find out if the man is still alone. You wait for us at the *tienda*, where the bus stops. When we arrive, you tell us if other men have arrived from Huajuapan. Today I will go to your uncle Patricio and ask for his help. If the man is still alone, we will proceed with the liberation of La Concha de San Miguel. And if there are more, we may have to return for reinforcements."

The poet liked the appellation he had invented for Concha on the spot—brave but not too heroic. And he also knew that legends were easily created in the currently devastated culture of the Alta. José had a grasp of Mixtec history that was second to none. He also knew how and when to use that knowledge.

He stood back on his rickety legs and put out an arm for one of his strong sons. Plato offered his thick shoulder, and the old man grasped it.

"Now I go to dig up my *cuarenta y cinco*, my .45 *automatico*. It has lain silent these many years, since the days of my grandfather, and the Revolution. I have cleaned and oiled it every year for all this time, and now it will pay for its keep. But *espero a Dios*, I hope to God that it will not have to speak in its strong voice, for in the hands of my father it spoke the names of many men. And they have been in Hell, cursing his name since those bloody times."

He reached out one hand and clasped that of his old friend. "Ildegardo, come down with us, and we will call together the men of the *Sociedad de los Animos Ancianos*. We must make our plans and say our prayers to begin preparing for the solstice celebration. Even though the Heart of the World has not yet been returned. You are welcome, my friend. None of what has passed was your fault."

Ildegardo went inside the hut and patted his weeping wife on the shoulder to comfort her, then he picked up his machete and slung it over his shoulder to leave.

The four men were a hundred meters down the path when José stopped, glanced up the hill toward the Osorios' *ranchito*, and said to Ildegardo, "I did not want to upset my cousin Lilia with it, but I have other news, and it is not so good either."

"And what is this news, Amigo?"

"Cenovio is in the jail in Tlaxiaco. They have arrested him for the murder of two policemen in Culiacan."

Ildegardo felt the news like a blow to his chest, and he grew dizzy. Socratio saw him shudder at José's words and reached out to steady him.

"Both my children are prisoners. How can this be?" He turned his eyes to the smoky heavens and said, "Please, my God, spare my children. My eldest, Demetrio, is disgraced and my other two are prisoners. I pray, Lord, that you will set them free, in the name of all that is holy."

José put his hand on Ildegardo's shoulder and said, "Ah, *mi compadre*, it is useless to keep the rest from you."

"More?!"

"I am afraid so. It is rumored that El Profesor Ward is dead, and I am afraid that it is possible his death came at the hands of Cenovio. He is being held for the murders of three men, no less. When he phoned from El Norte that he was returning with the Heart of the World and your family book, it was glorious news. But something terrible happened that we will not know until Concha is freed and back in the sanctuary of our unassailable mountain bastion. The truth is that the Heart of the World is lost again."

Ildegardo felt weak. He walked a short distance to the shade of a large pine tree and let himself down slowly into the needle duff at its base.

The three Gorostiza men watched him, waiting, and after a moment, Ildegardo waved them down the path toward the village.

"Go," he said, "I will join you later. My heart cannot bear these burdens and support my legs too. I will join you when I have regained my strength." Tears were coursing down his weathered face.

"We will wait together, then," said José as he lowered himself carefully to the ground beside his old friend.

"Go!" he said, motioning his two sons down the hill. "We will meet you in Santa Catarina. And then the great cacique, Don Armando Pacheco, will feel the force of our strong hands!" And he shook his bony poet's fist at the end of a thin and flaccid arm.

MiT

When the Aero Mexico flight made its turn onto the last leg over the Oaxaca City airport, Berto pointed out the window and said, "Monte Alban."

Tom leaned over him and looked down to see a big hill, flat on top, and on it sat several enormous buildings and pyramids.

"Whoa, what is that?"

"Monte Alban, it was the major city of the Zapotec and Mixtec people long before the Spaniards came. It was the major trade and religious center of this whole area for hundreds of years. Some of the greatest treasures of Mexico were discovered there in the 1930s.

"Practically, no one in the States knows about the Mixtec people, but it is suspected that Mixtec taught the Aztecs how to write. They were the most famous astronomers and astrologers during that time. There is a story that Moctezuma the Second was carried on a litter from Tenochtitlan, Mexico City, to consult with the Mixtecs. He hoped that they could tell him what the future held, hoping that it would guide him in devising some way of dealing with the Spaniards.

"The Mixtecs are one of only two people, the other being the Maya, who have maintained their culture to any real extent, and they are the only survivors of the calamity that fell on us from Europe."

Tom thought for a moment before saying anything. "You have deep admiration when you speak about your people, but at times I hear almost disrespect. It puzzles me."

Berto stared out the window for a long moment before he said, "It puzzles me too. I am not sure how I feel about my blood, about the genes that made me this short, and my face this broad. I don't know if it's something to be ashamed of or something to be proud of. I just don't fit in anywhere."

There was another long silence, and then he added, "It's the same thing with your minorities in the States. "You hear them speaking of Black Power, Black Pride, Red Power, Red Pride, but you can hear a terrible ambivalence beneath all the rhetoric."

He sighed. "I feel one way half the time, and another way half the time. You see, down here it's no different than in the north. The general Mexican populace often speaks with pride for its indigenous peoples—look at the Ballets Folklorico and all the other dance companies that celebrate those traditions. But in the daily practice of their lives, they look down on anyone with indigenous blood. We're the niggers of Mexico, to put it plain and simple. There is prejudice everywhere." And there was a profound bitterness in his voice.

It was early evening as they drove through the city. Tom saw that it was a mix of old and new. The old part of the city, though, was exciting. It reminded him, in a way, of the old colonial parts of Saigon. It spoke of real culture and a long urban history.

The Veracruz hotel was clean and modern, with a restaurant next to the lobby. While Berto arranged for rooms, Tom stepped out to the sidewalk, and an old, one-eyed man walked up to him, holding a beautiful rug woven in browns and beiges. The design was beautiful.

"*Buenas noches*, Señor. You would like a rug, perhaps. Genuine Atzlan. Very real, very good, very good price."

"I'm sorry but I don't have any pesos," Tom said, patting his wallet.

The old man smiled, "Ah, Señor, dollars even better. I give you special price for you give me American dollars. No problem."

Suddenly, Berto was at Tom's side. He waved his hand at the old man and said, "*Fuera, gusano. No somos turistas.*"

The old man looked hopefully at Tom until Berto waved his hand again and said, "*Andale, andale*," then muttered "*chingaso*."

The man left, his head down and his face neutral. There was something that he recognized in Berto that had made him respond cautiously. Tom guessed that he suddenly smelled them as cops. Some things didn't change, no matter where in the world you were, especially in places where cops had arbitrary powers that American cops had been accorded only in the South before Martin Luther King changed things.

He sighed inside, then said, "What about dinner?"

Berto smiled. "I know a place that will blow your socks down. It's in the boutiquey part of town near the *Zocalo*. It's called the *Cebolla y Ajo*."

Tom pursed his lips and searched his memory. He suddenly smiled and said, "You have to be kidding, no one would name a restaurant The Onion and the Garlic!"

"Hey, *Chavo*, that's good. Real good!" There was a genuine delight on the man's face that Tom had been able to pick the Spanish equivalents out of his brain. "But it's true, The Onion and the Garlic. But don't worry, the food is great. We'll get a taxi just as soon as we put the luggage in the rooms."

"How far is it?"

Berto frowned. "Hmmm. I'd say it would take about fifteen minutes to walk there."

"Hell, let's walk."

"Why?" Berto's voice was genuinely puzzled.

Tom looked around. "I haven't been out of the States for a real long time, and I like the feel of this." He waved his hand up and down the street named *Avenida Heroes de Chapultepec.*

"Okay, Amigo, if you want to walk, we'll walk."

"Great," Tom said. He looked up and down the street, listening to the conversations of the people passing by. It had a . . . magical feeling to it—a whole new set of impressions, a whole new way of seeing and feeling things. It was great; this was going to be a real good time.

Half an hour later, they were sitting in the restaurant, drinking coffee and waiting for their food, when a group of tourists came through the door.

Tom nodded at the people and said, "Oaxaca must be a major tourist town."

Berto nodded. "Yeah, Monte Alban is one of the primo tourist attractions in Mexico, and that's what most of them come here to see. Also, Oaxaca is famous for its rugs, pottery, and carvings. As a matter of fact, the Aztec royalty ate exclusively off what is known as Mixtec polychrome dishware. It's red and black, beautiful stuff."

"For a cop you sure seem to know a lot about Mexican archaeology."

Berto shrugged, "It was my minor in college. I had a real good prof."

Tom nodded his head. "Same with me, only my favorite prof taught lithology." He smiled at the questioning look on Berto's face and added, "It's a specialty in the study of geology. It's the study of rocks themselves—how they form and what they look like. That kind of stuff."

"Sounds boring to me."

"Yeah, you'd think so, but it was fascinating to me." He toyed with his spoon, tipping its blade and rocking its handle up and down. "You know, when I was a kid, being a cop was the last thing that ever crossed my mind as a profession."

"How'd you get into it?"

"The military. I ran out of money for college and had to go back to work. When I knew that I was going to get drafted for the war, I decided to volunteer. Draftees were mostly rocket fodder, so I thought I'd have a chance of sorts if I joined." He laughed a dry little laugh. "It didn't keep me out of the war, but I only had to spend a little time in the boonies."

"You were in the military police?"

Tom nodded. "Yeah, you could say that. It was a special kind of duty, but I learned to be a cop there. And when I got out it just seemed like the thing to do. Get a job, get married."

Berto was surprised. "You're married?"

"No, divorced." He flicked a finger at the door of the restaurant. "Look at that guy."

A big man dressed in white with a green and black sash tied around his waist stood in the doorway with another man and a blonde woman. He wore huaraches on his feet, his hair was drawn back in a silver ponytail, and there was a presence about the guy that you couldn't miss. The guy was charismatic.

The man looked around the restaurant for a moment, and then the maître d' approached them. The big man spoke in fluent Spanish to the maître d' who led the three to the rear of the restaurant. There they joined the group of tourists who'd come through the door earlier.

"*Californios*," Berto offered.

"How do you know?"

Berto shrugged. "Just a guess, but after a while you get where you can pick them out by the clothes they wear, the way they act. Remember, I lived there for a long time."

Tom smiled. "You know, we're actually quite a bit alike. That's one of the little games we play in Jackson Hole too—Name the Tourist. The ones from the Midwest are easiest because they usually come in tour groups. The men mostly wear hats with the names of farm machinery or grain companies on them. The women are always snapping the elastic on their huge underwear. On a hot day the group sounds like a popcorn popper."

Chapter Nineteen

It was late when Plato saw the lights of the pickup truck coming up the hill from the direction of San Miguel Achiutla. The driver parked it across the street from the *tienda*, the little store that sold little items from gum to Panadol headache pills to batteries. The truck belonged to Patricio Gorostiza, brother to José and the past president of the *ejido*. He was a very respected man, and *un hombre muy macho*. He was known, like his brother, for his intelligence, but he was not the intellectual José was.

In the front of the truck, Plato saw Ildegardo Osorio. In the back, with Plato's brother Socratio, were his two cousins, Juan and his brother Raul. They were *famosos*—men famous for their willfulness. Many believed them to be bad men, even banditos, and some said they were *narcotraficantes* who cultivated a field of the famous Oaxacan *mota,* but no one knew for sure. The brothers had never done anything to draw the attention of the local law, but they disappeared for weeks at a time, always returning with money. It was a tradition that the personal business of the men in the little towns and villages of the mountains was strictly their own, as long as it did not bring dishonor to the reputation of the people.

But there were two things that everyone did know about Juan and Raul Gorostiza: they were absolutely fearless, and they carried excellent, American-made guns. Also, and most importantly, they had been initiated into the Sociedad de los Animos Ancianos, so their discretion and loyalty to the community were unquestionable.

Patricio got out of the truck and crossed the street to wait for Plato.

"What news?"

"The man is still alone. Concha sleeps between the two old people, so they will know if she tries to get up. The guy sleeps on the other side of the room near the door."

"Good," Patricio said, nodding his head. "And they are sleeping now?"

"The guy was still up when I left, sitting by the fire." Plato smiled. "But he was drinking *Las Lagrimas de Dios*. He should be asleep by now, if he has kept lapping at The Tears of God since I left my hiding place among the agaves."

Patricio smiled, "Yes, pulque is good for sweet dreams."

"But it makes a man feel like a stallion too. We should hurry."

"Hmmm. If he has taken liberties with Concha, it will mean his life, I swear to you. Come on."

They abandoned the pickup about a kilometer from the Mendez *ranchito*. The two elders, Ildegardo and José, were left with the vehicle, then Patricio led his son and two nephews quietly through the dim moonlight. Though the waxing moon was more than half full, the smoky air had dimmed its light. But the fires had been burning for so long that few no longer noticed the smoke or the pulsing red beds of embers that glowed on the hills where groves of trees had been.

Once hidden in the agave field, the men sneaked to its edge, fifty meters from the poor ranch, and watched for over half an hour. Then, suddenly, the guard appeared on the veranda to brace himself unsteadily against an upright and undid his pants to relieve himself.

There was a pool of smiles in the agave field, the white teeth of all the men showing in the dim moonlight overhead. This man was no professional. He was drunk.

They waited for half an hour, smoking their hand-made cigarettes and saying nothing until Patricio motioned them to put their heads together.

"Juan and Raul, you will come with me inside. Socratio, you will wait beside the door with your machete. If he comes through the door, kill him. He must not escape. Plato, you go to the back door next to the hearth and oven. If he comes out there, you will do the same."

Socratio sucked on his teeth, making the sound of disgust or contempt. "He will not escape."

"He has a gun. If he is alerted and knows how to use it, the three of us could be taken out. So be careful with this man, take nothing for granted. *Vamonos.*"

The five men carefully made their way to the wattle and daub house and arrayed themselves at its openings. Patricio and his two nephews squatted near the door to listen until Raul pointed at a wall to indicate he had located the man by his light snoring.

Patricio nodded, then reached under his shirt and took out the venerable Colt .45 automatic of his father. Raul retrieved his pistol while Juan, the largest of the three men, left his in its holster. In his hand was a leather thong.

Patricio entered first and, after a few moments, appeared in the doorway and described with his hands the man's location and the direction his head was lying.

Once all three men were inside, they moved to the sleeping man's side, and Patricio kneeled at the man's head.

"Who is there?!" Old Man Mendez suddenly cried out from the other side of the room.

Instantly awake, the guard woke and pulled his gun from under the blanket that served as his pillow. The little house filled up with the blast from the weapon, its flash lighting the faces of the rescuers.

As he struggled for possession of the gun, Patricio put his thumb over the pistol's hammer so it would be harder to pull the trigger while wrestling with the gunman's strong arm. Then the guard screamed, and his grip gave it up. Then he screamed again just before Patricio brought the barrel of his pistol down across the man's face.

"Stop, for the love of God, stop!" the man cried. Then he shrieked again. "Stop! A-i-e-e-e, stop. Please!"

Raul, his voice low and tense, said, "I will let go, but if you move a muscle, I will shoot you. Believe me!"

"Yes, yes. Oh, yes-s-s-s." The man's voice trailed off in relief.

"Roll over on your face, *piojoso*," said Juan. The man obeyed, and the light slap of the leather thong could be heard in the dark as Juan secured the man's wrists.

"Not so tight," the man protested, between his gritted teeth.

"You shoot me in the face and then ask for pity?" Patricio growled in the man's ear.

"Are you hit?" asked Raul.

"Not badly. I can talk, so my jaw must not be broken, but my face is burned. It was a close one, I tell you."

"Hey, Mendez!" Juan said, then repeated himself. "Old man!"

"Yes?"

"Light a lantern, we need light!"

"Who are you?"

"We are from San Miguel. You are safe with us."

"Yes, yes."

They heard the old man rise and take down his lantern from a roof beam lighting the room enough to see Plato and Socratio's tense faces in the door. And they also saw Concha sitting against the wall, Old Woman Mendez cowering beside her. In Concha's hand was a long, wicked-looking butcher knife, and her eyes were as calm as if she were watching a sunrise rather than the lamp being lit.

"Concha! It is me, Patricio Gorostiza."

"Yes, I know."

"Ah, good. You can put the knife down; we are here to take you home."

"I knew as much. When I saw Juan and Raul, and they pretended to not know me, I knew that you would come for me. Thank you."

She stood and put the knife on a table and then helped Old Woman Mendez to her feet. "What are you going to do with him?" Concha asked, gesturing to the man who had been guarding her.

Raul smiled. "I think I have done enough to him!" He turned to Plato and said, "You were right, the pulque had made him like a stallion, but it gave me one great handle with which to make him beg. Did you hear him?"

Then, in mimicry, he cried out in an agonized voice, "Stop! A-i-e-e-e, stop. Please!"

And the men roared with laughter, clapping one another on the back, but it was a laughter of relief, not meant as teasing of the man bound on the floor. They felt strong and clever, *listo*, and these are not feelings common to the peasants of the hills—men and women more used to being victimized than victorious. It was a very good feeling for all of them, a very good feeling indeed.

MiT

Pete Villareal turned out the light and laid his head on a big feather pillow. The hotel they were staying in, the *Señorial,* was an old Belle Époque building on Oaxaca City's main plaza, called the Zocalo. The wood was dark and polished, the furnishings heavy and ornate, and the bed was much too soft for his taste. He doubled a pillow and flattened it under his head, then lay back to consider the day.

Some of it had been spent wandering through the Mercado, the major city market, and the smaller *Mercado de Artesanias.* Everyone in the group had loaded up on stuff, though Pete had listened to Olga and put off his shopping for the return trip. No sense in lugging it down to Tamazulapan, over to Tlaxiaco, and then back to Berkeley. So, instead of shopping, he had spent the day just looking around the old town, playing the tourist.

Olga had gone with him in the afternoon, taking him to some out-of-the-way places like the Tamayo Museum and the old Spanish aqueduct. They had enjoyed one another's company and, he remembered with a flush, that at one point, he had put his hand on her shoulders as she stood in front of him, and he had seen her quiver and goose flesh appear on her skin. At the restaurant that night, she made a point of sitting beside him, insisting that one of the group move down a place to accommodate her. Hmmm.

The meal had been excellent but heavier than he was accustomed to—loaded with Oaxaca's famous chilies/chocolate/cinnamon mole sauce, and there had been a lot of superb Chilean wine. He had been surprised at how good they had been, equal to the California wines he was used to.

He closed his eyes, feeling the wine way down deep in his body, pooling in little burgundy puddles that began to slowly widen into a pond, then a lake, expanding, expanding. Finally, he looked down, and he was standing up to his ankles in the deep red wine.

Suddenly, the top of a pine tree rose out of the lake, followed by rocks and then a field, gradually replacing the lake until a forest surrounded the meadow, and that became the main feature—a wine-red alpine meadow with dark green pines and a night sky trembling with stars.

A white sliver of a moon, shaped like the Cheshire cat's smile, rose above the trees like something buoyant had been released from the bottom of a pond. It caused a bubble of laughter to rise to Pete's chest, and he heard himself laugh.

Across the meadow, along the edge of the enamel-green trees, another sliver of white drew his attention away from the midnight-blue expanse above him.

The sliver grew larger, seemed to bend at its middle with a regular rhythm, and then he recognized the object as it grew larger. It was the white horse again, illuminated from one side like the fingernail moon above, and it was cantering toward him. This time it was riderless.

He watched it approach until it was about fifty yards away, and then it shied, rising to its back hooves, spinning away from the trees at the near edge of the meadow. It came down on all four hooves, hunching its back as if in pain. And then, suddenly, Pete was aware that, unnoticed, another animal had sprung from the trees and was now eclipsing the top of the white horse's broad, luminescent body.

The beautiful horse stood, transfixed by the feline animal's strength. It was a cat of some kind, a leopard—a jaguar.

The big, muscular cat's claws dug into the animal's flanks and shoulders, though drawing no blood. The beautiful white horse seemed to be in no pain, but its eyes spoke of helplessness.

Help me, it said with its eyes, *Help me*, and it moved its hooves up and down in place to make a *thock*, *thock* as they came down—a soft *thock, thock, thock* in the wine-red meadow.

Pete woke from the dream with an explosion of breath. He felt his heart pounding, and there was sweat on his hot face and bare chest.

Knock, *knock*. *Knock*.

Pete strained to return to his senses, trying to remember where he was.

Knock, *knock*, *knock*.

He remembered where he was and realized the sound was someone tapping on his door.

He threw back the sheets, went to the door, and when he opened it, Olga stepped quickly inside. Before the woman pushed the door shut, he saw that she was dressed only in a thin robe and slippers.

In the sudden darkness, he heard the robe drop to the floor, and then she stepped to him. He felt her pubis against his leg, kneading the muscle of his thigh. Her breasts were soft, and hot as the mouth and tongue she was placing, again and again, against his chest. He pulled her head back by the hair and put his mouth on hers, swallowing her sultry pants as fast as they came.

Pete picked her up and walked till his shins met the bed, then dropped her. He stripped his shorts to the floor, and he could smell her hot body, the fertile smell of her vagina.

He crawled on top of her wide-spread legs and entered her body as he moved up her writhing form. He heard her gurgle deep in her throat and felt her burning fingernails: first in his buttocks, then up his back as she thrust her pelvis up to spear herself. She screamed, and it was a feline yowl that made Pete's scalp tighten.

MiT

Tommy woke at dawn, momentarily disoriented by the songs of foreign birds outside his window in strange trees. Then he rose to put his feet on the floor and smile at the sensation of being in a completely new environment. It had been way too long since he'd gone anywhere and done anything this different.

Outside the window, he saw the baroque dome of the city's main cathedral. It reminded him of the night before when he and Berto had strolled back to the hotel.

He led him to the huge Santo Domingo church; they had gone inside, and it was wonderful in the original sense of the word. It struck Tom with a sense of wonder at the immense nave and the gold filigree of the ornamentation. One of the chapels had been decorated with a passion that was almost voluptuous—the vestment-draped mannequins were as opulent as the feathers of tropical birds, and gold was used in every element possible. It all spoke of a religious passion missing in modern religion, especially the saccharin music expressed on acoustic guitars and electronic pianos.

And as Tom gazed out over the rooftops at the foreign city, he suddenly had a little epiphany. The only element of passion in his life up north was Polly, and the hours they spent twined together—wound around and inside one another's bodies. Here, even the architecture spoke passionately to one's senses, and it was revivifying. This was his kind of place, but, perhaps, he should think about looking into finding a spiritual path a little wider than the ones Polly and Alcoholics Anonymous were affording him. Hmmm.

He looked at his watch and saw that it was a little before six o'clock. The bus to Tlaxiaco didn't leave until 7:30, and there was plenty of time for breakfast, so he decided to go for an early morning walk.

On the sidewalk just west of the hotel, Tom saw a sidewalk vendor's stand where a woman was mixing hot water and instant coffee for a customer. He walked down to the stand and asked for a cup of coffee with milk and sugar. He also bought a large sweet roll, which was more bread than pastry, but it was sweet and cinnamony—just different enough to help maintain Tom's sense of being in a foreign land. He relished it again: the sense of strangeness.

To the west, he reached a major intersection and then crossed The Avenue of the Chapultepec Heroes. Tom knew that Chapultepec was a fortress in Mexico City that had been defended to the death by cadets who eventually threw themselves from the parapets rather than surrender to American Marines. The Halls of Montezuma took on a very different connotation when one walked the streets of Mexico, especially in the light of America's misadventures in the Middle East.

We just never seem to be able to remember our history lessons, Tom thought. As a veteran of the war in Vietnam, he had a personal viewpoint that he mostly kept to himself. But it was a lesson he'd damn sure never forget.

As he walked up the street he'd wandered onto, Tom's thoughts turned to Polly.

She'd love this place, especially in an early morning such as this—a wide street bordered by huge trees full of birds singing exotic songs in other tongues and flitting in the nameless trees of Oaxaca, Monte Alban, Mixteca, Atzlan, Shangri-la, or Xanadu.

The traffic was almost nonexistent at this hour as the faces of the commercial buildings remained blank with sleep. Soon the smell of the city will transform with the morning with its rich slanting light and quiet houses.

This was a Mexico that Tom had never heard of—clean, modern, peaceful, and orderly. Thoughts of the stereotypes the American media fed the people in the guise of informed news made him sad and a little angry. Few American journalists went to other countries without preconceived notions that colored their reporting, and few American tourists ever escaped the busses, hotels, and resorts of the countries they visited. They came away knowing very little more than they knew when they got on the plane in the States, yet passed themselves off as experienced and knowledgeable (which they were in their own minds). Then they were free to continue the stereotypes they had left with in the first place.

Tommy shook his head to clear it of his old, critical mindset. This was a new place and a new time in his life, and it deserved an open mind.

CHAPTER TWENTY

Concha stood beside her mother in the smoky little *cocina* beside the sturdy wattle and daub house. They were making balls of cornmeal dough as she breathed the smoke from the open hearth beneath the steel sheet on which they would make the day's tortillas. She closed her eyes as memories of her childhood came back to her, memories of the countless times she had helped her mother like this. It was so good to be home, to have the hard-packed adobe ground under her bare feet. She felt connected to the earth here in Mexico.

Her thoughts returned to Wyoming and the enormous house she had lived in there. She remembered the deep snows, the bitterly cold days, and the magnificent view of the Tetons out the enormous front room windows. And the kitchen had more appliances than many Mexican stores had in stock. Her bedroom had been the same, her and Nathaniel's closet holding enough clothes to start a good business in this country. It had all been so much, so very, very much.

She glanced around the homely little house with its handmade furniture, very little more than was needed to live a simple and unadorned life. No paintings, no little tables with a sculpture on it, no glass cases full of Indian *muñecas* worth many thousands of dollars. And no secrets in the basement.

Here she was happy inside herself, while in the north, she had learned that happiness came to people mainly through the accumulation of things. And that's what she had used to fill the hole in her chest that echoed with longing for her home, and the loving warmth she now felt radiating from her mother. It had been love that had been missing in her home in the north. Now she could identify what it had been she'd missed. She knew now that the hole in her heart had been shaped like her mother's love.

She turned her eyes to her mother, whose bowed head over the cutting board diced tomatoes for salsa. The woman's hair had much more gray than Concha remembered, the braids now twined with as much white as black. She reached out and ran her fingers down her mother's nearest braid, and the older woman looked at her and smiled, then returned to her work. The woman was as content as it was possible to be on this earth now that her one daughter was home, and it showed.

Concha went back to her work, satisfied. She was home after a great adventure, and here she would stay for the rest of her quiet days as a widow. It was enough.

But, as she flattened a ball of dough into the first tortilla of the day, she remembered The Heart of the World and the book of her family's story. She tried to dismiss the thought, shaking her head at its persistence, but it would not go away.

The smoke from the family hearth was one thing, fresh and redolent of pine gum, and it was the same for the pit in which her father fired his pottery. But the stale smoke from months of forest fires that hung in the air outside was something else again. The corn they'd ground for these tortillas was some of the last from the little corn and bean *milpitas* that were the very foundations of rural existence in Mexico. But there was no money to buy corn from parts of the country that had not been cursed by the rain god whose heart had been stolen— stolen by a man of Achiutla, Marcos Albino, and her brother Demetrio—to be sold to her dead husband. Shame flushed her face.

Concha knew she must do something to atone for the greed that had prompted the selling of the people's very souls. But what?

Nothing would serve in place of the Heart, and nothing would ever replace the history book of her family line, lost through the greed of her elder brother.

And what of her brother, who had tried so hard to set things right with both the family and with Dzaui? The brother whose fate had passed to the taking of men's lives for the sake of what was inarguably correct? The unfairness of it all made her heart pound with the need to set it all right.

But surely this was useless pride. What could she, a small woman in the poor hills, possibly do? Even now, she was being protected from her own government through a watch set by the men of the village—a watch to warn of the return of the swarm of ruthless policemen who had scoured the village only recently for her and her brother.

As she stood, lost in her thoughts and automatically forming tortillas with the heel of her hand, she heard her mother say, *Oyez*. Listen. Concha froze when she heard the neighbors' vigilant dogs barking.

Her mother left the casita carrying her shawl and a handful of tortillas to call her husband from his wheel. Concha followed her quick steps up the hill, up the angling path that led to the family refuge, a limestone cave hidden in the brush above the *ranchito* that no stranger, even during the bloody time of the *capitanes*, had ever discovered. It was that secret sanctuary that was responsible for the fact that the bloodline of the legendary La Cacica de Teposcolula still flowed in the veins of the Osorios on this very day.

MiT

Tom was impressed with the bus. It was as good as any he had ever ridden in, and he had ridden in many when he was a soldier subsisting on a soldier's pay.

He had forgotten the rhythms and sounds of a powerful bus negotiating mountain roads, slingshotting out of the curves with the motor growling and the manual transmission meshing gears with soft mechanical noises.

He remembered the day in the Gros Ventre River valley when Berto said the mountains reminded him of the Mixteca Alta, and it was true. An hour west of Oaxaca City, they drove through mountains covered by pine forests and had been driving through them for two hours since.

There was something else that reminded him of home. The sun was a red disc in the smoke-laden sky, and the distinct smell of a burning forest took him back to the summer of 1988 when over a million acres of Yellowstone Park had burned. For almost five months, the smoke had been thick in Jackson Hole, and almost everyone had a sore throat and reddened eyes from the constant irritation. In the summer of 2001, another large forest fire burned above the nearby town of Wilson, and the scenario had been the same. Out the bus windows, he could see smoke plumes and thermal mushroom pillars could be seen in almost any direction, and the sour, pungent smells had seeped into the very fabric of the bus seats.

They arrived in Tlaxiaco at one-thirty in the afternoon, and when they stepped off the bus, Tom suddenly felt like he was in a Mexico often stereotyped by returning tourists. Everything he saw spoke of poverty.

The bus station was in the lowest part of town, the rest of the village rose gradually up a hill to the north. Here were dirt streets, cruddy walls, and litter everywhere. He could smell an open sewage ditch not too far away. The odor was laced with the otherwise attractive aroma emanating from the many little food vendors' stands near the small terminal.

As Tom stood surveying the place and its people, he heard Berto say, "Oaxaca is the poorest state in Mexico except for, maybe, Chiapas. Very little is ever done by the government down here, but things are changing."

"How's that?"

"The people are becoming very political, demanding more from the government. They learned it in the States, and they are bringing it back with them."

"Really?"

"Yeah. They are organizing the indigenous people to vote, to begin transcending their exclusive attachments to their home villages. The governing parties are courting them like they never have before, mostly because there are a lot shit disturbers coming back from the north with new ideas."

"I guess that's good, huh?"

"Sometimes."

"When is it bad?"

"When I have to listen to shithead felons whine about their rights."

"Huh?"

"Sometimes it reminds me of the States, where everyone snivels about their rights and abandons all responsibility to the community, to the country, and to the need for order. There has to be a line drawn somewhere, before we have a nation of armed punks who own the streets and men kissing each other on television." The jibe at the US was obvious and intended.

"Damn, Berto, what set you off? You've been in a shitty mood ever since breakfast."

"Ah, don't worry about it. My boss, Jesus Bernalillo, is at the hotel, and he's going to be nice as hell to you and roast my ass when he gets me alone."

"You told him I was coming, huh?"

"Of course I did. I phoned him from Oaxaca and told him. He wasn't happy." Berto stepped to the street and waved down a taxi. "Hotel Portal," he said when the driver got out of the car to help with their baggage.

The Hotel Portal was a nineteenth-century building on a corner and across the street from the central plaza distinguished by a clock tower set in its middle. In counterpoint, a tall pole had also been placed in the plaza from which Indians swung on long ropes wound around the pole, as they had done long before "civilization" had arrived. The portico of the hotel rose above the city square and commanded the view.

Inside, the lobby was modern, and there was a small restaurant across the entranceway. The smells from the kitchen made Tom's mouth water.

There was a courtyard with a fountain in the center surrounded by flowerbeds and hibiscus bushes heavy with blossoms. Nice.

"*Dos sencillos atras*, Santiago. Two single rooms in the rear," he heard Berto say, addressing the clerk by his last name. Apparently, he was a regular here.

"*Si, Rigoberto. ¿Quien es el gringo?*"

"*Policia, y entiende español.*" *A cop, and he understands Spanish*, Tom translated to himself.

"*Bueno. Numeros dies y once. ¿Bien?*"

"*Bien.* Hey, Tomás, come and get your key. You're in number ten and I'm in eleven."

Tom stepped into the lobby and picked up his suitcase. A smiling porter stepped up and took the bag from his hand. Tom smiled back and followed the little man across a courtyard that was ringed by tall, antique doors. Once across the patio, they passed through a door and into the parking lot of a modern motel. And it was unmistakably a motel because it had no charm whatsoever.

He was hanging his clothes when he heard voices in the room next door. Tom moved to the wall between the two rooms, but the words were unintelligible. The voice was not Berto's, so Tom assumed that it was the voice of the field supervisor.

Berto had given a thumbnail biography of the man during the bus ride from the city. Jesus came from a rich family, was a polo player and pilot, vacationed in the States and Europe. His hobby, like his father's, was raising thoroughbred horses and polo ponies. It was something familiar to Tom, who came from a town that had its own horsy set. Hell, maybe the guy would like to come to Jackson Hole and play some polo.

There was a knock at the door, and Tom opened it on a guy in his mid-thirties dressed in chino pants, Reeboks, and a madras shirt left outside his pants to hide his sidearm. He looked like he'd stepped out of an L.A. Times ad for the May Company.

"Hi, I'm Jesus Bernalillo," he said and stuck out a hand that sported a thick gold link bracelet.

"Tom Thompson. Glad to meet you."

"Rigoberto says that you are here to extradite Cenovio Osorio."

"No. I'm here just in case there is an extradition. Personally, I don't think it's going to happen."

"Oh? What makes you think that?"

"To be honest, I think the Mexican Attorney General doesn't give a shit what the US wants anymore. The Kiki Camarena deal has probably queered extraditions between the two countries for a long time, except for drug kings." Tom smiled disarmingly. "Also, I have promised Berto that I will keep my eyes open and my mouth shut. I will do everything I can to stay out of your road."

Bernalillo smiled. "You are frank, I must say. And I am glad that you understand things."

Tom shrugged his shoulders. "I try to be as open as I can be; it solves a lot of problems. I don't like secrets."

"Good, neither do I. But just so there are no misunderstandings, I am completely loyal to my agency. If they tell me that I am supposed to be, uh . . . circumspect with you, then I will do just that."

"That's more than fair. I have my loyalties as well."

"Excellent! We understand one another. This is good." He folded his well-tanned arms. "I suppose that you want to interview Cenovio Osorio."

"Well, sure. I'd like to know exactly what happened that night, the night that Ward was murdered. And why."

Bernalillo opened the door and said, "Well, we have made your job real easy. He has confessed to killing Ward and has given a complete confession. It's even written down on paper." He turned toward the courtyard, and wearing a model's smile, said, "Your work is done now that he's confessed. We'll take it from here."

Tom answered, "There's still a possibility that an extradition could happen, and he'd be exonerated."

"But the man has confessed! It is on paper!"

"No offense, but an American lawyer would probably have the confession disqualified."

"How?"

"A thousand ways. The lawyers decide how things go up north, despite any realities." Tom was being diplomatic. He knew that any good lawyer would claim duress for a confession extracted in this country and probably make it work. "It could be another problem between our countries."

They went next door for Berto, and Tom saw that the man was

sullen, having had his butt dragged over the coals for something that wasn't his fault. Tom sympathized. There was little that made him madder than to have to take a raking over for something that was beyond anyone's control. But it gave him an insight into the character of Mr. Bernalillo. The kinds of personalities who indulged themselves in scapegoating were usually unsure of themselves or incompetent. It was in contrast with the almost cocky sureness with which Berto had conducted himself up to this point. Then Tom remembered Berto's comment the day before about Indians being the niggers of Mexico, and it made sense.

Bernalillo was a member of the thin upper crust of Mexico's population, one of the rich few who either led indolent lives or skimmed the cream of the jobs. Because of their influence, they had their choice of what they wanted to do, and they never, ever started at the bottom. Rather, they were plugged in at the arbitrary levels of federal agencies and corporations, any place where they were competent or semi-competent to handle the job. It usually meant that on their first day on the job, they supervised people with years of practical experience. It was no wonder that Berto had fretted about their meeting with his boss because every day, he was in a lose-lose situation with this guy. And too bad because he was a good cop with good instincts. Berto was a pain in the ass in many ways, but independent thinkers usually were. Tom could see that being that sort of person in this relationship would be a damn hard assignment to labor under.

The three men walked out of the hotel and directly down the street, south beside the plaza. The municipal building was only two blocks away, directly across from one of the ubiquitous sixteenth- and seventeenth-century Catholic churches that are the architectural centerpieces of every Mexican town of any size. The original priests had been nothing if not ambitious, he would give them that.

The *Municipio* was a large building with tall trees and park benches in front. Tom saw there was a post office nearby, which was good to know. That was where one found telephones, and he had to phone Sam and let him know he'd arrived. His cell phone service didn't work in Mexico, so he would have to depend on landlines.

Inside, they walked down a short hall and into a large court with a cement floor and basketball hoops at either end. The back wall opened to a nice view of the west side of town and the mountains beyond. A smoky pall mostly obscured the mountains, but Tom saw that they were good-sized and covered with trees.

They turned left and walked to the end of the courts where a sign over the doors announced the police offices.

Jesus walked past the uniformed clerk, who only briefly glanced at the men, concentrating his gaze on Tommy. They were not unexpected, he could see.

The commander was a man in his fifties with silver hair. His name was Riley, and he spoke good English. Not the hip, Americanized English that Jesus and Berto spoke, but it was correct.

"Sit down, gentlemen. Please sit down." He motioned at three chairs arrayed in front of his desk. They had been expected, indeed.

Jesus introduced Tom and commented about his being a visiting officer who was there to observe procedure and get some knowledge of how the Mexican law enforcement system conducted things. There was no mention of extradition. Instead, he made it sound as if the case of Cenovio Osorio was a handy way to illustrate what Tom had come down to learn.

Riley nodded. "Very good. I will explain about Señor Osorio.

"An anti-smuggling patrol stopped him and two accomplices at a roadblock in the state of Michoacán. They were asked to open the trunk of their car, and when the Lieutenant and a soldier on the detail discovered contraband, Señor Osorio killed the two men with a machete. Luckily, there was another soldier who had been relieving himself in some bushes. He came back just in time to witness the murders and get a description of the car, as well as the number of the license plate.

"The car was found abandoned in Huajuapan de Leon, and officers were dispatched to the bus station and every other place that they might use to leave the town while a search was mounted. We received notice of the murders and informed who the car owner was through a computer link to the US authorities. Because Mr. Osorio is known locally, we sent a large detail to his village and searched for them.

"However, we were lucky. They might have escaped except we received a tip that they had boarded the bus from Huajuapan to Tlaxiaco at a stop outside the city, and when they reached Tlaxiaco, we arrested them. In the meantime, Mr. Bernalillo's office advised us that the Osorios were also wanted for murder in the United States."

Tom interrupted. "Who are we talking about?"

"Cenovio and Concha Osorio, brother and sister."

Tom decided to quit the charade that he knew nothing about the Osorios. "My government is curious, is Miss Osorio dead?"

Riley frowned. "Who said that she was dead? She is not dead, that I know of."

"Oh," Tom said, realizing from the withering glances Jesus and Berto were giving him that he'd broken his promise to keep his mouth shut. "Please go on, sir."

"So, the two were arrested, and Señor Osorio confessed to the murders of the policemen. As to his sister, she was released because she played no part in the murders. We could have held her on federal suspicion of smuggling, but we saw no point to it. If the *Federales* wish to pursue it, then we will have to try to find her of course, but we have received no requests."

Jesus leaned forward. "And you do not know her whereabouts?"

"No. We have informants in the San Miguel, but there has been no word of her since she left this building. That is a bit strange, certainly, but that's how these Indians are—they have family everywhere and an aunt is the same as a mother, so she could be anywhere in that valley. But if you need her, we can find her. It may take a while, but word always gets back to one of our daily patrols once we make it known what we need. A few pesos will get us anything, things being as poor as they are out there."

"Uh, Comandante?" Tom ventured, avoiding the glares of his partners.

"Yes?"

"Did Osorio say anything about the murder in the States, in Wyoming?"

Jesus stood up. "Well, thank you Comandante, I think that is all we need." He turned to Tom and said, perfunctorily, "Unless Señor Thompson can think of anything else."

"Oh, you are interested in that?"

"Yes."

"He said that he knew nothing about this when Señor Bernalillo asked him."

Tom hesitated, but his mouth went on, even though his brain was saying, *Don't do it!*

"I'd like to talk to Mr. Osorio, if it's okay. And I'd like to talk to him alone."

The three other men looked at one another. Riley paused for a moment and then said, "Certainly. I'll have the jailer to take you down."

When they stepped out of Riley's office, Berto leaned toward Tom and hissed, "My ass is going to be in a sling now, for sure. Thanks."

Berto left the office, then Jesus walked to the door and said, "I'll be here when you come up," and his eyes were blazing.

Tom felt more than a little sheepish about breaking his promise, but something down deep in him had prompted the words out of his mouth. He hadn't been able to help it.

Steep stairs led down into the basement lit only by bare light bulbs in sockets mounted to the cement walls. At the first landing, Tom caught the smell of human excrement and urine, and it got stronger the further down they went.

In the basement, they reached a stub wall and a barred door where a small man in a uniform sat on a chair at the door. He leaped to his feet when he saw Tommy, a puzzled look on his face.

"*Abrocharse*," said the jailer. The man unlocked and opened the door, then locked it behind them. The officer walked Tom to the second door, where a man was lying face down on the floor, his face pillowed on his crossed arms. In the corner was an enamel slop jar, accounting for the smell. The place was chilly but relatively clean.

"Osorio!" said the jailer, and the man on the mattress rolled over and sat up slowly, then leaned stiffly against the wall.

Tom took one look at the man's battered head and saw that any confession he'd made would not stand up for five minutes in an American court.

Chapter Twenty-One

When Concha and her mother came out of the cave, they saw a group of village men gathered in a pine grove near the Osorio casita. As they neared, José Gorostiza broke away from the group and called out to Concha, where the group gathered beneath the trees.

Her brother Demetrio and cousin Marcos Albino were waiting with José, Patricio, and their four sons. This was strange because her mother said that they were sent away from the community, exiled for their part in selling the Heart of the World. They never mentioned the fact that her husband had purchased the crystal, but now, perhaps, she was to be sent away as well.

Oh, God! Please do not let them send me away from my home! she prayed. The thought that she might be torn from her mother's side, just when she had regained a measure of peace for her soul, was more than she could bear.

She had not realized the pressures she had been living under until she had found herself back in the setting of her peaceful childhood. The little domestic chores she set for herself had dissolved the huge knot under her breast in the cold and beautiful country of her husband's home. When Cenovio arrived with the news that the Heart had been taken, the knot grew to an unbearable size. He'd said they knew that her husband had paid fifty thousand dollars to his agents in Tlaxiaco, who had bought it from Marcos and Demetrio for only two hundred dollars. ¡*Que desgacia*! Indeed, it had been a disgrace, and now it appeared that she would be accompanying the other *desgraciados* into exile!

As she followed José to the group, her heart fell as she looked out over the valley and its thousand clouds of smoke because the cost of the crime was obvious and becoming clearer. When they sent her away, she would kill herself at the first opportunity, throw herself into *El Pozo de Las Suicidas*, the Well of the Suicides, a common practice of hopeless Mixtec widows in the Alta.

As she approached the group, Concha noticed the hard looks of each of the men sprawled on the ground beneath the trees. It was obvious they had steeled their hearts for the occasion, and no mercy could be expected. She almost burst into tears.

Demetrio and Marcos stood back a bit from the group, their shame still written on their faces, though their eyes were hard too. No sympathy there either.

José took Concha's arm lightly in his dainty ink-stained fingers. "Concha," he said.

Her voice quavered as she said, "Yes."

"Tell us all you know of the cacique, Don Armando Pacheco. We want to know where his house is, what it is like on the inside, how many people are there. Everything you can possibly remember."

A little thrill ran through her body. "I do not understand."

"We know that he has The Heart of the World and the book of your family, and that he betrayed you to the police. We also know that he has decided he is not going to return it to us, except for a price. If we do not pay that price, and there is no doubt that we cannot, he is going to offer it to men in Mexico City. Then it will be gone from us again and *La Tierra Mixteca* will be ruined by fire and thunder—the lives of the Cloud People extinguished."

"But," Concha exclaimed, "he gave his word that the things would be returned to us. He said that he was of the family of the famous Cacica of Teposcolula, just as my family and I are. He promised that our holy properties would be returned as soon as he had recovered them! Again, I say that I do not understand."

José shrugged. "It is the way of men in this world. He found out that the Heart is worth tens of thousands of American dollars, and it is an opportunity that he will not pass up. However, give him credit, he had given us a chance to recover it."

"But how?" Concha said. "We have no money, no one has any money in these mountains. Oaxaca is the poorest state in Mexico, and we are the poorest of those poor."

José nodded and said, "That is true, there is no hope of raising the money for the return of our holy objects, so we will go to Huajuapan and tear them from this man's greedy fingers. And, if he will not give them up gladly, we will feed those fingers to the dogs of the street."

Concha smiled momentarily. She had forgotten José's florid speaking style. Then she looked at the men again and was now impressed with their air of resolve. Her successful rescue at Santa Catarina Tayata had inspired them with a newfound sense of competence. All too often, the people of the mountains were reliably passive in the face of any authority, legal or not. However, they had taken the bit in their teeth when they rescued her. It must have felt very good for a change.

This explained the hardness in the eyes of the men. Now, rather than fear, she felt a thrill. The night these men rescued her had been the most exciting time in her life, and apparently, it had been the same for them.

It also explained the presence of Marcos and Demetrio. They were being given a chance to redeem themselves with the people of Achiutla, and with the rain god, Dzaui.

"So you are going to Huajuapan to take back our things," Concha observed, "but is this possible? Have you considered the possibilities? Do you have a plan?"

Don Patricio spoke. "We have a plan for Tlaxiaco and Cenovio. But the reason we are here is to try to work out something for

Huajuapan. Only myself and my sons," he gestured at Juan and Raul, "have been to that city, but we do not know it very well. We will need your guidance. José wants you to go with us."

Concha was stunned. "You are planning to rescue Cenovio from the jail in Tlaxiaco?" She was horrified at the prospect because it would bring the police into the village thick as grasshoppers in a plague year. It was not a good idea. But she would hold her tongue for the moment.

However, a plan for Huajuapan stirred her. It struck her as being possible and being included moved something in her very soul.

"I can take you to Pacheco's house, and I know it on the inside. While Cenovio and I were waiting, I asked to go to the bathroom and was taken through the house from one end to the other. I remember how it is built."

"You must make a drawing for us then," Patricio said.

"Better, I will take you there."

She saw the men's eyes widen, though their faces remained impassive.

Patricio paused for a moment. "You are a woman, and this is ordinarily men's business. It will be dangerous."

"And what of it?" interjected Patricio's brother. "She has been away in the north for five years, so she must have learned many things. Is it not true that those who come back from there have a knowledge, an understanding that none of us could ever hope to learn down here?"

The look in Patricio's eyes was guarded. "That I cannot dispute. There is a great deal that can be learned in the north, but bravery is not one of them, and this will take someone with an iron will. It would take someone who is not afraid to go to jail . . . or die."

José snorted through his nose in disgust. "Did you yourself not tell me that Concha had taken a knife and was prepared to defend herself? Did you not say that you could tell from her eyes that she would have gladly cut the guts out of anyone who touched her?"

Patricio nodded, his eyes taking on a more thoughtful cast. "I did."

"And does not the blood of the great Cacica de Teposcolula and La Cacica Maria run in her veins, and are not the Osorio women famous for their brains?"

One could tell from Patricio's silence that he agreed this was something to consider.

"Then take her with you," José said with conviction.

Patricio looked at Raul, who nodded, then glanced at his brother. Juan nodded.

In turn, Patricio looked at Concha for a long moment.

He saw a small woman. But also, in that long moment, he suddenly saw something else that he had not expected and so had not initially noticed. The woman was completely at ease here at a council of strong men. Her eyes were confident, and he could tell that it was not false confidence that came from the need to thrust oneself forward. It was genuine.

He nodded slowly, thoughtfully. "Tell us what you think," he said.

MiT

Oz parked the van and watched in the rear-view mirror as Olga parked hers behind him. Then he turned in his seat to address the passengers.

"This is a holy place for me." He motioned out the windows of the van. "This is the Tamazulapan Valley, and this," he pointed through the windshield, "is the Mixtec pyramid I was helping to excavate when I had my vision and received my spirit animal."

Pete looked at the large mound. It was overgrown with small

trees and bushes, looked nothing like the wonderfully engineered structures on the top of Monte Alban.

So this is where the jaguar appeared, Pete said to himself. This pile of rubble is where the logo for Jaguar Travelers and where The Gate of Heaven 'shrooms popped into Oz's head. What a hoot.

A little bubble of cynicism worked its way into his head, despite his promise to the old hippie that he would take all this seriously. He was having some good tourist time, and there was no sense in gumming it up with a lot of pseudo-religious bullshit. He turned in his seat to look out the back window at the other van.

Olga was engaged in a lecture that, he assumed, both guides knew by rote.

He looked again at the big mound of rubble and let himself have another private little laugh at what appeared to be not much more than a big dump.

The groups piled out after the short lectures and walked on a path toward the hill. A short man in a straw hat who was plowing a field nearby waved his hand, and many of the group returned the wave, eliciting a big smile from him.

Oz led them to a spot at the base of the ruined pyramid, then pointing to a flat corner of a field next to a low rubble wall, he said, "I was sleeping here, next to a small fire. I was taking the watchman's place, a local who had to be with his wife who was having a baby.

"I was staring into the fire, my shoulders covered by a *cobija*, a blanket, because it was winter and the nights can get cold enough to freeze water. Anyway, I remember staring into the fire, and it began to flare, then it took on the form of an oval, and the flickering started to make sense.

"The flames had reduced to embers that had a bluish hue, then a deep bluish-green. It pulsed, then pulsed again. The second time it pulsed, it turned into a beautiful, iridescent blue-green bird with a longish tail and a brilliant black bead for an eye. And that eye had the most intelligent look I had ever seen.

"It was not the facial expression, birds' faces are immobile, but the look in the animal's eye sent a thrill through me. I began to get giddy with a sense that something unusual was about to happen." Oz's voice died away to a whisper. "And that was when I received my knowledge."

The knowledge of how to turn this whole thing into a lot of money, Pete thought, then turned to look at Olga. She pursed her lips in disapproval and jerked her head at Oz, bidding Pete to return his attention to what the man was saying.

Instead, Pete glanced down at the ground near his feet and saw a potsherd. He stooped to pick it up and examined the white clay decorated with an orange design. He jerked his attention away from the shard when he heard his name.

"Pete? Hey Pedro! Leave that shard here. It belongs to the people."

Pete felt a little sheepish because everyone in the group looked at him, their faces showing disapproval. Before they'd left the hotel in Tamazulapan, Olga had lectured them all on leaving anything they found. She also added something about it angering the spirits of the pyramid. He flipped the shard to the ground and smiled sheepishly.

"Okay," Oz said, "let's walk up this way. I'll explain how the pyramid was built and tell you some anecdotes about the excavation. Then, when we get to the top, I'll tell you some of what the Quetzal told me about the people of this valley and about my own life."

Pete had a thought. The jaguar, the jaguar of Jaguar Travelers! He thought that Oz's spirit guide would have been the powerful cat of Indian myth. It just made sense that the big man with the feline eyes, and manner, would be guided on his spiritual odysseys by that animal. But, instead, Oz's guide was a bird!

They stopped about halfway up the pyramid so the group could get their breath. Pete looked east and noticed a walled structure about a mile away, surrounded on one side by a grove of large trees. It looked cool and inviting.

Pointing, he said, "Hey, Olga, what's that over there?"

"That's a large natural swimming pool. It's fed by the springs that were the life of the ancient community that built this pyramid."

"Great! Let's go for a swim after we get done here. It's hot."

Olga smiled a secret little smile and whispered, "I planned to take you in there, but not today. It's a real sexy place at night."

Pete felt a flash of heat in his groin. He surreptitiously ran the heel of his hand down his groin, trying to quell the sudden tumescence there.

MiT

Comandante Riley sat in his office alone, thinking. Finally, his clerk tapped on his door and brought in the bottle of Coca-Cola Riley had sent him for, and then left.

The silver-headed man put his feet up on his desk and took a long drink from the cold bottle as he loosened his uniform tie.

Things were getting complicated, and he hated complications. He thought back over the chain of events that brought him to this moment.

First, the federal police had notified him that Osorio and two others, a man and a woman, had killed two police officers in the state of Michoacán and were thought to be heading this way. The American Federales had notified them of this.

Then Don Armando Pacheco had phoned with a business proposition. He explained that one of his nephews had been involved in some bloody business in El Norte, then again near Culiacan. He also knew the federal police would be looking for him and the Cenovios, who had stopped at his place in Huajuapan. He said that the Cenovios were on a bus to Tlaxiaco, then offered Comandante Riley a business proposition that would make his finances take a very healthy turn upwards.

This was something momentous because Riley had been worrying that very morning about his young mistress in Huamelulpan. She needed money for their two sons, so Riley had agreed to arrest Cenovio and hold him for the Federales, thus taking their attention away from the nephew. He also suggested letting the sister go, which was easy enough to do once Riley found out she was the wife of the famous scholar El Profesor Ward.

Then the federal cop Jesus Bernalillo had turned up saying that a gringo officer was coming down from the States and that this man's agency was seeking extradition. Bernalillo was scared silly that this gringo might get Osorio back to the States. He wanted Osorio to disappear, which was stupid as well as impossible now that so many people and their agencies were involved. The money Bernalillo was offering, on top of what Pacheco had promised him, would have been nice, but he could only do so much. Riley agreed to hold Osorio in custody until Bernalillo had a chance to try to work some things out. Riley had given him two days, and then Jesus had paid for three. Two extra pay envelopes in one week, and no taxes on either one. Not bad.

And then the gringo had surprised them all by asking for an interview with the prisoner. Riley had not known what to do. If the word came from the Attorney General that the gringo was to take receipt of Osorio, Riley would be in the position to catch some major political shit if the man complained that Riley had not been cooperative.

The choice had been a hard one. After all, Bernalillo was the chief field agent for the Mexican DEA's regional office, which had tons of US drug interdiction dollars in their inflated, mostly unaccounted, budget. Bernalillo had money to burn for law enforcement-related activities, and he could shove it to any police official he chose to. But money couldn't buy everything, although a man had to use a little discretion, especially when it came to the golden goose, Uncle Sam.

Riley took another drink of his soda and then smiled slightly. Bernalillo and Sandez must be sweating their asses off right now because this gringo could complicate their lives a whole lot. El Profesor Ward had been famous in the entire state of Oaxaca; both respected for his professional work and despised for his artifact trafficking.

Bernalillo and Sandez had been acting as his agents, and they were despised for everything they did, both as corrupt Mexican DEA and corrupt Mexican entrepreneurs. And that was why he'd hesitated only a moment when the gringo asked to interview Osorio—he had wanted to see the look on the faces of the two federal assholes who had been strutting around Tlaxiaco for the last two years, acting like they owned the place.

The Comandante was going to have to watch how this all played out and be damned careful. He liked the money but didn't want to get any more shit on him than necessary.

MiT

Tom, Berto, and Jesus sat on the patio outside the restaurant of the Hotel Portal while they waited for their food. They talked, but little of the conversation was in English, and neither of his "compadres" even pretended to include Tom. The other two men were clearly steamed about his interview with Cenovio Osorio, and he couldn't blame them. He had promised to keep his mouth shut and hadn't, so what the hell. And if these two knew about his and Osorio's conversation, they would be even madder.

Cenovio had gladly agreed to extradition. He knew that he would be spending his life in the deepest shithole in Mexico for killing the two Mexican cops. There might not be a death penalty, as such, in Mexico but life in prison for a killer of federal cops was short indeed.

Osorio had told him that he would cooperate with Tom, make a complete confession and describe the mitigating circumstances if Tom took him back to the States. Tom had assured him that if there were actual mitigating circumstances, his prison term could be as little as twelve years, and he would serve half that if he kept his nose clean. The man had jumped at it.

Now Tom had to get to a phone and talk to Sam. He desperately wanted to make contact with someone at home because, down here, he felt exposed. His partners were lying to him—and lying *muy* big time. Osorio had told him a lot about their real game down here.

When the food came, cheeseburgers and French fries, Tom took advantage of the moment.

"Hey, Jesus, where can I make a phone call?"

Jesus stabbed a couple of French fries, stuck them in his mouth, and pointed to the wall behind him. "Down the street half a block. There's a shop on the left with a phone booth right by the door. Tell the woman you want to make a call to the States, and she'll get you an international operator."

"Thanks."

"You're welcome."

It was Berto who couldn't stand it any longer. He glared at Tom and said, "What the hell were you doing, anyway?"

Tom shrugged and looked sheepish. "I know I gave my word—"

Berto broke in. "Yes. You did."

" . . . but I just couldn't help myself. My problem is that my mouth moves when I think."

"Then what the hell were you thinking about? Here we are trying to do our job and you butt in like you're in charge of the detail. This is a federal murder case, a Mexican federal murder case, and you are interfering. What did Osorio tell you, anyway?"

"I can't see how I interfered, not really. I talked to the prisoner, so kill me! All I wanted to do was try to find out how Ward got killed and why. Hell, I have to pretend like I'm trying a little. I've got to report in to Sam, and I can't tell him that I'm rocking on my nuts down here because I promised you guys that I would. Give me a break, I've got to give him something."

Jesus said, "Yeah, you've got a point. But try to stay in the background from now on out, okay? We have our job to do too." He wiped his mouth. "What did you find out from Osorio?"

Tom had known that it might come up, so he was ready with his answer. It might be half an answer, but he hoped it would do for the moment.

"Ward had this super religious artifact, some crystal that's sacred to the Indians, locked up in that monster safe of his, and there was no way that they were ever going to be able to get it, locked behind a door that size.

"Ward had a photo studio in his basement, next to the vault, and he used to take things out to photograph them for his customers—a new acquisitions catalog that showed what he'd come up with and what he was willing to sell.

"The night of the murder, Cenovio had heard that Ward had bought this sacred piece and had it at his house. He was working in Idaho at the time, so he and his buddy drove down to Alta and asked his sister if she knew anything about it. She said she didn't, and she was really upset.

"Anyway, that night Ward's wife took him down a cup of coffee and saw that he was photographing a book that was sacred to their family, which probably meant that he was planning to get rid of it for money. She went upstairs and told her brother and his buddy what was going on downstairs, so they went down to get their stuff back.

"When they went downstairs and confronted Ward about their property, he got angry, and they had a hell of an argument, which turned into a fight that eventually found its way outside. In the process, the professor got smacked on the head three times with a piece of firewood, eventually fracturing his skull.

"And now it gets pretty strange from my point of view. Osorio says he knew that Ward was dying. He was standing over the man and looked up at the Grand Teton and heard the mountain calling for the man's soul. I guess it's still a tradition down here and in South America, so an anthropologist in the States told me.

"Anyway, Ward had a ritual strangling rope in his collection, and Osorio and his buddy used it to kill Ward, then they took the body inside. There they washed the body, did some ritual stuff, and prepared him for burial according to their customs." Tom looked at the two men and asked, "What do you think about that?"

José and Berto looked at one another, and both shrugged. "So?" asked Berto.

"You don't think the story is strange?"

"No," Berto said, "the guy is an Indian, and I told you before that the folkways are still being practiced. There may be a relict burial practice still being observed in some communities. Didn't you believe me?"

"I believed you, but I thought of it in some superficial sense. Sacrificing a man to a mountain is a leap of the imagination that my mind isn't capable of making, I guess."

Tom looked around the patio, at the potted flowers, the climbing vines, and the sun-washed tiles, to reassure him of the orderly and present world he was used to living in.

"Well, as far as I'm concerned, an extradition wouldn't be a good idea. An American jury would be so unwelcome to a story like Osorio's that they'd want to kill him for witchcraft, as well as murder. I think he'd be better off being tried here in Mexico."

Berto and Bernalillo looked at one another, and something passed between them.

Tom had no idea what it was, but their faces showed some kind of relief when they looked back at him. Something was going on with these two, and he could guess what it was because the battered little man in the basement down the street had told him.

"But that isn't how the Honorable Nat Ward is going to see it, I can tell you. This has turned into a political deal, and politics is an unforgiving game. Besides, the warrant is from Teton County and the names on it are Cenovio Osorio, Concha Osorio, Valerio Trujano, and those are the ones I am sworn to take into custody, when and if the occasion presents itself."

"Okay," Berto said. "We'll see how it all comes out with our governments. But don't forget, this guy is wanted for two murders down here. Unless something outrageous happens, he's not going back to stand trial for killing a man under all those mitigating circumstances. Hell, he whacked the heads off two cops who were engaged in a lawful activity. No one in their right mind would think that killing Ward would take precedence over the outright assassination of two policemen. The extradition doesn't stand a chance."

He leaned back in his chair and took a big swig of his drink. "Why don't you relax and enjoy your stay down here. Hell, I just remembered something I was going to tell you. There's a rodeo down in my mom's hometown, Chilapa de Santa Cruz. You told me how you used to ride in rodeos, let's go down there, and I'll show you how it's done down here."

"You're going to ride?" Tom asked, surprised.

"Yeah. I was good when I was young. Hell, I'm still good."

Tom looked at the cocky grin on the guy's broad face and thought, *I just bet you were, Amigo, but time catches up with everybody.*

"I need to make that phone call." Tom shoved his chair back and asked, "Down the street and on the left, huh?"

"You got it," Bernalillo said. He looked at the check and said, "You owe two bucks."

Tom left the money and then walked through the door to the sidewalk to the shop, where he found a phone booth.

"Necesit*o un operador internacional,*" he said, gesturing at the booth.

The woman behind the counter glanced at a man sitting on a stool at the end of the counter.

"*No hay servicio.*"

"*¿No sirve?*" Tom asked, thinking that the phone must be broken.

"*No hay servicio a los Estados Unidos,*" the man said. No service to the US

How the hell did he know I wanted to phone the States? Tom wondered.

"*¿Cuando estaré servicio?*" Tom asked. "When will there be service?"

The man just shrugged his shoulders and looked out the door.

Tom looked at the woman, and she made herself busy tidying the counter.

Tom walked back out to the street and looked up and down. He would have to find another phone; there had to be more than one.

After half an hour, he found another phone, but the man there also said there was no service to *El Norte.*

A third man told him the same thing.

As Tom walked back up to the hotel, he was beginning to feel a little uneasy as he looked around at the foreign scene with its signs in a language that he could barely comprehend. Suddenly he realized just how vulnerable he was, and a vague fear began to come over him. He was alone and a very long way from home.

MiT

In Tamazulapan, the sun had been down for hours before the Jaguar Travel group gathered in the little hotel restaurant to eat. Pete was starving, not being used to eating as late as was the custom in Latin countries. After dinner, he pushed himself back and mentioned that he felt like a sausage. Olga said, "Why don't we go for a walk—that should help unstuff you."

They strolled to the main square and started down a poorly lit street that took them to the edge of town, then walked for about fifteen minutes. Olga lit the way with a tiny pocket flashlight. Pete carried towels she'd taken from her room.

The iron door to the swimming pool had been left unlocked, and when Pete wondered at it, Olga just brushed her fingers together to indicate a little money had arranged it.

Once inside, Pete could tell how large the pool was only by the number of bright stars reflected in the still, black water. It was a glittering field the size of a basketball court.

They took off their clothes and slipped into the water warmed that day by the hot sun. It was the perfect temperature, just cool enough to be refreshing but warm enough to give one a sensual feeling.

The only thing that was disconcerting was that the night made it impossible to see the edges of the pool until one's fingers touched them, but to his delight, when he rolled over on his back, he could navigate by the pulsing night sky.

They made a game of it, swimming side by side from Pegasus to Cygnus, over to Saturn, and down to Jupiter. The cascading water on Olga's firm wet breasts flashed with starlight.

After leisurely crossing the pool twice, Olga led Pete to the pool's north side, to where its spring-fed waters flowed from a limestone outcrop. She pushed him gently back to the rocks, flipped her hair over her shoulder, wiped her face, and stepped into his arms.

Her hot breasts flattened against his cool chest and her mouth opened wide as if to swallow him. She spread her legs and lifted her thighs to embrace him. He entered her mouth and her vagina at the same time, causing her to inhale a gasp. She thrust herself down, gripping him as she worked more and more of his shaft into her.

With all of him inside her, she breathed shuddering little breaths into his lungs and worked herself slowly up and down. She gave a little shudder and took her mouth away. The pale light of the stars lit her blonde hair and pale face, turned her brown eyes into black pools. Her wanton mouth was also a pool of dark as she continued with an erotic panting sound deep in her throat that made Pete even harder.

She lay back. Gripping his wrists, her nails burning their way into him, as she thrust her globed breasts and flinty nipples up to the dark sky, her blonde hair floated out onto the water in a large, pale aureole. Bubbles from the spring came up and mingled with the white hair and starlight. Her mouth made a dark oval, and animal sounds escaped her body.

He buried himself again and again and again. At every thrust, she quivered and gasped as her vagina became looser, and she felt more vulnerable to him as she neared climax. She no longer moved her hips, just waited to receive the thrusts that were coming faster and faster. Her nails dug deeper into his arms, her legs spread wider, her moans became more intense.

Pete could stand no more. He gave himself up to the moment and closed his eyes, so all his sensibilities were concentrated in finding the very bottom of her pelvis, the hollow little spot that led to her center. When he touched the spot, she gasped and then gave a little shriek. Her hands shook as she stilled his pelvis, holding herself rigid against the end of his shaft.

They came on the same heartbeat. Their hearts pulsed and sent hot ripples down their bodies to the place where their deepest essences were mingling. And a long cry, one that turned into a pulsing yowl, came out of Olga's throat. It sounded as if she had been stabbed in the heart.

Chapter Twenty-Two

After his abortive try to make a phone call, Tom took a walk around the mountain town. He needed a chance to think about his situation. When he needed to think something through, it was his habit to go for a walk.

He went to the hotel, walked across the porch, then turned the corner to head up the hill and into a part of town he hadn't explored yet. He walked no more than two blocks when he saw something familiar mounted on a wall next to a shuttered window. It was a small blue and white sign with the trademark double-A for Alcoholics Anonymous, and he felt immediate relief from the knot in his gut. Here was something familiar.

Tom had gone through treatment for his alcohol addiction at a Vet's hospital several years previous. His first revelation came when a crusty old counselor had said, "You people don't have a drinking or drugging problem. You've all got a living problem." It had gotten through to him.

The second revelation didn't come as quickly, but it was even more profound to his budding understanding of himself. He'd found out that he was a fear-driven person. All his adult life, he had felt himself a master of fear because he'd rodeoed, driven cars fast and wrecked more than one, joined the Army, and gone off to a shooting war. As a cop, he had gone into life-threatening situations, disarmed felons, and done other things that had satisfied himself that he was fearless—"ten feet tall and bulletproof."

While in the hospital, he discovered at his very center, he was still the frightened little boy who had cowered at the towering rages of his father and the phobic anxieties of his mother. Once he discovered that fact, he found ways to deal with his fear. AA meetings were the places he went to talk about the fact that he was a grown man who was afraid and was able to talk about it with no shame.

Tom walked to the sign and read: *Tengo Una Problema—Tengo Una Soluccion.* "I have a problem, but I have found a solution." It was one of the favorite mottos of the international organization, and it was as simple as it got.

The simplicity of it made Tom smile, and he felt the fear begin to ebb. He looked again and read *Horas: Lunes Miercoles Viernes* 2130—Monday, Wednesday, Friday at 7:30. The little street was suddenly sunny, warm, and quaint. There was a mix of flat-roofed stucco buildings and log houses with shingled roofs almost identical to the cabins sprinkled around Jackson Hole that were relics of the early days in the Teton Valley. The sight of them supplied some little reassurance that he might not be as alone as he'd been feeling.

He continued up the street to a corner and heard a familiar, buzzing sound. Turning left to follow the sound, he soon found himself at a small sawmill.

His grandfather had owned a sawmill— it had been the business of his mother's people since the pioneer days of 1840s Utah. The smell of freshly sawn pine and the sounds of sawyers always made him nostalgic for his bucolic childhood in Wyoming. He walked down the street to the edge of town and looked at the activity.

His practiced eye saw that this was a stud mill, specializing in two-by-fours eight feet long. By the huge bunks of the lumber, he could see that someone, somewhere, was building a lot of stick-built structures. The scene was another familiar reminder of home, where a local building boom was going on. Everyone was cashing out in the east and on the California coast to relocate to the mountain west. They were looking to escape all the problems they'd caused in those places, only to bring the same issues with them. The Mountain West, a historically friendly and neighborly place, was becoming as exclusive and class-conscious as any other place in America you could name.

As Tom looked around the mill, he wondered what had inspired all this activity in this little mountain place. On the way in on the bus, he remembered that he'd noticed two other sawmills on the eastern edge of the town. Come to think of it, he remembered that they were also stud mills. Indeed, someone had something going somewhere, and it wasn't small.

MiT

Concha rode in the back of Patricio's truck with Marcos Albino and another man from the village, who had been brought along to watch the truck during the raid. At their feet, there were baskets that appeared to be full of produce, though they were mostly cornhusks and underneath that, pistols and ammunition.

The pickup's bed had been outfitted with a pipe frame and a tarpaulin cover, making it a copy of the rural taxis that are a familiar sight all over Mexico. The pickup bore stolen plates taken from a hapless traveler's truck that happened to be putting new tires on his vehicle at the *Euzkadi* tire store in Tlaxiaco.

As they drove through Huajuapan, Concha guided them with hand signals to the neighborhood where the cacique's house sat. As they drove slowly by the big house, Concha pulled her *huipil* up to hide the bottom of her face. But there was no one who might recognize her near the big double doors that opened to the courtyard inside. They, and the small door that accommodated foot traffic, were closed.

Patricio drove the truck to a little park that he and his sons knew and stopped. Everyone got out and walked to the pump to refresh themselves from the hot ride over the mountains.

Once they had gathered under the trees, Concha explained the layout of the house again. Now that they had all had a chance to see the outside of the big structure, they wanted a detailed description of what they would find once they were through the door.

Concha described the location of Don Mario's office in the wing where he conducted business, hoping that the Heart of the World and the book of the family were being kept in that place. There would be only one chance to recover them, and that would have to be accomplished in a few minutes.

The plan they agreed upon was that they would get inside the door through guile. Juan and Raul would ask to see the cacique's secretary, posing as men with an artifact of great value for sale. They bought a watermelon and put it in a sack to represent the item.

They moved the truck to a point up the street from the cacique's house next to a sidewalk vendor's stand and got out. The baskets of produce had been left with people at the park and the weapons hidden in their clothes.

Juan and Raul crossed themselves and left, walking casually. The rest of the group crossed themselves too, praying with all their hearts that this would go well—that no one in their group or anyone in the cacique's household would be hurt.

But they had all sworn they would do whatever they had to do to recover the objects that were central to the future well-being of their community and the Osorio family. If it took blood, then let it flow. They would leave with their hands full, or they would die.

They watched the Gorostiza brothers go to the door and knock. Removing their hats, they stood on the sidewalk until the door opened, then spoke to someone the group could not see. When the door closed, Juan looked up the sidewalk and gave the hand signal, beckoning the rest of the raiding party to array themselves flat against the big doors.

When the door opened again, Pancracio's eyes bulged when he saw Patricio step from his place along the wall with his finger on his lips for silence while pointing a pistol at the secretary's chest.

The hapless man stepped back a pace as the Gorostiza brothers stepped through the door and pulled their weapons from under their shirts. He had a moment to understand what was happening, and then he took in a great breath to shout a warning to the household. But it was cut off by a stroke of Juan's heavy automatic on the side of his head.

The man reeled, gasped, and put his hand to his head, then fell to his knees and retched onto the courtyard bricks, a moment before another blow felled him into unconsciousness.

Concha quickly crossed the patio and entered the door that led to Pacheco's office wing. The men followed on her heels as she flew down the hall toward the tall door she remembered from her last time here, and as they were nearing the door, it opened.

A woman was backing out the door with a tea service in her hands. Concha slammed her hands on the woman's shoulders to thrust her into the office, making the silver service fly with a great noise onto the stone floor.

When the group burst into Pacheco's office, they saw the big man with thick glasses gape in surprise. The mouth of a man who sat in an upholstered chair opposite the cacique also flew open.

But, while the big man behind the desk was registering the scene with his eyes, his hands were busy. He pulled the drawer at his right open and put his hand inside. It came out of the drawer with a revolver and the big man fired it the moment it cleared the desktop.

Concha saw the flame from the muzzle, heard the report, and saw Raul drop his gun to the floor as a bullet hit his body. Without thinking, she stooped for Raul's gun as she saw Juan leap to the cacique and bring his pistol down on the man's thick arm. But the big man did not drop the weapon; instead, bringing it up again, this time to shoot the other Gorostiza brother. At that moment, Concha leveled the 9mm and blew the In/Out box full of papers off the cacique's desk.

The cyclone of paper and the loud report in the cacique's ear immediately affected the man. He dropped the pistol and raised his hands to his shoulders as he peered out the corner of his eye at the little woman with the gun held in a shooter's stance.

It had not been for nothing that Nathaniel had taken Concha to the pistol range and taught her how to use the pistols he had hidden about the house. Together, they had shot thousands of rounds on the pistol courses in Jackson Hole and Idaho Falls.

Patricio picked up the dropped pistol and said, in a menacing voice. "Give us our things."

"What things?" the big man said in a mollifying voice.

Concha aimed the muzzle of the pistol to his face and began to pull the trigger. The man's hugely magnified eyes saw the hammer raising and, worse, saw the look on the woman's face that grimaced over the gaping muzzle of the gun. He knew that she was beyond any bargaining or stalling. He understood that she intended to blow his brains out, then look for what they'd come for.

"Over there, over there!" he said in a strangled voice. One thick hand waved at a big carved wooden wardrobe standing against the wall.

Marcos dashed to the cabinet and opened the door.

"That's it," Concha cried. "The two cardboard boxes on the bottom shelf!"

Her cousin took out the larger box and opened it, then he nodded at the group, closed the box, and stood.

"Let's go," he said.

Patricio looked at his wounded sons and slashed his pistol down onto the cacique's skull with a sickening thunk, and the man's thick glasses flew to the floor. The man sagged against his desk and groaned. The heavy gun came down again, and the man fell from his chair, and this time no sound escaped his thick lips.

"Not me! Not me!" cried the other man, still in his chair and holding his hands over his cranium in defense against any blows. Patricio hit the man's fingers with the barrel of his pistol, and in reflex, the man took his hands off his head with a little yip. Patricio smiled and dropped the gun without a sound, except the solid sound of the blow.

When the group ran from the office and into the hallway, they saw the household staff scatter back into the rooms, the women shrieking and the men swearing.

When they all burst into the courtyard, Concha saw the man who'd guarded her at the Mendez rancho. He was coming from the back of the house, pulling his gun from the shoulder holster he wore. The memory of his hot hands trying to force their way between her clenched thighs came back to her, and without a thought, she fired as she ran.

The bullet took the man down. They heard him gasp as the bullet hit him in the chest, making a flat smack audible over the report of the 9mm. He fell, skidding across the tile on his face, then lay very still, his pistol falling from his hand.

Patricio's truck was waiting at the gate, the driver's face intent as he looked out the open passenger door.

Patricio and Marcos put the precious boxes in the front seat, and Marcos got in. Patricio and Concha clambered onto the tailgate and helped the wounded brothers into the bed of the truck. They almost fell back onto the street as the pickup accelerated down the road, throwing a cloud of dust into the late afternoon air and scattering the people drawn to the streets by the sounds of gunfire. And they were away.

MiT

It was an hour after the evening shift at the Municipio police station in Tlaxiaco. José Gorostiza had surveyed the building by asking if it would be okay to have a basketball game on the court—his sons and nephews wanted to play. The man on duty looked at the schedule, then said that it was available and approved the game. José walked to a side street where five men waited, all of them with gym bags.

"There is only one man in the office, and probably one more downstairs in the jail. There are the two guards at the door and one in the yard. Has anyone seen anyone else?"

Socratio flicked a hand for attention and said, "There's another one in the vehicle compound. He's changing a tire."

"Is he armed?"

"Not that I could see. Probably not."

"Very well. Plato, do you have the dynamite?"

Plato zipped open the gym bag at his feet, and they could see the fake sticks of dynamite taped together, the one in the center fused.

"Good, take the bag inside. I have told the guard to expect us for a basketball game, so when he sees the bag he will not suspect. Go to the office and ask the man on duty if the court has been reserved. He will say it has, then you act as if you are going back outside. When we see you come back to the door, we will take out the guard at the door. Then you go upstairs to the balcony and walk to the end, above the police office, and take out the dynamite. Demetrio and I will go to the office and then, God be with us."

José, plus the basketball team, Plato, Socratio, Demetrio Osorio, and two other men, bowed their heads for a moment, then crossed themselves. Their souls were as prepared as they would ever be. This was God's work now.

They held their breaths as they watched Plato walk up to the guard and say a few words. Then Demetrio and one of the other men walked across the plaza and past the guard, saying a good evening. The man with the carbine returned their greeting, though his face was alert and inquisitive. Suspicious.

"One moment," he said.

Sweat popped out on the two men's faces, but Demetrio whispered, "Keep walking."

The guard said, louder, "Hey! I said to wait a minute." His voice had taken on a deadly tone. These policemen suffered nothing that smacked of disrespect from the peasants.

Demetrio and his partner turned around and met the approaching man halfway. They were joined by Plato, who was already inside. Demetrio felt his pendulous lower lip trembling, so he sucked it up and took it between his teeth.

They waited nervously for the man to reach them.

"How come all of you are carrying new bags?" The fact that so many poor men could have the money for new gym bags had alerted his suspicious nature.

"We're here to play basketball, Señor."

Demetrio looked over the man's shoulder and, with relief, saw José and the other man walk up behind the guard.

They knew that the man could not help but turn to face the approaching men. Demetrio waited for his moment and, when the guard turned to cover his back, hit him with the leather sack full of lead shot. The man was knocked unconscious and fell, his carbine clattering to the cement floor.

“Close the door,” José hissed and picked up the rifle to hide it in the bushes. He turned to Plato and nodded his head up the stairs.

He turned to the rest of the men and said, *“¡Calmate, Calmate!”* even though his face was bathed with sweat. He felt anything but calm.

The four men, gym bags in hand, strolled around the corner and out to the basketball court. José then led them casually toward the watch officer, and once there they stopped just outside the door, he said, “Sir, I think you have a problem with a broken pipe in the lavatory.” He gestured to the corner of the court.

“Damn!” the man said and got up from his desk to join them.

The moment he was close, Socratio and another of the men grabbed each man’s wrists and slammed him up against the wall. José darted to the man and wrested his weapon from his belt.

Leveling the pistol at the man’s stricken face, he said, “Take us down to the jail. We are here for the prisoner Cenovio Osorio, El Liberador de Corazon del Mundo.”

He nodded his terrified face. “Yes, yes.”

“And, just in case there is a problem, I want you to look up there.” He pointed to the balcony walk above the gym. Plato was standing high above them with a bundle of dynamite in one hand and a Bic lighter in the other. He flicked the lighter, and a long orange flame hissed from it.

“*Si, si,* I understand. Down those stairs.”

“I know where the jail is, you bastard,” said José. “Half the people in these mountains know exactly where this jail is and what it feels like to be in it.”

Demetrio gripped the man by the neck of his uniform and followed him down the stairs to the stinking prison, lit by the naked bulbs that dangled from the high ceilings on long, twisted wires.

When they turned into the corridor, they saw the guard at the barred gate look up in surprise. They knew he did not have a weapon.

"Open the gate, you son-of-a-bitch!" José roared, brandishing the watch officer's pistol.

Their captive nodded his head. "They have dynamite! Do as they say."

"Ándale, ándale!" José said, his voice getting high-pitched with the tension.

Once the gate was open, they grabbed the jail guard and hustled him down to Cenovio's cell. He was waiting for them at the barred door, his bruised face bright with amazement.

The moment the door opened, he hurried through to make room for the cell's new occupants.

Clanging the door shut, José said, "I am going to wait up there and if I hear any screaming from you two, the dynamite is coming down those stairs. Do you believe me? Do you?!"

The two policemen inside the cell nodded.

Suddenly, a man in the cell next to Cenovio's stuck his hand out the bars, waving it for attention. "Hey! Hey! Take me with you."

José darted to the door and peered inside. "Hah! Fuck you, Dominguez. Everyone knows you belong right where you are, you thieving shit!"

The men turned and ran for the stairs, Demetrio leading the group and helping his brother, Cenovio. They had no choice but to run up onto the landing, praying to God that they would not be met with a barrage of bullets.

They saw only the pigeons coming to roost for the evening when the raiders flew out onto the court and past the unconscious guard. The whole rescue had taken just a few minutes, exactly as they'd planned.

There was something thrilling about their success, something larger than the almost unbearable excitement of the moment. They had planned the impossible and done the unthinkable. This was Mexico, and they knew they could not possibly escape the fury of the state. But all the same, the moment was sweet beyond measure. Corridos, those jubilant and bittersweet songs of the people, would surely be composed about this event. In the mountains and hills of this country, that was all the reward genuine heroes could expect. And certainly, immortality was enough. *¡Viva Mexico!*

MiT

Berto and Jesus were still not warming up to Tom. He tried to ingratiate himself with them at dinner, but they had been primarily polite, with little more. One thing had offered itself, however, when Berto had begun to chafe him a bit about being a rodeo cowboy when he was young.

"You don't ride in the rodeos anymore, then?"

"Nope. I'm too out of shape for that stuff, it's a young man's sport."

"You should give it a go, amigo. I am."

Tom looked at him blankly and said, "You're going to give what a go?"

"I'm going to ride a bull. I told you that I used to compete, didn't I?"

"I think I remember you saying something about it, yeah."

Berto beamed, his fifth beer glowing through the cocky smile. Tom knew he was being challenged in a small way. *Or maybe a small male way,* he thought—another little man with little-man problems. But he pushed the ungenerous thought aside. He had to get along with these guys, and he was a hell of a long way from home.

Berto continued, "I rode in the local rodeos that we have on feast days. I was damn good too." He took another drink of his beer, eyeing Tom as he drank.

"If you look around," he continued, "you'll see ads on the walls around town for a big feast day in a place called San Miguel Achiutla . . . rodeo, dance, cockfights, horse show, fireworks. Say, you think you'd like to get in a little bull riding during the feria? You said you only rode horses, but maybe you'd like to set your *cojones* down on a bull."

Tom winced mentally at the memories of hitting the ground, losing consciousness for a few moments, scrambling to his feet without really knowing if he was hurt or not, waiting for a flash of white-hot pain telling him that something was seriously wrong.

Yeah, if there was one thing from his youth that he did not miss, it was faking it until he got behind the chutes, then puking up his guts as the shock overtook him.

"Tell you what, Berto, you go ahead and ride. I'll be perfectly happy just watching you set your *cojones* down on a bull. As a matter of fact, I'd love to watch you do it."

"Ah, I don't want to have all the fun."

Tom grinned. "Go right ahead, I guess I'll just have to let you hog it all." He looked at his watch.

"I gotta go to a meeting," he said and stood.

Berto and Jesus looked at each other, and a cautious look passed between them.

"What kind of meeting?" Jesus asked.

"Oh, it's a fraternity I belong to."

"Fraternity?" Berto exclaimed. "Here in Mexico? You gotta be kidding, there's none of that frat rat crap down here."

Tom enjoyed the look of genuine puzzlement evident on both men's faces. "Trust me," he said, "I have brothers down here."

The walk to the building where he had seen the AA sign took only a few minutes. He was sure that Berto was following him, but he couldn't have given a rat's ass if the prick was.

He stood on the sidewalk outside the wooden door that opened onto the patio inside, where several rooms opened to the shrubs and fountain that decorated the interior. The strangeness of the surroundings was still intimidating him.

"Can I help you, Señor?"

Tom turned to see a man in a white shirt, tie, and dress pants standing behind him with a Big Book in his hand. Tom felt relief flood through him, and he said, "I'm looking for the meeting."

"You are in the right place, my friend. Come with me, my name is Juan Francisco Garcia." He put out his hand, and Tom took it.

"I'm Tom Thompson."

"And where are you from?"

"From Wyoming."

"In the United States, yes?"

"Yes."

"I think I know this place. It is very near the state of Idaho, yes?"

"Right next to it."

"I have friends from the federal government in Idaho, and they are coming down here sometimes to talk to us about *selvacultura* . . . I don't know how to say it in *ingles*."

"It's almost the same: silviculture. I have friends who work for the US Forest Service, so I know a little about it but not much."

They paused before an open door leading to a room where Tom could see a collective assortment of chairs in rows and a large placard on the wall with *Las 12 Tradiciones* printed in gothic script across the top. He could smell coffee brewing and cigarette smoke, so he felt right at home.

"That is very interesting, that you know of this *selvacultura*. We must have dinner together and talk. Please!" He gestured for Tom to enter the room.

When the meeting began, Tom felt more at ease because this was familiar. The rituals were almost identical: opening with a reading from the "24-Hour Book of Meditations," a reading of the "12 Steps" and "12 Traditions," then a choral recitation of the Serenity Prayer. The prayer gave him a very solid sense of who he was, and it was a blessing.

As the men around him began to share of themselves, Tom took a moment to give thanks for this place and the souls about him, a gift of understanding and acceptance. A few hours earlier, he had been full of fear, but now he was deep into a peace that always came to him when he did what was right for himself, and not what was right for others. First things first.

The understanding that there are no coincidences came to him again. Everything is exactly the way it is supposed to be, and the secret to serenity is to accept life exactly the way it comes, and when the student is ready, the teacher appears.

When it came his turn to share, José volunteered to translate, and Tom gladly accepted his offer. He wanted to share exactly what he was feeling and knew that only honesty about the way he felt led to the peace he needed if he was going to do be able to do his job.

He talked of his drinking history, beginning at seventeen and ending twenty-five years later when he started blacking out and engaging in bizarre behavior. He spoke of his anger and the violence that had become a big part of his life when he returned from his military service. At this point, almost all the men were nodding their heads in recognition.

Then he told them how it was now. He said that his life was still bothered by fear, but it seldom deteriorated into anger and never, so far, into violence. He described how it felt to be in a foreign country where the customs were obscure, and he didn't know what was going on around him. Without being specific, he described how confused he was about why he was here and what was appropriate behavior under the circumstances. He added that the fact that there was no phone service to the States made it hard because he needed to talk to his boss and family.

When he sat down next to Juan, the man asked him why he thought there was no phone service to the States.

"I went to three places, and all of them told me that there wasn't any," Tom explained.

Juan frowned. "That's not true. We have satellite service now, so there's always international service."

An alarm ran through Tom again. He now had more than a suspicion. The people who provided the service were instructed to lie to him, and he knew beyond a doubt who would have ordered it.

Juan patted Tom on the arm. "But that is alright, I have a phone in my office at the sawmill. You can use it after the meeting."

Thanking his new friend, Tom glanced around at the men in the room. Unlike him on the surface, but the same at their core. The understanding at the heart of his recovery came back to him. He was not alone; he was as common as bricks in a wall.

After the meeting, his new friend led Tom down the street that he'd walked that very afternoon. Smelling the familiar and comforting aromas of fresh heartwood, pine gums, and saps brought back memories from his adolescence and the wonderful times when he had worked at his grandfather's side, his thin muscles laboring against the weight of the heavy, sticky, aromatic wood.

"Do you only produce boards for construction of houses?" Tom asked.

"Right now, we are producing building material for a development company in Mexico City. They have ordered almost a million board feet of lumber for one of their projects just down the coast, at Huatulco, and we are one of the suppliers."

Tom waved at the mountains surrounding Tlaxiaco and said, "This must be national forest around here, then."

"Oh no. These are all *ejidital* lands here."

"*Ejidital?* What's that?"

"That means that it is owned by the communities organized into what is called *ejidos*. We buy trees from them, then harvest the wood with crews we hire from the communities."

"It is very expensive, then."

"Actually, the logs are quite cheap. It is the transportation that is expensive."

"If the logs are cheap, then the people must not be making very much money from the deal," Tom observed.

José shrugged. "A company in Mexico City makes the deals with the *ejidos*. And it is . . . brokered, I think is the word, by a local man."

"Then he is the one who makes the deal with Mexico City?"

"Yes," José said, and he made a face, "and most of the time he is taking advantage of the people." He shrugged. "But that is the way things are done here. The people do not trust the government, and they do not trust the *chilongos* in Mexico City. So they do business with a local man who is worse than the others. But they trust him more because he is a Mixteco. He is known down here as a cacique."

"It doesn't sound like the *ejido* people have much of a chance."

José shrugged again. "It is the way of the world. I am only a man who tries to turn trees into quality lumber. I leave politics to the corrupt."

When they reached the office, Tom saw massive ricks of wall studs piled about the lumberyard.

"You say there's over a million board feet here, and it's all for one project?"

"Yes. The Pacific coast of Oaxaca is . . . building a boom? How do you say?"

"There's a building boom."

"That is it . . . .A building boom."

"We've been having one of those in my town also," Tom said. "It's also a resort area, but in the mountains."

"In these mountains there is only poverty. The government and its investor friends are making a boom in Huatulco because it wants another Cancun to bring in tourist money. They are having very big plans down there."

Tom looked at the mountains of wood again and thought, *Huatulco? Why does that name sound so familiar*?

"Please." José was motioning to the open office door.

Once they were inside, the man dialed 0-9 for an international operator and gave the phone to Tom. Then she asked in perfect English for the number he was calling. He gave her the number of Sam's home phone and was relieved almost to tears when he heard the voice of Sam's daughter, Eleanor.

"Hi Ellie, this is Tom Thompson. Let me talk to your dad."

"It's good to hear from you, he has been really worried. He'll be glad to hear that you're all right."

That made Tom feel good, but it did not take long for that feeling to change when he heard the anxious note in Sam's voice when he took the phone.

"Tom! Where in the hell are you? Are you okay?"

"I'm in Tlaxiaco, and why shouldn't I be okay?"

"Sandez isn't who he says he is."

"I know, the Osorio guy told me. But how bad is it?"

"All I know is there's no one by that name working for the Mexican Attorney General down there. Failoni, the FBI guy, checked it out and the guy is bogus."

"I had an interview with the local chief of the regional police, and he seemed to treat these guys like real cops. But Osorio says they are the ones buying artifacts. They're smugglers for sure. He seemed to think they were federal cops."

"What guys?"

"Berto and another guy, last name Bernalillo. Jesus Bernalillo."

"How the hell do you spell that? H-a-y . . ."

"No, it's spelled like Jesus in the Bible."

"That's his name? *Jesus*?"

"Don't get upset, it's a traditional name down here—like Mohammed in the Middle East."

"Takes a hell of a lot of nerve, if you ask me. How do you spell the last name? I want to see if *this* guy's name comes up on the AG's list."

Tom gave him the spelling, then said, "You need to find out exactly what kind of cops these guys are." The question of the narcotics traffickers corrupting most cops in Mexico popped into his mind.

Sam said, "I'm going to get you some help as soon as possible. We'll get somebody down there ASAP, but in the meantime, play it their way."

"You sure know how to say the right things, Sam. You have just scared the shit right out of me."

"Just be cool. I'll phone Failoni right now and get things handled."

"Shit, Sam . . ."

"You'll be all right, just keep doing what you've been doing. You sound healthy enough. I'm thinking about coming down there myself."

"Bring some decent toilet paper."

There was a chuckle on the other end of the line—it made him even more uncomfortable than he was already.

"If it's of any interest, Osorio confessed to killing Ward," Tom said, "but there are a bunch of mitigating circumstances. And, whoever else these two assholes are, they were Ward's artifact suppliers here."

"Well, Ward's uncle still wants the guy, but that's not important right now, because an extradition is the last thing on my mind. I want to get you home safe before we worry about anything else."

"Thanks, Sam."

"Stay in touch."

"I'll try."

When Tom hung up the phone, the loneliness he'd been feeling before the meeting crowded back on him.

Juan and Tom walked outside, and as they were saying their goodbyes, Tom was suddenly aware of a commotion in the direction of the municipal center.

"What's all that noise about?" Tom asked.

"I don't know. It sounds as if it is coming from the *Municipio*."

"Let's go see."

"Señor Thompson, in this country one does not go toward those kinds of sounds. It could be very dangerous, and witnesses are never welcome."

"I'll be careful," Tom said. But he knew there was something about the sound of things falling apart that drew him like a bee to honey. Or a fly to blood.

Chapter Twenty-Three

When he reached the hotel, he saw Berto and Jesus jogging in the direction of the municipal building and caught up with them halfway down the street.

Every available police vehicle was being loaded with men, while what appeared to be civilian trucks were waiting to load other groups of police who stood with their rifles in hand about the square.

"What's going on?" Tom asked Berto.

"Some people broke your buddy out of jail."

"No shit? Was anyone hurt?"

"A couple had their heads rung, but that was all. The men were planning to blow the building, but something happened. This is some real serious shit. It could be Chiapas all over again." Berto referred to the native uprising that had taken place some years before in the neighboring state to the south, drawing international attention and *mucho* bad press.

Jesus pointed. "The sergeant who came for us is waving. Let's go down there and see what the hell is going on."

When they reached the entrance to the building, the sergeant told them that Comandante Ryan wanted to talk to them.

Once inside, the Comandante raised his eyebrows at Tom's presence but motioned them into chairs vacated by three of his staff. The deference made Tom wonder again. Who the hell are these guys, exactly?

Ryan began a torrent of Spanish directed at Berto and Jesus, which Tom could not follow for the most part. But the words *el*

Gobernador dice kept coming through: "the Governor says." He also picked out the names of two other Mexican states, Chiapas and Michoacán. The word repeated most often, however, sounded like Zapatistas.

Tom knew that Zapatista was the name for a myriad of subversive political organizations in the indigenous areas of southern Mexico. There were dozens of organizations whose acronyms included Z's for Zapata-EZLN, OOCEZ, and many others. He had seen graffiti by those names spray-painted on the walls of buildings in Oaxaca city and even here in Tlaxiaco. He had assumed they were typical expressions of toothless intellectuals all over the world. But it appeared those ideals had suddenly come to ground in this corner of the world, landing right in front of him. Recent unrest in Oaxaca City resulted in the deaths of schoolteachers who were members of the *Manzana* Union and could amplify that serious unrest.

Although he understood that the situation was serious, each time Emiliano Zapata's name came up, a picture of a cross-eyed Marlon Brando popped into Tom's mind, and it was distracting.

He concentrated hard enough to understand that they wanted to prevent a reprise of the upheaval in Chiapas when the Governor was kidnapped and his capture used as a major political card. Obviously, the new Governor wanted caution—demanding a sound assessment of the situation before he asked that federal troops be sent in. It was evident by the way the two law officers were invited into the situation's assessment that they were of one stripe or another.

Tom's assessment of the conversation was that Berto and Jesus were being briefed for an intelligence foray. Goose flesh crawled across his shoulders. When he was in the military, this had been his business, and a feeling of *dejá vu* gripped him.

There was also a surreal sense that came with the thought of something unthinkable in America until recently.

But today, genuine insurgents were readying themselves to have the heads of their oppressors. On the one hand, it seemed the stuff of B movies, but here he was, sitting in the middle of a planning session called to deal with what might be a genuine insurgency.

His paternal grandfather had been a US Marshal out of Fort Smith, Arkansas. There were family stories of him disappearing into Mexico for weeks or months at a time. Then he almost always returned with proof in the form of personal belongings such as pistols, rifles, or identification papers. The condition of gaining the reward *Dead or Alive* had genuine meaning when it came to stories of the real lawmen who led real lives in the real world back then.

Tom suddenly had the feeling that his presence in Mexico was pre-ordained. His Irish ancestors had been indentured servants who fled into the hills of Appalachia to escape their servitude. Then they fought the armies of the North as part of a peasant army. Insurgence ran in his bloodline as truly as his old hunger for alcohol—something else he had inherited from the same man with the gap-toothed grin and pearl-handled Colt who smiled from the family album.

Tom's attention returned to the room when Berto tapped him on the shoulder and beckoned for him to come with him and Jesus. More than a hundred police and soldiers mustered in groups outside. A familiar feeling swept over him, filling him with a sense as old as man.

Here were men gathered to hunt men. They were men galvanizing themselves for the ultimate experience, and he felt suddenly competent—fearless in the face of the unthinkable. He felt a sense of fraternity with these men and all the anxieties that had buzzed around his head for the last few days dissolved like wet Kleenex. He felt ready for anything.

Once they walked back into the lighted streets, the feelings began to wane. Tom had thought that his combative past had been buried. Now, he realized that the hunger to devour his enemies had only been lingering beneath the surface—a rage-filled creature as old as mud.

When they reached the porch of the Hotel Portal, Tom saw a group of people gathered there. Americans and they were looking down the street at the crowd of police and soldiers. Their faces were worried, and they defensively held their arms across their chests as they chattered back and forth.

Tom stepped out onto the hotel's front porch and bumped into a big man sporting a gray ponytail down to the middle of his back. Behind him stood a Hispanic guy and a blonde with exotic green eyes.

"Excuse me," said the man with the ponytail. "Can you tell us what's going on down there?"

"It's nothing for you to worry about. Some people broke into the jail and freed a local man. It's an issue for the police, but you don't have to be worried."

"Thanks, man, I appreciate it."

The guy turned to walk away when Tom recognized him from the restaurant in Oaxaca City where he and Berto had eaten dinner at the Cebolla and Ajo restaurant.

When Tom crossed the patio and pushed open Jesus's door, the man said, "Come in, now that you're already here, my rude gringo friend."

Tom said, "I was hoping that I don't have to be the turd in the punchbowl anymore. If there's no Osorio, there's no extradition, so I'm not going to be in the way. Can I get back on the team?"

Berto smiled and motioned for him to shut the door. "We forgive you, but you're still not on the first string." He turned to Bernalillo and added, "That's gringo talk for being competent."

Jesus smiled and said, "We need to make plans. Sit down and keep quiet so we can think this out."

The two lapsed into rapid Spanish so rapid that Tom had a hard time following what was said. And the old question came back: *Who the hell are these guys?*

MiT

In the village of Chalcatongo de las Cuevas, Patricio parked his pickup and turned off the lights. It was almost four o'clock in the morning.

His son Juan cradled his wounded hand as he went to the door of his great-uncle's house and knocked, then spoke quietly to the people inside. In the distance, the village's vigilante dogs barked as his father helped his brother Raul from the back of the truck.

The door to the house opened, and a tall man stepped outside. His silver hair shone, even in the smoky air, and he cradled a rifle.

"Is everyone safe?" he asked.

Juan answered, "My brother Raul has been wounded, ask Grandmother to get her medicines."

He turned and motioned to the people getting down from the back of the pickup. "And the rest of us need some water to drink, and we are hungry. The back roads are deep with dust and this smoke . . ." He waved his good hand at the stinking night.

"Mother!"

"I am not deaf," answered a woman's voice from inside. "Wake up Chano and get something from his tienda for something to eat and drink. Bring in Raul and let me look at him."

Once Patricio had helped his wounded son to the bed, he gave a handful of bills to Marcos and said, "Go for something for us to eat." When the young men were gone, Patricio said "Tio" and signaled for Concha to come to him.

"This is Concha Osorio Espinoza. She and her brother Cenovio are the ones who have returned the Heart of the World to us."

The tall old man nodded at Concha and said, "We have heard a great deal about you, Señora," he said, choosing the word for a senior woman.

Patricio said to Concha, "My uncle attends the dead kings of the Mixteca people, and he is the latest priest of a hundred generations, and more. He alone knows all the names of the kings and all their heirs, of which you are one."

Concha nodded. "They always laid the dead kings to rest in these caves That is why the town is called Chalcatongo of the Caves—the Caves of the Dead Kings. I have heard of this burial place of the Mixtec kings all my life, and know it is the most sacred place in all the Alta."

The uncle smiled, nodding to himself in the darkness. This woman had a good mind and an unusual appreciation for her people's history. He turned toward Patricio and his son.

"Bring me the Heart of the World," he said, "and let us take it to the cave of King Three Earthquake. Dzaui will be happy to know that it is being watched over by the spirits of the Mixtec kings, until it can be returned to its home beneath the pyramid of Achiutla. Tomorrow, if all goes well, we will take the Heart to its own home under the floor of the old convent in San Miguel. The feria will provide enough excitement that we should go unnoticed."

Concha suddenly remembered her brother and the other rescue mission from the jail in Tlaxiaco. "Do you know if my brother is safe?" she asked.

"Yes. All went well, no one was hurt, and they are up in the cave at this moment. We have heard, though, that there is a great deal of police activity in Tlaxiaco. One of my nieces has a phone business across the street from the Municipio—I have talked to her." His voice was concerned.

Concha asked, "They have not bothered our parents, have they?"

"No. Joséfina told me that the police have only gone to Santa Catarina and San Juan, but no closer. They are stopping all vehicles and searching them, but they have not descended on San Miguel and torn it apart as we feared."

"Where are the ones who went to the jail?" Patricio asked.

His uncle nodded his head up the mountain behind Chalcatongo. "In the Cave of the Wind."

"And all are safe, then?"

"Yes, although Socratio was thrown from the back of the truck when they hit a speed bump at the edge of Tlaxiaco. But it was more funny than serious. They are teasing him about it, but yes, by the grace of God, all are safe and back in the arms of their people."

He looked at Concha, and even in the dark, she could see the venerable old man's smile of approval.

"Now let us take the Heart to a safe place, to the cave of our ancestor kings."

Concha understood immediately she was being included in what was typically the business of the community patriarchs, and she was surprised by the immense respect she was being accorded. In her whole life, she had never heard of a woman receiving the deference she had experienced since her return home. It was something she did not understand, and she was becoming someone she did not recognize.

When Patricio returned from the pickup with the box, his uncle sucked his teeth in disapproval.

"You did not leave Him a hole!"

"What hole?"

"You must always cut a hole in the sack, or box, when you are moving these things—so He can see." His uncle put the box down on the table and opened its top. "There," he said with satisfaction, "that's better. Sometimes they are very ill-tempered, and that is not good."

"Who?" Concha asked innocently.

The older man looked displeased as if she should know better. "Why, the gods of course."

When Marcos and the driver returned, they ravenously ate a meal of tortillas, beans, sun-dried beef, and beer. Once finished eating, they began a slow climb up the mountain behind the hut until they reached hailing distance of a large cave with an enormous roof fall that hid most of its entrance.

"Socratio!" Patricio called.

"Yes! I see you," came the immediate answer.

"Don't shoot, it is Patricio and the others I have brought."

"*Pasale, Tio*. But I will shoot all the same if you have not brought us food. We are starving."

"Food, yes. And beer."

"How is it that there is any beer left? I would think that Juan and Raul alone would have taken care of it all!"

Socratio stepped from his sentry point and greeted each of them in turn as they entered the cave. His rough hand grasped even Concha's in the macho worker's thumb-grasp shake. It was, again, a surprising show of respect.

When they reached the large room behind the roof fall, the wounded brothers, Raul and Juan, went immediately to the back wall and lay down. They were injured but not bowed, still inspired by their success. Their wounds had been treated at a clinic in a small town where they stopped on their way back. They were not trivial ones, but it was not the first they had suffered, so they were taking them like the hard men they were. Not trusting the medico's work alone, they insisted that folk medicine also be applied by the famous *curandera* of Chalcatongo. Already, they both felt better.

The men in the cave fell upon the victuals like lions on their prey, drinking the beer with visible enjoyment. The fire cast the planes of their faces in bronze as they exchanged exciting stories about their successful raids against the state and the caciques. They crowed about finally drawing real blood through the seemingly invincible armor of the oppressors.

Concha went to her brother and knelt in front of him, tracing her fingers lightly over the lumps and cuts that deformed his face. He smiled shyly and said nothing, though his eyes filled with love and thanks for her touch and her loving tears.

He tore a tortilla in half and put it in his mouth, chewing carefully.

"You are safe," she said simply.

"And you."

"By the grace of God."

"Yes. And our things are here too. At last."

"Thanks to you. We did the easy part, to you fell the real burden." Her eyes searched his for the grief that had been there days before, but it was gone.

He smiled at her carefully, his heart reading hers. "I have been absolved."

"By the priest."

"By Jesus. I fell to my knees over there," he jerked his head toward the corner of the room, "and cried out for forgiveness. Suddenly I was filled with a sense of being loved. I knew then that it was all right, and I am at peace. I have prayed since then for your husband and his soul. Each time, I have had a awareness that it is well with him." He put his hand to her face. "And so, too, with you."

His touch lifted a great weight from her heart, one she had forgotten in all that had passed during the last two days. The burden of it all was gone—she had her gentle brother back.

"Concha."

She turned and saw Patricio and his venerable uncle beckoning to her.

"Go," her brother said.

"To where?"

"To the Cave of King Three Earthquake. I have heard them speaking of you, sister, and with much respect by these important men. Go."

In the dim, smoky light of dawn, Tio and Patricio led the way along a footpath that wound its way across the foot of the mountain. Patricio carried The Heart of the World, and Concha followed, her heart pounding. José followed, complaining the whole way, and helped by Marcos.

After a ten-minute climb, the group reached a vertical limestone escarpment. They followed the foot of the scarp for fifty meters or so, turned a corner, and stood at the mouth of a cave three meters wide and a little over a meter high. Stooping, they entered and walked to the heart of the mountain where an enormous room opened to them. Tio turned up the Coleman hand lantern he'd brought, carried it to a side of the cavern where a flat piece of roof fall sat. The limestone slab was perfectly shaped for an altar—as if purposely created for the task at hand.

Tio put the lantern down to light the top of the altar where someone had placed a piece of beautiful hand-loomed material on the stone. On each side of the material were three large beeswax candles, and in front were some small clay bowls. Patricio lit the candles.

The venerable man put a small bundle tied up in bleached homespun on the altar. He removed a peach, a plastic sack of black beans, and a tortilla. Two small bottles were opened, and Concha recognized the smells of *pulque* and *aguardiente*.

He poured the drinks into two bowls, put the beans in another, and added the tortillas. He reached into a jacket pocket and removed a *mamey* fruit, which he laid beside the peach.

"There," he said, satisfied. "He must be very hungry and thirsty by now." Patricio stepped forward, placed the box on the altar, then took out the Heart of the World and put the crystal on the center of the cloth.

"My brother José speaks your language, but I do not," he said to the eagle and the snake. Taking his cue, the poet stepped forward and removed his hat.

The crystal seemed to answer in semaphore as the candlelight pulsed in the cool currents that moved through the cavern. The rock crystal seemed almost to breathe in the apricot and lemon-colored light. The event transfixed Concha, and something touched her very deeply.

She stared at the eagle, which was posed with his head down and wings slightly spread. The work was delicately done, the artist's hand inspired enough that the feathers were realistic, but it was at the bottom of the piece that the sculpture lived.

The serpent that struggled to free itself from the eagle had wrapped itself around the eagle's legs. Its head was thrown up in defiance, poised to strike even though the grasp of the bird's talons had transfixed it.

That is my people, she thought. *One part of us is predatory and strong while the other is* listo, *clever and dangerous. The one part of us feeds on the other, even as that other part strikes back in defense of its life. And here we are, a thousand years after the artist's life is over, still struggling with our two hearts, always one against the other.*

And, at that moment, she realized that she and her people were the serpent in the talons of the eagle—born to be lowly but endlessly clever and dangerous. Here was their destiny, described for all time by the Mixtec artist from long ago whose own blood could possibly be mixed with her own. He knew then what she had come to know only in these last few moments—that the time to strike back had come and would surely come again as the obscure tide of her people ebbed and flowed through to the end of time.

The past two weeks had borne testimony to the continuing story of her and her people. Her gentle, heroic brother had recovered the rain god's heart at the cost of two tremendous and dangerous journeys and the lives of her husband and two other men. Then she and her brother had escaped captivity by the two of the most powerful members of Mexican society, the caciques and the police.

It was not over, she knew. The man she had shot, dead or not, must be atoned for. And the rescue of her brother, too, would have its price. But that was the story of her people—the eagle would always be stooping down upon them, but they would always be ready, *listo!* They might be gripped unto the brink of death, but they were ready to strike back once again. And to be willing was everything!

"Señora."

Concha turned her rapt attention away from the crystal and back to the cavern where Tio, Patricio, and José stood watching her.

"Concha, we must get back before it gets much more light. We never know who might be about, and all villages have their paid informants."

She nodded and then turned once more to gaze upon the eagle and the snake. The morning light warmed it, breathing lambency, and the crystal pulsed. The daylight from the entrance added shafts of white and pink to the yellow and apricot light of the candles. They danced with one another, twined, flew apart, melded, bloomed. It was the dance of life itself—everything and nothing, changing and unchanged.

Chapter Twenty-Four

In the morning's first light on the beach at Huatulco, the sun gave the ocean its first wash of color. The surf scored the shore with its regular beat, rasping at the sandy edge of the *Costa Chica* like a tireless artisan.

Polly was on the return leg of her morning run. Her light tread left perfect impressions of her feet in the sand just inside the wash of the surf. Pebbles of abraded shell and stone rolled up and down in the water, worn to grains small enough to form the matrix of the gracefully curved beach and fill her footprints.

As she jogged, she enjoyed the familiar smells of a life spent by the Pacific. Though this was the same environment where she had spent most of her life, her mind was in the mountains. Tom was somewhere north in the revolutionary Upper Mixteca while she ran on a beach in the modernizing Lower Mixteca. And while she was a part of the modernization, he mixed in with the old and dangerous.

She had learned about the area from a couple who worked on volunteer archaeological digs in Mexico and South America. On a map, they had shown her Tlaxiaco, the town Tom had mentioned. It was nearly ten hours by bus from Huatulco, but it did have a municipal landing strip, so a plane charter was possible.

She'd thought about taking a quick trip north, but it wasn't possible at the moment. The Mexican partners were a quasi-governmental corporation like many in the development business south of the border, and they were jockeying for a new position.

The instincts of Ferdie and Maria were to maximize their

business interests immediately with little or no eye for the long-term, so she couldn't leave at the moment. As much as she trusted Christina's business sense to temper the shorter visions of the other two, she was still too young to hold her own in a situation like this.

As her bare feet slapped lightly in the scrim of beach water, Polly felt a sense of uneasiness. But the business deal was not at the heart of her anxiety; it was Tom's penchant for living on the edge. He was in some kind of danger. She could feel it.

MiT

"Okay, Tomas, today you get to see my people having a good time." Berto pointed to a poster stuck on the wall of a shop near the *mercado*, the covered farmer's market where they had gone for morning coffee.

The coffee was sweetened in the pot, so there was no chance of getting it black. But it was good coffee, all the same, grown locally and called *Plumada de Oro*. Plumed in Gold.

"Look," Berto continued, puffed up like a Pouter pigeon, "rodeo, dancing, horse show, folk dancing, fireworks, and cockfights. You ever been to a cockfight?"

"No, can't say that I have. They're illegal as hell, though the Bascos over in Idaho still fight them, and the law there pretty much turns a blind eye to it. I've heard there's a fighting ring near Soda Springs, and that's not too far from Jackson."

"There's a lot to it, takes years to appreciate all the fine points."

"Some say it's a real cruel sport."

Berto grinned. "Life is cruel, Amigo. Especially down here in the Mexican mountains. We learn from the cocks—be fast, be brave, and have no mercy. The people who think it's cruel are only scared by it, and when the cruelties of life descend upon them, they don't fight because they don't know how. They're defeated by the smallest shit, and when things get really tough, they turn up their dainty toes and die a coward's death. But the cocks teach us where mortal competition can lead—*a la victoria*. To victory, even in defeat, man."

"So we can flap our wings and crow, even when our asses are on the ground."

"Even when our heart's blood is pumping on the ground."

"I guess it applies. I hope I never have to find out."

"You are right there. You better hope to hell you never have to see just how cruel it can get down here."

"I've seen a bit in my time."

"You mean your war?"

"Yes . . . Amigo."

"But there are no helicopters in these mountains. Down here we don't get to evacuate—we stand, and mostly die."

"Sounds more than a little melodramatic to me."

Berto grinned his infectious grin, accepting Tom's thrust with some grace.

"Well, I gotta admit, there's more than a little bit of melodrama down here too."

Tom stepped back from the wall till he could see the whole of a graffito spray-painted on the wall next to the poster. *Fuera al gobierno Fuera al PRI OOCEZ!*

He translated it to himself: Away with the government Away with PRI! He knew that PRI was a leading political party in the country, though there were others.

"What's OOCEZ stand for?" he asked.

Berto made a face, the one that signaled embarrassment. "It's a Zapatista organization. Buncha shitheads, schoolteachers, and other government employees mostly who think they're intellectuals but don't have one testicle in the bunch—just ten thousand cans of spray paint. We know who they are, and they're getting their butts kicked."

"The Zapatistas are the same ones who took over in Chiapas, aren't they?" Tom knew who they were, but he couldn't pass up the chance to make Berto squirm.

"Down there they were Indians, the real deal. They had guns and machetes, not spray cans. Hell, most of them don't know how to write, and they have real *cojones*."

"Wasn't that thing last night an Indian deal? Does that mean that it could really fall to shit here too?"

"Well, the poor people are sick and tired of being kicked around and shit on by every crooked dickhead with a government job or a little bit of money and influence. Who knows what could happen? It's one of the things we're going to try and find out when we get to San Miguel."

"Hmmm, that should be interesting," Tom said.

They were crossing the main plaza, and he could see a half dozen men hunched against the morning chill beneath their dirty serapes. They wore cheap straw cowboy hats, and their horny, black feet were bare to the cold in worn bull hide sandals. He knew that several times over the last 100 years, these same people had come down out of the hills in waves, shooting and slashing behind a peasant leader with little more than a great sense of what was right and just. It seemed implausible that things could come to that again. After all, this was a very modern society in most ways. Then again, last night, he had felt something in the air, something ponderous poised with a potential for great momentum. Even now, he could see glittering black eyes from under the ragged brims of the straw hats of the men on the south steps following him and Berto as they walked across the stones of the plaza.

"What time is Jesus going to get up today?" Tom asked, by way of a change of conversation.

Berto shook his head. "These *chilongos* lay in bed till noon, often as not."

"What's a *chilongo*?"

"People from the capitol—lazy bastards with too much money and social status."

"We call them rich skids in Jackson Hole—too much money and zero ambition."

"Same here. And the pity is, they set the course for everyone else. All the young people can't wait to get a government job so they can go to Mexico City, then do nothing but buy new clothes and strut, especially when they come back to their villages. *Famosos*."

"Hmmm, sounds too familiar."

Berto grinned again. "Some things are the same, no matter where you go."

Tom shrugged, "So, I guess we wait for Jesus before we go to the feria in San Miguel, huh?"

"Yeah, he's got the car. We got no choice, Amigo. He's in charge."

"Well, I guess that means I've got time to make a phone call to my son, then."

Berto's eyebrows rose. "I thought there was no international service."

"Oh, I found a guy here who lets me use his phone."

"Yeah? Who?"

"He's the manager of the sawmill up the street from the hotel."

"Oh? His name Garcia?"

"Yeah, José Something Garcia—Juan Francisco Garcia."

"Too bad about him."

"Too bad what?"

"He's in the hospital in Oaxaca City. They were talking about it in the market this morning, the women who cook the food."

An alarm went off down deep in Tom. Again.

"What happened?"

"Some Indians beat him almost to death last night. He even lost an eye. The police said the villagers had not been paid for their trees, plus the cutters took twice what the *ejido* had authorized.

"They said the local cacique, the guy who put the deal together, was selling the lumber to a gringo company with a bad reputation. I guess they are building a thousand condos on the coast and trying to buy up every tree in the mountains. The people say that they should be using cement, that to kill so many trees for seasonal houses is a crime against the earth itself."

Tom, who had just had a house built, knew how wasteful the construction trades were at home. Thousands and thousands of board feet were hauled to the Jackson Hole landfill and then burned at the regional dumpsite near Pinedale.

"It sounds like some people from the north have come down here with real wasteful habits."

Berto grimaced. "Same shit, different year."

Tom sighed. "Berto, listen. I know you think that we're a bunch of wasteful shits, and we are. I also know that you don't like anything about us, but I'm tired of hearing it, okay? I'm a gringo—so kill me!"

Tom expected the same old wry grin. Instead, Berto raised his hand, pointed a finger directly at Tom's forehead, cocked his thumb, and softly said, "Pow." After that came the grin, and the effect was genuinely frightening.

MiT

Pete, Oz, and Olga had a table for themselves in the Hotel Portal restaurant. The rest of the group filled all the other available chairs, and the one waitress appeared harried. She was not used to so many people so early in the day.

"Who are those guys?" Pete asked as he stared out the restaurant's door onto the plaza. He was watching Tom and Berto as they stood in front of a large graffito sprayed on a wall.

"I dunno," Oz said, taking a drink from his cup. "I talked to them for about two seconds last night, but they didn't give me their autobiographies. Good coffee, I need to see who the grower is—maybe do a little business while I'm here." His gaze followed Pete's out the door and watched the two men as they crossed the plaza toward the hotel. "You can find out from Santiago, the hotel clerk."

Olga looked at Oz and said, "What time do we leave for San Miguel?"

"The feria is always a bit slow getting started, so we won't miss anything if we're there by mid-afternoon. It's about an hour's drive from here, and the road is pretty bad between Santa Catarina and San Miguel, if you remember."

"I wasn't paying much attention last year, I guess."

"Too busy looking at the mountain and playing with yourself, probably."

Olga's mouth turned down. "It does have its own presence."

Pete turned his attention to the conversation. "What mountain?"

"Nindo Tocosho," Oz explained. "On its summit is the old observatory of the Mixtec astronomers/astrologers. It has been a place of celestial observation and ritual for at least a thousand years. They have carbon-dated fire scars, evidence of community ritual, to that date. But smaller pieces of evidence indicate that the site may have been used even longer than that."

"And still in use," Olga said with a bit of wonder in her voice. "Beautiful."

Pete said, "I take it that's the place we are going for the solstice gig."

"Yes," Olga said, "though it is used for other occasions too, like the spring fertility ritual." Olga's eyes seemed to dilate as Pete looked at them, and, at the same moment, he felt her hot hand on his thigh. The woman was insatiable.

Pete broke the gaze and turned his head in time to see Oz taking in the exchange. The look was cool, appraising.

The man dropped his eyes, took a big mouthful of the coffee, and held it in his mouth for a moment before swallowing. Pete saw in that action what a sensualist the man was. He'd already known it, but he was always impressed with the man's capacity to explore everything that came into his orbit with every one of his senses available to the moment.

Then, in a small moment of clarity, his mind went back to the apartment in Berkeley and the stoned girl he'd seen there. Oz's daughter. Pete glanced at the man's sensual face, his delicate grip on the coffee cup and watched his nostrils flare to inhale all the aroma possible from the hot coffee. And he suddenly understood the man's relationship with the girl.

Even that, Pete marveled, *this guy has enjoyed his own flesh. No,* he added to himself, *especially his own flesh.*

"Pete." Olga's voice cut into his little epiphany.

"Yeah?"

"There's a man here who buys premier handwork from the natives. I always go to see what he has available; do you want to come?"

"Sure. Why not?"

She smiled and nodded. "Good. I think you'll like the things you see. They are exquisitely made, and the colors . . ."

"First, I want to talk to Santiago. I want to know who those guys are." Pete got up from the table and walked to the hotel desk.

"Santiago?"

"¿Mande?"

"The men in rooms 10 and 11?"

"Yes?"

"Who are they?"

"They are policemen."

"The gringo is an American?"

"Yes, an American. I can let you see the hotel register, if you like."

"Please."

The man reached under the counter and retrieved the register from its place.

"There." He placed his finger on an entry and ran it down the next two.

Jesus Maria Bernalillo Morena
Lista Correos
Servicio Postal Centro
Oaxaca Oax

Rigoberto Sandez Sanchez
Lista Correos
Servicio Postal Centro
Oaxaca Oax

Thomas Eugene Thompson
P.O. Box 4563
Jackson, Wyoming USA

Two anonymous general delivery addresses and one P.O. box. They were cops, all right.

Hmmm. I wonder what this Thompson is working on. Drugs? It had to be. Oaxacan smoke is famous for its quality, and the nearby

"Little Coast" was a notorious offloading place for South American cocaine destined for transshipment to the States. But a Wyoming address? Hell, the only things in Wyoming were sagebrush, rednecks, and Yellowstone Park.

Pete had once made the mistake of hitchhiking through the state in his '70s hippie period. The whole damn state had been swarming with huge volunteer barbers with hot eyes, beer breath, and bottom lips bulging with Copenhagen snuff tobacco. They'd made his life hell all the way down the seemingly endless highway that crossed the southern part of the state.

"Muchas gracias," Pete said and placed a five-dollar bill on the counter for the man.

"And thank you very much, Señor Villareal."

Pete went back to the restaurant where the waitress was just serving their table.

"Find out who they are?" Oz asked.

"Fucking cops. I had a feeling that's what they were."

Oz put a small bite of omelet in his mouth and chewed carefully, his eyes on Pete the whole while. "Cops," he said, "what kind of cops?"

"I don't have the foggiest. Working the dope scene, probably."

"Well, all that has nothing to do with us. We are here in the interests of something universal, something larger than this . . ." he waved his fork at the window " . . . poor world and its quotidian affairs."

He poised another bite on his fork and said, "Pedro, this is going to be the experience of your life, my man. The experience of your life, and that's a promise."

Chapter Twenty-Five

In the Cave of the Wind, with its view of the valley and road below, Patricio looked at the people arrayed before him: José and his sons Socratio and Plato, his own sons Juan and Raul, Cenovio and Demetrio Osorio, Marcos Albino, and Concha, plus the two drivers.

With the exception of his sons, seasoned by action against the Mexican and American DEA, they were a ragtag, fortunate bunch of amateurs who had pulled off two raids on twin citadels of the Mexican establishment.

Where Patricio saw amateurs, José the poet and politician saw heroes whom he would celebrate in verse and song. José saw in them as brave people who had accomplished something never heard of in Oaxaca in many years, not since the state had put down the Triqui Combat and Unification Movement through the assassination of their leaders.

Or twenty years earlier, when the same had happened to Francisco Medrano, martyred by the soldiery. And before him, Ruben Jaramillo, who rode with Zapata himself. Pictures of him riding with Zapata through the streets of Tlaxiaco hung in many houses of that town.

These people standing before him would be the new heroes of Oaxaca's long resistance to tyranny. But, hopefully, they would not be more in the same long line of martyrs. And that included him!

Patricio stepped aside and let his brother take his place before the motley little group who were about to become national figures.

But José was not here to raise the name of Zapata only before these few. He was here to again raise the name of Zapata before the whole world, for to raise the fiery name of Zapata before the state beckoned the wrath of the state, and they could all be consumed in the fires of retribution. He knew these things well, having been a political organizer for the PRI for more than forty years.

What José saw was an opportunity to raise him out of the shit and into a position of true power using these heroes—and maybe-martyrs.

Here, with the successes of these few young people, José stood in a position of possible negotiation, virtually face-to-face and on equal terms, with the most powerful men of the country. Men who knew how to play the game as it had been played since the birth of the party in 1929, using the strategy of "compromise and corrupt."

He had a strategy: If the state thought that there was any possibility that a fervid populist sentiment was afoot locally, they would first consider force. If that were not a realistic option, then historically, the approach would be to negotiate while feeling out the strength of the opposition, and then, if the sentiment was weak, destroy the dissident parties.

However, if the sentiment appeared strong and organized, then the strategy would be to shower the dissident leaders with money in order to co-opt them by pulling them into the mainstream. Then the investment might be withdrawn and allocated elsewhere, leaving the original constituency back in the shit—unless a man made himself very useful.

But one had to use caution. The balance would be delicate—one would have to convince the government, and its military arm, that this tiny group represented a constituency influential enough to have to be acknowledged. Once they were acknowledged publicly, the money would surely follow.

José put his political strategies aside for the moment. First things first.

"Today begins the feria in San Miguel." He looked at the people and smiled. "We are obligated to honor our patron saint, but we are also obligated to share our successes with the people of our pueblo. They will want to see us there.

"The Heart of the World must be re-installed beneath the *Convento*, so Dzaui is appeased, making way for the rain clouds to return. But we must be careful. The police are stationed on all roads leading into San Miguel, stopping all traffic and asking questions. This is not an insurmountable problem. There are many, many vehicles going to the feria, and we can disperse ourselves among them in order to go undetected.

"But, let me remind you, we must use caution. Some of us are armed, but we must use force to defend ourselves only if our lives are obviously in jeopardy." He looked directly at the hotheads and chance-takers, Demetrio and Marcos, Juan and Raul. "Only," he emphasized, "in . . . defense . . . of . . . our . . . lives."

MiT

When Jesus, Berto, and Tom reached the police checkpoint, Jesus pulled over, and the three men got out. The lieutenant in charge had been in the comandante's office the night before and recognized them.

Tom listened while Jesus told the officer that they were going to the feria. Ostensibly to take part in the fun, but he said they would be looking for the Osorios as well as gaining intelligence on the *rebeldes*. Jesus claimed to have some informants in the village, ones that he could count on.

Rebels! Tom thought. *This is a little bigger than a jailbreak. And why aren't these people down in the village itself, establishing a strong presence?*

He listened carefully, trying hard to get the gist of the conversation. He was surprised to learn that two elite army units bivouacked a few miles away, waiting for orders. Also, a man from the Governor's office and some local officials had gone into San Miguel to contact the rebels.

Apparently, there had been another coordinated raid made at another Oaxacan town. That pointed to strong leadership, and this was a serious worry. The political current set in motion in the neighboring state of Chiapas and with the Apple union in Oaxaca City was lapping at the mountains of Oaxaca. They did not want it to turn into anything more than a gentle movement, given the history of indigenous unrest in this large state. There was a real need for caution.

Hell, this is serious, Tom thought. He remembered his days gathering intelligence in the *villes* of South Vietnam, and an all too familiar dread came over him.

Once back in the car, he asked Jesus, "What was that about two incidents?"

"Concha Osorio again. She led a raid on the most powerful cacique in the area. Apparently robbed him of a great deal of money, killed one man, and wounded some others."

"You're shitting me."

"Nah," Berto joined in. "Apparently this woman was trained in the States. That's what everyone thinks."

"And trained by the CIA, I suppose." Tom said sarcastically. The silence that followed gave him his answer.

Fuck me dead! he exclaimed to himself. The paranoia about one small agency of an enormous intelligence bureaucracy was unbelievable. Especially when many others in the intelligence community considered CIA to be the acronym for "Caught In the Act."

"Trained killer, huh?" Tom interjected with a sneer. He could not help himself; the thought was ludicrous.

"Mr. Thompson." Jesus turned a very cool eye on Tom. "Several eyewitnesses confirm that this woman took a combat stance and fired one round that hit a running man in the heart and killed him instantly. She led a raid on a very secure compound to rob a great deal of money and some priceless art objects, then escaped after also wounding a very important man and his bodyguard. Does that sound like an untrained amateur?"

"I have to admit that it doesn't sound like it, but to give the CIA the credit for her training . . ."

"And why *not* the CIA?" Jesus aske, angrily.

"Because you people give them too much credit, that's why!" Tom answered. "Hell, why not blame the FTD?"

"The flower delivery company?" Berto asked, genuinely puzzled.

"No! The Foreign Technology Division."

"Who's that?"

"Another member of the American intelligence community—and one that never gets any credit."

Jesus glanced at Tom again. This time there was more than hostility in his eyes—there was real paranoia. "You sure seem to know a lot about this kind of stuff."

Tom groaned aloud. "I give up; I fucking give up." It was hopeless. "Where's the damn rodeo grounds?" he asked. "I want to be someplace where I understand what's really going on."

MiT

At a roadblock outside Santa Catarina, two vans of Jaguar Travelers were unprepared for the police's thorough inspection of the vehicle, and the somewhat lengthy process of examining everyone's passports and visas. They could not recognize it for what it was—an outbreak of CIA Fever.

Once through the checkpoint, the ride into San Miguel

deteriorated the nearer they came to the town. In the distance to the east, they saw a range of wooded mountains nearing ten thousand feet, home to one of the few remaining virgin oak forests in the state.

The centerpiece of the range was Nindo Tocoshu, home of the locally worshipped spirits and the ancient celestial observatory site. Home, too, of the clandestine rituals that took place on the solstices each year. A place where a select few gathered to engage in one of the most powerful relict rites on the face of the earth—the propitiation of the sun and His wedding with the moon.

"There it is," Oz said, pointing. "That's the place, the summit of that tallest peak." He pointed to a wide spot in the road. "Pull over there," he told the driver.

Once the two groups gathered outside the vans, he said, "That is the mountain Nindo Tocoshu. If you look carefully, you see where a road has been built up to the pass under the peak. From there, we have to walk to the site of the observatory. The walk is quite steep in places and takes over an hour. That's why everyone who makes this journey had to prove them to be as physically fit as they are spiritually fit. The way is rigorous, in more ways than one."

For some reason, Oz chose the moment to stare at Pete. It was disconcerting, as the gaze of the whole group also seemed to be turned toward him.

Then Oz called their attention back to the beautiful, though smoky, valley below.

"There you can see the beautiful sixteenth-century Dominican convent perched on that point of land. If you look carefully, you will see the ruin of a chapel across the road. Above that ruin is a large unexcavated pyramid, one of the most important artifacts of the ancient Mixtec kingdom. It is several times the size of the excavated pyramids we visited at Tamazulapan and Huamelulpan."

An appreciative murmur came from the group.

"The fires seem to have died down quite a bit," Oz observed. "But it is still quite smoky. We will stop at the convent when we go by and take a brief walk to the pyramid so you can see it clearly. The place is the center of a great deal of spiritual energy, and you will feel it when you are there. There are also tales of secret grottoes beneath the convent, places where gold and other things are hidden. When the road was built, another rumor goes, the engineer in charge shut the job down for two days when a machine opened a tomb at the foot of the pyramid. The local people say that he carried away a lot of gold objects, as well as many things made of jade and other semiprecious materials. The story is very likely true."

Olga took the moment to add, "This whole valley is a vortex of great power." And, almost as if intended to underline her observation, the ground beneath their feet lurched and then trembled.

Pete's stomach pitched, and he saw from some of the others' white faces that they'd been affected in the same way. The whole group was from California, and it was something that excited more than a little reflexive fear in natives of that state. Except for Olga and Oz. Pete caught a look exchanged between the two, even as the earth shuddered beneath their feet. It was a look of excitement, a glance of sexual excitement, even. *Obviously,* he thought, *these two were into very big things.*

MiT

Concha was sick to her stomach, and her bowels felt loose, but it was not from anything she had eaten or drank. It was prompted by gut-wrenching fear. They were at a police checkpoint, and some cops were nearing the pickup she had hitched a ride on. There had been a dozen vehicles waiting when the truck she was riding arrived. Now it was their turn, and her mind was running wild.

A sergeant approached the driver while two soldiers beckoned the passengers to get out. Concha's mind flashed back to the events in Culiacan, not that long before, and in her mind's eye, she saw the officer's severed neck jetting dark blood onto the pavement in powerful squirts as the young heart emptied itself. She felt sick at the vivid memory of the hot, dark blood on the hot, dark asphalt.

"What is your name, Señorita?"

Concha managed to say, "Leonora Carmona Velasquez."

"Where are you from?"

"Chilapa de Diaz."

"Oh, really? Do you know my cousin Guillermina Garcia Martinez? She's from there, too!"

Concha looked at the man's eyes, and they had a foxy look.

"No. There is no one in Chilapa by that name."

The man waved his hand and said, "Pasale," motioning her to the other side of the blockade.

Her legs shook as she waited for the others to be questioned. A soldier looked her way, and she smiled. He smiled too, and for a moment, she was afraid he would mistake the smile for an invitation to make small talk. But he turned back to the business at hand.

The truck was finally allowed to reload its passengers, and they continued toward San Miguel. Not until they were far past the barricade did Concha lean over the tailgate and vomit into the white dust that billowed behind the truck.

Chapter Twenty-Six

San Miguel Achiutla had a population of two thousand, but up to five thousand people pushed through the streets during the feria. Some were visiting their home village, others were just tourists, but all were drinking, betting, dancing to multiple bands, and shouting over the noise of firecrackers and street musicians.

Tom loved it. The Fourth of July celebration in Jackson Hole had the same feel, but this was the real deal. There was an enormous sense of celebration, and it reminded him of the Tet holiday in 'Nam. Men in peasant clothes and masks grabbed well-dressed women and danced them along the streets while their normally deadly-jealous husbands smiled. Brass bands seemed to be under every other tree, and the sweating men turned music and alcohol into products best fit for the sensibilities of an auto body repairman or blacksmith.

Obviously, this fair was famous and popular. Tom asked Berto about all the cars and pickups with California, Oregon, and Idaho plates, and he reminded Tom of the Mixtec colonies that had flowered in those places over the last twenty years. More than half the men from the village spent most of the year in the north, returning at this time in an annual migration.

Earlier, a guy who'd noted Tom's cowboy boots had approached him and asked where he was from. When told Jackson Hole, Wyoming, the man had said, "Really? I work sugar beets near Rexburg, Idaho! Hell, man, we're almost neighbors." It made Tom feel a bit less of a foreigner.

"Here we are, Tomas," Berto said as they entered the patio of the elementary school. "San Miguel is famous for its fighting cocks; they've been breeding champions here for over two hundred years."

Three cockpits had been set up, and the place was a madhouse. Men were shouting, cursing, drinking, and laughing. And big money was being passed between men in bundles half an inch thick, accompanied by grim looks and fervent curses directed at the shamefaced handlers of the defeated cock.

"You stupid bastards!" Tom heard one say, "You just cost me six months of working like a dog! You and that fucking duck you passed off as a fighting rooster!"

The angry man pushed his way past Tom and Berto and went to a stand where several rows of hollow canes, about four inches tall, were displayed. The man picked up three of them in quick succession and drained them into his mouth.

"What's that?" Tom asked.

"*Caña*—sugar cane brandy. It'll put your dick in the dirt."

"The man is not happy," Tom observed dryly.

"No, but that man is." Berto pointed his chin at the jubilant recipient of the angry man's wad of bills. He was taking money from another dozen men who were waiting to give up their hard-won money as well.

"He musta bet the underdog," Tom said.

"Yeah. Some days it's chickens, some days it's feathers. But he'll be damn lucky if he leaves here with much of it."

"Some things are the same, no matter where you go."

"I've heard that before. Maybe because you keep saying it."

"Screw you, Berto."

"That's more like it, Compadre." The old grin.

"The heck with a bunch of chickens, where are the bulls?"

"Nah, nah. C'mon, let's go watch the fights. You'll get a kick out of it once you get some idea of what's really going on."

As they pushed their way toward the cockpits, Tom asked, "Where did Jesus disappear to?"

"He's looking for a local who gives him his information. After all, we're here on business, right?"

"If you say so."

A hundred yards away, Jaguar Travelers arrived in San Miguel. The vans parked beneath a large tree, and Oz gathered his group for a lecture.

"Okay, this is what's going on." He raised his voice to be heard above all the brass bands and competing PA systems down in the village.

"This is the celebration of the Catholic patron saint's day. Normally the Feast of Saint Michael is held in September, but the old solstice festival was never really superseded. Due to its ancient importance as an art and religious center as well as the money its men bring back from the north, San Miguel can afford to have one of the largest fairs in the Mixtec Alta.

"Because of the syncretism of Catholicism with some aspects of the ancient animistic belief, you will see a mix here of both religions. However, what makes San Miguel different is that it still has a very strong tradition of practicing the pre-Hispanic rites of the Cloud People. Select village elders, who may also hold responsible positions in the *ejido* and the church, maintain the ancient traditions. They have a mostly secret society, The Society of the Souls of the Ancients. It is responsible for maintaining the traditions pretty much the same way they were practiced in pre-colonial times.

"These practices are pagan in the extreme and were not acceptable to many of the Catholic priests, though it is impossible to think they know nothing about them. Things have changed a lot since the Vatican realized, about twenty-five years ago, that accommodation to native religions was necessary because it would smooth things with the natives. However, the Pope also realized that there were very real universal values intrinsic to native religions that Catholicism shared. However, some serious resistance from the local Catholic priests persists, but there is no church in San Miguel proper, so it's moot here."

Pete broke in with a question. "So what remains about the local religion that is so objectionable to the priests?"

Again he felt swamped by the unanimous look of disapproval from the group, and this time, it was accompanied by a pinch from Olga.

"Sorry," he apologized.

Oz went on. "We, Olga and myself, have been blessed by the fact that Olga's parents were the first resident anthropologists in San Miguel. That was in the early 1950s when the place was accessible only by horse or mule. They spent many years here, and became a part of the village's cultural fabric, so to speak. They were the first outsiders to ever become acquainted with the unbroken traditional continuum maintained by the Society."

Pete wanted to know what the unbroken continuum was, in this context, but he thought he'd keep his mouth shut and ask Olga later.

"Now," Oz said, wiping his forehead of the smoke-grimed sweat, "go ahead and enjoy yourselves. There are lots to see and record. Look for the things that represent the mixture of pagan and Catholic belief, like the maskers. Enjoy yourselves. Tomorrow is the solstice, and we will be readying ourselves for the events by fasting and washing. This is your chance to enjoy the world and its earthly manifestations before we purify ourselves of its influences and begin the cycle again, in synchrony with the infinite."

As the group broke up, Pete had some questions for Olga, but she said, "I have to go with Padrito. We are meeting with our spirit guide, the shaman of the Society. Enjoy yourself. I'll find you when we are through." And the two of them walked into the surging crowd that filled the dusty, noisy street.

Concha's parents' house was on the north side of San Miguel, in the forest above the *barranca*. The raiders met on the opposite side of the town because all knew that the elder Osorios would be under scrutiny, if not by the police, then surely by informants. It was important that their children not be caught. But it was more important that the rituals were observed as soon as possible, and the rain god returned to the home grotto from which Demetrio and Marcos had stolen him. The shaking of the ground that morning, with the lingering and pungent smell of recent fires, served to remind them that the sooner the re-installment rite took place, the better.

It was the sight of the withered corn and bean fields that supported both the life of their community and inspired them. Dzaui must be mollified; the rains must be summoned. The loss of their physical lives meant nothing compared to breaking the eternal cycle of rain, sun, and the produce of the *Milpitas*.

Concha stood beside the Milpitas of Señora Anna Laura de la Rosa—gray stubs of stalk and crumbling furrows instead of green corn and moist clods turned by the good and placid oxen.

Shading her eyes, she looked at the sky, cloudless still, even though Dzaui's heart was nearing its home. The big bowl above her head was a hot, washed out, old denim blue instead of roiling with the towering thunderheads that typified a late June sky in the Mixteca Alta. And were they not known as the Cloud People?

She turned her gaze to the west, to the pyramid and its sister Dominican convent. Her eyes followed the hill's contour down to where the little stonework dam lay hidden at the foot. Beside the green pool behind the dam lay the hidden entrance to the grotto.

It was in that cave that the re-installation would take place this afternoon. At the moment, the men were inside the house putting on their clothes and masks for their trip through the crowded village with the sacred bundle.

A quarter-mile away, Tom and Berto stood under a dusty tree. Tom sipped from a bottle of cold orange Mirinda as he thought about the cockfight he had just witnessed. Something about it had touched him in a very powerful way.

Initially, he was surprised by the frenzy of the fighting roosters. The slashing of the little curved steel spurs sent blood flying for meters out into the crowd, spattering faces and clothes with the fine red spray. The loud flapping, the slashing, the triumphant crows of the victors, the frantic exertions of the handlers, the screaming of the crowd, and the ebb and flow of money had been exciting, and there had been a palpable feel of antic death.

That had been expected. After all, he wasn't completely ignorant of what made up the sport. What moved him to the core had been the actions of one particular cock that had ostensibly been defeated in every sense of the word. His chest had been pierced by a cruel spur, with powerful jets of reddest heart's blood had shot onto the hard-packed dirt of the pit.

Tom was close enough to the ring to see the eye of the dying cock. It was golden, hard as amber, fixed on his crowing and wing-flapping triumphant foe. Tom had seen in it a final summoning of absolutely every mote of will left to the dying bird. He saw the eye pulse and glow with the gathering of all that was left, draining the very sheen of his luminescent feathers to aim a last kick, one that drove a steel spur into the femoral artery of the crowing victor. At the moment of the piercing, Tom saw the pupils of the prostrate cock's eyes dilate and his body go limp.

The victor staggered, his wings drooped, his head cocked in disbelief as he turned an eye down and saw his spurting ruin. A croak escaped his throat, and he fell on his side, dying of shock, even as his frantic owner gathered him from the floor of the ring and placed his mouth over the rooster's beak in an effort to breathe life into the slack body.

A great confusion arose from the crowd of sweating, screaming men. Money given up moments before was snatched back. Fists flew, and bodies thumped to the ground. Knives flashed, but the hotheads were pulled back from their intended victims by strong hands and cooler heads. The men who had been targets moments before bared their chests and shook their money in the faces of the would-be knifers. Tom was glad to get the hell out of the melee, and fast. He knew everything he needed to know about being stabbed.

Standing in the shade with a cold soda in his hand, he could not relieve his mind of the golden eye of the dying cock. Barely alive, but still hard in a way that transcended life itself, it was a concentration of the will, the likes of which he had not witnessed since the war. Something long buried in him was resurrected in that moment. It was the memory of the will to never, ever give up.

When Oz and Olga walked away, Pete decided to brave the crowd alone. He had met everyone in the group by now, and, without exception, none were his type. Not only that, they made him uneasy. There was something about each of them that made him feel creepy. These were not daffy astrological types or the intellectuals who still followed the teachings of mystics like Gurdeev or the Maharishi—the usual run of Bay Area goofs. Doctrinaire did not describe them either, but there was something inflexible about them that he couldn't put his finger on. Maybe it was the icicles up their asses.

Thirsty, he stepped into the shade of a small storefront and bought a bottle of cold beer. The hot and dusty, smoky air in the winding main street had dried his throat.

He was leaning in the broad doorway when three men in peasant homespun, wearing palm hats and old wooden masks, jumped into the store. One threw a little bunch of firecrackers at his feet, and they burst with ear-splitting pops, throwing paper bits and acrid smoke into the shop.

Another of the men leaned toward Pete to display a small magazine conspiratorially. Pete glanced at it and saw a picture of two men engaged in anal sex.

The clown in the mask gestured at Pete's long hair and trade bead necklace then pointed to the picture. It was a very pointed insult to his manhood, and for a moment, his temper flared. Then he remembered stories his grandmother had told him of old traditions still practiced in Mexico. These clowns played a very old role, originating in pre-Christian celebrations that survived into the modern world. These were the levelers, the busters of inflated egos and pomposities, and it was a brave bureaucrat or popular figure who ventured to a feria where he was known. The maskers descended on them like African bees, intent on filling their hide full of stingers.

Pete decided instantly to join the fun, so he put down the bottle of beer and made a gesture as if to grab the masked man and kiss him. The man stepped back; his fingers flew to his face in a coy pantomime and then shook a hand in an emphatic *No, no*. However, another of the three clowns turned, dropped his pants, and spread his buttocks to show his stained anus.

The other onlookers in the shop gasped and made exclamations. The women averted their eyes as the men, Pete included, roared in amusement at the daring of the clown. The three maskers then waved goodbye and, miming romantic farewells at Pete, disappeared into the crowd. Grinning, Pete paid for his drink and stepped down to join the river of flesh and noise.

The maskers, Juan, Raul, and Plato, joined Socratio in the street, where he stood with a bundle slung over his shoulder. The wooden masks were hot, almost suffocating with the dust and late June heat, to say nothing of the ambient smoke. A large fire had flared on a flank of Nindo Tocoshu, and the smoke was drifting down on the surging, noisy village.

"Did you see that gringo's face when I shoved that picture in his face?" Juan said.

"What did he do when I showed him my asshole?" Raul asked.

"He was pretty good about it, just grinned. But you should have seen the women, they almost fainted. It was great!"

"Let's work our way down behind the clinic and toward the river. This mask is suffocating me, and my side is hurting like hell."

Juan lit a string of firecrackers and threw it behind an older man who was lurching drunkenly through the crowd. At the beginning of the sharp little explosions, he picked up his heels and danced crazily, knocking about well-dressed men and women. For a moment, they were annoyed, but once they got a good look at the terrified and dancing old geezer with the silver stubble and dirty sombrero, they pointed and roared. "¡*Viva Mexico*!"

The four men in the masks jigged and made obscene gestures and returned obscene retorts with even more obscene mimicry. Socratio joined his index fingers and thumbs together in a triangle, flexing them between his legs into a clear representation of a large vagina to insult a large, elegant woman dressed in silk and adorned with gold jewelry. She shrieked in outrage and made a grab for Socratio, her face contorted in rage as her husband collapsed against a nearby wall, tears of laughter coursing down his face.

After a dozen minutes, Pete found an eddy in the river of bodies, and he stepped into a small side plaza with a large wooden corral set up in it, people crowded around its circumference. Pete edged his way through the crowd and saw a man getting ready to ride a bull.

The animal stood braced at the far side of the round enclosure, two men holding its head by the horns, and its face and eyes were covered tightly with a large piece of cloth while another man held its tail. A rope circled the animal just behind its front legs, the rope wound tightly in a double strand, and the mounted man's hands forced between it and the angry, quivering bull. At a nod from the rider, the men shook the rag loose and freed the animal's tail.

Pete had seen American rodeos and was somewhat familiar with the sport. But this was quite different in detail. But the result was universal, and as usual, the bull won. The intense, stocky little Indian rider made it halfway across the arena then found himself sticking out at a quickly widening angle. And at an increasingly sickening speed as the merciless laws of physics, and rodeo, overwhelmed his strength and skill.

The sight of the man trying to loosen his hands from under the tightly twisted rope, his bulging eyes considering his impending trajectory, sent a pulse of empathy through Pete. Empathy turned to concern at the moment of impact as the rider was thrown to the ground with a resounding *thump*! and an aurora of dirt and dung flew into the air.

"Fuck me!" Pete heard a nearby gringo voice exclaim.

He turned his head and recognized the guy from the plaza the day before, the Wyoming cop.

"That looked like it hurt," Pete said to the guy.

The tall, stocky man with bright blue eyes grinned and shook his head. "It had to hurt. There were a lot of rocks out there, and I tried to tell him be real careful."

"You know the guy?"

"Yeah, he's kind of a partner of mine."

Pete looked again. The rider was being helped from the arena; his hair was hanging down onto his grimacing face. It was the man that Thompson had been walking with in the plaza. Another cop, but a Mexican.

"Rodeo riders, huh?"

"Not me, anymore. And not him anymore, either."

"Not the same as Wyoming, is it?" Pete said and was amused at Thompson's wary reaction.

He didn't say anything, just turned to stare at Pete, with his thumb hooked under the strap of a small daypack where, Pete was sure, the man carried his sidearm. The man's eyes had turned an icy blue.

"Relax," Pete said, "I just did a little detective work back at the hotel in Tlaxiaco. I'm Pete Villareal with the PD in Berkeley, California, and I'm working undercover. Don't blow it for me."

The man's eyes warmed only a fraction. He didn't like being found out, and Pete could empathize with being in the same situation. It made a man feel exposed and vulnerable—and that was the last thing any cop wanted to feel.

Pete stuck out his hand, and Tommy took it. Then he looked around and said, "I need to find the little dickhead who got dumped by the bull."

"Who is he?" Pete asked.

Tom shook his head and said, "I'm not quite sure. He and another guy claim to work for the Mexican Attorney General, but it looks like a cover of some kind. I'm sure they're federal cops, but I have no idea who they really work for. My boss is working on it with the FBI, though."

"Not knowing who your partner is can't be pretty, especially down here."

"Tell me about it."

They found Berto at the local clinic where a doctor was casting his forearm. He looked pale, even under the dark hue of his skin.

Pete, in perfect Spanish, inquired about Berto and found he'd also suffered a concussion and would be staying the night.

"He was lucky to get in early and get one of the beds," the doctor had said. "By ten o'clock tonight we will be putting them out on the patio."

When Pete surprised Tom at the rodeo, his first impression was negative. The guy was too hip, for one thing. His hair was too long, and the bead necklace was passé—reminiscent of a time that refused to pass into oblivion. Too many people were still working hard to keep the '70s alive for his taste. People stuck in the past made him wary.

However, once Pete explained that his beat was the Berkeley street scene, Tom relaxed. The guy had credentials, and once they had begun to confide in one another, some amazing things came to light.

When Tom had mentioned Doc Ward's name, Pete looked incredulous. Ward's name had come up in Pete's investigation of a new boutique hallucinogen that was the current rave in Bay Area high society. Comparing notes, they made some connections that would help untangle cases in both Wyoming and California. When Tom told Pete they had Ward's computer files, the guy's eyes lit up. It sounded like exactly what he needed to make his case against the guy selling the 'shrooms to the pseudo shamans in the Bay Area. Ward's files might even include info on distribution. Perfect.

Tom was glad for the new company. He had been feeling more and more disconcerted by his working relationship with Berto. And most especially now that Jesus was in charge of things. He confided the whole history of his investigation.

"So you don't know who these guys really are, huh?"

"No. Sheriff Harlan said that the Attorney General's office had denied any association, but that doesn't mean a whole lot really. I've worked with US intel groups, and disavowal can be routine, a way of keeping things compartmentalized and secret. I do think that they are legit cops, their training shows. But there's something else not kosher about them, and that's a fact. I do know that they've got a smuggling sideline going, but that doesn't explain it all."

Pete took a drink of his cola, looked at Tom out of the corner of his eye. "Why didn't you hop a bus out of here when you found out these guys were dirty?"

Tom looked abashed. "There's a political angle to this, and some powerful people want an extradition."

Pete put his empty bottle down and wiped his face. Then he said, "Thompson, you want some real good advice?"

"Sure, go ahead."

"Get the fuck out of here. You're in way over your head."

Tom nodded. "Maybe you're right. This could be a fool's game."

Pete flipped his thumb at the clinic. "Your previous relationship with that guy could be the only thing keeping your ass alive. You're a real problem for these guys, especially if they're dirty."

"Things don't get done the same way down here, that's for sure. You should have seen my suspect's face and hands."

Pete shrugged. "It happens every day in L.A., Chicago, Houston, Miami. Name a city, and I'll find you half a dozen guys whose specialties are confessions."

"Doesn't happen in Wyoming."

"Maybe I'm just a cynic, but I'll bet you dollars to doughnuts that you've got the same percentage of sick cops there as any other place."

Tom remembered Ben Pobeda. The Jackson PD had one for sure. And he had his reservations about what one or two of the sheriff's deputies might not do in a given situation. Hell, maybe it was the way of the world, and he just didn't want to know about it.

Pete stood. "I've got to go find my people, though I'd rather spend some more time shooting the shit. It's been a pleasure talking to someone who speaks the same language."

"Mind if I tag along while I look for Jesus? I need to tell him what happened with Berto and get a ride back to town, so I can pack up and get out of here. It'll be a relief to have some backup for a change."

"Sure, c'mon. I'll introduce you to Olga and Oz."

"They sound like a pair."

"They're different, all right. Only in California."

As the two gringos walked up the street from the clinic, moving toward the noisy bustle of the village, they met a woman and two men walking the other way. Masks were hanging from strings around their necks.

As they passed, Tom looked a second time at them. The men were hard, and their eyes recognized Tom's interest and flashed resentment. One, with a pendulous bottom lip, looked positively evil, and Tom averted his eyes from the man's aggressive gaze.

"Friends of yours?" Pete asked.

"I am glad to say that I have never seen them before in my life."

"Cute," Pete observed, describing the woman.

"And ugly as home-made sin," Tom replied, describing the men.

"So what is Bernalillo up to?" asked Villareal.

"He's supposed to be on an intel run. The police want to know what is going on here. The jailbreak and a raid on the biggest godfather in the area have both been connected to San Miguel, which is known to be full of Zapatistas. They're afraid that the problem in Chiapas might have given the Indians here big ideas. They're scared shitless, I think, that their record with the Indians in Oaxaca might be shoved into the international spotlight. The world press is looking for a chance to roast any Latin country whose human rights record isn't spotless, the hypocritical bastards."

"Speaking of which, there are a couple of TV camera crews here to record the festival."

"You saw them?"

"Yeah. They parked their outfits next to our vans, and I saw their equipment. They had a hand-lettered sign in the window that said *PRENSA,* and one of them had *Televisa* stickers on their equipment cases."

"This place has gotta be big news of some kind then."

"Don't worry, it will be news whether there's a real story behind it or not," Pete observed ironically.

Tom stopped, then spun around.

"What?" Pete asked.

"That woman!"

"What woman?"

"The one you said was cute."

"What about her?"

"It was Ward's wife!" Tom looked down the street, but all he saw was a brightly colored crowd, dancers, balloon vendors, kids, and drunks.

MiT

At the meeting place of the Society, José Gorostiza was a busy and nervous man. He had been busy feeding Jesus Bernalillo disinformation about the *rebeldes* when *El Padrito* arrived with *La Leonessa.* Now that he had finished planting his disinformation with Bernalillo, he needed to get rid of the two Californios so he could hurry to the grotto for the re-installment, then keep his appointment with the press. He sat the two gringos down at a table and explained the schedule for the solstice ceremony.

"The moon will rise about eight o'clock. We will begin the prayers at ten o'clock, and the blood rite will take place when the prayers end. The moon will witness this event because we will pray until the moment there is one finger's width between her bottom and the top of Dzaui's effigy on the pillar.

"The climb takes a bit more than an hour and a half, so you must have them ready to leave the road's end by seven thirty. We will be waiting at the summit, and will bring all the things needed, except the offering. That is your responsibility only, not ours. We want no knowledge of that until you point it out to us."

"Yes, of course. We are aware of our responsibilities, and we understand that they are serious ones," Olga said. She paused, wanting reassurance. "But the Society should be prepared for any event. This one could prove to be difficult."

"Please do not worry," José said and pointed to Olga's gold Rolex. "What time is it?" he asked.

She glanced at the watch and said, "Almost five."

"I must be going. I have other people to meet."

"Thank you, *Viejo*," Oz said and touched the fingertips of both hands together in a respectful gesture. "*Hasta luego*."

"*Va bien*."

José waited until the two gringos were gone, then took a black balaclava from under his shirt and put it in the shoulder bag carried by most men in rural Mexico. After Chiapas, it was what the world expected a sinister mountain peasant demanding the rights of his people to wear.

MiT

As they neared the grotto, Concha, Demetrio, and Marcos were frightened. They had looked over their shoulders and seen the two gringos turned, and the tall one was pointing in their direction.

"Who are they?" Marcos asked.

"Gringos, that's all I know," Demetrio had said.

"They are talking about us," Concha said. "Cenovio said the American from Wyoming was tall and had blue eyes. That describes the one on the left."

"Then they are both cops from the north." Demetrio's mouth turned down in a grimace of hate. "The bastards are here for our brother!"

"Jesus Bernalillo is here too," Demetrio said.

"You saw him?" Concha asked.

"No. But I heard that he is strutting around the village in his gringo clothes and gold chains, the *chilongo* prick."

"He has come back for the Heart, surely." Marcos's voice was thick with hate. "But when I tell Juan and Raul the DEA bastard is here, they will be glad to know it. He is the one who led the police to their marijuana field, and they burned it. And because of him, I will carry the stripes of disgrace until the day I die."

"We will do what we have to do later, but right now we must get to the grotto, the others will be there by now."

They walked to the dry, gravelly river channel that fed out of the mouth of the barranca, then followed it to the junction with the river below the dam. Mounting a masonry aqueduct, they followed it to the toe of the limestone mountain on which sat the convent and the pyramid.

Glancing around to make sure that they were not being watched, they pushed their way into the thick brush that grew below the vertical wall of limestone that anchored one side of the dam. Once inside the first fringe of growth, they found the path cleared for initiates. On both sides of the pathway were net bags, and inside them were the dried bodies of snakes and poisonous lizards—warnings to trespassers not to go any further.

Concha sent the two men ahead so she could shed the men's clothes she was wearing and prepare herself. Her heart beat rapidly as she stopped to take a newly loomed huipil from the sack she had carried through the village. She removed the hat, mask, and shirt and donned a blouse and the huipil, which identified her as a Mixtec woman and a resident of the village of San Miguel.

She undid her hair from the braid she'd put under the hat and brushed and re-braided it with ribbon. Taking out a bottle of water, she washed her face, hands, and feet, then put the bottle back in the sack for the men to wash themselves with.

Patricio was waiting at the mouth of the cave. He'd had second thoughts about the election of Concha to the Society; as a matter of fact, he was dead set against it at the beginning. But his doubts had slowly gone away over the last couple of days. She had the body of a woman, that was clear for all to see, but she had spiritual strengths that were apparent to all who could get past their prejudices.

In Tlaxiaco, there was a public bath called the *Baño de Cacica Maria*, named for the last cacica in the Mixteca Alta, almost two hundred years ago. Now, another woman with a will as strong and a mind as acute as any man's had appeared. Patricio was convinced that it was a sign that the times were truly changing. Everything else turned on its head, why not the traditional roles, especially in times as troubled as these?

He stood aside as the three dipped one knee to the ground in respect and entered the holy place. It was a practice integrated from the Catholic customs they'd learned as children. The Cloud People had learned they needed every shred of spiritual help available if they were going to survive.

The altar was prepared. One hundred and thirteen hand-dipped candles were lit to throw their golden light on the wooden *Santo*, a representation of the Archangel Saint Michael, who was the patron of their town. It was carved in the sixteenth century by a local artist and recently restored by another artist. The new paint and gilt glowed warmly, making it vibrant, almost alive, to their minds.

On the other side of the altar, a flat rock was set in mortar and decorated with flowers of every color imaginable. It was from this pedestal that Marcos and Demetrio had taken the Heart of the World. They were now stripped of their shirts and knelt before the altar, their lips moving in real penance. The stripes on Marcos's back were a bright red, the welts still healing.

Juan brought the carefully wrapped box with the hole cut in the top to the altar and cut the cords securing it. He looked up at the benevolent *Santo* and crossed himself three times, lifted the crystal, and set it in its proper place, at last.

There was a thump and a giddy lurch from the base of the mountains. Dust and bat droppings fell from the cavern's roof as a tremor rolled through the ground. Murmurs escaped the mouths of all present as they steadied themselves.

Patricio advanced to where Demetrio and Marcos knelt. He took a grip on the quirt, a symbol of the authority of the elders. As the volume of Demetrio and Marcos's vocal penance rose in anticipation, he slashed each one once. He was careful to avoid the cicatrices on Marcos's back, moving the blow to the man's buttocks. After each stroke, the men shouted, "*Perdoname Señor*!" And it was over: Dzaui had been mollified, according to that part of the ritual.

The two kneeling men rose and donned their shirts. Demetrio pulled his shoulders forward to relieve the burning stripe on his back while Marcos rubbed his buttocks. Patricio had not spared anything in the stroke that each of them was given. But it was a small price to pay to have their banishment lifted.

Two acolytes, one an old man and the other a younger man learning the rites, began setting the altar with vessels for the food and drink on which Dzaui would feast. Then the ceremony would be confirmed and sanctified, with the shedding of blood on Nindo Tocoshu. All that was left was the long chanting of the vocal ritual. José, the only one who knew the complete text that would take place when he returned from his appointment with the international press in the tule grove beside the river, would do that.

Chapter Twenty-Seven

It was dark, and Tom, Pete Villareal, and Jesus had been talking for an hour at a little bar not far from the village plaza. Bernalillo had been very interested in Tom and Pete's sighting of Concha. He got up once and left them for a few minutes, then returned for particulars. He was probably checking with informants, sending them around to look for the woman.

Bernalillo and Pete drank a few beers and sampled the wares of the pulque vendors who dipped their Tears of Christ from plastic buckets, using an incised gourd cup that everyone shared in common. Tom settled for Mirinda and Squirt his thirst increased in the presence of the drinking men. At one moment, he had a strong impulse to taste the pulque, just a taste, out of curiosity. But the second he'd raised the mild liquor to his lips, a voice in his head echoed a cavernous *Don't* at the last possible moment, and he'd given the gourd cup back to the vendor.

It shook him. After years of richly rewarding sobriety, he had come so close to a swift slide into his own customized hell, and it was depressing. He had come within a literal half-inch of a loss of all that was good in his life.

Then he had looked up from the raucous crowd at the tables and turned his eyes to the fireworks bursting thunderously overhead. They cast the boisterous, laughing faces in brilliant hues as the lights flashed and the gunpowder roared, and he had a little celebration for himself. He said *Thank you, God* ten times, silently to himself.

Then he turned to watch the other two men descend into a part of their personalities best left unaroused in him.

When he handed the cup back to the vendor, Pete had asked why, and he answered simply, "I quit drinking, and my life got better." It had only served to amuse the other two, but Tom recognized and deeply felt the life-changing power in that simple statement.

Tom joined the conversation only occasionally and saw they both talked too much, revealing things they would have been silent about when sober. Pete was on assignment in pursuit of law enforcement business, but one of his drunken revelations was he ate a mushroom being trafficked illegally in California. He scoffed at the gulls in his group at being fleeced by Oz and Olga. However, when the good-looking blonde showed up to claim him, Pete went with her gladly enough. He said he'd see them later, but Tom suspected not. The guy could not be depended on to do what he promised—that was clear enough.

Jesus, too, had shown more of his hand than he intended. He pointed out villagers, telling stories that only someone who had spent a lot of time trafficking with them could know—but trafficking in what, exactly, besides intel? At the rate that Bernalillo was putting them down, Tom figured he wouldn't have long to wait before the man tipped his hand enough for his real job to be revealed. And the two pretty *muchachas* he herded to their table were asking for a bottle of mescal. It damn sure wouldn't be long before his tongue started wagging if he dipped into that stuff.

The pretty girl with the intoxicating floral perfume was named Maria Cristalina, and miracle of miracles, she was making eyes at Tom. He was flattered but had to tell her that he had a *novia*, that he was engaged. She still smiled seductively, dragged her fingernails lightly over the fabric of his Wranglers, and galvanized an instant response that took him by surprise.

"I think I'll go check on Berto," he said and stood up from the table.

"Well, hurry back, Amigo. I can't handle all this by myself." And Jesus wagged his beaming, drunken face in a circle that took in the two pretty women, both with raven hair and crimson lips in the Latina style at its most seductive.

O*hhh*, Tom thought, *to be younger and dumber.* Hot, slippery mouths and hot, slippery bodies were what made him go when he had been young, dumb, and full o' cum.

The crowd now verged on madness. Mouths were thrown open to the dark sky, shouting obscenities, exclaiming in drunken happiness or penance as eyes flashed, hands touched, arms clasped in friendship. A half-dozen men took Tom's hand as he pushed through the crowd saying "America good" or "I am work Kentucky Winn Dixie store, ver' good my fren'." It made him feel good.

When he finally made it to the clinic, it was as the doc had predicted. The patio was half-covered with injured or sick people, and two nurses were busy monitoring the casualties.

Tom spent only a minute or two in the room and left after commiserating with the little guy. "The doc says he wants to keep you here until tomorrow, so he can keep an eye on you. I'll check in again before we leave for Tlaxiaco, and maybe he'll let you go with us then." Then he remembered the treacherous mountain road they'd driven in on. He had to try to talk Jesus out of the car keys and talk him into moving his party to Tlaxiaco, where it was safer.

Man, some men never learn to quit following their dick around, he thought as he hitched his daypack around and looked at his watch. Not even 8:30 yet.

On the other side of the village, Pete and Olga had found some of their pilgrims eating at the open-air stands near the market. They were sitting around the tables "like good little girls and boys," Pete mocked to himself as they approached the soul tourists.

"You need some food," Olga said in a disgusted little way. *She didn't drink at all,* Pete remembered.

"Sure," he said and sat down on a bench where she indicated.

In the Tule grove by the river, José, Patricio, Socratio, and Plato held the press conference.

Sweating under their hoods or bandana masks, they blinked, and perspiration drenched them as José fulminated against the government's treatment of the indigenous mountain people. He spoke of the poor health services and schools, of the horrible conditions of the local roads, and the lack of bus service of any kind. And he spoke of the revolution of 1910 and the ruling party's betrayal of the principles that inspired the bloody event. Finally, he spoke of Emiliano Zapata and his love and understanding of the needs of the little people.

This was what the *Televisa* folks had come for. The cameraman panned to José and focused on the man's masked face, gradually zooming in on the zealot's eyes and the poet's lips. After a full five minutes of sound bites, any one of which would give a news director the hots, José smoothed a sheaf of papers and began to catalog the movement's demands.

The TV crew's director motioned her second camera to a profile angle while the Mexico City correspondent from *Time* magazine and the woman from *Reuters* scribbled furiously.

Plato listened to the fireworks in the village and thought about the fun he was missing. Dropping his hand below the range of the cameras, he gave the sign for "*screw this*" to his brother.

Socratio snorted back a laugh and threw out his fist in a revolutionary salute to cover the snort. It punctuated José's demand of the moment perfectly. The cameramen recorded it faithfully, and the next morning it would be the primary image fed to the whole world.

And it would be that image that prompted a grim President of Mexico to turn to his most trusted cabinet members and say, "Get your asses down there. Fix the road, hire more doctors, buy some busses, build a new school and market, double the electric service, and whatever else has to be done."

His eyes were hard as obsidian. "Fix it all, and find that fucker." He pointed at the television and José's image. "Whoever he is. Make him rich, buy him a house, buy him a *whorehouse*, I don't care. I want his ass back in front of the cameras as soon as possible, with his bare face hanging out and praising the PRI."

One of the people in the room said, casually, "It would be a hell of a lot cheaper to kill him."

The President turned to the man, a member of the incoming president's team, and hissed, "One: This is not the north; this is the south of Mexico where most of the population is indigenous. Two: These images are being seen all over our country and are going to be re-broadcasted all over the world. The print media is going to do the same. Three: You don't understand shit. Get him out of the room."

The man paled. He was undone, and his career for the next six years, at least, would find him condemned to sitting in a Conasupo office, checking the count of grain sacks or supervising the party's slogan-painting crews in the rural backcountry that made up most of Mexico.

In San Miguel, Tom was pushing through the crowd again, making his way back to the tavern where he'd left Jesus. Pete was also making his way toward the same place because he'd asked Oz if they could give Tommy a lift back to the hotel, and he agreed.

Tom arrived first, but Jesus was gone, the table where they'd been sitting now occupied by other people.

"Dammit," he muttered to himself, "where did he go?"

He glanced around, then, on impulse, walked to the side of the patio and looked out into the relative darkness. Jesus leaned on a big tree with one hand and held a very unhappy *muchacha* by the wrist with the other.

Drunken dick head, Tom thought and decided he'd better give the girl a hand. It looked like she needed it pretty badly, so he started toward the couple at the edge of the noisy night.

At that moment, Pete Villareal walked into the bar and saw Tom step out into the dark. He started across the room to catch Tom, to tell him he could go back with the tour group because he'd known that Jesus would not be interested in leaving the feria before the party was over.

Tom was at the rear of the building when a man in peasant's clothes and a bandaged left hand stepped from behind the tree and blew Jesus's brains out into the night. A burst of fireworks overhead drowned the sound of the girl's scream, then she put her hands to her head and ran past Tom toward the whirlwind of the street.

Tom's trained instinct was to go for his pistol, but it was buried in the bottom of the daypack he had slung over his shoulder.

The shooter began to walk quickly to the corner of the building, where Tom was rooted with the insane thought that he would go unnoticed.

When the man saw the gringo standing at the edge of the light, his hand came up like a striking snake, and his eyes never left Tom's. The big .45 rose, and Tom heard the hammer thumbed back. From a distance of ten feet, Tom saw the man's cold black eyes clearly and knew the shooter was going to pull the trigger. Before the flash and the blackness, Tom's last sensation was the knowledge that something hot was flooding his legs. His bladder had released, and he was pissing his pants.

Pete saw it all from the rear of the tavern: Jesus pawing the girl, the shooter step from behind the tree, the terrible distortion of Bernalillo's head as the bullet blew through it. Then the body fell behind a stack of beer bottle crates. Its winking Reeboks were the only things visible in the showers of cascading fireworks overhead.

He saw Tom and the shooter face one another, then another man step quickly forward and slap the Wyoming cop across the back of the head with a sack of some kind, the blow collapsing his legs as if he had been shot.

Pete stepped into the shadow and watched as the two men dragged Tom's limp body along the patio and then disappear into the dark. Then Pete heard a man hiss, "Get the backpack, Juan!"

The man who hit Tom snuck quickly back and grabbed the pack. Then all Pete could see was Jesus's immaculate white shoes winking pink and blue as they reflected the crackling fireworks bursting overhead.

Chapter Twenty-Eight

Tom woke in a panic. Something was crawling under his shirt, making its way scuttling through his chest hair! In the foggy outer banks of his mind, he tried desperately to open his shirt to rid himself of the many-legged thing that tickled his flesh as it ran in zigzags across his stomach, then over to his ribs and back again.

"*U-h-h-h-h.*" His traumatized brain could make his mouth form nothing more intelligible than a long, tormented grunt. He opened his eyes and saw a wall made of wattle and daub, the horizontal matrix of bare sticks visible through the adobe mud. A rude cupboard hung on a wall, and there was a rubber tub half full of water against another wall.

"*U-h-h-h-h!*" he moaned. Tears ran down his anguished face because he was terribly afraid, and he hated nothing more than being helpless. Nothing.

Tom swung his legs and kicked the cupboard, causing it to fall from the crude wall with a crash.

The noise helped clear his head enough that he realized his arms were bound tightly to his sides, just above his elbows. They were secured with something that ran across his back.

Horrified, he remembered it had been the same practice used on prisoners during the war. He was a captive! He screamed.

An Indian woman with long gray braids pushed open the flimsy door, and she carried a wicked-looking knife in one hand.

Tom's mind focused. "*Insecto! Insecto grande en mi camisa!*" he said, clenching his jaws at the sensations inspired by the frantic bug.

The older woman hesitated for a moment, then opened Tom's shirt. She chased the insect down, then cupped it in her hand, dropped it to the floor, and ground it to a paste with her bare heel. The damn thing had been the size of a Bic lighter and made a smear the size of a fried egg.

"*Solo un' cucaracha*," she said.

"It's *just* a cockroach to you, maybe," Tom said. Goose flesh covered his body like he'd just emerged from a cold river. *Ugh!*

She pulled the door shut, and Tom heard her shout, "Agustino!" then the padding of her bare feet as she moved away.

He looked around to see he was in a little bathhouse, and the objects spilled from the cupboard were toiletries. His eyes focused on a plastic bottle of Pert Plus, and he was moved to make a disoriented laugh. The object was so American that it verged on the hallucinogenic. He'd felt for days that he was a stranger in a strange land, and he'd not been smart enough to take the myriad hints that told him to pack his shit and git. And now this. He moved his feet to where he could see them.

"I'll be damned," he muttered. He was wearing antique leg irons, nineteenth-century relics. He'd seen equivalents at the old prison museum in Laramie, and the sight of them amused him. He chuckled and said, "Fuck me dead. I'll never smile again."

He heard soft footsteps hurrying toward the bathhouse, then the door opened, and a small man peeked inside. He had the wrinkled face of a man who worked in the sun—wispy, white whiskers and eyes shining in a gentle way that highlighted his smile.

"*Muy buenos dias, Señor*," he said in a soft voice.

"And a good day to you too, Amigo. Where are my pants? And shorts?" He willed his brain to work in Spanish. "*¿Mis pantalones y cortes?*" He was naked from the waist down.

"*Ah si. Yo lavó, secandolos ahora.*" He'd washed them, and they were drying.

Tom remembered the hot rush of urine as he'd looked into the muzzle of the gun and was humiliated by the memory.

I shoulda quit drinking that damn orange pop before it got me into trouble, he thought. His irony processor was still warm apparently.

"*¿Tienes hambre?*" the man asked, inquiring if Tom was hungry.

"*No. A tengo mucho sed,*" Tom answered. He was thirsty as hell.

"*Momentito,*" the little man said and pinched his thumb and index finger together to indicate a moment of time.

He was back in minutes with a gourd cup full of water. He helped Tom sit, and a pulse of emotion ran through him because the water was sweet as the well water from his kitchen tap. For a moment, he was afraid he was going to cry.

"Ahhh, *gracias.*"

"*Para servirle.*" The man was excruciatingly polite.

"*¿Como te llamas?*"

"Agustino."

"*Bueno*, Agustino." Tom wagged his head at the walls of the hut. "*¿Es baño?*" asking if it was a bathhouse.

"*Si, es baño.*"

"*Yo quiero bañarse.*"

"*Ah, si.*" the little man pinched his fingers together again and left, pulling the stick door shut.

Minutes later, he returned with Tom's pants and the older woman, her knife in hand. Sharpened over time to a slim curve, it had evolved into a boning knife that made Tom's skin crawl at its wickedly efficient form. The woman was undoubtedly the author of its evolution and knew how to use it, absolutely no doubt.

Agustino took a leather thong from around his neck and knelt at Tom's feet. There was a key on the thong. With a cautious glance at Tom, he inserted the key into one of the locks.

He struggled, twisting at the key and fighting the lock. He tried the other lock, and after a minute of twisting the key while squeezing the latch, the cuff released.

"*Muy oxidado*," he said as if Tom hadn't guessed the problem was rust.

"*Son antiqüedades*," Tom observed. And antiques they were.

The little man smiled. "*Si, tengan muchos años.*" He stood and then took the woman's knife as she brought in a plastic bucket of soapy water. Tom realized that he was going to get his bath, but he wasn't going to be the one to give it.

"No, no," he tried to protest, but one hard look from the crone told him he was going to get bathed whether he liked it or not.

She washed him thoroughly from the waist down, and it felt damn good. Then Agustino put on Tom's pants, re-cuffed the free leg, and unsecured Tom's arms. They'd bound him with a nylon strap with clamp fasteners so the bonds couldn't tighten and cut off the circulation to his arms, so that was good. Grandma stripped Tom's shirt and finished the bath. Then they re-secured his arms and legs.

He was still a prisoner, but he was clean. Refreshed, Tom leaned against the wall and said, "*Gracias a ustedes.*"

Agustino smiled, but Grandma whetted the wicked-looking knife against the wood of the rickety door, then jerked it shut. Tom was having a hard time liking her.

MiT

Not wanting to explain everything, Pete Villareal took a taxi back to Tlaxiaco. He then phoned the Teton County sheriff's office, and Dispatch gave him Sheriff Harlan's home phone number when he explained what happened. Sam told Pete three men were sent to look for Tom from the Mexican Attorney General's office. They were in Tlaxiaco at the moment. He also said that he was chartering a plane to Salt Lake City, where he would make a commercial connection to Mexico first thing in the morning. Pete gave him directions to Tlaxiaco.

Pete was impressed with the man's calm, efficient approach to things. The man obviously knew how to get things done with a minimum of motion. It looked like he would be there by the following evening.

Pete went to the police station and reported the murder of Jesus Bernalillo and the kidnapping of an American law enforcement officer. The effect was to electrify the command center set up in the gym. The Zapatistas, it seemed, had upped the ante.

El Comandante arrived, his face pale and tense, and his first phone call was to the Governor of Oaxaca state. The Governor's first call was to the President, and that man's first call was to his Minister of the Interior, whose responsibilities included the maintenance of order in Mexico.

Historically, that ministry was responsible for the deaths of more Indians than the Conquistadors, so their experience was invaluable. The minister and the President conferred for twenty tense minutes, trying to interpret the night's events. After that conversation, the minister phoned the negotiation team in Tlaxiaco.

"Yes, Mr. Minister?" the ranking officer said expectantly.

"The President says to find out what they want now. He's given his word on the new road and the other infrastructure. Find out why the escalation and the price for the return of the American. What with immigration reform and all the other politics going on, he doesn't want any bad press about a kidnapped gringo. The economic future of our country hangs in a delicate balance here."

The negotiator felt the weight, and it was enormous. "What about the Mexican officer, Bernalillo?"

"What about him? He was involved in dishonest things; he was corrupt."

"Yes sir," the man said quietly, but he was alarmed. If death were now the price for being corrupt, two-thirds of the government's employees would be doomed. After all, if a man couldn't steal, why go into public life at all?

Chapter Twenty-Nine

The next morning at 11:00, Sheriff Harlan phoned Polly's office in California from the airport in Mexico City. The office called her in Huatulco, and Polly chartered a plane to Tlaxiaco, beating Sam to the Hotel Portal by two hours. When he arrived, the hotel manager, Santiago, sent for Polly immediately, a fifty-dollar bill still glowing in his pocket.

"Sam, what the hell is going on?" Polly's usually cool composure was coming apart at the seams.

"How did you get here so soon?"

"Chartered a plane. Where is Tommy, Sam. What is going on?"

"I came from Oaxaca City with a man from the Ministry of the Interior, and he says Tom has apparently been kidnapped by revolutionaries. The government is trying to establish contact with the guerrillas responsible, but there appears to be more than one faction, and there is some confusion as to who has him."

"He's alive isn't he, Sam? Tell me that he is alive. Please."

At that moment, Pete Villareal and Olga entered the reception office. He stuck out his hand, identified himself. "Pete Villareal, you look like you might be Sheriff Harlan."

"Yes. And this is Polly Anaya, she's Tom's fiancée. She was down here in Mexico already, so I thought she might as well be here too."

He turned to Polly and said, "Polly, this is the man who saw Tom taken after they met at the fiesta. He was good enough to phone the department and let us know what happened." Pete and

Sam had worked out a cover story, so they wouldn't blow the fact that Villarreal was working a case.

Pete saw that the man was a pro, despite Pete's prejudice against men in cowboy boots. His long-ago haircut beside a highway in Wyoming was still a prominent feature on his emotional landscape.

"What happened?" Polly asked Pete.

"Uh, I'm Olga Blavatsky, with Jaguar Travelers. Mr. Villareal is with me."

Polly looked at the other California blonde and said, "How do you do?" then turned back to Pete.

Olga's green eyes flashed at the curt dismissal.

"I was drinking with Tom and Jesus . . ."

"Jesus?"

"The Mexican guy Tom was with—the one who was killed. I was with Tom for a couple of hours . . ."

"Thomas doesn't drink."

"Lady, he drinks Mirinda like it's going out of style."

"He does everything like it's going out of style," Polly said, her eyes softening. "I apologize for interrupting, please go on."

"I went back to get Tom, so I could offer him a ride back to Tlaxiaco because it looked like he might be stranded. I walked into the bar, asked where they were, and the waitress said they'd moved to the patio out back.

"I walked out, stepped to the side of the building so my eyes could adjust to the dark. I saw Tom walking toward Jesus, who was pawing one of the girls we'd been talking to. I think Tom was going to do something about it. Bernalillo was pretty drunk.

"It only took a second, but a guy suddenly stepped from the back of a big tree and shot Jesus at point-blank range. Then he saw Tom, and pointed the gun at him. Tom put up his hands, stepped back . . . Man, I thought he was dead for sure."

Pete shook his head at the memory. "Anyway, he stepped back and almost bumped into another guy I hadn't seen, and he slapped Tom with a sap. Then they dragged him off."

Sam said, "I'm going to get a room and join the task force. Polly, you go back to your room and wait until I can find out what the plan is. Pete, thanks for your help, it's always refreshing when a civilian takes the chance to help in police work."

Sam signed the register, took the key, and walked out. Polly followed him, and once they were away from Pete and Olga, she said, "Sam!"

He stopped. "What, Polly?"

"If it's money they want, I have money."

"I know that, but let's wait for them to make a move before we make any offers."

"Sam," Polly said, and her eyes were hard as sapphire, "I want Thomas back. If it costs me all I have, I want him back and I want him back *safe!"* Her voice broke on the last word.

MiT

Hidden in the hills above San Miguel, Patricio was beside himself. He needed time to sort out the implications of what had happened the night before, and he couldn't decide whether it was a curse or a blessing.

"It's a blessing," José declared. "This is a gift, Patricio, and we must use it with care, with delicacy, with respect—as all great gifts must be received."

José had seen things in a completely different light, and his brother was almost always mystified at the difference in their perceptions. Oftentimes, what was completely ambiguous to Patricio seemed clear to José, and this was apparently one of those times.

"Explain this to me, then," Patricio said. "I cannot see how a dead officer of the Mexican Drug Enforcement Agency and a kidnapped

American policeman is anything but an excuse for the army to come into these hills and leave us all in pieces." He was having some very real pains in his chest lately and was having them at this moment. Joséfina had called from Tlaxiaco to report that five hundred soldiers of the dreaded and blood-soaked *Ejercito* battalion from Tapachula, Chiapas, were bivouacked in a field outside the town.

José smiled. "If the government had any idea we were a dozen ignorant peasants, they would have us for dog meat already. Your fears are not entirely misplaced, my brother. But if we inflate ourselves like the puffer fish, though our spines are few, we can give any predator second thoughts about trying to consume us." He smiled. "And if our masquerade is discovered, so what? Better to reign one day as a lion than live a thousand years as a sheep."

Patricio hated metaphors. "First we are fish, and then we are lions and sheep. You don't live in the real world, José."

"The real world stinks," the poet said and took down a bottle of the local mezcal. "Yet, my brother, I have a plan that should sweeten the air considerably." He took a drink. "*Televisa* is in town and *Time* magazine wants to interview the rebels. We are going international."

MiT

Agustino was having a hard time with the leg irons again. Tom needed to take his daily drizzly and was beginning to think he was bound for another pissing embarrassment before the locks yielded.

In an inspired moment, he remembered there was a small spray can of WD-40 in his daypack.

"Agustino."

"*Si, Señor.*"

"*¿Donde esta mi maleta de espalda?*"

"*En la casita.*"

"*Oye, hay una bote de lubricante alla-WD-cuarenta.*"

"*Ah, conozco. Me voy par' la.*"

"They must sell WD-40 everywhere in the world if he knows what it is," Tom said as he watched Agustino leave.

When the little philosopher came back, Tom's respiration rate began to climb because sandwiched between his sweater and rain poncho should be his loaded Sig P-220 and two clips.

"*Pistola se fue,*" Agustino said with a grin, having read Tom's mind. *The pistol was gone.*

"*Lastima,*" Tom said with a wry smile.

"*Sea una buena, dice Demetrio.*" *A good one, and someone named Demetrio had it.*

Tom told Agustino how to unzip the junk pocket that held the WD-40, along with a broken signal mirror, snakebite kit, surveyor's tape, waterproof matches, a can opener, and other mostly useless stuff. All of it mystified and amazed the simple peasant as he removed them one at a time and asked Tom to identify them.

When the little WD-40 can came out, Tom audibly exhaled because he'd had a secret hope stashed in his mind ever since he'd remembered the lubricant.

The key on the thong around Agustino's neck showed the lock mechanism of the irons was a simple two-plate affair. If lubricated well enough, the mechanism shouldn't be too hard to manipulate if he ever got the chance. He blessed the lessons on locks he'd learned from DaddyO back in Jackson, what seemed like years ago now.

But, at the moment, his priority was to get to the outhouse before he had an accident. Black beans and chiles with tortillas for breakfast were making his stomach sound like surf on a beach—wet and powerful.

Agustino sprayed the locks liberally, as Tom directed. When he twisted the key, the mechanism clicked like it hadn't since the day it was assembled.

"*Ah, buenisima*," he said. Score another one for the gringos.

Tom was raised mostly on a ranch, so an outhouse held no mysteries for him. He knew what to expect. However, he'd forgotten the sensation of flies doing touch-and-go's on his bum.

Agustino re-secured Tom's arms after he finished, then they began their shuffle back to the bathhouse. Tom took a good look around while he had the chance. He saw there were no men visible except his escort. The village appeared populated only by women and children, and they all came out of their huts to stare when Tom was escorted from the privy.

He also observed that they were pretty high above San Miguel, and he could see the convent about two miles away to the west. That gave him his sense of where he was, which helped his state of mind, which the damn vigilante dogs did not.

The suspicious animals sniffed at the bathhouse door, growling, as Tom sat and pondered his fate. When he kicked the flimsy sticks the door was fashioned from, they growled and snarled. When Agustino took him to the outhouse, the dogs barked insanely, baring their teeth and dashing at Tom's legs. Agustino screamed at them and plied a stick, which didn't seem to impress them very much.

"Gusano! Golfo! Oso! Perra!" he would yell, but the fuckers still dashed at Tom and snapped their wicked-looking teeth. It took only one trip to the crapper to give him a real hate for the animals. They were going to make any run for it dangerous, even if he could get out of his shackles.

Back in the bathhouse, Tom felt less exposed, but it was time for the lectures again. His mind reeled at the thought of the seemingly endless political observations and rhetorical questions the little man was pelting him with.

The whole morning was spent with the man perched in the sunlight outside the door on the bath stool. He held discourses on the history of US/Third World affairs. Vietnam had been covered quite thoroughly, especially once Tom admitted to being a veteran of that one.

Agustino was gracious enough to take a few minutes to comment on France's sins in Asia and Africa—an appreciated attempt at being polite to the guest. But he had not been very long in returning to his main thesis.

Cuba, Grenada, and Panama were covered thoroughly, not to mention the Dominican Republic, with Iraq as a sidebar. The man was kind enough to confine himself to the last forty years. However, the US's earlier incursions into Mexican and Latin American affairs were inferred by the whole running discourse.

The form of his observations followed the Greek model for argumentation, the little man lecturing gently and spicing his words with a mostly rhetorical: *"¿Es cierto, O falso?"* True or False? Only occasionally did he wait until Tom made an observation or objection.

He was gentle and often acute, but his worldview was evident from the lower-left corner of geopolitics. Tom found himself agreeing with much of what the little man had to say, despite being forced to these considerations by his helpless state. Funny how being raised lower working class forged one's perception of the world, no matter how far one progressed up or down the social ladder.

The early afternoon was spent on the history of America's sins against Nicaragua, El Salvador, Guatemala, and especially Cuba. Tom would nod his head or shake it in disagreement as the noon meal came and went, and the sun began its lazy arc down the afternoon sky.

Tom laid his head back against the wattle and daub wall, mouthed *cierto* at appropriate moments, inspiring a satisfied nod from his little philosopher guard. A *falso* from Tom would send a corrugation of perplexity up the man's brow. But he would purse his lips, re-frame his argument, then, smiling, drive the refashioned point home again. To argue was useless.

While watching Agustino wrestle with a rebuttal, Tom came to a very disquieting realization. He was taken prisoner by the two most politically ruthless groups in the world—women, and philosophers. So, as a redneck male born and bred, he understood he could expect no quarter and, certainly, no mercy. He was de facto guilty of everything wrong in the world. And he just might have to listen to this guy till he died, possibly at the hands of the granny with the boning knife.

Chapter Thirty

Concha stared at the script. Although it was written in José's florid hand and larded with metaphor, she was satisfied it was the truth about the state of her people. There was little in that she could not say with a whole heart.

She looked over to where José set up a table and two chairs, one for himself and one for her. The TV crews from Mexico's *Televisa* and the one from CNN were set up, and there were also three reporters sitting on camping chairs.

José sat down and, with a nod, cued the directors of the crews and the cameras to start rolling. José spoke for a minute or two, identifying himself as the "Subcomandante," and then stood and gave Concha a nod. She walked out of the dark and sat down at the table.

Her composed, pretty face was a startling contrast with the hooded and menacing males who had, to this point, been arrayed in front of the cameras. The cameras caught it all—her striking little figure in the brilliant Triqui huipil, her light step, the long black hair framing the handsome Indian features, her bare feet, and most of all, the fire in her eyes.

After a moment, she forgot the script and began to speak from her heart. She gave a brief history of the rich cultures of Mexico's indigenous people, especially the Zapotecs and Mixtecs of Oaxaca State. She reminded them that Benito Juarez, one of Mexico's greatest reformers, was a Mixtec Indian—a man who stood with Abraham Lincoln in his belief that "justice for all" was more than a theory. It was something that had to be put into actual practice, even if it meant another civil war.

She spoke of the divided soul of Mexico and illustrated it with the story of the eagle tearing at the snake and the snake looking for its opportunity to strike its tormentor to its death—the seemingly eternal struggle of Mexico against both its past and its future. That is to say, against its proud indigenous history and its progressive possibilities.

Then she spoke about the low estate of Mexico's women and the impending death of family life as America sent its poisonous, false liberalism deep into the heart of the great country of Mexico. She called on the mothers of the country to both rise and nurture, a task that a country even as great as the United States seemed incapable of. Finally, she talked of her own life in the north and what she had seen there. She warned of what was bad and described warmly of what was good and worthy of emulation.

She pleaded on behalf of the indigenous people of the country. Then she demanded respect and equality for both men and women, and the passion in her voice, the heat in her eyes spoke of a soul on fire.

The press members had been given background on this woman. They learned how she led a strike against a powerful cacique and shot a man who had once tried to force himself on her. But this was but their first look at her, and it would certainly not be the last. She would make an indelible impression on the world's zeitgeist, where the time for women had come at long last. This woman would surely become an emblem of that fruiting struggle, and the press could hardly wait to get it out to the world. This was real news.

When the cameras were turned off, Concha sat down with the print reporters, one of them a woman from an international Spanish language magazine, and spent an hour talking.

Everything she had felt and held inside for so long came out: the education she'd been denied by the Mexican system but had been afforded by her husband, the breadth of her experience as a child from an indigenous village who had grown up as a millionaire's wife. The fact that he was an intellectual from a famous family, and had been murdered, added elements to the brew fermenting in the journalists' minds.

The hereditary acuity of her mind shown and made the journalists' work easy. She was the sanguinary heiress of the Mixtec queen, Cacica de Teposcolula, was she not? The Mexican media people could barely contain themselves.

The *Televisa* people in the broadcast truck were doing a quick edit. The beautiful, bilingual reporter had already done her intro in both English and Spanish. A sixty-second report would be ready in thirty minutes, in plenty of time for the ten o'clock news in the States, and it was a shoo-in for a spot on all the international feeds. With much more to follow.

MiT

Because he didn't understand one whit of Spanish, Sam had no idea what was going on at the tactical center. There had been an impressive communications system with single-sideband radios, satellite commo, and other gear he wasn't familiar with. There were military men in uniforms and a couple of men in expensive suits. There were also younger men who preferred designer jeans, expensive running shoes, and thick gold watches, but all carried sidearms ostentatiously. This was a cop's world, and Sam's long experience gave him a real good idea of what was going on. But it wasn't enough, even when his companion from the Interior Ministry's office spoke perfect American English. But Sam could tell that the guy was evasive about the details, which wasn't good. He needed to know what the deal was, and this would be the one who would know. When the officer introduced himself as being from the Ministry of the Interior instead of the Attorney General's office, Sam knew something new had been added. While the Attorney General managed most of the country's law enforcement agencies, the Ministry of the Interior and the CIA were sisters under the skin.

Tom Thompson was his number one officer, and Sam had lost him. One is supposed to keep good tabs on the inventory and personnel, and losing a guy was bad for business, in more ways than one. Losing him in a foreign country was bad for the political side of his business, and when a county officer gets mixed up in an international mess, it's, well, an international mess.

Besides, though Tom Thompson didn't know it, Sam had designated Tom his successor. The office of US Marshal for Wyoming was coming up for grabs soon, and Sam had his eye on it. But he needed a successor whose reputation would be as immaculate as possible. Tom was competent, well-liked, and a local son. The pruning he had gone through when he came to the end of his drinking and now his imminent marriage to a smart and personable woman made him the only man Sam knew he could pass the Stetson on to. He had talked to the old pols who made things happen in Teton County, and they mostly agreed. The only hitch was that Tom hated politics, but it was something Sam planned to work on.

As he left the command center with the Ministry of the Interior's man, Sheriff Harlan felt God himself had taken a dump in his lap.

"What's the deal?" Sam asked his escort.

"The deal is that we don't know what we have for sure, but most of us think that we have been had."

"How so?"

"The press conference and the Marxist rhetoric after the violence in Huamelulpan, then the movement of people in the San Miguel area, made it seem that we had a major incident on our hands. As you may know, the people in the south of our country have been very restive lately."

"Do you think that the murder of Bernalillo and Tom's kidnapping are related to that?"

"Now that the feria is over, we haven't detected any suspicious goings-on. Our intel people have concluded that there appears to be no traffic between the group that appeared in the media yesterday and the organized groups here in the south."

"So these guys are bogus?"

"Yes. We are getting ready to go in."

"What do you mean by 'go in'?"

"We're organizing a complete sweep of the area; a thousand army troops are being readied, and the operation will begin at daylight tomorrow. Five hundred crack troops with experience of this kind will spearhead the ops. They are from Chiapas, which will reduce residual enmities here in Oaxaca."

"What about Tom?"

Sam felt an alarm run through him. His man may have been written off as a casualty of the coming situation. He knew that if the kidnappers saw a sweep coming, they would like as not kill their captive before sprinting for the mountaintops.

"Let's hope for the best." The Interior Ministry's man didn't look Sam in the eye when he said it.

It didn't help Sam's peace of mind to look up at that moment and see Polly standing on the porch of the hotel, her face haggard from the wait for news.

Behind her, in the hotel lobby, an argument was going on: "You are going with us. Period!" Olga's face convulsed with emotion.

"I guess maybe you don't understand, Olga. An American cop has been kidnapped!"

"I . . . don't . . . give . . . a . . . *damn!*"

"Pete's face flushed. "But . . . I . . . *do!*"

Olga realized she underestimated Pete's feelings about this Thompson's predicament. As a result, she would have to take a different tack.

Oz saved her the maneuver by asking, "Pete, why?"

"Why what?"

"Why do you care so much? You only knew him for a few hours, so what's the big attraction, exactly?"

Pete could not blow his cover now. He took a deep mental breath. Today was the solstice, the day he would find out exactly what was driving this mushroom-and-money scene. He had to get back to his original priorities. Besides, Thompson's boss was competent and had the support of the Mexican Ministry of the Interior's agent. Pete shrugged. "Simple. I liked the guy."

Olga glanced at Oz, and Pete caught the look. Something was going on between these two. They were nervous as whores in church.

MiT

José and Patricio had played all their cards. Their chance at the game had come, and they had gone for the pot, which was large. But they also knew if they overplayed their hands, they and everyone else in the group were dead as dry donkey dung.

Juan and Raul's killing of the DEA agent and kidnapping the American pushed the ante so high that there would be no going back. By playing the *Televisa* card, the ante rose even higher, and the game was now dangerous for both sides.

The government could not afford to throw fuel on the moment because a blood bath in the Oaxacan Sierra could flare the general situation out of control if the incident were large enough. But José was one of the few who knew that there were only a dozen people at the heart of the situation—a political Potemkin Village.

His strategy had been to keep the situation inflated through the media but not inflate it too much. However, because of last night's escalation, the strategy now was to inflate the action just enough so that the government wouldn't react with magnum force but have to resort to its historical reflex of larding the situation with money in order to co-opt the populist sentiment by corrupting its leaders.

Corruption was what made the wheel go around in his country, and this was their chance to get on the money wheel with everyone else. And if the strategy worked, they were *chingons*—clever fuckers. If it didn't work, they were *chingaron*—fucked completely. It was a dangerous game, but there was no going back.

Vamos a ver, he thought. *We'll see what happens.*

But at the moment, he had to turn his mind to the other business at hand. Now the duties of the Sociedad de los Animas Ancianos took precedence over everything else. The last rites of the rain ceremonials had to be celebrated before it all could come to fruition. It was time for the blood sacrifice.

After José sang the long hymn of the Heart in the grotto, he had stepped outside to see a few cumulus clouds already moving across the face of the moon. This morning the clouds were larger, grayer, and pregnant with promise as they scudded slowly across the sky to the west.

Patricio had taken down the linen-wrapped bundles from the scaffold in the back of the cave. He untied them and shook out the brilliant *huipils*, the vestments woven by the local women on backstrap looms. He unrolled the silver-dressed leather belts and straps, the feathered caps, and other hand-made adornments. He went to the scaffold, then reached to the back and dragged a heavy sack to him that musically clinked as it moved.

He loosened the neck of the sack and shook its contents onto the table beside the other ritual objects. They were obsidian knives fluted by hands whose craft secrets were lost for all time.

The blades were given shapes that galvanized the artist in anyone with any sensibilities. The handle of the first was the head and neck of Murcielago, the bat king. His folded wings devolved into a blade fluted to an edge sharp as any chef's instrument. The obsidian was gray, the color of Murcielago, and came from the volcano Popocatepetl. The other, heavier blade was fashioned from the rock glass of Orizaba, another volcano home of the ancient gods. Orizaba obsidian is green—the eye color of some rare cats and some even rarer people. The handle of this instrument had been worked into the head and shoulders of the jaguar, and its blade was even keener.

MiT

Agustino had re-hung the bathhouse cabinet and replaced the articles, except for the American-made toothbrush that had fallen into a corner.

Tom stared at it as his lecturer pointed out that the moon was out during the day, the drunken slut. Early this morning, Agustino had seen her making her way toward the western horizon, pale from her debauchery at the feria in San Miguel.

Before the Creation, she was wedded to the sun, and it was always light, so she followed at his side. But when Adam and Eve were driven out of Paradise and night fell on the world, God set the sun and moon on opposite sides of the sky, and she was alone. She was fascinated by the sounds of song and music and the captivating little lights and explosions that sometimes flared below when the little humans celebrated. The intoxicating smells from pulque, caña, and aguardiente jars rose and made her giddy. She thought,

It is so lonely up here while the humans are celebrating, and they are enjoying themselves so much while I am so lonely!

Finally, she could not stand it any longer, so she waited until one night when she was the size of a fingernail clipping and then lowered herself to the earth. There she stole a *huipil* to disguise herself and joined the villagers to discover what the people did at a feria. She sang, drank cups of liquor, was dragged into the circle of firelight, and danced. At first, she danced after the fashion of the demure women. Then, because she was the moon herself, she danced with the men and welcomed their hot hands and hard members. She drank more pulque and danced until, in the moonless dark, she was coaxed into the woods and experienced the physical passion of one of the men who had seduced her down to the earth with his music and laughter.

The next morning, she woke, and it was already day. When Father Sun saw her abroad in the daylight, he was very angry. She was shamed and, for a long time, did not venture down to the earth, just sailed slowly above it and looked down at the lights, listened to the songs, smelled the liquors, and felt the itch.

"Who knows," Agustino said, "perhaps the moon herself walked the streets of San Miguel last night, drinking and singing and hot. Perhaps one of our own young men was lucky enough to be the man who mated with the moon, so his sons will be strong, and his daughters full of passion. It is said that the famous cacicas of the Mixteca were the daughters of such couplings."

Tom loved the story. It reminded him of his youth before television had decimated his society. He remembered when most men had been storytellers, and he sat at the edge of their circles to hear stories of soldiering, work, hunting, drinking, and women. This little story was a generous thing to share and reminded him of his quickly retreating youth.

Agustino had also given Tom back the little Mag-Lite flashlight from his pack, hoping that it could be fixed. Stumped by the switch mechanism, which required a twist of the head, Tom promised the man to try to fix it. Another thing Tom needed now was the little mirror from the wall, and he needed it broken. If he could get several shards of glass, he could use them to fashion a key from the toothbrush on the floor. It wouldn't have to be all that strong now that the mechanism of the manacles was liberally bathed in WD-40. All he had to do was get the mirror down from the wall and break it.

He stared at it for a long moment, galvanizing his will to do whatever it took to gain the prize because it could mean the difference between living and dying. And he wanted very badly to live—at least long enough to fix the bastard with the evil eyes who had murdered Jesus and then come within half-a-breath of adding Tom's brains to the mess on the patio.

Chapter Thirty-One

Anderson Cooper looked into the camera as he introduced his guest, Jorge Castaneda, a writer, columnist, leftist intellectual, and professor of political science at the National University of Mexico in Mexico City and NYU.

"Didn't you announce the death of Marxism in Latin America?" Cooper asked. "From many reports it seems to have quickened, first with the teachers' union *Manzana* movement, and now we have this Zapatista unrest, both of them in the state of Oaxaca. And who is this new heroine of the people down there? Have you heard of this Concha Osorio woman before?"

"No one I know has heard of this woman before. But remember that I did not predict the end of militant unrest among the indigenous peoples of Mexico. Quite the contrary . . ."

In the presidential palace, the President of Mexico put his folded hands under his chin, and his stare turned as hard as the grim line of his mouth under the impeccable mustache. He was alone in the big room, just him and the television.

On screen, Cooper was asking, "And who is this Concha Osorio Ward?"

"She just might be another Rigoberta Menchu," Castaneda said brightly.

Cooper stared into the camera and editorialized, "Professor Castaneda is referring to the Nobel Laureate of 1992, an Indian woman from Guatemala who captured the attention of the world and focused it on the plight of the native peoples of Latin America."

In Mexico City, the President stared at the colorful box-of-bullshit, pressed the mute button on his channel selector, and then sighed. Governing Mexico had turned out to be like working the bridge of an enormous oil tanker that was ponderous and slow to respond to its captain's guidance: first steering it right and then left to keep it off the shoals. Guiding the ship of state had to take place long in advance of any measurable response. Ironically, the recent gain in Mexico's momentum was due in large part to his economic reforms.

Recently he had steered hard right in order to bring the country into the competitive world that lay ahead, intending on raising on raising Mexico to the head of the second rank of nations and poising her for entry into the first rank. Ruthless businessmen ran the giant economy of her neighbor to the north, and after Clinton's NAFTA, they had transformed the frontier states into models for the rest of the country, but things had changed since. Dealing drastically with the narco wars in the north was a very complicated but unambiguous matter. However, negative international publicity about suppressing indigenous unrest in the south would make his presidency lose way if he steered too far to the right.

The French say it best: "On the right is the wallet, but on the left is the heart."

The Socialist revolution of 1910 was the patriotic matrix of Mexico, and its ideals were the stuff of its soul. The *frontera* with the US was where the future, and the flesh, of a healthy economy took its form. Mexico seemed, like man himself, to be condemned to an endless struggle between the soul and the flesh.

This woman, Concha Osorio Ward, had described it perfectly with the metaphor of the eagle and the snake. In fact, the eagle and snake motif was an icon of Mexican culture that was even found on the national flag itself. Unfortunately, in that context, it showed the snake as a helpless victim about to be devoured by the eagle.

El Presidente raised his remote control to condemn Anderson Cooper and *Licenciado* Castaneda to gray. Instead, he picked up his secure phone and pushed the button for his Minister of the Interior's office.

"Yes, Mr. President?"

"You've been watching CNN?"

"Yes."

"Call in the dogs."

"Sir?"

Call in the special units, but leave everyone else on alert. The world is watching, and I don't want those people harmed."

"That woman is dangerous." The minister referred to the clips of Concha's speech, which were being featured on all main cable channels.

"Yes, very," the President agreed. "But she may also prove to be useful."

MiT

Tom had worked himself up to the edge of hysteria, and he wanted to cry like a child because he felt as afraid as any helpless child. In spite of this, the stress had gotten to him, and his fit was giving him a lot of relief.

He cursed Agustino and kicked the cabinet from the wall again. He'd screamed, cursed, and challenged them all. When he had the women, the children, the dogs, and the one man in the upper village to watch him throw his fit, he told them all to go fuck themselves. *¡Chingan todos!*

They waited until he was through, then all but the scabby dogs left. After that, a beautiful little girl dressed only in yellow underpants, gold earrings, and a shy smile brought him a sweet roll.

Mexicans are passionate people who understand that when a man has to lose it, he has to lose it, and they take no offense at his anger.

Now, if he could figure out some way to kill all the barking, snarling, pissing dogs, his day would be perfect. Tom imagined watching a mountain sunset with a cup of good coffee, a shy smile from a pretty little girl bearing a gift, and all the mangy dogs in Mexico dead. Best of all, the reality was that in his mock frenzy, he had knocked the mirror to the cement floor, and it now lay there in shards of keen glass.

MiT

Oz and Olga had everyone ready on the turnaround at the end of the mountain road. All the flashlights had been tested, and everyone was gathered for the trek up the mountain to the sacred grove.

"Remember, no food until after the ceremony!" Olga emphasized. "The Society of Ancient Guardians will have everything prepared for us, including the meal after the ceremony. All you need is your flashlight, your water, your Gate to Heaven, and a reverential attitude."

And your bullshit detectors are in the Off *position*, Pete thought.

His mind was on the police action in Tlaxiaco while he was here with a bunch of dickheads with no common sense, too much money, and way too much time on their hands. He couldn't wait to put a major kink in all their lives when he chopped this action in the ass back in Berkeley.

Oz gave a little speech about the history of the cultivation of the monster 'shrooms—how rare they were, how privileged this group was. They were also the only people in the whole world who were going to share in this secret ritual thought lost in the fogs of antiquity.

Olga's voice joined Oz's in the dark. "This climb is also a

meditation walk, so use the time to prepare and strengthen your minds. You will need to create a reservoir of mental strength to participate in this ritual because it is from another time and another world."

They started up the dark mountainside, their flashlights throwing wan circles of light onto the dark ground and scorched night air.

MiT

Sam went to Polly's room, then knocked, and she let him in.

"You can relax, the raid is off again," he said and saw relief soften her face. Sam had been brutally honest with her earlier and said that Tom's chances of surviving a military operation were not very good. In his mind, he knew the chances were a flat zero, but he hadn't wanted to deprive her of any hope.

"What happened?" she asked.

"The Minister of the Interior phoned and told the military and the police forces to stand down. Ten more minutes and it would have gone off. The troops were in the trucks and ready to roll."

"Why did he call it off?"

Sam shrugged. "Who knows? This is Mexico, and you should know more about it than I do."

He stared at the wall for a moment and added, "What the hell are Tom and I doing down here, anyway? We don't know the language, and we don't know any rules, so we can't know what the hell is going on."

Polly answered, "I know the language, and I know some of the rules."

"What are the rules, then?"

"The basic rule is to not do anything until you have to. After that you make it up as you go along."

"They're not big on planning, huh?"

"Only the technocrats in Mexico City and the industrialists in the north use planning as we know it. The rest of the country either doesn't know squat about planning or actively sabotages what everyone else is up to in order to steal the spoils. Down here it's, *Ready, Fire, Aim.*"

"What makes it different down here?"

"It's always the year 1910, and Emiliano Zapata, the greatest hero of the peasantry, is as alive as he can be. His picture hangs in most of the schools of the countryside, in the place where the presidents would normally be."

MiT

The first thing Demetrio Osorio did when he came into the bathhouse was to order Agustino away, then shine a bright flashlight in Tom's face. The second thing he did was lean down, breathe his stinking alcoholic breath in Tom's face, and curse him. The third thing he did was kick Tom in the stomach to make him groan with pain. Then he laughed and left with another man he had called Marcos, who had leaned in through the door to watch.

Now, lying in his puked-up sweet roll and coffee, Tom remembered his vow never to kill another human being. But that vow meant nothing to him at the moment. In his mind's eye, he felt the pistol buck against his hand and shock spreading over the man's face the moment he understands that he is killed. Shock, fear, thoughts of his mother, and her name come to his lips. The fragile shucks of his manhood fall away, and the baby boy receives the wound. Then the slackening of the limbs and darkening of the eyes as his soul flies away.

Even in the dark, he thought he knew who the man was—the one with the pistol who had made Tom piss his pants in fear. But what goes around comes around, the bastard's time would come; it would come at Tom's hands, and he could hardly wait.

Most of the Society of the Ancient Guardians gathered around a fire at the summit of Nindo Tocoshu. Some were not qualified to participate in the *Rito Grande*, the Grand Rite, while others who were qualified had chosen not to participate. However, all members were present to honor, and mollify, the anger of their rain god.

José stooped at the edge of the fire to stir the contents of the blackened clay pot simmering at the edge of the flames. He put the tip of a small finger in it to test the temperature, then carefully washed the finger and wiped it dry.

"A few more minutes should do it," he said, then stood and looked at a cloth spread on the ground. On it were twenty-four small gourd bowls set in a circle.

José pointed to one and said, "That bowl is for the elected one. Remember that we start with that one because the extra ingredient takes a bit longer to have its effect. Patricio, you are in charge of this part of the ritual, so remember that the liquor must be poured into the bowls from the one with the red rim then into the others. It must be handed out in the same order. Do not forget."

Exasperated, Patricio said, "I have participated in three other Grand Rites—in every one that you have."

"I apologize, brother, it's just that you know how important it is that everything be done in exactly the same manner that our ancestors did it in other times of peril for the Mixtecos. You know how important this is."

José turned to look at the edge of the clearing, to remind himself why they were here. Fallen logs still smoked, glowing embers veined the sides of standing trees, and the air was thick with the smell of fresh smoke. Half the circumference of the ceremonial glade had been consumed, and the fire still glowered.

But they were gathered here to bring an end to all that. The fires would be quenched; the convulsions in the bowels of the earth would be stilled. That was why they were gathered here to celebrate the Grand Rite. It had been called for only three times in the almost forty-five years the Gorostiza brothers were active in the Society. Three times the earth had shaken, and the clouds abandoned the people. But none of those times had been half as bad as this one. Never had Dzaui been so angry.

This one, of course, would be somewhat different. It would be only the second time that a non-Mixtec person would witness the rite and the first time to serve as the elected one. The father of *La Leonessa* had been the only one previously invited as a witness, and that was more than forty years ago. So, it was fitting, in spite of the fact she was a woman and offering them the elect, and a great deal of money, for the other gringos to witness the sacrifice.

Surely Dzaui would appreciate the magnitude of that offer and respond with his presence by again dragging his robes of rain behind him. The fires would be doused, the earth stilled, the corn and bean flowers beckoned. It had been so for the whole long history of his people, and it would be so this time too. Dzaui would be awakened, and then he would rise in joy when he smelled the blood.

Chapter Thirty-Two

Polly knelt by her bed, her hands folded in prayer as she begged for Tom's deliverance.

She shook with fear, both for him and for herself, because this was more than she could bear. Having to accept this as something beyond her control was not what she was used to. Her intelligence, beauty, social standing, and money had insulated her from this feeling of helplessness for almost her entire life. Not since the troubles of her first pregnancy had any obstacle yielded to her after she brought all those resources to bear.

But this night, she had cursed the fates, she cried, she paced the floor and took showers. She even sent the night watchman out to buy her a pack of cigarettes but threw them in the trash after one nauseating puff.

Surrendering, she finally fell to her knees in a position of wordless supplication. And at that moment, she remembered something Tom always said, something that mostly amused her in the past: "Finally, we have absolutely no power over people, places, or things."

He had repeated it many times, and she had not believed. She had power over all those things at the times when Tom was repeating the homely motto. The one word she missed, it was clear now, was the first: *Finally*.

She then remembered something else that Tom repeated in some of their most private talks: God is real, and he works real miracles in our lives when invited with a whole heart.

That had all been too simplistic for her. She was raised High Church Episcopalian, and its rituals made her feel a glow when she took her daughters to Christmas and Easter masses, but she had never had to ask God for anything.

Now, she was alone and far from her church, her family, and too far from the man she had promised to marry. She was alone, but if Tom was right, perhaps that was not true. With tears of helplessness running down her face, she raised her hands in honest supplication.

MiT

When Tom heard approaching footsteps in the dark, he rolled over, put his manacled feet against the rickety door, hoping to keep the *pistolero* from entering again. He promised himself he was going to resist in every way he possibly could.

Earlier, he was lying in the acid stench of his vomit and the blackness, feeling sorry for himself. The helpless emotion had begun to corrode him at the core, threatening to collapse him and his will.

But he had forced himself to halt the descent into self-pity. What inspired him was the memory of the dying cock and its final kick, the one that sent his adversary to its end. Tom remembered the golden eye, hard as amber, and the unexpected flash of the deadly spur.

Never, ever, *ever* give up, he remembered from the cockfight, and it had come back to him again this night.

He felt the push of a hand against the door, then a voice whispered, "Señor Tonson? Señor Tonson is Cenovio Osorio."

Concha's brother? Tom rolled away from the door and said quietly, "Come in."

The man pushed the door open, entered, and shut the door behind him. He then turned on a dim flashlight, shining the weak beam toward Tom. Then, miracle of miracles, he heard the sound of his backpack and running shoes drop on the floor of the hut!

"Why are you here, Cenovio?"

"I am coming because they are say to kill you."

"Who wants to kill me?"

"Marcos Albino an' Demetrio, an two more *malditos*—ver' bad mens."

"Who are they?" Tom asked, thinking that Cenovio was talking of the two men who had kidnapped him, the ones who had left half an hour earlier.

"*Marcos es mi primo*, me . . ."

"Cousin," Tom supplied. "And who is the other one?"

"Is me, brother."

"Brother!" It was hard to believe that this big man with the drooping lip and murderous eyes shared the same bloodline as the other two gentle people.

"Yes. They are drink mezcal with two *otro malditos,* an' they talking to kill you. I am talk them that to killin' you only make police come for all our family, but they are *muy borracho*."

"So there will be four of them coming?" Tom asked, and the thought frightened him. Two, maybe. Four, no way.

"Yes, so you mus' run 'way. Don' be go through San Miguel, you mus' go over mountain to valley on 'nother side." The beam of light ran up the east wall of the bathhouse.

"How am I going to find the way? And what about the dogs?" Those damn barking, snarling, biting, mangy, rib-pooched, skeletal dogs. But Cenovio chose to ignore that part of the question.

"Is *campo* . . ."

"Field."

"Yes, is big field there." This time the beam of light pointed to the north wall.

"I've seen it. It runs to the edge of the trees. Then what?"

"In corner of field is *camino* . . ."

"Trail, yes. How big?"

"Is big one. You following it for two kilometer and is coming 'nother *camino*, down from mountaintops. This one is going over mountains an' when you is over tops is *barranca grande*."

"Canyon."

"Si, *cañon arbol*."

"Wooded canyon."

"Is two *caminos,* and you taking one on the left."

"Okay. I go up this trail to where it meets another trail, one that goes over the ridge. I stay on that one until I get to the head of a wooded canyon, and then I take the trail to the left. ¿*Correcto*?"

"*Si*. This *camino* is going to *camino de carros*."

"A highway."

"Yes. Is road an' many *carros* and *camionetas* are going there."

"What about the dogs?"

"You mus' be waiting for the rains. Then dogs are go inside and don' be hearing you when is coming these rains."

"Rains! What rains? It hasn't rained here for over a year, and the place is burning up."

"Tonight is coming rains."

"How do you know?"

There was a long silence, and then Cenovio said, "Dzaui is come again. The Guardians are on Nindo Tocoshu, and is coming the rain when they are singing an' they are . . ." The voice trailed off in the dark.

Tom shook his feet to make the chains on his ankles rattle. "What about these?"

The flashlight came on again, and Cenovio handed it to Tom to hold. Tom almost gasped when he saw the thong and key that Agustino had worn around his neck. He guessed that Cenovio was going to kick him loose, and the proof of the rescue was enough to make him want to bawl in relief.

When the chains and strap that tied his arms had been removed, Tom stood and stretched them. Oh! It felt good. But then a little voice said, *Not yet, not yet.*

"The dogs will go inside when the rain comes, but what if it doesn't come?'

"Is come, *seguro*." The voice was so confident that Tom believed.

"And what if the *malditos* come before it rains?"

The silence in the little room was disturbed only by the buzz of the crickets outside. The confidence that Tom had felt a moment before was disturbed as the thought of four men and a half dozen dogs tearing at him made his heart skip.

"Can you come with me? The dogs won't bark if you come with me."

"I mus' go down to *casita* where they are drinkin' and try to stay them. If I am do this until the rain is coming . . ."

"And if they find out that you have helped me to escape?"

"They will maybe kill me, but is okay. I am dead man jus' the same."

"Why?"

"I have kill policemens, and that is something that I cannot be helped for. They will come. Me and Demetrio and also Marcos, Juan and Raul, José and Patricio. We all are dead mens."

"You don't know that for sure."

"I have know this from my dreams, and there will be many others dead mens too. Only my sister is living a long life."

Tom had heard the same prophetic note in the man's voice when he predicted rain and had no doubt of its truth this time, either. The little man was a prophet.

He heard Cenovio step to the door and open it, though the only evidence was the sound. Then Tom saw the stars.

"Adios, Amigo," Tom said as he heard the man's bare feet

padding away. A dog barked down the hill, and the crickets chirred even louder than before, a sure sign of rain.

MiT

José had been chanting for an hour, raising his voice to the stinking black sky and the muddy stars to summon Dzaui from his deep sleep. Calling his name, calling his name . . .

Patricio relieved him at intervals, calling for intercession by others in the ancient Mixtec pantheon. He asked them to raise the god who had turned his face as two acolytes fed the fire and warmed food for the meal after the ceremony. Two other acolytes cleaned the altar of wiry grasses sprouted between the stones. They were dressed in their ceremonial gear of feathered caps, necks hung with jade ornaments, armbands, plumed bustles, and skirts of bleached homespun.

"I am glad that this time we did not have to carry those turkeys all the way up the mountain. Last year I thought I was going to have a heart attack before I got up here with the damn things."

"Ah, but this year we will not have *carne de pavo* for our families, and that is a pity."

"Hmmm, yes. They will be disappointed that we do not come home with turkey meat. And why not? Why is it that there will be no turkeys to shed their blood for Dzaui?"

"Because Dzaui is very, very angry with the people. They say he would not be satisfied with the blood of birds."

"But what reason? What is it that we have done to make him so angry at us?"

"Some say it is because many are worshipping with these new people, the *Evangelistas*."

"Hmmm, that is possible. The padres have always left us some of our father's religion to feed our souls, but these new people, they are different. They say the love of Jesus is all we need."

"Both my sons and one daughter worship with them. But they seem so happy, it does not seem right that Dzaui would begrudge them this happiness."

"But that is what the priests of the *Capitanes* said long ago, then they killed everyone who was content with the love of the old gods of the people, like Dzaui."

The other man tugged a grass bunch from between the stones and shrugged. "The business of the gods is complicated because they are very temperamental. One never knows what they will do, and besides, it is every man's lot to suffer. That's just the way it is."

At the lower edge of the clearing, Plato and Socratio saw the bouncing procession of lights coming up the trail, announcing the arrival of the gringos.

"It is very pretty, is it not?"

"Yes, like a serpent of light," Socratio agreed.

When the Americans reached the edge of the glade, they gasped at the priest's appearance. They looked as if they had stepped off the walls of Monte Alban, the royal city of the Zapotec and Mixtec kingdoms.

Olga and Pete were the last to arrive. Pete was chagrined he had been the one to lag, as Olga patiently waited for him to catch his breath at many of the zigs and zags of the trail. Many of the group were in their fifties, even sixties, but had kept up the pace Oz set. This was a very unusual bunch of senior citizens, even for the fitness-goofy Bay Area.

Plato and Socratio escorted them to the fireside, where they saw José and Patricio standing in front of a stone pillar. On the pillar was set a stone visage about the size of a large pumpkin. It must have been buried at the ceremonial site because it was dark with water it had absorbed. The damp sculpture was striking for the effect the water-darkened surface gave as firelight shone on its matte surface. The reflections heightened the contrasting eye sockets that were black wells into which the light fell and did not return. The gouged mouth was open in what appeared to be a screaming grin.

The two elder brothers stood in front of the pillar with their arms raised and their voices chanting together in a sing-song wail. The song line rose and fell, turned from duet to solo and back to duet as the two priests twined their voices in a song old as the stones.

The men's dresses were just as striking, with plumes and ornaments of a magnificent variety. The costumes were readily recognizable for anyone who had seen codices of the ancient Mixtec civilization. There was a breathtaking extravagance about the costumes that underlined the intricate vocal celebrations. The effect the scene had, lit by a fire that the other men were feeding, was striking. Exciting.

Pete's hair stood on end, and from the looks of the other gringos' faces, they were having the same sensations as the singers' voices spiked the night and twisted their voices into a cable of sound. The group gathered at a place indicated by Oz, and after a couple of moments, the song line fell to a solo by José. Patricio turned and strode to where a ceremonial cloth was spread on the ground with small gourd cups set in a double circle. A man dressed in feathers, jade, and silver jewelry filled the cups half-full from a blackened clay pot.

Patricio stepped to the cloth and reached to the center of it for a cup. He turned, raised it to the smoky night, then walked to the group. Pete felt his sleeve pinched, and Olga tugged him forward. The man in the stunning ceremonial dress handed him the cup.

"Drink it," Olga whispered. "And hurry, while it's still warm. It tastes awful when it's cold."

Pete raised the cup and sipped at the liquor. He could tell it was alcoholic, but except for the familiar rush of the alcohol, it tasted like nothing he had ever tasted before. Not good, but not all that bad. And he could tell that Olga was right: the stuff was definitely better warm. He drained the cup, lumps and all, and handed it back to the priest.

Patricio handed the empty vessel to a helper, who broke the clay vessel on a stone, and returned for another cup. He did that until he had given each in the group of Anglos a portion. Then he filled the balance of the cups, and the members of the Society drank.

Pete noticed the cups were handed out from the center of a serpentine, the coil of vessels unwinding slowly. And as he watched the uncoiling, he distinctly saw the form of a serpent take shape on the cloth. It slowly unwound as the priest took the cups from the cloth. Finally, its tail was pinned to the cloth by the last cup. When that cup was picked up, the serpent moved slowly, sinuously off the cloth and into the darkness outside the fire's light. It moved toward a pile of rocks at a distance from the fire that two men had been tidying up when the group arrived.

Whoaaa! he thought. *The drink was hallucinogenic, and it was quick, having taken only minutes to begin its effect.* He turned to Olga and looked at her.

Olga stared back at Pete, and she was smiling. There was nothing seductive about the smile; it was more a smile of approval. But it was her eyes that struck him with more than the smile. They were a luminous green, and the fire's light was dancing in the dilated pupils flashing red, green, red with green, red, then green again.

Pete was aware that the hallucinogenic drink was at the heart of the striking effect, and he let himself embrace it. He was visually oriented and color-sensitive, so when he was stoned, that faculty was enhanced.

I don't know if I want to eat a mushroom on top of this. God only knows where a trip like that could take me, he thought. But when Olga told him to, he ate it.

The night air was warm and heavy with the smell of fresh smoke from slowly dampening fires still flaring on the mountain. It sure as hell didn't feel like rain was on the way, but the crickets seemed to think it was.

Tom unzipped his backpack and searched the inside to take inventory. On the top was a light wool sweater, then the sweatpants. His rain poncho was packed next, and under that was a pint water bottle, but it was empty.

Oh well, he thought wryly, *I won't need this if it rains the way Cenovio said it's going to.* The next item confused him, his fingers not recognizing it. Then he remembered his slingshot he used to kill grouse during the hunting season.

He stood and stretched again, for the twentieth time since he was left alone. The tedium and the tension of waiting were getting to him, but he knew he had to wait for Cenovio's promise. Twice he opened the door to the bathhouse and stuck his head outside. Both times two of the emaciated mongrels stood from their beds beneath the bougainvillea at the side of the little ranch house and growled.

He sat down again, his hand on his pack, and tuned his ears to the sounds of the night: crickets, a distant radio, a cock crow answered by others. A burro brayed and wheezed for a few moments. In the village far below, a pack of dogs barked insanely to mark the passage of a stranger.

While the barking was faint, Tom could also pick out the voices of different groups. Dogs were an ancient warning system, and one with teeth.

He had come to understand that the dogs, which during the day were little more than filthy, scarred, flea-bitten flesh, filled a real ecological niche. They ate the human excrement dropped randomly in the dark and made night walks a tentative affair. They also gleaned the garbage and other offal that drew flies, and they were an alarm system for each owner's property. They were ignored almost totally after they were pups, and the death of a dog meant little more than food for the others. No sentiment was wasted on them when they were grown, and when a dog had served his purpose, he was killed and pitched as easily as corn husks were discarded. Feral dogs filled the ancestral niches once filled by coyotes and wolves, so they could be a real threat to anyone who dared to walk alone in the night. Tom smiled grimly at the thought of the contrast with the canine darlings of *El Norte*, on whom more money was spent than given to charity and could receive more affection than the children of the house.

Suddenly, his attention was seized by the sounds of drunken men's voices coming from down the hill. There was shouting, cursing, and he focused all his senses in that direction, trying to interpret the ruckus.

Only an occasional word was distinct enough to be recognized, and almost all of the swear words being shouted for emphasis. The sound was universal enough. Anyone who has spent any real amount of time in bars, and other places where alcohol is consumed in quantity, can learn the language of drinkers and translate it. He feared the moment had come when the four *malditos* decided to execute him. His choices would then be to run and risk the attacking dogs or stand and face the men. It was a lose-lose situation.

He gauged the volume for any indication that the men were heading up the hill, then understood it was only a drunken argument. The ruckus died away, leaving only the sounds of music from a radio and the crickets' chirring barely discernible over the thunder of his pulse in his ears.

The pilgrim group sat on the ground to watch and listen as José sang. He occasionally stooped to take powders and liquids from various bags and clay dishes at his feet. He sang for a few minutes, then bent to put his fingers into one or another of the vessels, stood, and flicked his fingers at the pillar and effigy. Oz circulated among the group and prompted them to finish their mushrooms and drink their water.

Pete enjoyed the show, watching the firelight play off the singing priest's glowing feathers, the silver, and green jade. The singing man turned into a pillar of pure meaning. The songs, his body, the fire, the feathers and jewels, the night and the stela with the stone head were joined in a crucible of significance that transcended thought. It was everything except thought and intellect. The drink had given Pete a glow and feeling of peace that made him willing to acquiesce to every sensation. He was not afraid; he was ready to step through the great Gate to Heaven.

There was no sensation of time's passage. He only knew when the singer stooped, took Pete's hand, lifting him to his feet, and was now leading him to the pillar. And Pete gasped at what he saw.

The moon rising above the horizon was the same globe under the sombrero of the skeleton rider in Berkeley!

The trees behind the stela danced in the firelight, framing the pillar and head with its open mouth in a feathery flow of night and heaven. A feeling came out of the dark mouth, a feeling that filled Pete's chest with a beauty he had never known before.

Peace. Peace. Peace, it bid him. Pete raised his hands as tears of joy washed his face.

Two waiting priests took Pete by his hands and gently led him to the stone pile he felt he was bound for the moment he stepped into the glade. He raised his arms again, and the men removed his shirt.

He turned and looked at the visage again. The moon glowed above the trees; the stars made silent music and joined in a harmonic wave of love that caused Pete's face to wash again with grateful tears.

The priests sat Pete on the low altar and motioned him to lie down. When he did, two beautiful birdmen took his hands and held them lovingly. Two others put their hands on his legs, removed his shoes and socks, and held his bare ankles in the same loving way.

Pete turned his wet face from the starry sky and looked at the four wonderful bird creatures who held him. They were joined by the most beautiful animal he saw: its coat a mottled blanket of liquid gold and black. Its eyes were deep emerald green with a resonant ruby set in each center. The red of the pupils beamed at him and transfixed his will with a rush of feeling centered in his groin. The beautiful beast rattled in its throat, flashed its teeth, and slowly lashed its tail. The cat stepped lightly to the foot of the altar, put its paws on the stones, and lithely vaulted up.

The animal's breath filled his lungs as it placed its cheek against his. Its breath smelled of roses and was cool and damp as it blew across his face like a freshening breeze. Then the animal put its paw on his chest and said, *I am the Jaguar.*

Yes.

I am the rain. Can you feel me?

Yes.

I want the rose you carry.

Yes.

I will take it now, for it is mine.

Yes.

The Jaguar removed its paw from his chest, and a red bloom came into view. Pete was overwhelmed by the physical sensation of the blossom widening its petals. It welled, grew larger and larger, and the red color took on a metallic sheen as the firelight ran over it. Then its petals scattered in brilliant shards of red light. Then Pete was watching the scene from above.

The instant change was not surprising, it seemed only a different point of view, but he knew his part was done, and it was time to go. He was not surprised to see himself lying on the stone altar in the firelight with the brilliant priests holding his limbs and Olga kneeling between his legs. In one bloody hand, she held a glowing green blade, and in the other, she held Pete's heart, which she had taken from a wound in his chest.

He turned away from the scene toward the darkness below the moon to look for his spirit animal—the white horse with the beautiful eyes. It would come from the dark, and he knew to look for its glimmer. Pete waited in the perfect dark, but the shining horse did not come. Only at that last moment did he realize he had made a terrible mistake. Many terrible mistakes.

Chapter Thirty-Three

Tom woke when the thunder rolled. He cursed himself under his breath for having fallen asleep, for leaving himself vulnerable.

Stepping to the door, he opened it and put his head outside. When the lightning flashed, he saw the dogs were gone from under the bougainvillea bush. He waited for another flash and, without any conscious decision, put his feet to work as the thunder boomed from the dark sky. He stumbled over the furrows of the field but kept running in the direction of some woods he saw illuminated by flashes of lightning.

The thunder faded, and the only sounds were his ragged breath and stumbling footsteps over the dusty clods. He tuned his ears for the sound of barking dogs in hot pursuit, but they didn't pick up any noises, except those of his running stumble.

He fell, then picked himself up, wiped his hands, and adjusted the daypack. Overhead was a full moon whose light helped a little, but he still ran awkwardly, tripping and staggering on the uneven ground and stubs of corn stalk.

The field ended, and his feet felt the smooth forest floor, then suddenly, a great light flashed, and he was struck down! Lying on his back, feeling the pain spread through his head, he knew he was hit by lightning and feared he might be dying.

Oh God, please not now! Not now. He'd been through too much to die now that he was free!

A throbbing pain spread through his head, and he tasted blood. Then, raising his hand to his face, he felt a sticky wetness and knew what had happened. The lightning flashed again and confirmed his guess. He had run into a tree.

Waiting for another flash, he rolled to his knees and moved carefully in the direction of a clearing that presented itself in another pulse of bright light.

He did not want to get too far into the woods because he needed to find the trail as soon as possible. Running his tongue over his split lip and wiping at the blood that ran from his nose, he turned in the direction he had come. His forehead throbbed, and he fingered a big knot that pulsed painfully.

"Damn," he said and then grinned. He was away from the effing house, and there were no damn dogs, so a lump on the noggin was a very small price to pay for even this small amount of liberty!

More lightning came and went, and he saw no one crossing the field. His escape was still undiscovered, so it would be safe to use the flashlight.

Putting the pack on the ground, he rummaged in the junk pocket where he put the little Maglite after Cenovio left the bathhouse. He turned the focusing ring, and the little instrument shed its precious light. Tom turned his back to the field and pointed the lens away from the direction of the casitas. Holding it as close to perpendicular as was practical, so its light could not be seen except from yards away, he zigzagged the clearing until he intersected the trail, then started up it as fast as he could go.

MiT

Concha could not sleep. She was back in Chalcatongo with Tio and his family, waiting for word of José and Patricio's negotiations with the government's team in San Miguel. It hardly seemed possible, but they'd heard the President himself promised to accede to all the demands José had made in the original press conference.

The same thing had happened in Chiapas, and, apparently, it had worked well enough that the process was being followed as a model.

But what was genuinely amazing was the Governor of Oaxaca wanted to meet with Concha to talk about what she had recommended in her TV interview. He, too, was taking his cues from the events in the neighboring state to the south. International publicity was a lever with a very long handle, and God damn, Ted Turner.

In Chiapas, the governor was sacked, along with much of his administration, to be replaced by a man sympathetic to the needs of the Indian peoples. It was an object lesson for other governors of states with large indigenous populations. The Oaxacan governor even sent word that the President might be interested in meeting Concha, if it could be arranged.

But it could be a trap. It would be better to arrange these things through José. He was the local political operative and knew the ins and outs of many of Mexico's political snakes' dens. She and her brother had barely escaped the first levels of the country's septic political system. It was best that she didn't agree to anything at this point.

She stood near the entrance to the cave and watched the sky, where nimbus towers were building in the bright moonlight. They were lit at the top by the orange moon, and their bottoms sputtered with dashes of lightning. Storms were building as Dzaui stirred from his long, troubled nap.

Breezes built and blew the stink from the sky. The night turned cool, and lightning flashed over the mountains to the south. After a minute or so, she heard distant rolls of thunder. The lightning danced on the summits of the mountains, limning them in instants of dazzling white light and again, louder this time as the thunder muttered and grumbled.

She took in a deep breath, and her lungs filled with the clean smell of the cool air moving in from the east. Rain. Her intuitions ran down from the soles of her bare feet, searching the earth itself for another sense of change for the better. Good. The ground itself felt solid again. Dzaui seemed satisfied.

Concha turned her mind to the events of the last month and was amazed at how much had transpired. The death of her husband, then her flight, and the horrible event south of Culiacan. Then she'd lost Dzaui's heart and been held by the cacique's man until she'd been rescued. Pictures of the string of events ran through her head like a movie that ended with an image of the camera lenses pointed at her and earnest reporters asking her questions. And, somehow, she had known all the answers.

How had she gotten here? As a child, she was anonymous as any person could possibly be in this world, raised in one of the most poverty-stricken places on the face of the earth. Then she had been taken as a wife by a rich man and gone to a land where the grass grew only half the year, then was a land of ice and snow the other six months.

True, she learned a great deal while she was there, and she had seen things. Her education there was not a trivial one. But to flee the powerful country to the north, then find herself a fugitive in her own country, only to end up being told the governor and the president wanted to meet with her was hard to believe!

She pulled her shawl tighter around her shoulders and buried her hands in it as the air grew cold. Lightning danced closer and closer as it moved in all directions from the summit of Nindo Tocoshu.

Walking to a tree, she leaned against it to watch the drama of the sky and wait for the first drops of the blessed, blessed rain. Her people would be happy, and that made her gladdest of all. The dangerous task of returning the Heart of the World to the Mixteca had fallen to her and her brother, and she was genuinely grateful they were chosen. Life itself was riding on these winds.

Destiny. Was there anything to all that? Was it true that each person was given a task to do, something important in the scheme of universal things? Something given to her and her brother that could change the fate of her people? Surely not.

But perhaps it was true. After all, she was an Indian woman from the poorest corner of the land invited to meet with the most powerful men in her country. Amazing. Perhaps there was something to the idea of destiny after all. The worst part of being human is that the gods keep us so pitifully blind to all but what we need for the moment, and it's dolled out in such small amounts—only one day at a time.

MiT

Thunder woke Polly, and at first, she didn't know what had brought her out of her troubled sleep. Her body smelled of perspiration and smoke, so she stripped off her clothes and went to the bathroom to turn on the water in the shower and wait for it to warm as lightning flashed outside, and opalescent, blue flickers lighted the bathroom window.

She slid it open to let fresh air rush inside. The smell of smoke was gone, and the air was heavy and sweet. She opened her mouth to let the water from the showerhead rinse away the taste of the cigarette. The stream washed down her face and over her breasts and cleaned the stickiness from her back. She took in a deep breath of the fresh air spilling through the window. Then she dropped her chin to her chest to loosen the muscles in her shoulders and shook her head slowly from side to side, relaxing. Then she remembered Tom.

Polly snapped her head up and felt the muscles in her shoulders tighten again. She put her face closer to the window as if somehow she might sense what was going on with him by smelling the air.

Closing her eyes, she sent her senses out the window and waited for an intuition, but there was nothing there to comfort her. Thomas was still gone, and now it was raining. And again, she felt absolutely helpless. A sense of deep depression overwhelmed her, and she began to cry, the tears falling down the shower drain into the void of a heartless land.

MiT

Tom was making good time up the trail, given that he was running by the grace of a small flashlight. His breathing was labored, but he'd been running in the mountains around his house for months and was in pretty good shape.

Thank God for Polly and her exercise program. A year ago, he would have been puking from the effort, but at the moment, he was breathing hard and little more. The grade up the side of the mountain was steep, but his legs were holding out, and he was doing fine.

And then the rain hit. It began with a few big drops then quickened steadily, so he decided to stop and don the poncho. When he stepped back onto the trail, it was already slick. The earth apparently contained a lot of clay, so he would have to walk, no matter how much he wanted to maintain the fast pace. At any rate, he reassured himself, he was a long way in front of any pursuit. From the sound of things, the only ones likely to chase him were probably passed out by now. They had been pretty damn far into the mezcal jar, and drunk men don't make good athletes.

The rain slacked a bit, but it still came down steadily, and he had to stretch his steps to stay on the rocks in the trail. He still slipped, making for slow going. But the day was about to begin, and there was just enough light to turn off the flashlight. Tom stepped off the slippery trail and into the shelter of a big pine tree, then he dropped the pack and knelt to put the flashlight inside. The smell of the pine needles and the wet air suddenly flashed his mind back to his house in the mountains of Wyoming. For a moment, he was overcome with a longing for home. He wanted to be in his house; he wanted to be with Polly; he wanted to be safe.

He shook the thought from his head in order to stay focused on where he was and what he had to do. The mountain was steep, the trail hard, and God only knew what waited ahead. Or was gaining on him.

The duff under the tree was comfortable. He put his hand down and felt its resilience, a softness he had not felt in what seemed to be centuries. His butt was sore from the two days spent sitting on the cement floor of the bathhouse, so he decided to take a little rest. He put his back to the tree and stretched his legs. In his hurry to get up the trail, he hadn't realized the toll the steep trail was taking on his body. Winded and hungry, his feet hurt and legs ached.

He took off the poncho, turned it inside out to dry, and let the sweat on his body dissipate. He was very thirsty because he'd lost a lot of water while hurrying under the raincoat, and dehydration was a dangerous possibility if he didn't find someplace to get a drink.

But I'm free, he thought. The fearful memory of being held against his will kept trying to surface, but he turned his mind away from it. This was no time to indulge in thoughts of anger or revenge because he was free, and that was enough. All he had to do was keep his mind in the "now" and stay vigilant, and right now, the most important thing was to find the branching trail.

Cenovio had not given him any notion of how far up the mountain the trail split, and he was worried that he might have jogged past the junction. Then he suddenly remembered that the rain alone might not obliterate the signs of his passage. He looked at the path and saw the evidence of his flight in the inch of mud that had been dust an hour earlier—long gouges where he'd slipped on the mud. And where he hadn't were the distinctive track of his running shoes. He quickly rolled up his poncho and stuffed it into the pack, his mind racing. He would have to stay on the grass and duff beside the trail unless it began to rain hard enough to wash out his tracks.

Shrugging his pack on, he looked around for something he could use as a walking stick. He wrenched a limb from the rotting base of an oak, then laid it on a rock and broke it to a convenient length with a stomp of his foot. The going would be steep, but if he took his time, he could make it without having to leave more floundering tracks.

At that moment, something caught his attention. His heart began to pound in his ears as he concentrated, making it hard to hear, but the sound was unmistakable. It was the frantic barking of a pack of dogs, and they were getting louder.

Chapter Thirty-Four

Sam and Polly were drinking coffee in Polly's room. She had packed several packets of Starbucks Arabica instant coffee and a heating coil that boiled water in a mug. The restaurant didn't open until 7:30, and the coffee in the *mercado* was loaded with sugar, per the local custom.

"It sure smells good out there," Sam said. "It musta rained pretty good for a while, there's major puddles in the courtyard."

"The lightning and thunder woke me up. It rained real hard for ten minutes or so, but then gradually slowed to this." She waved her hand at the window, referring to the damp morning with monster gray and black clouds piling up slowly on the eastern horizon.

Sam said, "I've seen it rain out on the plains, in the Powder River Basin, and I thought I'd seen clouds before, but when I was coming back from the tactical center . . ." He left the sentence unfinished to indicate how impressed he'd been with the size of the threatening clouds.

"What's going on over there, anyway?" Polly looked terrible. Her hair was piled carelessly on her head, and black circles made her blue eyes appear washed out.

"They made contact with two of the leaders and are negotiating. One of the things asked was where Tom is and if he's all right, but that's not important to anyone but us. The cops and soldiers over there are mad as hell, and they want to go in and break some heads. The powers-that-be are in favor of negotiation, but the conservatives think that the government gave away the store the last time this happened. They think this incident could encourage every political splinter group to buy ski masks then call a press conference in order to stick up the government."

Polly frowned. "Well, if they had let the money intended for the communities go to where it belonged instead of their pockets, they might not be in this position. Only one peso out of ten thousand ever makes it past the grasp of the police and government officials. It's the story of Mexican bureaucracy. They're just pissed because they're going to miss out on what they've come to think of as their share. I have no sympathy whatsoever."

"But they are right, in a way."

"What way?"

"When people only have to don hoods and carry guns to get what they want, it's not a recipe for public order. You can't stick up the government every time you please, using the media as a weapon. The police have to be free to do their job."

"Sam, if you knew what the job of the police has been down here since time immemorial, you would be shocked."

"After finding out what Jesus and Berto were up to, it's easy enough to believe. They've got Berto sitting in the jail over there, and it doesn't look good for him."

"What was that all about, anyway? What were they up to?"

"They were dealing in artifacts, but only the world-class artifacts that Ward dealt in. Their angle was that they used their offices as cops to get them. Besides being on the take, they were letting narcos off the hook in exchange for world-class artifacts, and that's what happened with the Osorios. Growers could use artifacts to buy their way out of a bust, then keep on growing their crops."

Sam continued. "I guess there are a whole lot of important cultural things that have meaning to a family or a community, or even an entire culture which has been hidden for centuries.

Sanchez—Sandez, whoever—knew about all this because he's a Mixtec Indian and was probably corrupted by his supervisor, Bernalillo.

"Berto told Jesus about some of the stuff that he knew was hidden by particular families and others that were related to secret religious ceremonies. Because this is a big dope-growing state, they would barter with people they'd arrested. I guess they found a lot of very important pieces that way, and now Mexico wants to get them all back. This is turning into a political shit storm, because a lot of the robbers are some of our best politicians."

"So they were robbing those families or communities of their patrimony, their history, their religion, and without a second thought? Pretty typical bureaucrats, Mexican or American."

"They were working with the late Nathaniel Ward."

"I'm not surprised."

"The guys from the Interior Ministry have been interrogating Berto, and I think, they are giving most everything they've gotten out of him to me and the FBI."

"Did they say what Sanchez was doing in Jackson Hole?"

"He was there to do damage control."

"What kind of damage control?"

"Find out what he could about the investigation into Ward's murder—whether he and Bernalillo had been compromised. Unfortunately, we shared some information with him that we probably shouldn't have. Tom told him about the computer files the Feds were working on, and he relayed that back to Jesus. We have phone records that show calls to Tlaxiaco, but there was something bigger going on."

"Like what?"

"One or more of Ward's customers hired Bernalillo and Berto to do what they could to find out the extent of the damage. Then Bernalillo sent Berto north to assassinate Ward's wife, thinking she might know their names. We almost enabled a rogue operation and been a party to her murder and the killings of others.

"But then the Osorios turned up in Mexico, and I sent Tom down here with the hit man." Sam shook his head. "But, besides the shitty little deal that those two were doing on the side, they have led us to some important info on the smuggling and artifact dealing scene: a customer list that Jesus had in his briefcase. He wrote down some names Ward mentioned while they were doing business."

"Why would he do that?"

Sam shrugged. "Maybe to blackmail Ward, or he might have been planning market directly to the collectors. The list includes Germans, Swiss, Mexicans, Canadians, Americans, and one of the biggest names is The Honorable Nathaniel "Nat" Ward."

"You are kidding!"

"Nope. And, unless I miss my guess, it was Congressman Ward's collection that inspired the nephew's interest in archaeology. It also inspired him, unless I'm wrong as hell here too, to become a dealer in illegal artifacts. Who would be a better person to connect a professor with a network of multi-millionaire collectors, and vice-versa?"

Polly grimaced. "And this guy is the one who's responsible for Thomas being down here, then."

"No, I am responsible for that. I can't point the finger at anyone but myself, and now we have no business being here. We're in the middle of a foreign operation where the rules are different, and the values are inverted." Sam looked out the window. "I just want to get Tom back, then go home where I know the rules."

MiT

Tom wasn't jogging now, he was running. There was almost no traction on the muddy trail, so he was trying to travel on the rocks and grass that bordered the track. It was slippery, and he had fallen, but he was able to push himself to the limit in good areas.

His breathing was ragged as his brain tried to stay ahead of the body that burned oxygen faster than he could get it into his lungs. A black border fringed his vision, and perspiration ran over his eyelids, making it even harder to see. He was falling into serious oxygen debt.

Louder baying of the dogs told him he was being overtaken, but he hoped he could maintain a lead to where he might make a stand. The men would have to be practiced runners to catch him, and he didn't think that anyone who had been drinking all night was any match for the steady pace he had set. Then he heard a panting dog.

He turned and looked down the trail to see the big mongrel named Oso standing in the middle of the trail, looking back over his shoulder with his tongue hanging out a foot. He maniacally barked when he saw Tom, and apparently, he could also see the pursuers, so they could be no more than two hundred meters or so behind! Tom vaulted up the trail. The brief respite had given his body the rest it needed, and the rush of adrenaline the dog inspired was pumping through his body.

He ran, taking little steps and jabbing the sides of his feet into the grassy soil. The first fifty meters were comparatively easy going, but then he was in the first rock band, and the going was bad. Rocks rolled under his feet, and the dirt that had accumulated over the dusty winter was a film of mud that made the rocks shrug his feet away.

Tom's mind worked as he scrambled, trying to concentrate on where each foot should go, looking for bare rock that might afford enough friction. The dog was going to be on him by the time he reached the top of the rocks, he knew that, and he would have to stop to give the dog some attention. He was not going to let the bastard bite him, he promised himself. Not by the fucking mongrel who had made a point of pissing through the flimsy door of the bathhouse every time he walked by.

When Tom reached the top of the rocks, the dog was right behind him and barking so insanely that it said the pursuers were close. When he turned to face the animal, his lungs were burning, and his throat was raw. In his blurred vision, he saw a rock the right size for throwing. He bent to pick it up, but this was a Mexican dog with a sixth sense for the distance any man can throw a rock accurately. He dodged back down the trail, then stood at the bottom of the outcrop and bayed.

His strength was failing him, his legs were numb, and his chest on fire. But those were things he could prioritize, push down, put away. It was some other physical realities that were putting a damper on his flight. The air was thin, he was not young, and he hadn't had anything to eat for too many hours, and the machine had worn parts. No amount of adrenaline or inspiration could make up for those facts. Tom had to make a stand.

He turned to face the animal and saw it reaching out to take his leg. He lashed with the walking stick, but the animal's reflexes threw him backward at the last moment. He bounded back ten meters and bared his teeth in a grimace that made Tom shake.

"You . . . son . . . of . . . a . . . bitch!" he gasped and looked around for a rock. But there was nothing more than wilted grass, and the dog knew it as he turned his head to let the pursuers know that he had his quarry. He alternately looked at Tom and bared his teeth, then lolled his tongue to gasp for air.

Then Tom remembered the hunting slingshot he'd put in the daypack the last time he'd gone hunting. He dropped the pack to the ground. He put his left hand in the pack while holding the stick in his right to keep the dog away. When his hand found the slingshot, he pulled it out and dropped it to the top of his pack, then felt for the sack of steel ammunition for the Wrist Rocket. When his hand closed on the sack, his lips moved in thanks.

Tom realized that it would be impossible to load the slingshot without getting bit, so he gritted his teeth and stuck out his left foot while he loaded his weapon.

The dog was on his foot in a heartbeat, and the pain was paralyzing. Tom shrieked as the dog's teeth ran their full lengths into the sides of his foot. Snot flew from his nose, and his hands shook as he tried to make his brain concentrate on loading the slingshot while the animal pulled him downhill. Tom put all his will into the weapon, and his brain went into slow motion to cope with the pain. It was almost more than it could stand. Almost.

He did not remember aiming or releasing the steel shot, but his brain scored the effect of the missile. The animal was killed instantly. At a distance of only two feet, the round shot pierced the dog's skull and destroyed its life. The jaws released, and the body slipped on the slope, then hit a protruding rock and stopped.

Tom glanced at the slack body, then scrambled up to his backpack. The pain from his wounded foot rocketed through his body, but he switched his brain into a lower mode, and the pain decreased.

He reached the pack, threw it on, and grabbed the stick because he would have to use it as a crutch. Then he turned back up the steep hill to begin his flight again.

Tom left the trail when he saw a rib of rock that angled up the slope. It would give him solid footing, but it would also give him cover from the eyes of the men behind him. Then he remembered he had not heard voices for some time. He stopped for a moment and glanced over the rock rib. There was no one in sight on the trail. He was outpacing them again because they'd stopped to examine the body of the dog. He strode uphill as his legs summoned strength where there should have been none. His lungs were on fire, and the rush of air seared his throat, but he was almost there. He glanced up. On the skyline, a man on a big mule holding a pistol in his hand shouted down the hill to the other men. Above the pounding in his ears, Tom heard answering shouts, and he wanted to scream—anything but to be held prisoner again. As if that were an alternative to the reality he was facing.

The man on the roan mule was the one with the big lip and the murderous eyes. But now, his eyes were mocking and alight with humor. He sat on the mule with a pistol held casually in his hand as he shouted down the hill to describe Tom to the others, saying how pathetic he looked. The goading was painful enough, but even more painful was the sight of the pistol in the man's hand because it was Tom's personal service arm.

Perhaps it was that final insult that inspired Tom's brain to remember the lesson of the fighting cock: *Never, ever, ever, ever give up*. He dropped his pack and raised his hands, and Demetrio pursed his mouth, worked his throat, and launched a huge gobbet of spit.

Tom stooped and retrieved his backpack and unzipped it as he began a slow walk around a huge agave to put it between himself and the mounted man.

The rider responded by jabbing the mule with his heels and riding to the other side of the agave as he raised the pistol and sighted over the barrel. He was smiling and in no hurry because his compadres were in sight now. The gringo was trapped, and the time to kill him had come. When he rode around the agave, Demetrio was puzzled at what he saw. The man with the funny headband, the wet and muddy clothes, and the bloody shoe had his arms raised in front of his face. Demetrio dropped the muzzle of the pistol, curious as to what this man was doing. The pose was so odd.

The steel shot entered Demetrio's eye through the upper lid and rolled it back to expose the upper part of the orb in a flash of white. The instant he released the projectile, Tom knew it was going exactly where he had willed it to go. But he was still surprised by the instantaneous effect the impact had on the man. Demetrio didn't utter a sound, simply threw his arms over his head and fell backward, hitting the ground. Then he rose to his elbows and knees and put his hands to his face. The surprised mule ran a few paces and whirled to look at the fallen man. Then came the scream. If Tom had not been scrambling for the pistol, he might have felt a twinge of pity, but he did not.

Once he recovered his pistol, he popped out the clip and checked it. Then he glanced at the screaming man and dismissed him for the moment. He looked around the agave and saw three men standing down the hill, about fifty meters away. They were soaked in sweat, with hats in their hands and mud splashed to their knees. One was wearing a holster and had a .45 in his hand, the other two wielded machetes. Their black eyebrows and mustaches stood out in stark contrast to their pale and sweating faces.

It took a moment for them to understand what they were seeing. They had watched the gringo walk to the other side of the agave, then saw Demetrio ride behind it. Then they heard screams and saw the mule run into sight again to stand with its ears pricked as it stared at something. And now the gringo was pointing a gun at them.

Tom shot the man with the .45, which made him drop the pistol, then grab the thigh the bullet had pierced. The other men dropped their machetes and ran. The wounded man dragged himself to his feet and hobbled down the hill for the shelter of the rocks. He never made a sound except for a gasp when he'd been hit. He'd been shot before.

Tom turned swiftly to Demetrio. He sat with a hand over the ruined eye. He was not screaming but sat with gritted teeth and his one good eye on Tom. There was more hate on his face than fear.

Tom might have left him sitting there on the ground if the man had shown fear rather than malice. But the one defiant eye moved him to walk to the man, raise his pistol high over his head, and smash him on the skull with it. The defiance left the face, and the man groaned, rolled onto his stomach, and grasped the top of his head. He groaned again and alternately dug his feet into the hillside, his legs moving in spasms.

Tom stepped to the fallen man and aimed the pistol at the back of the shaggy head that was seeping blood through the fingers of the clasped hands. But something in his head said *No,* and his promise came back to him.

Tom turned his back and walked toward the mule, his hand out. The mule lowered her head, pricked her long roan ears, but didn't move away.

"Ho, girl," Tom said softly, "Ho, girl, c'mere."

She responded to the English words, and her eyes softened, her lip pulled up in a bit of a grin, and she met Tom halfway. She even made a pleased little sound when Tom took the bridle then rubbed her forehead.

Leading the animal down the hill, he checked to see if the men behind the rocks were visible, but they were not. So, he pointed the pistol down the trail and slowly pulled off three rounds. The recoil of the gun, the muzzle blast, and the sound of ricocheting bullets gave him a feeling of deep satisfaction. He felt in control again.

He retrieved his backpack, then mounted the mule from the uphill side and sat for a moment. His hands and arms shook, and his stomach was doing vaults. His eyes ran tears, and he was hiccupping.

After a minute, Tommy wiped his eyes, then turned the mule uphill toward the skyline. His body rejoiced at the feel of the strong, muscular strides of the beast. It was as if it were his own renewed and unfettered strength that propelled them up the hill. He was strong again. He was going to make it.

Once on the ridgeline, he stopped and turned to look at the wounded man. He was still curled in a tight ball, and his muddy clothes and posture gave Tom a twinge. Not a twinge of conscience, but a twinge of empathy because he could see himself curled in the bathhouse, lying in his own puke, and it had not been that long ago. *What goes around comes around*, he said to himself. There was a satisfying symmetry to the situation.

MiT

When the heart of the rain finally arrived, it came in bucketsful. It came in tubsful. It came in swimming-poolsful. It made so much noise, it woke Polly from her profoundly depressed sleep.

Groggily, she rose from the bed and went to the window where she could barely make out the cars in the courtyard, only meters away. The rain pounded on the roofs and hoods of cars, raising a tinny din. Rain spouts formed water in arcs thick as a man's leg.

Polly walked to the nightstand, turned on the lamp, then went to the bathroom to wash her face. She looked in the mirror, and her reflection appeared to have aged ten years. She then brushed her teeth and then returned to the bedroom for her hairbrush.

Standing at the window, she watched the deluge as she brushed her hair. It felt good. She closed her eyes and counted the brush strokes . . . *twelve, thirteen, fourteen, fifteen* . . . but the usually soothing ritual just added to her headache.

She walked to the bed, sat down, and put the brush down beside her. "What am I doing here?!" she asked herself aloud. "Why am I not in Huatulco with my family when I know they are worried sick about me and this dangerous relationship?"

Thoughts of Ferdie, Christina, and Maria crowded her fevered thoughts. "I have been so selfish, and I treated my family badly by moving to Wyoming. Ferdie is a good father to the girls, and he is brilliant and reliable, even if he has been unfaithful to me. Now I have abandoned them for a man who is vulnerable but reckless, and whose ambitions are limited. In only one year, he has been stabbed almost to death, and I almost died with him. Now he is kidnapped deep in the mountains of Mexico, and I am here alone. I must be insane!"

Polly picked up the bedside phone, and the desk answered.

"*¿Mande?*"

"*Llamame un taxi, por favor. Pronto.*"

"*Si, Señora.*"

"*¡Inmediatemente!*"

"*Si, Señora.*"

She hurriedly packed, then grabbed her purse, left the room, and walked across the patio toward the office, heedless of the pouring rain. Weeping from fear and emotional exhaustion, she stopped beside a large potted camellia and took off her engagement ring. One last time, she looked at the engraving: *You And No Other,* then gently dropped it among pink petals battered from the bush by the rain. Then she dashed across the wet patio and out the hotel door to her waiting taxi.

In the darkness at the edge of the patio, one of the kitchen girls had witnessed the scene. After Polly was gone, she went to the camellia pot and retrieved the ring. Then slipped it on her finger—it fit perfectly.

Chapter Thirty-Five

Tom found the wooded canyon and followed it down the mountain. As he rode, he looked over the Nochixtlan Valley at the morning sky and was impressed. The bulging clouds were piling and piling as the morning light turned them to brassy billows. As he watched, the towering clouds grew and continued to build. They kept growing until it outpaced his whole experience of clouds.

He had seen storm clouds over the Great Plains and thought them impossible to surpass, but this was a new standard. The storm front became an immensity that staggered his perceptions of what a sky would generate. The bottom of the formation grew blacker, the swollen sides turned brassier, and the edges were now a molten red. The enormous clouds boiled and pumped, rising and rising and rising as they ballooned even larger. Lightning snapped from the bottom of the mass, and thunder growled like a pride of lions over a kill.

The drought would be battered beyond memory by the angry immensity sweeping down the heavens to blot the earthscape from view. It was something of the gods' making, larger for having been held at bay for so long. Nature was pouncing on the occasion with a vengeance. The first cold winds came in blasts that frosted Tom's face a few minutes before the lightning.

The first bolt landed less than fifty meters from him and blasted the top of an oak into sparks and splinters. The circle of smoke was drowned instantly by the wind. The mule hunched her back and skittered but did not try to buck. Then came a blast of raindrops the size of grapes, and hail was right behind it. He was cold to the bone in moments, in spite of his sweater and poncho.

The trail soon ran with water, and it grew softer by the moment. It would be impossible to travel on it before long, but the lightning was what was gaining his immediate attention. More than one of them landed so close that it was impossible to distinguish the flash from the booms that literally shook the ground.

I've got to get out of the open, Tom thought.

Moments later, he saw a small side canyon, and he rode into its mouth. The place was lower than the rest of the terrain and somewhat protected from the dancing lightning bolts. He dismounted by some bushes, and he tied the mule to one of them. Large animals attract lightning, and he did not want to be sitting on top of a lightning rod. He ran his tongue over the split lip and felt the large bump on his forehead. Hell, he'd already been hit by lightning once today.

In the inundating rain, he looked around for a safe place. Then, as if to underline just how pressing the situation was, a lightning bolt flashed above him and rent the air with an ear-splitting *CRACK*. The top of the tree fragmented, sending a vein of fire plunging down the side to explode in a ball of sparks on the wet ground.

"Shit, fire!" he exclaimed and looked anxiously around. Another flash lit the canyon, and the thunder assaulted his ears. Finally, he chose a spot in the bottom of the arroyo and anxiously walked down to it. The place he chose was running with a few inches of water, so he stepped to a place above the rivulet.

He thought the rain could not get any heavier, but it did. Then it changed to hail with balls of ice the size of rice at first, then getting progressively bigger until he had to put his hands in the hood of his poncho to keep the pellets from hurting. After a couple of minutes, his hands were tender from the pounding, and he was flinching at each stone.

The pounding hail was bad enough, but he now had another problem—he was up to his ankles in water. He was standing at the mouth of a sizeable ravine, and he realized it could be catching huge amounts of water further up the mountain. It might even be dammed and be getting ready to release a wall of water and debris he wouldn't be able to escape. He decided that it would be safer in the trees and began to walk through the growing stream of icy water.

But lightning struck immediately above, and a deafening crash of sound made his heart almost jump from his chest. He retreated to the ravine, but it was now running water just below his knees, and the water was full of balls of ice that, mercifully, had stopped falling. The rain was still coming in sheets, and icy air was being driven by the freezing wind. Tom was now starting to shiver from the cold. Hypothermia was setting in.

"God," he said, "I don't want to die here! Not now, not like this. No one will ever find my body."

Tom was genuinely frightened. He could be struck by lightning, or he could fall into hypothermia and collapse into the roiling rush of muddy water and ice. He was shaking badly now.

Snatching a passing stick from the flood, he used it to brace himself against the surge. He turned to face upstream, then moved his feet apart and put the point of the stout stick into the bottom of the flood to form a tripod, something he learned in the army's survival school.

The water was now rushing above his knees, and he could feel pieces of debris banging his shins. Some of them were large enough to hurt his numbed legs, so there was a real danger of being knocked from his feet. If that happened, he would never gain them again. It was time to get out of the flood, lightning or no.

He moved the point of the stick and poked it into the arroyo's soft bottom, then he slid one foot to the side and followed with the other. Using the tripod, he braced himself against the current and inched carefully across the stream. At one point, his foot went into a hole, and he almost lost his balance, sending a flash of panic through him. But the water became gradually shallower as he went, and he was finally out of the rush and standing in ankle-deep mud on the slippery edge of the rushing waterway. If he could perch here without slipping until the flood passed, maybe he had a chance of survival. Twenty minutes later, the flood had passed, and he slogged toward the mule, who stood hunched against the rainstorm. Thank God she had not bolted.

Tom's pack was slung over the saddle horn, and in that pack were waterproof matches and firestarter—part of the survival gear that smart hunters carry in snowy Wyoming during the hunting season. If the mule had run away, he would now be a dead man walking.

The hunt for sticks and wood for the fire warmed him as he moved around the canyon, gleaning pieces from the aprons of the trees. He snapped dead branches and rusty insect killed boughs that would kindle readily and put the small pile under the shelter of a pine tree, then placed a stick of firestarter on it. The stuff lit at the first match.

Tom piled more tinder on the fire and then added larger sticks. Even in the drizzle falling from the tree, the fire grew with each piece of wood. Ten minutes later, he had a fire with flames a meter tall. He raised his poncho, let the wonderful heat under it, held out each hand and sodden foot in turn, and let the glow work at the muddy balls they had become. His shaking was lessening with each moment.

Thank you, God, he said silently. I'*m going to make it. I'm going to make it.* In order to warm his back, he turned around and almost jumped out of his skin. A man dressed only in pants had been standing behind him.

The specter's long, black hair hung in strings over his face. The feet were bare, the eyes vacant, the face a bluish-white. Tom saw the man's skin was waxy, and there was no goose flesh—symptoms the body was barely responding superficially because it was cold deep at the core. Even his heart had been chilled. However, the most notable thing about the body was a raised and raw weld that ran from the base of his throat down the length of his sternum. It was Pete Villareal, and he was dying of exposure.

MiT

Polly sat in the waiting room of the Cristobol Colon bus station. It was crowded with Indians—some traveling but most just sheltering from the storm. She found a seat in the corner of the dreary place and closed her eyes. She was completely exhausted. *Goodbye, Thomas*, she thought, *I'm sorry I wasn't strong enough for you.*

Her chest felt tight from withheld emotion, but she had made up her mind. She would go back to Ferdie and lose herself in the development deal they had worked so hard on and for so long. They would have a family business again; they would *be* a family again. She and Ferdie could re-marry quickly while still in Mexico, then he would go back to his womanizing, and they would return to their separate bedrooms in California. She felt numb inside at the thought, but it was better than constantly tripping along the precipice of utter disaster.

The conversations among the Indians swirling around Polly were suddenly hushed, and when she opened her eyes, she saw Sam Harlan towering over her. The whole bus station was silent, and the peoples' eyes were turned toward the enormous gringo and the *rubia* in the plastic chair.

"Not now," Sam said, "not till we know if he's alive or dead, and we get him back. You can leave him later if you want to, but not now."

"Sam, I can't take it anymore, I need to feel safe again. I am not cut out for this sort of thing!" she cried. "I can't sit and worry constantly about Tom. I am going insane with the constant insecurity!"

Huge sobs came galloping out of her chest, and Sam reached down to pat her awkwardly on the shoulder. An Indian woman stood and beckoned him to take her seat, so he sat and put his arm around Polly's shoulders.

She grasped him as if she were drowning and began to sob, hanging on with surprising strength, as he continued to hold her until the storm inside her passed.

At last, she released him and wiped her face on her sleeves.

"Polly?"

"Yes?"

"I'm scared, too, and *I* need you here. You need to stay until this is all over, no matter the outcome. It's the only decent thing to do."

"I know that. If I had been doing the right thing, I would have felt good about leaving, but I only felt numb." She attempted a smile but only managed an ashamed grimace.

Sam stood. "Give me your ticket, and I'll get your bag."

"I only have this one. I'm glad you found me before the bus arrived. Sam?"

"Yes?"

"You are a true friend."

"Thank you."

They left the bus station as a break in the clouds allowed a shaft of sunlight to bathe the town as they waited for a taxi to take them back to the hotel.

Back inside her room, Polly opened the door and turned on the light. The first thing she noticed was something on her pillow. It was a napkin from the hotel restaurant, and on it sat her ring.

MiT

It was four in the afternoon when Sam knocked on Polly's door. When she opened it, he smiled then gave her a huge hug, and she knew what it meant. She grasped him as if she were drowning and sobbed until he had to pull her arms from him.

She finally walked to the bathroom, and he could hear the water running in the sink, muffling the sounds she was making. After a minute or two, she reappeared in the doorway, wiping her face with a towel.

"Where is he?"

"At a village over the mountains. An American missionary phoned and said some villagers found him leading a mule out of the mountains with a dead man tied to the saddle. He said that Tom is going to be all right, though he was very cold and dirty. And he has a wounded foot from a dog bite. The missionary said the local doctor has treated him, including a rabies shot."

"How do I get there?"

"I guess it's a long ways because there are no roads over the mountains. We'll have to take the highway that I came in on and then cut south for quite a ways to get to this town called 'No-Shit Something'. The guy from Interior said the police will take us. They are real interested in what Tom was doing coming out of the mountains with a dead man."

"I'm interested in what Tom was doing coming out of the mountains with a dead man too. Nothing's *ever* simple with him, is it?"

"Absolutely not. He's a one hundred percent pain in the ass."

The missionary was a tall man with bright red hair and beard and a beatific look in his eyes. He had a wife and three daughters, the smallest of whom was sitting in his lap as he puffed on a pipe.

They, and a half-dozen villagers, were sitting around a bonfire built in front of the missionary's stone house. Tom was wrapped in a blanket, and his thickly bandaged foot was elevated on a small wooden stool.

"Still cold?" the man asked.

Tom dragged his eyes away from the fire, where he had been staring, and nodded. "I thought I'd been cold before, because I grew up in very cold and snowy country, but that rainstorm just about did me in."

The man nodded. "You were in pretty bad shape. How's the foot?"

"It's okay. Those ibuprofen bombs you gave me are working. It throbs a bit, but it's not too bad." Tom stared back into the fire for a time, then said, "Mike?"

"Yes?"

"At the feria, when he was drunk, Pete told me he was going to go to some kind of ritual in the mountains, to a ceremony that was a thousand years old where the people ate hallucinogenic mushrooms. He was investigating the drug trafficking end of it, but he was getting real interested in the religion part. So, I have a question."

"Yes?"

"I guess it just seems impossible that kind of stuff would still go on. I thought those sorts of practices were ancient history."

The man took his pipe from his mouth and said, "Hardly. There are a lot of places where shamans, witch doctors, and the like are very much a part of community life. In Africa, Asia, Siberia, even America."

"America?"

"Sure. What do you think all this New Age stuff is? It's a reversion to the primitive, something right off the walls of Lascaux."

"Is it evil?"

The man puffed on his pipe and furrowed his forehead. The little girl on his lap turned her face up, waiting for an answer. Finally, he said, "There is a great deal of evil in the world. And, in spite of the influence of monotheistic religions like Christianity, Judaism, and the Islamic faith, there is a large number of people who still believe in the primitive animistic practices of the past. There are millions and millions of people who still practice the rites of religions as primitive and superstitious as those of the Neanderthal culture. They deify animals, sing, drum, and spill blood—sometimes human blood. And it's interesting that it is still a part of Christianity's most solemn ceremony, the Eucharist, though in a highly symbolic form."

"Jesus said, 'Drink of my blood, eat of my flesh'."

Mike nodded and waved at the dark night. "It's why I'm here. Many of the people don't know the meaning of a religion that offers them access to a God that loves. Instead, they hang on to the old religions and fall into the old follies. We Christians speak of Satan and his temptations, but it is only a useful personification of the evil that thrives where people are ignorant of an alternative where love and forgiveness are at the heart of existence. It's part of the same old cycle."

"What cycle?"

"The cycle of spirituality declining into religion, of faith degrading into law and ritual, of love being traded for the stuff of the world. The God part gets lost after a couple of generations, and the people begin to suffer, so they look into the old caves of the past, and many are lost there. Then their children find themselves in spiritual agony, and they begin their own search until they 'discover' the teachings of a man who said that God was love. They bring together small communities of people like themselves and go back to a simple religion that gives them great comfort and, we believe, eternal life.

"But then the children of those children begin to interest themselves in the trappings and ritual, in the superficial aspects of the spiritual experience. They begin to build bigger churches, mount bigger productions, dress their priests in grander raiment. The teachings become encrusted with interpretations, like barnacles on a ship's bottom, and the thing flounders under its own weight. The spiritual love is lost, and the children of the ones faithful to the practices, instead of the spirit again find themselves in agony, and they, in their turn, disperse in search of love. Many find themselves back in the caves or dancing around the fires as they raise the fearful spirits of the old pantheon. Then the cycle begins again."

"And it just goes on and on."

"Just goes on and on. We believe that it will all end though. And we look forward to it."

That was little comfort for Tom at the moment. The body of a man he had hardly known but liked very much was lying in a wooden box with his body piled with ice. Tom shared the man's last terrible hour, and if there had been any doubt in his mind before, it was dispelled forever: evil was real, horrible things were practiced, and souls were lost.

And then, with the background of conversational murmurs and gentle people digging aluminum foil-wrapped corn out of the fire, he thought about love.

He had it, lost it, been given it back only to almost lose it again, along with his life. He was tired of taking chances, of riding the roller coaster. He wanted Polly, and he wanted to simplify his life. He wanted what this man with the child in his lap had. He wanted inner peace.

"*Carros.*"

Cars. The word broke Tom's reverie, and he looked up to see the headlights of three vehicles moving off the road, then park next to the few houses of the *pueblito*. Something told him the cars were there for him, and a lump filled his throat. He was feeling safer by the moment.

When he saw Sam get out of the first car, he was exhilarated. When he saw Polly running up from the second car, he was stunned.

Polly saw the man in the blanket, with a bandaged foot propped on a stool, and she stopped because this was barely her Thomas. The face was gaunt and haunted. She went to him, and he shrugged the blanket off one shoulder to hold out his hand to her. As she walked into his grasp and held his face to her body, she felt how cold he still was.

A very long moment passed, and then he looked up at her. She took his face in her hands, ran her thumbs over his temples, and said gently, "Let's go home."

EPILOGUE

Tom stepped onto the deck and looked out over the valley. He was happy way down deep because he had a whole new sense of things. He felt blessed being born in America at this particular time in its history—something that sprouted in the aftermath of the events down south. The first thing he did upon his return was take the TV to the Saint John's thrift store and cancel his newspaper subscription.

After their marriage in Mexico, Polly quit her partnership in the family firm and gave her position to Christina, then taking a place on the board in its stead. The wedding she planned in the Chapel of the Transfiguration in Jackson devolved to a civil ceremony in the beach resort town of Ixtapa. Sam Harlan was best man, and their daughter, Christina, was a grudging bridesmaid. Polly's other daughter had been absent, but hell, nothing was perfect—except this sparkling morning in the mountains.

Polly was outside gardening in the morning sun because it was October and bulb time. He walked back inside and went to the coffee machine to pour a cup, then stepped to the west window of the kitchen.

Outside, it was brilliant with high autumn light on the yellow aspen leaves of the several trees in the yard. Polly was on her knees at the edge of the wildflower garden she'd put in the spring before. Millie lay in the sun and watched Polly divide gladiolus bulbs and sort them with some new tulip bulbs bought the day before. A tendril of wheat-colored hair fell from her Gibson-girl hairdo, and a diamond stud earring beamed a needle of light at him.

California women! She wore a University of Wyoming sweatshirt, gloves, Wrangler jeans, whacked-out tennies, and five thousand dollar's worth of earrings. What had he ever done to deserve her? As far as he could tell, nothing. Just plain dumb luck.

He thought about the call he received to investigate a burglary at Teton Village that led to their reunion, then of their adventures together in the two years since. In the middle of his thoughts, the door opened, and Polly came inside, followed by the dog.

"Hi, Mil," he said and reached down to twiddle her ears and run his finger down the top of her nose.

"I want some too," Polly said and put her arms around his neck. He pecked her on the forehead and reached up to pull the comb from her hair. He held some hair in his hand and stared at it. It was alive. He put his nose in it and drew in a breath. A tear ran unexpectedly from his face and fell onto her cheek.

She pulled her face back and looked at him. "What is it?"

"I love you."

She put her face back on his chest and kissed his shirt. "We're going to town."

"What for?"

"To buy a pumpkin. The PTA is selling them in the square downtown."

"You go."

"*We* are going, Thomas." He could tell by the note in her voice there was no use to argue. She reached up and wiped his cheek with her thumb. "You're leaking."

They parked in front of Stone Drug on the sunny side of the street. Fall was slipping away, and winter was waiting somewhere up north. But, in the meantime, the days were wondrous with their creamy light, and the nights glittered with the promise of winter nights cold enough to burst trees like artillery rounds.

"I'm going to get an ice cream cone. I'll see you over there."

"Get me one too. Vanilla."

"See you in a couple."

He went inside and walked to the old soda counter. It hadn't changed much in the whole length of his life. He remembered coming in here with his sister, brother, and cousins to get ice cream after the Saturday evening movie. They would then go to the Wort Hotel and sit on the curb to listen to the music and watch the gamblers through the open doors.

In the old days, the bandstand was right in front of the street entrance, so the music of The Sons of the Pioneers, The Sons of the Golden West, and other bands would flood the sidewalk. It pulled the tourists in like netted fish. He loved to look at all the interesting people the night brought to downtown Jackson Hole. They couldn't have been more strange and exotic to Tom than if they'd been New Guinea cannibals dressed like Birds of Paradise. They sat on the curb, licked at their cones, and their eyes popped at the massive turquoise jewelry, sequined shirts, and silver-dressed boots popular with the women in those days. The men with their piped shirts, expensive hats, and glassy boots were only a little less impressive.

"One vanilla and one strawberry, LaDonna."

"Haven't seen you for a long time, Tommy."

"I was gone for a while. Mexico. Got married down there, then honeymooned in Ixtapa."

Her eyebrows went up. "Jeepers. Running with the fast crowd now, huh?"

"Nah. A lot of it was police work."

"We paying you guys in the sheriff's department to vacation down in Mexico now?"

Tom grinned. "It's Yuppie Town."

"Hell, I guess," she said and handed him the cones. "There you go."

"Thanks, Hon." He held his hand out for the change, but she winked at him and dropped it in the plastic tip jar.

"Thanks, Tom. I'm saving for a trip to Mexico," she said. It made Tommy smile.

Tom crossed the street and stepped onto the sidewalk. He stopped. In his mind's eye, he saw the little Trique Indian child looking up at him, her cedar knot eyes full of anticipation, her dirty little hands outstretched. It was a memory from Tlaxiaco last summer.

"*Sientase*," he said, and the child sat. He handed her the ice cream bar. A brilliant smile cracked her grimy face, and she closed her eyes. Licked. Licked. Like one of the little native kids who used to sit on the curb and listen to the music in Jackson's primitive past.

Other thoughts of Mexico occurred to him. Only the night before, he and Polly were watching a television news program when Concha Osorio appeared. The subject was the new socialist movements in Latin America. After the familiar faces of the presidents of Cuba, Venezuela, Brazil, and Ecuador, a segment was shown of her being interviewed on the plaza in Tlaxiaco—right under the noses of the police who tried to kill her months earlier. Except for the cops: Berto, who was somewhere in the Mexican prison Archipelago, and Jesus, who was dead. Small world.

Glancing into the bright park that bustled with people, the first thing that caught his eye was a world-class mommy butt in lavender spandex. The tall blonde in the dermal pants made political conversation with a plain as a sparrow woman in a beige jacket and felt clogs. Nouvelle Jackson Hole in a nutshell.

Tom's eye roamed the park. There were three tables set up with holiday cakes, candies, and cookies—thick cookies with Jack O'

Lantern faces in creamy sugar frosting. He made a note to buy a half dozen. It was for the PTA, after all.

As he looked at the crowd, he saw that it was made up mostly of women with toddlers, and he was struck by how old many of them were. Lightly graying ex-career women in their late thirties and early forties who probably gave up their politics and ambitions to get back to the real world before it was too late. Not very many natives, he noted. Rachels and Muffys rather than Lawannas and Lynettes. But anymore, that was just fine with him. *Hell,* he thought, *everybody's gotta be someplace.*

He finally saw Polly, pointing toward a big pumpkin, and a man wearing a change apron was grinning. The pumpkin's stem drooped and was frayed into a small broom. It was wizened and cocked to one side with creases half an inch deep, and it was ugly as hell, but he knew she would turn it into something striking..

As he walked up to her and the man selling the pumpkin, he handed her the cone and said, "You always have to pick the ugly ones, don't you?"

She looked him dead in the eye and said, "It means some work, but they always turn out just the way I like 'em." She took a lick of the ice cream and winked.

MiT

In Oaxaca, the brothers Patricio and José Gorostiza were walking on a trail through an oak thicket, and as they walked, they talked. They spoke of their village their past duties, and how they had given to the community of San Miguel. They laughed about many funny things that seemed to jump into their memories. Then, they remembered their long-dead parents and their one teacher in the little adobe schoolhouse, Profesora Ordoñez, who had given José his love of poetry.

They talked of Concha Osorio's new status as an international celebrity and the recent events that had pulled them into the main current of the Mexican state. And they laughed at the money they had both received since their little deception with the world's press. After exciting the world, they were given the local distributorship for *Modelo* beer and *Rey* bottled drinks, both peeled off the local cacique's action. They even received a small truck to deliver the items along their route—a gift from the regional PRI leadership.

But the best part had been their elevation in the party. They had sat at the table with the local war chiefs, and as representatives of the indigenous community, their input seemed to be considered seriously, and *that* was something new. In the past, the local cacique, another Indian, had been the only one to sit at the privy-council table. And there they had sat, across the table from the man who'd ended up having to share his business and political pie with two old farts, one of whom could barely write. He had not been a happy man, to be sure. They'd even tweaked his nose publicly a couple of times just to let him know that he was not the only wealthy Indian in town anymore, and it had been fun. The memory of it made them laugh. But all that came to an end when the new national president was elected.

José leaned over and chortled to his brother, "Looks like we're going to have a *bunch* of company!" The brothers howled with laughter as they did a little calaveras jig on the edge of an abrupt limestone escarpment. Both had just seen the bottom of this remote canyon, and it was littered with bones and cloth tatters—the remains of more than a hundred years' worth of the state's local enemies.

"Okay, that's far enough," said the sergeant in charge of the police detail.

The two chortling older men turned around, tears of laughter running down their cheeks, to face the policemen who had brought them to this isolated place in the beautiful southern state of Oaxaca, home of the Cloud People. Then, hands tied behind their backs, they took in two identical breaths and raised their chins to offer their hearts to the traditional instruments of the state.

"No bugles, please," said José, "I'm not partial to martial music. And no last cigarette either, I'm trying to quit."

He couldn't help himself. Dignity and humor were all the little people of Mexico have when standing before the instruments of the state.

The End

The Jackson Hole Mystery series
by J. Royal Horton

Murder in Jackson Hole (Book 1)
Murder in the Tetons (Book 2)
Murder in Moab (Book 3)
Murder on the Red Desert (pending)

Other books by
Jon R Horton

Gib
Snuffy Johnson's Cowboy Christmas

ABOUT THE AUTHOR

Jon R Horton was another one of those kids who read under the covers by flashlight, devoured the library's fiction stacks, and hoped to be a writer. After one year as an honors student in English at the University of Wyoming, he served in the U.S. Air Force as a Russian linguist and intelligence analyst. With his GI Bill, he earned a B.A. in Russian Language and Literature from California State University at Northridge then entered the D.A. program at Idaho State University as an English major.

The academic gender wars of the 70s prompted a career move into the international oil exploration business, where he was as a Helicopter Operations Safety and Security Supervisor, specializing in remote ops. After retiring, he started writing in earnest and self-published five novels, all five-starred on Amazon. Jon has also been published in several literary magazines and written articles for general interest magazines. He was last published in the premier issue of the British literary magazine Ronin.

Printed in Great Britain
by Amazon